FIGURES IN RAIN

Chet Williamson

FIGURES IN RAIN
WEIRD AND GHOSTLY TALES

Ash-Tree Press
ASHCROFT, BRITISH COLUMBIA
2002

Figures in Rain
First published
by Ash-Tree Press
P.O. Box 1360
Ashcroft, British Columbia
Canada V0K 1A0
www.ash-tree.bc.ca/ashtreecurrent.html

ISBN: 1-55310-039-5

Typesetting and design by Ash-Tree Press
Printed and bound in Canada by Morriss Printing Company Ltd.
1745 Blanshard Street, Victoria, British Columbia

CONTENTS

For Laurie,
then, now, always.

Preface

THE STORIES IN THIS COLLECTION are in the chronological order of their publication dates, though that order doesn't perfectly correspond to the order of their composition. I've resisted the temptation to revise them, with one or two exceptions remarked upon in the story notes.

You'll find those notes in their holding pen at the back of the book, where they won't disturb your reading with their insistent '*I, I, I . . . me, me, me . .* ' If you peruse them, please do so *after* you read each story, as they contain a few spoilers, but may give you a look at what went through my befuddled mind before and during the writing process.

My thanks go out to Barbara and Christopher Roden for publishing this collection and helping to select the contents, to my ole pard, Joe R. Lansdale, for writing the introduction, and to the agents who marketed and the editors who bought these stories in the first place. Thanks too to my family and friends who have been so supportive over the two decades in which these pieces were written.

Thanks, most of all, to the readers. I hope you'll enjoy reacquainting yourselves with the characters in the stories you may have previously read, and meeting for the first time those you haven't.

Chet Williamson
Elizabethtown, PA
June 2002

Introduction

I'M MORE THAN A LITTLE PLEASED to see this collection of Chet Williamson's work, because I have been a fan for years. If I were the jealous sort I'd be jealous. He's certainly worthy of jealousy. Tremendous talent. Tremendous guy. But even if I were the kind to be jealous, you can't be jealous for long. Not of a guy like Chet. He's got so much class it rubs off on you. Or it rubs off on me as much as I can absorb class. My skin is a little resistant.

Frankly, and Chet may not know this, a lot of writers of our generation were jealous when Chet came onto the scene. They said stuff like, 'Hey, who is this guy? How did he go out there and get a novel published so easily? I'm trying all over the place.'

Then they read him and said, 'HEY, WHO IS THIS GUY!' Because they wanted to write like him.

Too bad. He's one of a kind. His own man.

This all took place during the horror boom of the eighties, and I suppose if Chet had been willing to stay with that horse, he might have become a household name in the field.

It was a horse too small for him to ride, however.

Chet has written in a number of venues, and in venues that can't be identified other than as Chet Williamson stories and novels. You see, he wasn't willing to do the same thing over. Even if he might have thought he should, he couldn't. It wasn't in him. Even within the horror field he was confusing. Same reason. He didn't like to repeat himself. Didn't go for the same effects.

Most successful writers do just that. Repeat themselves. Same kind of book, or in some cases, the same book, over and over. They do this because, sadly, most readers want it. They want the same exact story time after time.

This book is not for that kind of reader. It is for someone who wants to have a new experience with every story. An experience that has echo; stories where more is going on in the scene than just the scene.

Chet is a master at that.

ཞ ཟ

I don't remember the first short story I read of Chet's. I was introduced to his work by his novels, which are also excellent, but after the impact of the novels, I was struck even harder by his short work.

I have a sneaking suspicion that Chet, like me, actually prefers writing short stories.

Oh, novels are fun. I enjoy them as well. I know Chet does. But there is something indefinable about a short story. Something wonderful. I know writers who have published numerous books who get all dreamy thinking about having their own short story collection.

I think one thing that is so appealing about short stories has to do with being able to write in so many different story-telling veins. Moving from one idea to another quickly. Instead of six months to a year or longer on one idea, one set of characters, you can experience half a dozen ideas, numerous characters and experiences, by writing a number of short stories during the same time span.

This is not to say that short stories aren't hard work. They are. That's why a volume of this size by a writer of Chet's stature, his quality, should be treasured like a bottle of fine wine.

Only it's better. Unlike wine. You can take this volume off the shelf and re-experience it time after time.

Another reason to cherish this book: a writer who writes short stories these days is a rarity. Markets are slim, money is slimmer. Many just won't bother to do it.

Let me give you another reason.

Chet does what so many writers wish they did, and that is, no matter what the story—and in this volume they are all of the creepy variety—it's the characters and style that count the most. A lot of writers say that, and mean it, but they don't have the chops to back it up.

Chet does.

Chet knows people and he knows how to write about them. His style is vastly different from most of the writers I know who write horror and horror-related material. It's softer. Not dull. Not weak. Soft. He sneaks up on you. He can come at you like an express train when he wants, and he can be as nasty as any of the so-called nasty writers, but it's the simple beauty of the prose that marks a Williamson story. It wraps itself around you slowly, and then starts to squeeze.

And the characters.

A Williamson hallmark. They are living, breathing, human beings. They stay with you long after you lay the story down. Even if the plot slips away from your memory, the mood, the way the story made you feel, the attitude of the characters, remain.

His ideas aren't anything to sneeze at either.

Sigh. Maybe I really should pause here and feel a little jealous. This guy can do it all.

Even a seemingly traditional idea in his capable hands can surprise you. In fact, he uses your own expectations against you.

So, to repeat, in case you haven't been listening: there's nothing standard about any of these stories, and if one or two at first remind you of something that has gone before, keep reading. Pretty soon you will see that Chet is leading you down the primrose path.

From a writer's viewpoint, there's certainly plenty to envy about his work.

And there's yet another reason to cherish this book.

This dude is big. You get a lot of stories, a lot of bang for your buck, and no padding. Just good, honest, literate, entertaining fiction.

ꕤ

Which stories do I recommend?

All of them.

Chet doesn't write bad stories.

In fact, I'm keeping you away from them by writing about Chet. He deserves someone to stand on something high and yell his name. He's earned the right to be recognized as one of the finest writers of our generation. And generations beyond, I'm sure. But it's time for me to get out of the way. It's time for you to see that this isn't just ballyhoo.

It's the truth and nothing but the truth, as they say in court.

So, find a nice comfy spot. One light directly on the page is best. The rest of the room dark. It would be nice if, just by coincidence, it were raining outside. Maybe a roll of thunder and a flash of lightning now and then.

And if there's no rain, no lightning and thunder, it won't matter. Chet will get you anyway. Within a page you'll fall under his spell.

I envy you the experience. I know this is a book I will cherish and that any reader of fine fiction will treasure, and will return to again and again.

Joe R. Lansdale
May 2002

FIGURES IN RAIN

Offices

IT BEGAN LATE ONE FRIDAY NIGHT. I'd stayed in the city to see a film that ended around eleven, and walking back to my car I remembered that I'd left some copy that I wanted to work on that weekend in my office. I signed in with the night man and hopped the elevator to the sixth floor. A trio of widely separated lights provided the only illumination, but I had no trouble finding my way to the suite of twenty cubicles that was the advertising department. Without turning on my desk light, I slipped the copy under my arm and started out.

Then I saw Larry Donaldson in the office across the hall.

He was sitting in the semi-darkness, his elbows straddling the black bulk of the typewriter in front of him. He was staring through thick-lensed glasses at the empty carriage, and I heard a low sigh press timidly against the thick silence.

Seeing him startled me. I'd noticed no other name on the sign-in sheet, and I wondered if he'd been here since five o'clock. Hell, on a Friday night?

'Larry,' I called, and shook a little at the odd feeling of my spoken word just hanging in the air. 'Larry,' I said louder, 'what are you doing here?'

He didn't move or turn or speak; he just sat staring at that empty typewriter. And then, almost imperceptibly, he began to fade, and I suddenly realized that I was seeing *through* him, as if through cloudy water. By the time I felt any astonishment, he was gone.

'Jesus Christ,' I said softly.

Then the thought came over me like an old warm blanket with just enough holes to let a little chill in: I had seen a ghost. Somehow, since I last saw him that afternoon, Larry Donaldson had died.

It was possible. Larry was in his mid-forties, smoked a couple of packs a day, didn't exercise, was a little overweight. . . . Hearts have given out for less. Or maybe it was just an accident; maybe he got smashed at that bad junction where U.S. 30 joins 283.

Whatever had happened, I felt sure that Larry was dead. So it surprised the hell out of me when, the next day, there was nothing in the paper about an expired copywriter for Maitland Products, Inc. It *really* threw me when I walked into Al's party Saturday night and there was Larry with his wife, puffing on a Marlboro and hoisting a Schlitz, his five-foot-nine hundred-ninety-pound frame looking more corporeal than ever.

'Kenny,' he slurred at me, and clapped his cigarette hand on my neck, dribbling ashes over my shoulder, 'you know my wife, doncha?' I smiled, and she managed one too, a little crookedly.

'Excuse me,' I said, 'I'd better get a drink.' I wormed my way to the bar through the smoky, boozy crowd of slogan scribblers, section managers, and commercial artists, poured myself three fingers of Jim Beam, and thought about Larry's miraculous resurrection.

What the hell had I seen? Not a ghost, for damn sure. So what was going on? A crack-up? I didn't much care for my work, but it wasn't all that demanding, merely a necessary obeisance to Mammon to put food on the table.

Then I saw Walt Barnes maneuvering his way into the kitchen, and smiled in spite of my worries. His disapproving frown was firmly in place behind a newly grown beard flecked here and there with gray. He noticed me and gestured toward the living-room, where the population was less concentrated.

When we got there, he grinned. 'Another command performance party, eh?'

I nodded. 'The director's the director. Besides, I'd rather drink his stuff than yours. He can afford it.'

He laughed. We knew that neither one of us was offering the Gettys any competition. I wondered if I should tell him about seeing Larry's 'ghost', but decided I'd rather try to forget the whole thing.

'How's the writing?' he asked.

I raised an eyebrow. 'Fantasy or real?' Fantasy was the company work, the things that didn't matter. Real meant our own stuff that we did at home, over lunch, or during office hours when the manager was away.

We talked until Al and Marie came over. Walt quickly drifted out the door, and another fifteen minutes saw me slipping back to my apartment and a night full of funny, half-remembered dreams about dead people and typewriters that made music that sounded like symphonic disco played through Jello speakers. I had a headache when I woke up.

By the end of the weekend I had nearly forgotten about Friday night, putting it down to tiredness or job dissatisfaction. I arrived late as usual Monday morning and waited impatiently for the elevator, hoping that Al wouldn't step off it.

Finally the door slid open and I entered. Chuck Dieter was standing at the back of the car. 'Morning, Dieter,' I said, and threw on a slightly embarrassed and harried smile that I hoped said 'caught in traffic'.

Dieter didn't reply. He might have nodded in my direction, but I wasn't sure. He was still standing there expressionless when I got off at the sixth floor.

I scooted down the hall and made it to my office without being spotted, then began the normal routine: turn on the lights, unlock the desk, bullshit with Walt. He was in his office, toying with the script for a radio ad. I asked how it was going.

'Awful,' he answered. 'Somehow I can't throw myself into the shoes of a housewife whose sole concern is how to make her silverware sparkle for the bridge club.' He leered. 'Maybe I should throw myself into her panties.'

I grinned. 'Talk like that and they'll shuffle you back to the halls of academe.'

'Let 'em,' he snorted. 'The pay was crap, but the *MLA Journal* beats hell out of *Advertising Age*.'

I checked my watch. 'Almost time for the *Smooth 'n Soft* meeting. You going?'

'It's delayed.'

'Why?'

'Dieter's out this week.'

'Out?'

'Vacation.'

'But I just saw him on the elevator.' I was starting to get that funny feeling again.

Walt frowned. 'Must have been somebody else. He and his family went to the shore for a week.'

'Uh-uh.' I shook my head sharply. 'I *saw* him, Walt.'

Walt picked up the phone and punched three digits. 'Nan? Walt. Is Dieter in? . . . Do you know when they left? . . . Okay, I'll get to him next week. Thanks.' He hung up. 'Left Saturday morning. You still think you saw him?'

I didn't know what to say. I was as certain of having seen Chuck Dieter as I'd been of having seen Larry Donaldson on Friday night. I felt spooked as hell, and my stomach started to churn. 'No,' I answered softly. 'No, I guess not.'

Walt seized the chance to talk about 'poor old Dieter', who'd been a free-lancer several years back. He'd taken a job at Maitland after his first novel had hit the remainder shelves like a bullet, and he hadn't turned out a piece of fiction since. He talked about it from time to time, but all that came out of his typewriter was copy.

It was a pattern I saw over and over again, and Walt had noticed it too. 'Big business is like a protective mother,' he said. 'Forget all the obvious faults. Its real danger lies in what it considers its *best* quality—the ability to provide jobs.'

I knew what was coming. 'You oughta go back to teaching, Walt. You'd get that need to lecture out of your system.'

'Goddammit, I'm serious. When Dieter came to work here, he was bright, eager, creative—ready to sell out, sure, but maybe he could sell his soul by day and buy it back on the installment plan at night by writing. Old Big Business crushed him to her massive tits and said, "Here's money, here's

Blue Cross, here's security!"—and he grabbed that nipple with both hands. But it didn't work out the way he'd planned. It sucked *him* dry.'

'Hell, Walt, a lot of these clowns *love* their work. They come in early, they leave late, they find creativity in it.'

'Maybe so, Ken, but *I* know I've only got so much to spread around. And if I give it all to Big Mama, I won't have any left for me. It happened to Dieter, to Donaldson . . . hell, to *all* of 'em.'

I smiled. 'And the goblins'll get *you* if you don't watch out.' He laughed, and I stood up. 'I'd better get back to my office.'

'Offices,' he corrected. I looked at him curiously. '*Holy* offices,' he explained. 'Got to take this work seriously.'

ꕤ

I took it very seriously Wednesday night. I was working late on Femi-Dri, a project I knew little and cared less about, and I was bored and angry. It was ten o'clock, and I'd just about decided to kick my desk in and write filthy words all over the glass office dividers when Wendy McCormick walked past in the hall.

It had happened twice before, and this time I almost expected it. Not for a moment did I think that the physical body of Wendy McCormick was in that office. But I hoped I would find out what the hell *was* there.

I stepped into the hall and saw her walking slowly away from me. I called her name loudly, commandingly, but she didn't stop. I yelled it, then hurried after her.

She looked absolutely real. I can remember everything about her—her dress (a nicely tailored black print with, so help me, little apples on it), her jewelry (gold hoop earrings, small engraved gold locket), her complexion (pale as a frozen corpse), and her reaction on seeing me (none whatsoever). There was no doubt. This was the Wendy McCormick I knew and had dated and even slept with once about a year before, but when I tried to grab her shoulder, my hand slipped through it.

My stomach knotted like a fist. I told myself that maybe I'd missed, and tried to grab her again. Nothing. I'd always thought grabbing a ghost would be like sticking your hand in cold oatmeal, but this was just—nothing.

She walked on until she reached her office, then sat down at her desk and simply stared straight ahead into the darkness. I turned on the light, but there was no change.

My watch read ten-thirty, and I was sure Walt Barnes would still be awake. I ran back to my office, called him, and asked him to come down.

'Jesus Christ, do you know what time it is?'

'Yeah, I know. Can you come?'

'Look, Ken, I don't get paid overtime, so I don't work past five, all right?'

'This doesn't have anything to do with work. Not directly, anyway.'

'Is it important?'

'It's important enough that I think I'm going to go crazy if you don't get down here.'

There was silence on his end for a second. Then he said, 'Okay, I'll be down', and hung up.

After waiting fifteen minutes, I decided to wait for Walt at the elevator. As I left my office, I became aware of a form sitting at the desk in the office diagonal to mine. It was Charley Landon, big as life, staring at nothing. I didn't need to touch him.

☙ ❧

Walt arrived just after eleven. I knew I was nervous, but when the elevator doors slid open with their mechanical whisper, I felt every hair on my body jump to attention.

'This had better be good,' he announced gruffly as he stepped from the car.

I told him everything. I told him about seeing Larry that first night and Dieter Monday morning. I told him about Wendy walking in, and about Charley sitting like a robot in his darkened office. Then I told him about putting my hand through Wendy, and he laughed.

'You asshole! You got me out of a hot tub for a *Shock Theater* rerun?'

'Walt, listen to me, I am not shitting you!' But his face still wore that damnable mask of academic cynicism. 'They are *real*! They're in there right now!'

He looked at me as though I were crazy. 'Okay,' he nodded at last. 'Sure. Let's go see them.'

I followed him down the hall. He looked frequently over his shoulder, fearful, no doubt, that I'd go for his jugular with my teeth. Then he stopped cold in front of Marty Petrocelli's office. 'Christ, Marty,' he said, 'you gave me a start! What are you doing here?'

I shouldered Walt aside. Marty was sitting at his desk, the same as the others. Walt spoke again.

'Marty? Hey . . .' He turned toward me suspiciously. 'What *is* this, Ken?'

'Come on,' I said as I continued down the hall.

There were more of them now. Nearly half of the small offices were occupied by the seated forms of the people I worked with every day. I was nearly at Wendy's office when Walt caught up with me. His complexion was pale.

'Ken, what the hell *is* this? Why is everybody here? Is this a joke or what?'

I pointed to Wendy's office. 'Ask her.'

Walt's temper, never long in abeyance, flared. 'You're damned right I will! Wendy!' he shouted. 'What's all this about?'

There was no answer. 'Wendy?' The voice shook.

Nothing. No reply at all.

'God *damn* it!' he yelled, and reached for her shoulder to swing her around. His hand went through her and he lost his balance, falling against the desk and knocking over a cup of yellow pencils that clattered like dry bones on the floor. He staggered back, making a sound that only utter astonishment kept from being a scream.

Wendy's figure hadn't moved. Walt's gaze darted from her to me to her like a trapped animal, his mouth trying to frame a question that made sense.

I smiled gently. 'Welcome to *Shock Theater*.'

He didn't laugh. His eyes just got wilder.

'Walt,' I said firmly, 'it's all right. I don't know what they are, but I don't think they even know we're here. They can't hurt us. They're like . . . like shadows.'

'Could it——' His voice was pinched with fear. 'Could they be, uh, projections?'

I cocked my head.

'Projections,' he went on, apparently afraid to take his eyes off the Wendy-thing for too long. 'A gag—a joke done with projectors.'

'In every office? I don't know how or why. Besides, I've seen them walking. They look too real for projections.'

Then I touched 'Wendy' again, and my hand disappeared into her body, reappearing when I withdrew it. I heard Walt's breathing turn ragged. 'Jesus!' he stammered, 'Jesus Christ, don't do that! Let's get out of here. Let's go somewhere and . . . and talk about this. I can't stay here anymore!'

I felt funny myself, somewhere between hysterical laughter and the dry heaves. I walked into the hall, Walt close behind, and as we headed toward the elevators we saw them. Only a few offices were empty now, and in all the rest sat the images of their workday occupants, still and unmoving, as much a part of the tableau as the telephone, the In–Out boxes, and the desk calendars all faithfully turned to dates that had no meaning in that timeless night.

The cool outside air was like a tingling embrace that welcomed us back to a world full of life. The stars, moon, and city lights burned brighter and cleaner than the white incandescents that had illuminated the things six floors above.

We walked a few blocks to Dornan's. Walt ordered a double Scotch, I had a bourbon, and both drinks were drained within a minute of their arrival. We were halfway through a second round before we started talking about it.

'Kenny,' Walt said, staring at the drink he held in his shaking hands, 'what *were* they?'

I just shook my head.

He looked at me sharply. 'What's the matter with you? You seem . . . relieved!'

'I am a little,' I smiled. 'At least I know I'm not crazy, now that you've seen them too.'

'But what *were* they?' he pressed.

'I'm not sure. But I've been thinking.' I took another sip, trying to make sense of it all. 'I think maybe it has something to do with what we talk about all the time. The draining effect this kind of junk-work has.' I stopped again. 'Shit, this sounds like some paranoid fantasy.'

'No,' Walt said, 'it's no fantasy. Go ahead.' His hands, cupped around the glass, seemed to be praying that I'd bring order out of the chaos reality had become.

'They're trapped,' I said softly. 'Everyone we saw is a person who's been at Maitland and seems content to stay. They don't *want* to go anywhere else or do anything else. They're ready to give up and play the game and have "Maitland Retiree" as the second line in their obituary.

'And when they gave up, when they accepted it, they *lost* something. Call it—what's the word—a *Ka*, a piece of their soul—their creative self, maybe. Anyway, *something* is trapped in that building.' I took a long swallow, not knowing if I really believed what I was saying.

'But why did *we* see it?' Walt seemed calmer now. 'Everybody works late at times. Why hasn't anyone mentioned it before?'

'I don't know. Maybe it takes somebody who still wants out badly enough to see them. Maybe if you're already trapped, you don't notice.' I had another thought. 'Maybe they only show up when the person's sleeping. That would explain why I didn't see them in the early evening.'

Walt nodded. 'And why there were more of them the later we stayed.' He stopped suddenly. 'But what about Dieter? You saw him in the morning.'

I wasn't sure. 'He was on vacation. Sleeping late, maybe.'

'But he showed up at the office anyway. Jesus, I wonder if that's it. When you're sleeping.'

I didn't know. It didn't matter.

We sat in silence finishing our drinks, then ordered more. Finally Walt asked the question I'd been afraid to.

'What do we do about it?'

I looked for a long time at the translucent pearls my ice cubes had become, rolling the glass in my hand so that they moved around and around and around until the warm air diminished them and they were gone.

'Nothing.'

'Nothing?'

'What *should* we do?'

I could tell that Walt didn't know either. 'Jesus, Ken, *something*. . . . Maybe the police?'

'And tell them what? Our theories aren't worth shit. And besides, who gives a damn? Not our spooky friends up there—they seem very content. There's something else too.'

The 'something else' made me very sad, and I dug my nails into my palm to keep from getting drunkenly weepy.

'There's no crime,' I said. 'Whatever's going on up there, and in a million other buildings tonight, whatever it is, it isn't against the law.' I took a deep swallow, but it didn't get the lump out of my throat. 'You can't steal a guy's car, or his money, or his goddam jockey-boy lawn ornament, because that's against the law. But what you *can* steal . . . what you *can* . . .'

I left it unspoken. Walt knew.

Then I laughed, laughed long and hard until the tears came. 'And there's another reason we can't go to the cops.'

And Walt was nodding and laughing too, and the people at the bar and the fat bartender and the skinny waitress with the dirty white tennis shoes all looked at us and heard Walt choke out, 'Why *can't* we?'

And they heard me shout back, 'Because we're drunk, you asshole!'

And we were.

❧ ❧

I stayed at Maitland another three weeks. Neither Walt nor I saw anything strange after that Wednesday night. I refused to stay late; I took all extra work home with me. Walt talked about quitting, but had no job to go to and wasn't confident enough to free-lance.

Neither was I, but I did it anyway. Whether what we'd seen in the office was real or a joint hallucination, it gave me the excuse to get out of something that had slowly been sapping me of imagination, creativity . . . joy. The day I left I told Walt, only half jokingly, to watch out for the monsters. He smiled and said he would.

I ran into him one evening several months later, and we hopped into Dornan's. He was still with Maitland, had gotten a small promotion, and had even been elected captain of the department's softball team. He'd been working late that night, and when I asked him if he'd seen any more spooks, he said he hadn't, not a one.

We talked for a long time about a lot of things, and around midnight we left the bar and said goodbye, with a promise to call each other soon. I watched Walt walk down the street, and saw for the first time the back of his softball team jacket. The emblem glowed softly in shining red and gold—a cartoon death's head, and underneath it the legend that he, as captain, had chosen: *Maitland Zombies*.

At least he hadn't lost his sense of humor.

A Lover's Alibi

HAROLD DODGE HAD BEEN AFRAID he would choke at the last second, but he didn't. He brought the gun up smoothly from where he had hidden it under her chair, pressed it against her right temple, closed his eyes, and pulled the trigger. When he made himself look, he saw very little blood. He was glad. He'd been afraid that there would be a spattering of it, like in the movies, that his sweater would bear red blotches that would brand him to all Manhattan as a wife-killer.

But there was only a thin trickle that was almost indistinguishable from her auburn hair in the dim light. He looked at his watch even though he'd checked it only a minute before. It had been 8:32 then; it was 8:33 now. No time warp had sprung from the force of Carol's death to either stretch time or compress it. It was somehow reassuring. In the space of time it had taken to pull a trigger, he had changed immeasurably. But not time. And not the alibis that time supplied.

He took a few deep breaths and tried to relax. There was no rush, not really. The walls of their condo were thick enough to contain the sound of thousand-decibel rock bands at Carol's goddamned New Year's Eve parties without drawing the neighbors' fire, so to imagine that the cozy pop of Carol's purse-sized .22 would carry through brick and plaster was a paranoid fantasy.

Harold wiped his prints from the blued metal and pressed Carol's fingers (were they growing cold so soon?) around the butt and trigger. Her prints were already on the cartridge shells inside. She had loaded them herself months ago after the Clemens woman was attacked out front. Harold had thought she was foolish to buy a gun. Now he was glad she had.

He left the building by the fire stairs, meeting no one during his descent. The twenty-floor walk made his legs rubbery by the time he hit the street, but he ignored the pain and walked briskly toward his car five blocks away. He edged the Jaguar out into traffic and headed for the tunnels. Once free of the city, he took the road for Newark.

It was 9:47 by the dashboard clock when he pulled into the parking lot under Susan's apartment house. He climbed the fire stairs to the fourth floor, peeked through the tempered glass window to make sure the hall was empty, and dashed into her apartment.

She was in his arms before the door had finished closing, and he couldn't even remember her ever holding on so tight, not even in bed.

'Did you do it?' Her words were a rough whisper.

'Yeah. Yeah, it's done.'

'Any problems?' she asked anxiously, pulling back and looking at his face.

He shook his head. 'You?'

'It went fine.' Her voice shook, and he wasn't sure if she meant it. 'The pizza kid came at 8:15.'

'Did he buy it?'

'I think so. He gave me a funny look.'

'What did you say?'

'Just what we'd planned. I had the shower on, the bathroom door open a little, and I yelled, "I'm taking the pizza money from your wallet, okay?" and I waited a bit, and then I said, "Harold?"'

'You're sure you called my name?'

'That was the point, honey. I didn't forget. And then I shrugged like you couldn't hear me and that was it.'

'At 8:15, huh?'

She nodded.

'Okay, good. What time did I get here?'

'About 6:30. We went right to bed, made love, slept a little, and I called for the pizza at a quarter to eight.'

'That's perfect,' he said, smiling openly for the first time. 'We'll make it fine, baby, not a thing to worry about.'

'Was it . . .' Susan paused. 'Did she suffer at all?'

'No,' he answered quickly. He almost wished she had. God knows she made him suffer enough, with that desperate possessiveness of hers. *I love you, Harry*. She would say it over and over and over again until it sounded obscene.

He *had* loved her years ago when they'd gotten married. Not more than kids out of school, really, though she was out of Vassar and he was out of a small state teachers' college. It hadn't been for her money, though. He'd have married Carol if she'd been poorer than he was. That way it might have worked.

He'd wanted them to live on his salary and she'd agreed. But before too long it became humiliatingly apparent that he couldn't make enough to satisfy Carol's tastes, and she started dipping into her trust fund. His financial dependence on her grew like a slow cancer, and in three years they were in Manhattan, living in a two-storey twelve-room condo, and he was a gentleman of leisure, to whom small-town journalism was and would always be a thing of the past.

The thought that he'd married her for her family's wealth came over Carol only a few months later. And then the questions started.

—Do you really love me? Really?

—Do you know how much I love you?

—Do you know that I would do anything for you?

—Do you love me?

—Do you?

—Do you?

It was a litany that nearly drove him insane. He *did* love her, he told himself, and told her as well. But it was like trying to fill the Grand Canyon with a whisper. No words could have satisfied her, no loving touches or little gifts could have fed that hungry irrational need. And as her need became greater, his ability to fulfill it shrank, until her worst fears and suspicions were created by the Frankenstein's monster of her own insecurity.

ꝏ ꝏ

The women were an afterthought at first. He turned to them like he turned to numismatics, Yankee ball games, the countless films she had no desire to see—as an escape from her cloying possessiveness. But then he met Susan at a Kurosawa festival, and everything had changed. Here, he thought, is the woman I *should* have married, and her response was the same. They met often in large, anonymous hotels, and Harold occasionally drove to her place in Newark.

Carol's paranoia had trebled when Harold started sleeping with Susan. It was as if she could see a fat scarlet *A* emblazoned on his hairless chest, and it made him nervous. There had been no informant, no seedy private detective with grainy Polaroids. Why then the new string of questions? The pleas? The entreaties?

—Harry, there's something wrong. Won't you tell me what it is?

—Oh, darling, please don't hold anything back from me. Don't you know how much I love you?

—Share with me, Harry. I'll understand. Don't you love me anymore?

No I don't, you grasping bitch! But he never said it.

He could have gotten a divorce easily enough, but in the eight years he'd been married to Carol, he'd grown increasingly fond of the things one could do with money.

The only answer, then, was to kill her.

He had broached the subject with Susan quite delicately, and was relieved to find that she considered it a valid option. The idea of making the death appear suicidal was hers, and Harold had sprung at it. Carol had a reputation among her circle for being neurotic and moody, so a suicide would not come as a great surprise. And his affair with Susan would give Carol an overwhelming motive.

It was perfect. Goodbye, Carol. Go to hell and take that clinging-vine love of yours with you.

'I'm glad.'

Susan's words brought him back from his reverie. 'What?'

'I'm glad she didn't suffer.'

He held her then, and kissed her hard. In a few minutes they were in bed together, and it was good, better than ever before, as if the danger they were about to face had made their lives that much more real, their feelings more intense, so that they clawed at each other in a wish to take it all. It was not so much like making love, he thought oddly, as making hate.

Afterward they couldn't sleep, so they got dressed, ran the cold pizza through the garbage disposal, and threw the empty box and some dirty napkins in a waste can where they could be found later if anyone wanted to look. Then Harold called a garage a few blocks away and told them that he needed a jump-start. They promised to be there in fifteen minutes. He kissed Susan goodbye and went down to the garage to turn on his lights before the truck arrived.

—Yeah, I guess they must have been on since 6:30 or so. No, battery's dead, no use to try it. Just hook it up and I'll start it.

Perfect. And if they told him to try it first, he could always fake its not starting.

Only when he stepped off the elevator he noticed his lights were on for real. He stopped dead and thought for a moment. Could he have done it subconsciously, left them on to give himself a stronger alibi?

Just then a rusted Volkswagen jerked around the corner, a scruffily bearded man behind the wheel. When he saw Harold he slowed and opened his window. 'That yours?' he asked. Harold could smell the reek of beer from inside the bug.

'Yeah, it is.'

The man shook his head. 'Gonna be deader'n shit. I pulled out around seven and they were on then. You want a jump?'

Around seven?

'Uh, no, no thanks, there's a service truck coming. . . . When did you say you saw my lights on?'

'Seven or so.'

'Are you sure? I . . .' *Don't say too much. He's right. Remember that. He's right.*

'Sure I'm sure!' The voice was testy. ''S'when I left for the friggin' game.'

Harold nodded. His heart was pounding and his face felt as if the blood had deserted it.

The man grunted, and the car shot away up and around a corner. Drunk, Harold thought. It must have been more like ten when the man saw his car. Drunk, that was all.

In a few minutes the service truck pulled into the garage. There was no reason to fake, though—the Jaguar's battery was actually dead. It was charged quickly enough by the truck's heavy-duty job, and Harold wrote the mechanic a personal check. Then he drove back to Manhattan.

His watch glowed 12:14 as he turned off the ignition in the garage beneath his building. He walked in the front door, exchanged a few purposeful pleasantries with Sam the doorman (including a dirty joke Sam would be sure to remember), and rode up to his apartment.

Carol was still there. The little blood that had dripped on the carpet had nearly dried, and her skin had acquired a waxen pallor. The eyes, partially open, had already started to shrink into themselves. Harold shuddered and called the police.

A small army entered the room twenty minutes later, and a detective named Tompkins took Harold into the den. While the army clicked and measured and probed in the living-room, Tompkins did the same to Harold's brain.

Harold played it exactly as planned—no, he left hours ago. Where was he? He couldn't really say. Don't hold anything back, Mr Dodge, don't try to protect anyone or it could be bad for you. Do you really have to know, Lieutenant? A woman, Mr Dodge? (A nod from Harold, a patented understanding smile from Tompkins.) We've got to know who, sir. I understand, I understand.

And then the details—the place, the name, what was done, what was said, who was seen, and we can keep this private, can't we, Lieutenant? Of course, but you understand, we have to check. It's routine. Surely, Lieutenant, I understand. Could we have a recent photograph of yourself, sir? It'll be returned. (Check away, check away, boyo, and if you catch me I'm dumb enough to deserve it.)

They took Carol away then, and Harold went to bed. He felt slightly ill, as much at Tompkins's close examination as at any guilt he felt, but he was exhausted as well, and slept soundly.

The phone woke him at ten in the morning. The memories of the night before jolted him into consciousness, and his voice was crisp and unfogged when he answered.

'Harry?' Susan's voice. 'I just heard. The police were here. Oh, Harry, how awful!'

At first he wondered what she meant, but then he realized she probably suspected a phone tap. Smart girl, he thought. Worth killing for.

'I know,' he said, playing the game. 'It was such a shock to . . . to find her like that. Horrible.' His voice choked dramatically.

'I've got to see you, Harry. Got to talk to you about . . . us.'

Careful there, love. Don't overdo it.

'All right. I need some fresh air. How about the park? Fifty-ninth Street entrance.' No bugs there.

'Fine. Give me an hour, okay?'

'All right. Goodbye, love.' He hung up and took a shower. The phone rang again as he finished toweling himself dry.

'Mr Dodge,' the voice said, 'this is Lieutenant Tompkins. We checked up on your story, sir, and it all fits.'

'You talked to Miss Denton?'

'Yes, sir, we did. Now that in itself wouldn't be enough to establish an alibi, considering your relationship with her, but the kid who delivered the pizza identified your photo . . .'

'He . . .'

'. . . and one of Miss Denton's neighbors saw you enter the building around 6:30. That, with the testimony of the service man who started your car, puts you in the clear, since time of death was determined to be about 8:30.'

'A neighbor . . .'

'Yeah. Uh . . .' Paper rustled over the line. '. . . Mrs Staedelmeyer. Sixtyish widow. You helped her on the elevator with groceries, she said.'

'I . . .' *What the hell!* 'Oh, yes! Yes, I remember now . . .'

Is he trying to trick me? Entrapment?

'I just wanted to let you know that it was okay. I'm sure you have enough on your mind. There'll undoubtedly be a ruling of suicide, but since she didn't leave a note, we've got to look into all the possibilities. You understand.'

'Yeah. Yes, thank you, Lieutenant.'

'Thank you, Mr Dodge. We'll get back to you soon.'

Harold hung up, his mind whirling. *Jesus, the pizza kid? Mrs . . . what was it, Staedelmeyer? What's going on here?*

It had to be a trick, he thought, and he'd been goddam stupid enough to fall for it.

—There *is* no Mrs Staedelmeyer, Mr Dodge. And the pizza kid never saw you or heard your voice, just the shower running. You want to tell us about it now?

Asshole! There were probably a couple of detectives on their way up now!

ꕥ ꕥ

Harold dressed frantically and practically fell down the fire stairs. All he could think of was finding Susan, finding out what the hell went wrong. He emerged breathlessly from the stairwell onto the street and began dogging the seven blocks to Fifty-ninth Street. He entered the park and waited, watching the entrance from behind some thick trees. When Susan arrived, he made his way through the trees to several yards from where she stood looking for him.

'Susan!' he hissed. A crosstown bus drowned out his voice. 'Susan!' he called louder, and she turned toward him.

'Harry!' she said. 'What are you doing in there?' She walked toward him, but he stopped her with a gesture.

'Are you being followed?' he asked.

'Followed? No, why?'

'*Why?*' he repeated, then impatiently gestured for her to join him. When she did, he grabbed her arm roughly and dragged her deeper into the trees. 'What did they ask you? What did you say?'

She seemed confused. 'Why are you so upset? I told them you were with me. That was what *you* told them, wasn't it?'

'Of course! But what's this about the pizza guy seeing me? And this Mrs Staedelmeyer?'

'I told that Lieutenant about them . . .'

'*Why?* Jesus Christ, why did you do that?'

'Harry, you're hurting me! Let go!'

She wrenched away from him and he could see the pale marks where his fingers had dug into her arm. 'Why did you *do* that!' he roared.

'I . . . I thought it would help. . . .'

'Help? That cop tricked me today because of your goddam help! How the hell could you be so stupid as to make up such an obvious lie?'

She shook her head back and forth slowly, her face drawn into a puzzled grimace that reminded him of Carol's death rictus. 'A lie . . .?'

'Yeah!' he barked. 'Yeah! A lie! You know? The things that get you *caught*?'

She still looked confused, but the determined independence that had first drawn him to her was coming to the fore. 'What are you talking about, Harry? What lie?'

He heaved an exasperated sigh. 'The pizza boy didn't see me, for Chrissake, and I don't even know who the hell this Mrs Staedelmeyer *is*. Tompkins caught me on it—he fucking well *caught* me!'

Now she looked concerned, and there was a trace of sympathy in her eyes that Harold couldn't understand. 'Harry,' she said quietly, 'now you listen to me. I know you must be upset by this, and maybe you even feel guilty after what we talked about and . . . and even planned. But there's no reason to now. She was unbalanced, you know that. And you know that that boy saw you when you came out of the bathroom. . . .'

'What are you . . .'

'And you know that you helped that woman with her bags, Harry—I saw you with her when I opened the door for you.'

'No, you . . .' Harold stopped and looked around, sudden suspicion turning his ruddy cheeks pale. 'Where?' he whispered, his eyes darting. 'Where are they?'

'Who?'

'The police, whoever, the people following you. . . .'

'Harry.' Her voice was shaking as if she might suddenly cry. 'Harry, there's nobody else here.'

'Then why are you *saying these things!*' He started to hyperventilate then, and grabbed his head in both hands, trying to press the nausea back inside along with the fear that coated him like dry sweat. When Susan touched him he gasped at the contact, and she stepped quickly away. For a full two minutes he stood there shaking, gasping for sanity until he fell to his knees and rolled slowly over onto the grass, the feathered sunlight slapping his flushed face through the leafy branches overhead.

When he opened his eyes, Susan was standing looking down at him, a tear rolling down her left cheek.

'What time?' he said, his voice quieter now, flatly calm. 'What time did I get there last night?'

She swallowed before she answered. 'Six-thirty.'

'And what time did the pizza come?'

'Eight . . . eight-fifteen.'

When he looked at her face he knew she was not lying.

He lay there for a long time before he spoke again. When he did, it was so low that Susan had to kneel to hear.

'What? What did you say?'

'I killed her,' he repeated.

'No. No, it wasn't your fault.'

'I was there. I shot her. You know that.'

'You were with me.'

'I was with her.'

Susan rose. Her shoulders were hunched, her hands limp. 'Call me,' she said. 'I'm going home. Call me later today.'

He didn't answer.

'Will you do that?' She waited a moment longer, then turned and walked away, out into the roaring of Fifty-ninth Street.

After a while he stood up and walked out onto the street himself. He traversed the seven blocks as though in a dream, nearly getting hit by a cab as he crossed Sixty-fifth against the light. He didn't look to see if people were following him. He was afraid they weren't.

ཨ ཨ

As soon as he entered the apartment he noticed the note peeking slyly from under the chair in which he had shot her. It would have been impossible for the police to have overlooked it the previous night. It read:

> My Dear Harold—
> I have decided to take my own life. My constant depression is more than I can bear, and it is not fair that it ruin your life as well. Be happy, my love.
>
> Your loving Carol.

It was unmistakably his wife's handwriting.

He slumped into the chair, the note held tightly in his trembling fingers. It was the last piece of the puzzle that made up his perfect alibi, but there was no feeling of elated relief in him. Instead there was the numbness of dislocation, of sanity sliding under the door. One-word questions pattered like boiling raindrops inside his skull—*How? Why? Who?*

But he knew who.

He found her other note taped to the mirror on the medicine cabinet in the bathroom when he went for his pills. It was as if she knew he'd need them.

> Darling Harold,
>
> I love you, and have always. I don't know why you did what you did, why you felt it was necessary to end it that way. You should have talked to me, told me what you felt. I would have understood. I understand you far better than you know.
>
> You've never realized how much I love you. Now you'll know. I loved you enough to die for you. I knew what you intended. Even though you wouldn't tell me, wouldn't share with me, I could see it.
>
> Women have died for men before. But has a woman ever died at a man's hands and come back to bless him with safety, to guard him with innocence? That is what I've done for you, to show you the depth of my love. I have given you, my murderer, innocence of my death.
>
> Is that enough?
>
> Do you love me now?
>
> Do you?
>
> Do you?
>
> Then share with me. Love me. Be with me. You can.
>
> Open the cabinet.

His tongue was dry, and he thought that he had stopped breathing. He looked at the door of the cabinet and saw his own face reflected palely in the neon glow. He already looked like a dead man.

His fingers touched the metal knob of the cabinet, then hesitated. He looked back at the note and wondered if those words at the bottom had been there before.

> I would do anything for you.

The cabinet door slid back noiselessly. The straight razor sat alone on the bottom shelf, a cobra ready to spring. His hand captured it and it glittered in the white light.

There were more words on the note. He could see them forming now.

> Share with me. Love me. I need your love.

His whisper was ragged and choked. 'My love was nothing—it was a lie. . . .'

And then he heard Carol's voice in his ear as something gently raised his arm with the razor so that the edge touched his throat, cold as ice, hot as flame . . .

'Mine wasn't.'

. . . drawing it across his skin like a bow across a cello's strings as the love song softly dies away.

Lares & Penates

THE HOUSE WAS SMALL AND WHITE, tucked neatly between two slightly larger houses, divided from the one by a narrow driveway, from the other by five yards of grass. The grass was thin, its sparseness due to the ancient maple in the front yard that served as a huge umbrella, shading both house and grass from the sun. Everything was shaded at the Morgans' place—the little porch set back only a few feet from the sidewalk, the flowers just off the porchfront that somehow grew without sunlight, the windmill and wooden ducks and flamingo and jockey boy that stood close together on both sides of the little walkway that led from sidewalk to porch. Everything was in shadow except the Morgans, Abner and Dorothy.

Abner and Dorothy. For years the sun had seemed to shine on them, and their neighbors looked at them with affection and envy, affection for the affection they gave, envy for what they had become. Not for money or property or fame, but envy for the so difficult achievement of growing old happily and gracefully, for living together in a house, humble as it was, with green shutters and flowers that tried their best and lawn ornaments on what could only with kindness be called a lawn. Abner and Dorothy in their eighties, *sans* rest home, *sans* live-in nurse, *sans* mooching off their children, for there were no children, and that perhaps was unfortunate, but they seemed such a perfect unit that a child might have been an intrusion, a book pushing apart matched bookends.

And on a warm summer's afternoon in this quiet neighborhood on the outskirts of this quiet city, if one goes off the shaded sidewalk up the little cement path, past the flamingo and the ducks and the coal black stare of the jockey boy pretending to hold a lantern that has been missing since 1947, one might hear Abner Morgan say to his wife, Dorothy, 'We can't live anymore.'

'Can't live?'

'It's too much. It's all too much.' Abner vaguely waved a hand at the white mass of bills on the desk top before him. 'Electricity, oil, insurance, groceries . . . and doctor bills. So many doctor bills.'

Dorothy looked down, and her mouth wrinkled like an old leather change purse. 'It's my medication,' she said as if scolding herself.

'Oh no, it's not just that. It's my doctor bills, too. We're old, Dotty. Two old cars so broken down you go broke yourself trying to keep them in shape.

But what else can you do? When it's your life and not a car, what else can you do?' He shook his head and smiled ruefully through his thick white moustache. 'We shouldn't have gone away. That's what did it.'

'Abner, that was . . .'

'Now don't tell me any differently. We didn't have to go. I didn't have to see those places.'

'All your life, Ab, you wanted to see Rome, see Greece, all the places you taught about.'

'A lot of people want,' he answered. 'But they've got better sense.'

'You saved years for that. For us. I loved it just as much as you did. More.'

Abner tossed the pen on the desk, knocking over the pile of bills. 'I just wish we could have gone when we were younger.'

'I don't begrudge it,' Dorothy said dreamily. 'Not at all.'

'You travel,' Abner snorted, 'and what do you have to show for it? Memories, an albumful of photos . . .'

'Souvenirs,' Dorothy smiled.

'Souvenirs,' he repeated, picking up a small stone figure from one of the recesses in the rolltop.

'I love that,' Dorothy said.

'We don't even know if it's authentic.'

'I believed the man,' she said. 'It *looks* old.'

'*We* look old,' Abner replied, hefting the figure in his hand. 'A second mortgage,' he said. 'A second mortgage for this.'

'Not just for that.'

'What else have we got to show for it?'

'What you said. Memories.'

'We can't pay bills with memories.'

She looked at him oddly, as if finally understanding the gravity of his complaints.

'We can't pay the bills,' he said again.

'The mortgage?' she asked in confusion.

'No. Not enough left.'

'But we . . . we had it figured out . . . we could do it all right. . . .'

'That was three years ago, Dotty. Before three more years of inflation and fuel hikes and real estate tax going up all the time.' He ran his fingers through his thin hair. 'Maybe we didn't think we'd live this long.'

'We can cut corners,' she said. 'The telephone—no one calls anymore. Maybe we could . . .'

'Dotty,' he said quietly, 'we haven't had a phone for six months now.'

She looked surprised, but her eyebrows met in remembrance, and she nodded. 'Your pension,' she said, 'the social security, there are increases . . .'

'Not enough. Not for the mortgage. And for the bills.' He looked again at the stone figure. 'Damn it. How ironic. A second mortgage for a *lar*. We lose our home for a *lar*.'

'What? A what?'

He turned toward her, smiling thinly but with kindness. 'A *lar*. I've told you, you remember. *Lares* and *penates*. What this is.'

'*Lares*.' She said the word like the name of an old friend unseen and unthought of for years. 'Yes. *Lares* and *penates*.'

Abner nodded. 'Household gods. Supposed to guard your home, keep it from harm.' He shook his head back and forth, back and forth. 'Only now no home to guard.'

'Is it that bad?'

'That's what I've been saying, Dorothy!' Abner's temper flared, but just a little. 'That's what I've been telling you. We can't pay. We don't have enough money.' With the help of his cane, he got up from the desk and walked over to where she sat on the recliner. 'Our *lares* and *penates* have deserted us, my dear.' He rested a thin-skinned hand on her shoulder.

'What can we do?'

Abner sighed. 'My lodge home, perhaps. I'm still a brother. We could give them everything that's left,' he looked around the small living-room at the shabby acquisitions of sixty years of marriage, 'little as it is.'

'I don't want to go there, Ab,' Dorothy said simply.

'No,' said Abner, 'neither do I.'

'What about my sister?' asked Dorothy. 'What about Julia? Her husband is a doctor. Maybe they'd loan us . . .'

'I won't ask your relations for a loan, Dotty. I wouldn't think of it.' Abner didn't remind her that both Julia and her husband had been dead for ten years. It was easier and less painful to go along with the delusion.

ꕥ

The two of them went out and sat on the porch until supper, talking to each other when they had something to say, lazing in the silence when they didn't, saying hello as neighbors and acquaintances and what seemed like a hundredth generation of children passed by on the sidewalk in front of their home, slowing to enjoy the cool shade of the big maple, the younger children looking at the jockey boy, ducks, flamingo with unfeigned interest, the older ones with a tolerant amusement, the adults not at all, their eyes passing over the statues of painted wood and iron to drink in the couple sitting lovingly on the porch, to smile and say hello and envy. Abner and Dorothy.

Abner and Dorothy. They went to bed when it was still light and awoke with the dawn, so as to use no more electricity than was necessary. On the cool summer mornings Abner would awake first, often before six o'clock, dress in a shirt and bow tie, and sit on the porch until Dorothy arose, watching the day grow bright, feeling the air become warmer as more and more cars would pass on the street.

But on this particular morning, when Abner pushed open the screen door, he heard a metallic jingle. Looking down, he saw that the opening door had knocked over a small stack of coins, a few of which were still piled in no special order. There were pennies and nickels and quarters and dimes, and two large half dollars. There was even a 1922 silver dollar, green with verdigris. All the coins were coated with earth, and some were streaked with grass stains. Abner noticed quite a few pre-1964 silver coins among the dimes and quarters. But where had they come from? Who had set them on his porch in the dark, piled up like some child's play tower?

He was still looking at them, cupping them in his left hand and examining them one by one with his right, when Dorothy came out onto the porch in a dressing-gown. She was smiling, as though the problems of one day could not conceivably be carried over into the next. Abner thought she had probably forgotten. 'What have you got there?' she asked.

'Coins,' he said. 'Somebody left some coins on the porch last night.'

'Why?' She seemed puzzled.

Abner shrugged. 'I don't know. Maybe somebody thinks we're a charity case.'

'That's silly,' Dorothy said, and Abner was sure that she *had* forgotten. He felt ashamed. Holding the coins made him feel like a beggar.

'I never asked,' he said, half to himself. 'I never complained to anyone.'

'A silver dollar,' Dorothy said, taking it. 'You don't see these much today.' She put it back in his hand. 'What are you going to do with these, Ab?'

'I don't know.' He thought hard. Kids? But why? 'Take them to the coin shop, maybe. There are some old ones here.' He might as well keep them. He might as well. Somebody wanted them to have them. And God knew he could use them.

'Oh, you've moved a duck,' Dorothy said.

'What?'

'You moved a duck. Look—the last one.' He looked and couldn't see any difference, but Dorothy was probably right. One day she'd forget her own name and a minute later she'd remember at what theater they'd seen *Yankee Doodle Dandy* in '42.

'The last one,' he said, stepping down to where the mama duck and her four ducklings were frozen in the permanent waddle they'd held for decades.

'Put it nearer the others,' she said, and he moved it as she directed, brushing a bit of dirt from its wooden bill. 'Goodness, but they're dusty,' Dorothy said as Abner rejoined her on the porch. 'I'll wash them a bit after breakfast.'

They went back inside and while Dorothy made breakfast, Abner set the coins on the desk and counted them. They totaled $7.38, but he thought the silver would bring more from the coin shop, and it did. The coin man asked Abner if he had a metal detector, but Abner told him no, that these were just some coins he'd found over the years. He didn't like to lie, but the truth was too improbable, and, to a man as proud as Abner, too embarrassing.

'Look,' he said when he arrived home. 'Forty dollars.'

'From the coins,' Dorothy said. 'That's wonderful. But come sit down. Such a long walk.'

Abner *was* tired. It had been ten blocks each way to the coin shop. 'Not enough, though,' he said, shaking his head. 'Part of the oil bill, that's all. Not enough.'

But the next morning there was enough. Neatly stacked in a small pile was $185, mostly in tens and twenties. It had been raining, but the money was dry under the porch roof.

'What shall we do?' Abner asked rhetorically.

'Keep it,' Dorothy shrugged.

'Dotty, we can't keep it. Not this much. This is a lot of money!'

'Somebody wanted us to have it. It didn't walk up on our porch by itself.'

'But it might be stolen.'

Dorothy laughed. 'Who'd steal money to give it away? Robin Hood? Besides, we kept the coins. What's the difference?'

Abner didn't know. His first inclination was to report it to the police, but then he wondered if that meant he would have to tell them about the coins too, and why he had spent them but reported the bills. Besides, maybe Dorothy was right. Maybe someone knew they were in trouble and wanted to be their friend, someone with enough money not to miss a few hundred dollars, someone with enough sense to know that a flat-out offer of aid would be refused. But gifts in the middle of the night (*scarlet ribbons*, thought Abner, *scarlet ribbons*)—well, that was another matter.

The money was enough to meet the bills that month, but Abner did not allow them to splurge on anything. They kept the electric use low, using the radio only for a little music with supper and the morning national news at eight. Though he was tempted, they didn't resubscribe to the newspaper they'd dropped months before, so they didn't find out about the killing down in the ward.

ஐ ஐ

Not that a killing in the ward was anything out of the ordinary, but it was the nature of the crime that earned it more than a back column in the city's sole daily. A young black man of dubious legal reputation was found stretched in an alleyway, his body bearing the signs of innumerable shallow puncture wounds, and blows light enough to daze but not kill. He had bled to death after what appeared to have been a long struggle. Screams had been heard, but screams were frequently heard in the ward. The young man's empty wallet was found by his body.

Dorothy heard all this in great detail from her friend Esther, who visited every Sunday. 'Oh, they just kill each other down there all the time,' Esther was saying. 'They're like *animals*, Dorothy.'

'It's a shame,' Dorothy said. 'Such a waste.'

'Hardly a waste,' Esther replied. 'I'm just glad they're all down there and not in *our* neighborhoods. But I'll tell you this, it's not even the colored that are so bad down in the ward as it is those Puerto Ricans. It was a Puerto Rican that did it, I'll just bet you. . . .' And Esther was off again. Dorothy had heard her vilify the Puerto Ricans so often that she turned off Esther's voice, thought about something else, and didn't mention the killing to Abner when he returned from his walk in the park.

Three weeks later Dorothy's doctor changed her prescription. 'They're more expensive, Ab,' she told Abner as they walked home from the medical center, 'but Dr Long said Medicare should cover most of it.' It did, they learned, but not all. Two days later the compressor in the old Kelvinator broke down. With labor, fixing it cost over a hundred dollars.

The thunder woke Abner at five the next morning, and he lay for a while wondering what they were going to do and listening to the rain slapping the wide leaves of the maple, splashing on the worn shingles of the roof. Unable to go back to sleep, he got up and dressed, the rain-smell sweet and damp in his nostrils. He made a cup of instant coffee and took it onto the porch. There was no wind, and the rain came straight down, saturating the tiny front yard, but leaving the porch dry so that he was able to sit on the swing without first wiping it.

It was too dark to see the money at first. Only after he had finished his coffee and the sun had turned the sky from black to a flat gray did he notice it, three fat piles of bills a yard away from his slippered feet. His hands trembled as he picked them up and counted them. There was $650. He felt his heart trip and race, then sat back, making himself relax, making himself think slowly.

Who? Who could it be? And how could they know how badly he and Dorothy needed it? And why on the porch, where it could be stolen, why not in the mail? And *who*? And *why*?

He thought of not telling Dorothy at all, of not worrying her with it, but they had shared so much over so many years that the act of deceit would have been impossible. He took the money inside and put it in a desk drawer. When Dorothy came downstairs he showed it to her.

She seemed only a bit surprised, as if something that she'd been expecting had come in the mail, but far sooner that she had hoped. 'Do you know?' he pressed. 'Do you have any idea of who could be doing this?'

'*Lares*.' She smiled.

'What?' His ears marked it as a person's name at first.

'*Lares*,' she repeated. 'Those household gods.' She picked up the stone figure in the desk cubbyhole. 'Maybe him. He won't let us lose our home.'

'Dotty,' he said weakly, 'oh, Dotty, he can't move, he can't go out and bring back money. It's someone else. Someone else.'

She sighed, turning the figure in her hands. 'You must be right, Ab,' she said, 'but it's such a nice thought.'

'I'd better go to the police.'

'No,' Dorothy said. 'There's no reason. We didn't take it from anyone. It's a gift. Someone wanted us to have it.'

Had it not seemed so magical, she might not have convinced him. But it *did* seem to have magic in it, glamor in the ancient sense, as he had taught the word to countless members of his English class over how many winters. Glamour, magic. The finding of treasures, the gifts from gods to men. Might not questioning the sources anger the gods? While Dorothy made breakfast he looked at the *lar* she had been holding. Impossible, he thought. Not this. Not this tired and worn old piece of stone whose household, even if he were truly a *lar*, had perished long ago, whose members were dust, whose doors and walls and windows no longer existed even in memory.

But then, damn it, damn it, damn it, *what*?

They kept the money and it kept them. Abner did not tell the police, and Dorothy did not tell Abner what Esther told her three days later of the two numbers runners found dead in the ward earlier that week. 'Same way as the other one,' Esther said. 'All those little wounds. Some sort of Puerto Rican weapon, I'll just bet.'

ᘓ ᘐ

And the weeks passed into months until October came and it was time for the reckoning of the fuel oil budget. According to the bill, they owed \$130, and the monthly rate was going from \$40 to \$65. The next morning Abner found the money again, \$350 this time, in \$50 bills. There was no question of not spending it. It was, he had decided, magic, if not of a household god, then the magic of a friend who knew their needs even as quickly as they did.

A policeman came to the door a few days later, a short, stocky, balding man in his mid-fifties who showed his identity card and badge before he would pass through the door Dorothy held open for him. 'Someone's here,' Dorothy called to Abner upstairs, who came down slowly, one hand on the railing, the other on his cane.

The policeman's eyes narrowed for a moment, and he gave a small smile, the gentleness of which seemed ill at ease on his coarse features. 'Mr Morgan,' he said. 'You taught English at Rutherford?'

'Yes, that's right.'

The policeman laughed softly. 'I had no idea you were the Abner Morgan I had to see. I'm Randy Nolt. I had you when I was a junior. Class of '45.'

'Oh my,' said Abner. 'That was a long time ago. You were . . . Kathy's brother.'

'Right!' Nolt smiled. 'She was a year ahead of me.'

Abner maneuvered his cane to his left hand and shook hands with Nolt. 'It's nice to see you again, Randy. What can we do for you?'

They sat. 'I'm with the police, Mr Morgan. A lieutenant. And I came over to just ask you a question or two.'

Abner stiffened, and Dorothy seemed to lose her composure as well, her fingers darting about suddenly like freed birds. Nolt noticed the transition. 'A question,' Abner repeated thickly.

'Is something wrong?'

'No, no,' said Abner nonchalantly.

'No,' Dorothy parroted.

Nolt looked at them for a minute, then went on. 'We're trying to trace some bills,' he said. 'Now, on Tuesday last, Mr Morgan, you paid a bill to Hollister Oil with three fifty-dollar bills. According to the serial numbers on them, those are some of the same bills that were stolen in a break-in at Woolworth's downtown a couple of weeks ago. We have a suspect under suspicion . . . or had one . . . so if you could remember where *you* got the bills it would really help us out.'

Abner and Dorothy looked at each other, then Dorothy turned back to Nolt. 'I really don't remember, we had them for . . .'

'No, Dotty,' Abner said. 'We're going to tell the truth. We found the money,' he told Nolt.

'Found it.'

'On our porch. There were seven bills. The others are right here,' and he took them from his wallet and handed them to the policeman.

'Found them,' said Nolt. 'You swear to that.'

'On my life.' Then Abner told Nolt about the money he had found the other times, and Nolt's face grew paler and his expression grew more grim.

'Mr Morgan,' he said finally. 'I didn't tell you everything at first because I didn't want to upset you.' He paused. 'It's not just a theft I'm investigating—it's a murder.' Nolt looked down at his hands so that he wouldn't see the old people's eyes. 'That suspect I mentioned . . . he was found killed the other night in the ward, his pockets emptied of money. It was the same M.O. as some of the other recent ward killings, and from what you've told me, Mr Morgan, you've been finding your money the morning after each of those murders. And the amounts correspond fairly well to the amounts these people were supposed to have been carrying.'

Nolt looked up at last, and saw the horror and fear etched into the pale faces along with the wrinkles of age. 'Look,' he said reassuringly, 'I don't for a minute believe that either of you are responsible in any way for these deaths. The victims were strong, big, young. But someone *might* have committed these crimes to get money for you. Do you know of anyone who might do something like that?'

At first Nolt thought Dorothy Morgan had begun to say something, but she was only going, 'tsk, tsk, tsk,' over and over again, shaking her head in short jerky motions, like a feeding hen.

'I don't know of anyone who would do that,' Abner said. 'Not kill. Not even steal for us.' He looked at Nolt with pleading eyes. 'My wife . . . she's upset. Could you leave us alone for a while, wait on the porch perhaps?'

'Just a minute,' Nolt said. 'Then I think we'd better go downtown.' Abner looked alarmed, but Nolt's next words were soothing. 'Just till we decide what to do with you.'

'Do with us?'

Nolt shrugged. 'Protective custody, maybe. I mean, there's a possibility that whoever did this could turn against you—get mad at you for telling the truth.'

The next morning, while Abner and Dorothy were still sleeping in the quiet motel room in which the police had put them, the morning papers hit the streets with a front page story about 'The Robin Hood Slayer', which a boozed-up sergeant had let slip to a reporter. The story was picked up by a wire service, and that evening Abner and Dorothy heard their names mentioned by Frank Reynolds.

After a week, they were permitted to return to their house, and Abner shook his head as he saw the pile of bills that had accumulated in the mailbox. 'What to do now, Dotty,' he said. 'Worse than ever.' It was far worse. Besides the $350, the other money, he'd been told, might have to be returned as well, if and when a link was definitely established. It could, if a killer was not found, take years.

But Abner and Dorothy's finances were resolved in far less time than that. Two days after they arrived home, they received a visit from a representative of a Los Angeles film production company. His clothes and car bespoke money, as did the offer he made them to turn their experiences into a TV movie. 'But there's no story,' Abner protested. 'We don't know who did it. They may *never* find out.'

'We'll take the chance.' The man had smiled. 'Might be more intriguing if they don't.'

They didn't. Six months went by, and Abner paid all the bills and paid off the mortgage as well from the option money the man had given them. There was not the slightest lead, nor the barest hint of who might have been responsible for the killings. Esther continued to blame the Puerto Ricans, 'though why they'd give good money to white people like us is beyond me, I'll just tell you. . . .'

ജ ര

The next spring the leaves came back onto the maple tree, and Dorothy's flowers grew in shadow, and Abner thought that maybe there was a little more grass on the front lawn than last year. In May the big check came, the check that meant they were really going to make the film, and Abner paid to have the house repainted in June. The following October they watched the movie on a windy Friday night, feeling somehow detached from the shadow show on the screen.

After it was over, Dorothy turned it off and said, 'You know, Ab, I'm glad they didn't catch him.'

Abner's eyes widened. 'He was a murderer, Dotty.'

She thought for a moment, as if trying to recall something, then smiled. 'You're right. Yes, he was,' she said, then turned and went upstairs.

Early in the morning, around two o'clock, two drunken college boys who had seen the movie stopped in front of Abner and Dorothy's house and took the heavy jockey boy as a souvenir for their apartment. The jockey boy was back when Abner stepped onto the porch the next morning. It had not rained the previous night, and this time Abner saw the blood. He stood for a long time looking into the deep black eyes, then at the sharp beak of the flamingo, and finally at the wide flat bills of the wooden ducks, thinking, thinking until things finally started to come together. Together, like Abner and Dorothy, glamour and magic, *lares* and *penates*.

He went back into the house, came out with a wet paper towel, and carefully, almost tenderly, cleaned the blood from the lanternless fist. The paint was chipped in a dozen places, and he reminded himself to get some at the hardware store. It was, he thought, the least he could do. For *lares*. *Lares* and *penates*.

I'll Drown my Book

LATELY I'VE THOUGHT OFTEN of what Prospero says in *The Tempest* when he renounces magic:

> I'll break my staff,
> Bury it certain fathoms in the earth,
> And deeper than did ever plummet sound
> I'll drown my book.

And now I renounce my magic as well, and end my career before it's begun. It's knowing what *he* knows, J. M. Wingarden, writer, literary artist, spinner of sorceries, mystery man extraordinaire, that makes me turn my back on words.

When he vanished seventeen years ago, the literary world—by which I mean the world of all who read—was shaken. He had been prominent for only a year, yet in that time there had appeared two novels that some consider the finest in the language. *In the Shadows* brilliantly examined in less than two hundred pages the dark soul of twentieth-century man, and *Over the Border* screamed a warning to civilization with searing sanity. The books were praised, bought, read, and shivered at, then read again. And the name of J. M. Wingarden became universally known.

Then, as suddenly as his star had gone into nova, he became a black hole. J. M. Wingarden vanished utterly. Whether he died or dropped voluntarily from sight no one knew, but the latter was the guess of most of the *literati*, as his books were never reprinted, despite the staggering demand. Only contractual machinations by the author himself, went the reasoning, could have produced the situation, for the publishers were reputedly livid at having to suppress the books.

So J. M. Wingarden disappeared, but the mystery remained, greater than that surrounding all the other literary riddles of our time: Traven, Salinger, Pynchon. At least we have the works, if not the men. But Wingarden became more than a riddle. He became an enigmatic legend, the Sphinx of Letters.

He called me on the telephone three months ago. I thought it was a joke, but the voice sounded so sincere, so unfailingly *right*, that I believed him within a few sentences. He said:

'Mr McPeel, this is J. M. Wingarden.'

The voice was heavy, rich with something beyond years. I didn't answer.

'The writer. I wrote *In the Shadows* and . . .'

'Yes,' I interrupted. 'I know you.' I had to add, 'If this isn't a joke.'

'No,' he said. 'It's not a joke. I'm alive.' I hadn't suggested otherwise, so the comment seemed odd to me. 'I would like to give an interview.'

'An . . . interview?' I could barely speak.

'Yes. Do you think it would be profitable for you? I mean to say, do you think you could get it published?'

Could I get it published? Only in every damn magazine in the country. 'That would be no problem at all, sir.'

'Are you certain? It's very important to me that it be disseminated as widely as possible.'

'I can guarantee that, Mr Wingarden.' My mind raced as I thought of possible markets. 'But why have you decided to grant an interview after so many years?'

'I'll explain that when we meet. That is, if you want to do it?'

'Oh, yes sir, definitely.' In another second I would have crawled into the mouthpiece. I wanted to get the details—where and when—quickly, as I had this irrational fear that at any second he'd say *very well*, hang up, and disappear again. But instead he told me where he lived and how to get there (I scribbled the directions frantically), gave me his phone number (listed under 'Johnson, M.'), and asked me if the following Thursday would be all right. I said it would, and he quickly hung up, as if unused to human contact.

My heart was literally pounding as a dozen questions sprang to mind: Was he planning a comeback? Was there a new novel or at least a plan to reprint the first two? And why *me*, for God's sake? Why not Updike or Fowles or Mailer or a hundred other writers who would have tossed their paperback rights onto a pile of flaming film options just to sit at the feet of J. M. Wingarden?

It didn't matter. All that mattered was that *I* was going to do it. My few dozen stories and articles, my three paperback originals—all that was nothing. From now on I would be known as the man who found J. M. Wingarden, and when I thought of the doors that would open, I felt giddy.

I cancelled the interviews I'd scheduled with some potters for an *Art News* article, dug out my copies of *In the Shadows* and *Over the Border*, and re-read them twice that weekend. On Monday I hit the New York Public, went through the 1968–69 *Reader's Guide* and *Book Review Digest*, and O.D.'d on Wingardenian microfiche. Tuesday held more of the same, and by that evening I figured I knew as much (or as little) about J. M. Wingarden as anyone except the man himself.

I got my notepads, tapes, and clothes packed and took a flight to Philly the next morning. From there, a rattly commuter jerked me to Lancaster. I rented a car, found a Holiday Inn, and called Wingarden to make sure everything was still go. It was, but he didn't seem talkative, and I hoped his reticence wouldn't carry over into the interview.

The following day I drove south-east to a small town named Quarryville, and another mile east to Wingarden's farmhouse. My mentioning this is no breach of confidentiality. It makes no difference now. The house was large and boxy, set far back from the two-lane. A weathered barn and several smaller outbuildings surrounded it on three sides. Though the grounds seemed well kept, the paint on the house was chipped, and a large limb lay untouched at the base of a huge elm in the front yard.

It took several minutes for him to answer the door after I knocked. At first I thought he was a servant in his checked wool shirt and worn poplin trousers, and his apparent age also fooled me. The dust-jacket photo taken seventeen years earlier showed a man in his late thirties, an unlined face beneath a cap of dark, curly hair. But this man appeared to be at least seventy. A light halo of white hair fringed a mottled scalp, and the lines in his face were scarred with far more than fifty-five years of frowns. He didn't smile. That whole day I never saw him smile.

He introduced himself and invited me in. There was a large bookcase in the foyer, and in the dim light I could see that it was packed with multiple copies of his two novels. The books were in varying conditions, and there seemed to be no semblance of order in the way they were arranged on the shelves.

Wingarden led me into a room on the left, a den with a lounger, a large color TV, a couch, and a coffee table. There was no desk in the room. The walls were lined with bookshelves, all packed solid with only two titles—*In the Shadows* and *Over the Border*. He sat in the lounger, and I on the couch. I put the tape recorder on the table and took out my notepads, but he held up a hand.

'No notes, please. You may use the recorder, but I ask that after the tape is transcribed you destroy it without making a copy.'

I agreed, turned on the recorder, and began.

'May I ask you a personal question first? How did you come to choose me to interview you?'

'I called Dan Rhodes and he suggested you. Said you were a good writer. And an honest one.'

I nodded. Dan was my agent. He'd handled Wingarden at the beginning of his career, but I hadn't made the connection before. 'I couldn't help but notice,' I went on, 'that your bookshelves are filled with your own work.'

'I don't read anyone else,' he said coldly. 'I can't concentrate long enough.'

I didn't want him hostile and made a mental note to come back to the subject later. 'How long have you lived here?'

'Seventeen years. Ever since I dropped from sight. I have a large garden out back that keeps me busy.'

'Do you still write?'

He shook his head. 'I never write. The money I made from the books has been enough to get me by. I bought real estate with it years ago, invested. I live on interest.'

'Why did you stop writing? Why disappear?'

He sat quietly for a moment, then weakly waved the question away. I decided to go back to the books. There wasn't much else to ask. 'Why have you collected all these copies of your work?'

'I needed them.' He said it and stopped, as though it were enough, but it wasn't, and I looked at him and waited. He sat uncomfortably, then added, 'I couldn't destroy them. I'd worked too hard on them to do that.'

I scanned the shelves. 'You know you've got a tidy fortune here. Your books are fetching high prices in the out-of-print market.'

He nodded. 'That's become a problem to me.'

'How so?'

'I've been buying up copies ever since I dropped from sight. The book dealers I work through think I'm one of them—M. Johnson. But, as you say, the prices have accelerated tremendously, and it's becoming more difficult for me to buy them.'

I didn't understand. He didn't seem a megalomaniac, or even a grand eccentric.

He stood up. 'Come with me. I want to show you the house.'

I switched off the recorder and followed him, while he barked out 'kitchen', 'sitting-room', 'dining-room', as we entered each dim chamber. But none were so dark that I could not see the floor-to-ceiling shelves full of books that covered nearly every wall on the two floors.

Then he took me into the basement. It was huge, packed nearly solid with piles of cardboard boxes. I lifted one of the lids and found what I'd expected—a box of J. M. Wingarden's two novels, the same books that sat on every shelf in the house.

'Let's step outside for a moment,' he said, and when we were on the porch he pointed to the barn, whose top was at least fifty feet from the ground. 'It's full of them,' he said quietly, 'hundreds of cartons of them, stacked on skids.'

I had to ask, 'How many? How many altogether?'

'Of *In the Shadows*, one hundred and thirty thousand, eight hundred and fourteen. *Over the Border*, two hundred and eight thousand, five hundred and forty.'

I wanted to laugh in my discomfort, but didn't. 'Why have you done this? How many copies of your books do you want?'

'All of them,' he said and walked back into the house.

Back in the den he sat in the lounger and waited for me to turn on the recorder before he started to talk. I didn't have to ask a question for a long time.

'It began in '68, just after *Over the Border* came out. The reviews were good, and it sold very well.' He shook his head. 'Too well. It was a few days after Christmas that I felt it for the first time. I awoke just after midnight to the sound of something inside my head. I lay in the dark for a moment, and it was as if someone were there in the room watching me. More than just watching, really—it was as if my mind were being probed, looked into, as if my thoughts were no longer mine alone, but audible for anyone to hear. It was a feeling of intense . . .' He waved his hand in the air, reaching for a word, '. . . *discomfort*, an obscene intrusion. And I could not shake it off. Finally I took some pills and dropped into sleep.

'But the next day the sensation was back, and now it seemed as though *several* people were with me, prying into my brain, discovering everything I'd hidden from the world. As the days went by the sensation grew stronger, until I was afraid I was actually going insane, that the tremendous critical and popular success had been too much for me to handle. Yet I wasn't aware of any such change in myself. I only wanted to write more, to use the success as a base from which I could reach higher.' He laughed without mirth. 'I found myself, after writing a book about madness, going mad.'

Sighing deeply, he reclined the lounger so that he stared up at the ceiling. I felt like a psychiatrist. 'And then,' he went on, 'I realized what it was.

'I *felt* them reading me.

'I couldn't imagine what caused it, and I've not come up with a fully logical answer in all these years. I suppose it may have been due to my sensitivity. I've always been aware of other people's reactions, emotions, and such. Somehow my books my have acted as a sort of storage battery, so that there is actually not only a part of me, but *all* of me in every one of those books.'

He sat without speaking for a minute, then said quietly, 'An author has the limitless accessibility of God. He can reach out and speak to millions, each at a different time, precisely when they want to hear his voice, read his mind, reach into his thoughts. But unlike God—lucky, lucky God—he is incapable of turning them away. If they own the book, they own him. His thoughts . . . *my* thoughts . . . are there at their command. They read me, and I must speak to them.

'The first few years were the worst. Shortly after these . . . visitations, shall I call them? . . . began, I ordered my publisher to stop reprinting. They were furious, but I had my rights. The power of a good writer, eh? The damned books were everywhere, and I would have gone bankrupt trying to buy them up, so I bided my time. I had no choice.

'It was agonizing. Millions were reading the books, and I felt them all, prying and probing. Laudanum was the only thing that gave me peace, and I became addicted, but at least the sensations diminished enough to let me sleep, though fitfully.

'The books already in print disappeared from the stores quickly, as they were *the* books of the season, and their mysterious author caused no end of unwanted publicity. I was read and read and read over and over until my brain was so swollen I knew it would burst. I had to start collecting the books, in the hope that by gathering them up I would be gathering the pieces of myself that I needed to become whole again.

'I wrote to book dealers under my pseudonym, inquiring after copies, and was able to buy them cheaply. Condition was unimportant, and since my investments were showing an honorable return, I was able to amass several thousand copies in the first few months. But it became more difficult. Although the readership dropped, it was still high enough to cause terrible pain.'

He suddenly straightened the chair and looked at me. 'Think of your own work,' he said. 'An article appears in a popular magazine, and for a month or two the odds are good that whatever the time of day, your words, your thoughts, are being read by someone somewhere in this country.'

There was horror in his eyes. The thought had occurred to me, particularly at the beginning of my career, and with pleasure. But from the perspective of J. M. Wingarden, I began to feel like an actor who was always on stage in front of an audience that never went home.

'Now,' he said, his voice thick, 'multiply that by several thousand over a period of *years*, and you'll know what I've gone through.'

'But it would be impossible,' I said, 'to gather *all* the books. Why even try?'

'I must,' he answered, rising and crossing to the shaded window. He reached out a hand to pull back the shade, but let it drop to his side. 'I simply must try to get them back.'

'Hasn't readership of your work fallen off considerably? Certainly that must ease this feeling of yours.'

'It's changed it, not eased it. Before it was like a torrent. Now it's a faucet dripping in an inconstant rhythm. It stops for a time, and you think, peace at last. Then someone somewhere picks up a book, and it starts again.'

He drew in a breath, and the air in his throat rippled in a sob. 'That's why I asked you here, so that I could tell them, *beg* them all to read me no more, to send me the books . . .'

'Send them? Why not destroy them?'

'No!' he cried, with more force than I had imagined him capable of showing. 'No. I'm part of them. Too much of my life went into them to see them destroyed. Otherwise, why shouldn't I have destroyed all these? No. They must send them to me. They'll be returned upon my death, I promise that. But I can't afford to buy them anymore, that's impossible for me now.'

I tried to grasp some bit of logic in his ramblings, tried to find some way to break down his psychosis. 'What if it backfires?' I asked in as reasoned a voice as possible. 'What if it creates a renewal of interest, and your books begin to be widely read again? And why should people send you books worth a hundred dollars and up?'

'They must,' he said, looking at me with hurt, frightened eyes. 'After I've given them everything I have, would they refuse me so little?'

He sat down and reclined the lounger once more. 'As for the renewal of interest, it's a chance I have to take. I can't go on like this much longer. I was able to give up the laudanum years ago, but I must resume its use if things continue as they are. If I do, it will kill me.' He craned his neck to look directly into my eyes, and I'll never forget his look of pleading desperation. 'You're my final hope, Mr McPeel.'

He wouldn't talk about anything else. Before I left, he gave me some papers that would corroborate my story. He stood on the porch as I drove away, his head down, shoulders hunched as if against a heavy wind. But there was no wind.

When I got back to the city the next day, I transcribed the tape and edited the hard copy. The cassette I erased, dismantled, and threw in the garbage. Then I called Dan, and he told me to bring over the interview first thing Monday morning. He hadn't arrived by ten, so I left it and the corroborating papers with his secretary. He called me that evening.

'This is for real?' he asked.

'For real. He's crazy, Dan. Truly.'

He sighed. 'Crazy or not, I can place this high. Give me a week.'

It took less. He called me on Thursday to tell me that *Time* was the winning bidder with a figure so high it was embarrassing. The piece appeared three weeks later with a cover photograph of J. M. Wingarden. It was an eight-page, removable, center insert. My by-line, though not on the cover, was firmly ensconced on the first page, along with a photo Dan had supplied.

Wingarden had been amazingly right in one way. Copies of *In the Shadows* and *Over the Border* poured in to *Time*'s offices for weeks. But they never got to Wingarden.

Wingarden was dead.

He died the day after his *Time* hit the newsstands. It was a combination of a cerebral hemorrhage and a massive coronary. The doctors couldn't explain how both had hit at once. But I can.

Quite simply, his mind imploded. He couldn't withstand the real or imagined input that must have buffeted his brain as literally millions of people read his words at one time. Perhaps he thought that because they were only spoken, they would not have the power that his written words had had years before. At least, I think he believed that; he seemed so sure it would not harm him.

Yet he was wrong, and that's what I find so frightening. If it was all paranoia, delusion, he shouldn't have died, for he hadn't imagined that outcome. And even if he had—if the whole thing had been a suicidal plot—what human mind could shatter both brain and heart in one cataclysmic moment?

In that impossibility lies my terror. In that and more.

It started the evening Wingarden died. I awoke just after midnight to a touch as light as a strand of spiderweb or the wings of a moth, and a low buzzing inside my head.

I took a few Seconals and finally got back to sleep. But the next day was a nightmare, and before noon, before I'd even heard of Wingarden's death, I knew that his awareness was now mine. I talked to Dan about it, and he suggested a psychiatrist. I'll see him, for what it's worth, but I'm not going to stop what I've been doing for the past few weeks—going to every used book shop in Manhattan and buying up those originals I wrote in a mad burst of hack creativity two years ago.

If any of you send me copies of *Heart of Space*, *Timeframe 2000*, or *Within the Giant's Grip*, I'll send you a dollar for each, plus postage. Fifty cents for any magazine with one of my stories in it.

And please don't read them first.

Prometheus's Ghost

ON FIFTH AVENUE, THE OLD MAN howled. He lifted his black and weathered face, empty eyes glaring at cathedral spires, and howled long and loud. David Ormond stopped walking and turned to look. Usually Ormond ignored the street crazies, but the blind man had been on Fifth Avenue for so many years that Ormond thought of him as an institution. Winters and summers Ormond saw the man and his dog, a mixed breed that reminded him of a large bear cub. The sign the man bore on his back was nearly as creased and stained with years as the man's face. *Here but for the grace of God go thee. Buy a pencil.*

'What's *wrong* with you people?' Ormond was close enough to see the yellowed teeth, the dark holes where others were missing. The blind man's nose was running, and moisture clotted his untrimmed moustache. '*I* know! *I* know! You're all *ghosts*! This city is fulla ghosts! I *hear* you—I hear you walkin' and talkin'—but you don't buy no pencils no more, I ain't heard no fuckin' plunkin' in my goddam cup. . . .' The words rushed out, the irregular puffs of vapor making a frenzied smokestack of the man. Ormond caught his balance as someone jostled him from behind, and decided to move again.

He walked down Fifth, listening to the old man's cries of '*Ghosts*! Goddam *ghosts*!' diminish, swallowed up by traffic and voices and the scuff of shoes on cement. He did not look back, but the old man stayed beside him, becoming in Ormond's mind another old man, his father.

Ormond counted the months and came up with seven. It surprised him that so much time had passed, but then he supposed that the experience would always seem near, even if he grew old. His father had been so sad at the end, so full of despair at leaving a life that had never been very good to him. Burdened with various cancers since his fifties, he had fought back and held on long enough to see his ever-healthy wife die of a stroke just before their fortieth wedding anniversary. Even then, with machines doing the work of half his sundered organs, he feared death more than he hated what he'd become. He'd not been comforted by pastoral words, nor from his only son's lying assurances that soon he and his wife would be reunited. A few nights before he died in pain, not being granted the grace of coma, he had held Ormond's hand in his, squeezed with what little strength remained, said, 'If only I knew, Davey, if only I knew, I wouldn't be so scared,' and they had both cried. Ormond had thought that cry his father's own, but later he realized that it was that of each bit of humanity damned with the unwanted leisure to slide slowly into the dark rather than fall headlong. If only we knew, he thought again as he walked.

Then the two previously disparate concepts collided within him. The blind man had cried of ghosts, and his father had wished for life. And what were ghosts if not some evidence of the survival of life?

It was Saturday. Ormond walked past Saks, where he'd intended to buy some shirts, and continued down Fifth until he came to the main library. The subject catalog on 'Ghosts' was impressive, and after an hour of consideration and browsing, he withdrew four books: two on parapsychology and related fields, an older volume on ceremonial magic, and a thin chapbook on ghostly folklore and traditions. He spent all afternoon reading, gathering snippets of spectral lore and making notations on a yellow pad.

When he finally glanced out his window, Ormond was surprised to find that night had fallen. He had not realized how deeply he had been immersed in the books. It was as if for the past several hours someone other than himself had been controlling his actions, encouraging his dilettantism in the field of the supernatural. He had never had any interest in the subject before; he didn't care for horror movies, and even as a child the ghost stories the other children shivered at had left him bored, impressed only by their silliness. Why, after forty years, was he now seeking out such tales?

The answer was simple, and it came to him simply. He was haunted, not by ghosts, but by death itself, by its reality and finality, by its might and surety in claiming his father. Yet it was not for his father that he was now seeking some spectral sign of assurance, but for himself. He'd thought a thousand times, not only since the death, but since his father had contracted his first, gentle carcinoma, about the hereditary aspects of cancer, the other death that might be waiting for *him* in the years ahead, years that might not prove as long as he would wish. At times he thought it inevitable that the genes bequeathed to him should someday turn rebel and devour their fellows. And then he would tell himself that death was inevitable for *everyone*, that it was the price one paid for the experience of life. But that knowledge did not comfort him. The only thing that could do that, he realized, was the knowledge that what he had been reading about was real.

Ormond poured himself a double scotch and looked out to the lighted windows of the apartments opposite. The liquor warmed him, and he began to wonder if he were serious, if he were willing to make the search in earnest. Dim forms passed behind glass or curtains. He wondered what those people were looking for tonight, what they were planning, what they wanted to learn or acquire. Money that would eventually be left to relations or the state? Position that could be snatched away long before death? Sex that would not matter a jot when he was shrunken and withered, she dry and barren in the earth? Those things made his own quest seem not nearly so absurd as he had first considered it. He looked for nothing more nor less than the calm certainty of immortality, the ability to face death in peace, and surely such a search was worth time and money.

He sat down and looked at the pages of notations he had made. Medieval superstitions, backwoods legends, parapsychological theories were all there, and running through them was a unity, a sense of purpose, a message he could not ignore. *Seek and ye shall find* was the essence. To open oneself, to be willing to listen and believe, was essential. *Self-delusion*, he thought. *Hallucinations. You expect to see ghosts and you will, but only the ghosts of your own mind. That's why most apparitions are horrible, because we're afraid of them and we project that fear.* He told himself that he had to retain doubt, if only to avoid creating his own ghosts. He could not afford to lose his disbelief. He would have to see a ghost *in spite* of his lack of faith. That was the only way in which he could believe in one.

But where, for God's sake?

Then he thought of Mallory Stewart, his father's partner. Mal had taken over the real estate business a few weeks after the funeral, paying Ormond a healthy sum for all the years and energy his father had sunk into it. In truth, Mal had been the strong one, doing the lion's share of the work once the first illness had claimed his partner. Ormond had felt guilty taking the money, but Mal had insisted, and told him that if he ever needed anything to let him know. Perhaps Mal could help him now.

When he called, Mal sounded as jovial as ever. 'Davey, good to hear from you. What's up?' The voice was harsh from years of Camels, but that was the only effect that the four decades of nicotine had had.

'Well, I was wondering if you were going to be home tomorrow. Thought I might drop by.'

'Just happen to be in the neighborhood of Utica?' Ormond heard the good-humored irony in Mal's voice. There was no reason to dissemble.

'There *is* something I'd like to talk about.'

'Sure. We'll be around. Anytime after one.'

Ormond arrived early the next afternoon. He chatted with Mal and his wife for a bit until Mal stood up. 'Shall we talk turkey?' he asked.

Ormond nodded. He and Mal put on jackets and went outside, where they strolled in a fair-sized reproduction of an old English garden, Mal's favorite spot on earth. It was where Ormond had played cowboys and Indians with Mal and his children, now grown and moved away, and it was where Mal had made Ormond the offer for his father's half of the business. The narrow paths through the faded beds and brown vines were rich with memories. It was a place Ormond thought of often. 'You should've been here a week ago,' Mal said. 'I had some bleeding hearts.'

'So late?'

'Mild autumn. Had roses almost till October.' He stopped and turned to Ormond. 'So what did you want to talk to me about?'

Ormond sighed. 'This is going to sound strange.'

'Try me.'

'Have you ever come across any houses that were supposed to be haunted?'

'Haunted?' Mal smiled gently. 'What brought this on, your dad?'

They sat on a bench, and Ormond tried to explain as best he could, suspecting that every word he said sounded like that of a lunatic trying very hard to act normal. But Mal did not laugh, and, when Ormond finished, he looked intently at the younger man, leaned back, and lit one of his Camels.

'Okay,' he said, 'you came up here to ask me a question and I'll answer it. But first just let me say something.' He made a slow, broad gesture, leaving ash droppings on the dirt. 'I think I've learned things from this garden. I mean, every year I see all these things die, and every year they come back to life again. Now I go to church, and I think I believe what I hear there, but all *this* is what makes me sure.'

'People aren't plants,' Ormond said softly.

They sat in silence for a while. 'So you want to see a ghost,' Mal finally said. 'You figure if you see a ghost, then you'll know.'

'Yes.'

'I'll tell you the truth, Davey. I've got no haunted houses listed. I've been in realty for a helluva long time, and I've never even heard of one. Ghost stories aren't real life, kiddo. I don't know how many hundreds of houses I've been in and sold and tried to sell, and people had died in them, sure, and there were some where people were murdered or went crazy and killed themselves, but no ghosts, Davey, not even a hint of it, not in any of them. I'm sorry.'

'Maybe you just didn't know how to look.'

'Why would I *want* to look?'

'How about an *old* house then? One that's been around for a while, one that a lot of people have lived in over the years.'

'Davey . . .'

'Mal, you said if I ever needed your help. . . .'

'All right. Jesus.' Mal threw down the butt, stomped it out, then field-stripped it, slipping the paper into a jacket pocket. 'Oldest place I've got listed now is a place a little north of Remsen. Old farmhouse from the mid-eighteen hundreds. It's beat to hell. Been up for almost three years, heirs in Syracuse want too much for it. Eighty-five-five, and it'd be at least another thirty to fix up. If you want, I'll give you the key.' He shook his head. 'But there aren't any ghosts. When you want it, this week?'

'No more vacation days. How about next Saturday?'

'Stop by the office. I'll be there till two or so. Just tell me one thing. When you don't see anything—and you won't—you gonna give up? You gonna admit it's stupid and forget it?'

Ormond smiled. 'I don't think I'll forget it. But I'll probably give up.'

He passed the following week without the impatience he had anticipated, as if the knowledge that the search was coming was enough. Often he considered just what steps he would take once he was inside the house. Try as he might, he was unable to imagine himself drawing pentagrams on the floor, or chanting unpronounceable names. The spells for raising the dead were grisly and time-consuming, calling for the 'operator' to spend days in graveyards and dress in clothing that had been worn by corpses.

But he did not want to raise the dead, had no wish to see some moldering corpse by the side of its grave, waiting zombielike for orders. He wished only to see a ghost, a revenant, a spiritual souvenir of a soul that had passed on to some higher plane. He decided he would simply go to the house with some candles, remain there overnight, and keep himself open to whatever might choose to manifest itself.

Mal Stewart was out showing a house when Ormond arrived at his office late the following Saturday morning, but a secretary gave Ormond the key and directions. In another forty-five minutes he was pulling off the two-lane onto a long driveway of loose stones. The house itself sat back two hundred yards from the road. Distance made it look grander than it was, and by the time Ormond was halfway down the lane he could see the immense disrepair into which the place had fallen. Shutters hung cockeyed, paint had vanished from most of the woodwork, and more shingles were missing and askew than were in their proper place. But the house itself seemed sturdy, constructed of large red stones that glowed warmly in the October sun. Aside from the cosmetic deficiencies, it appeared to be worth the price asked, especially if the surrounding land went with it.

Once inside, however, Ormond thought Mal's thirty-thousand-dollar repair estimate was low. A damp dust not far from mildew coated the building's interior, and it took a long while for him to get used to the smell. Boards creaked wherever he walked, even when he merely shifted weight, and those which did not creak felt spongy beneath his feet. Small piles of cracked and fallen plaster dotted the floors like old droppings in a beast's cage. The windows were unbroken but filthy, turning day into twilight, and Ormond returned to the car for the Coleman lantern he had bought that week in SoHo.

He went through the first floor, and found the kitchen to be the only room with a recognizable function. An old Kelvinator sat in one corner, its once-white finish yellowed. A large double sink was near it, rusty pipes visible beneath. There were no cabinets, no counters, and Ormond wondered who could have lived in the place only—what had Mal said?—three years before.

Ormond tried the cellar next, and found only a large room, seemingly bare of anything but an ancient coal furnace and an equally aged water pump and heater. The floor was divided into quadrants by thick lines of dust and debris, as if there had once been walls there. He was about to return upstairs when he noticed in one corner a yellowish lump which proved to be a pile of newspapers roughly two feet high. Ormond blew the dust off the top of the stack and found himself looking into the grim face of the Ayatollah Khomeini. The issue of *The Utica Press* was from 1980, and announced the freeing of the Iranian hostages. So, Ormond thought with satisfaction, someone *had* been there just a few years before.

Gingerly he looked through the papers, dropping one on top of the other as he read the headlines; the events were self-dating. Whoever had saved them had saved only special issues. There was a bicentennial Fourth of July issue, whose red and blue masthead was uniformly green with mold; there was the Nixon resignation; the Bobby Kennedy and King assassinations; four issues on Jack Kennedy's death and burial; the Cuban missile crisis; and more. They went back to Korea, to V-E and V-J Days, D-Day, Pearl Harbor, repeal of prohibition, Roosevelt's election, and the stock market crash. The issue on the bottom of the pile announced the Armistice. It was stiff and boardlike, and when Ormond tried to unfold it, it cracked into large chunks, enveloping him in a choking cloud of flakes.

Coughing, he dropped the pieces and went back upstairs. Only when he went outside in the autumn chill was he able to stop. Nevertheless, he was glad he had found the papers. It told him the house had had long-term residents and, if he was correct in assuming that the issues had been collected by one man, a resident of age and determination, continuing his collection as he had for over sixty years. He wondered briefly if that determination might extend as well to things of life and death. And then, as quickly as the thought had come, Ormond smiled at it. Already he was projecting, wishing too much. In another minute he might make himself see an old man in bib overalls rocking on the porch, reading a crisp, brand new *Utica Press* from the 1920s. He cautioned himself to be careful. The place was atmospheric, and he felt sure that men wiser and saner than himself had allowed themselves the luxury of seeing things that weren't there.

He resumed his examination on the second floor. There were seven rooms, each as empty and neglected as the rest of the house. Wallpaper hung in damp strips, and he saw, above the broken plaster of the ceiling, support joists like the skeleton beneath the skin. Dirt was everywhere. Ormond opened the closets in each room, and was startled by a mouse that skittered past him and into the hall. *Maybe that was a ghost*, he thought, smiling. *Maybe I've seen one now, so I ought to just get the hell out of here*. He made himself laugh, and slammed the closet door.

In the last second-floor room he entered, what he assumed was the closet door was wider than the others he had seen. When he opened it he found, instead of a wall two feet away, a winding staircase going up, which he followed. The attic was high-ceilinged and as vacant as the rest of the house, but the smell of dampness was not nearly as strong. Ormond looked about, went back downstairs, and waited for evening.

He stayed in his car, trying to read a book, afraid that he wouldn't have enough fuel for his lantern to last the night if he remained inside the house. When he analyzed his feelings, he realized that while he'd been in the house he had felt nothing. There was no sensation of a presence, there were no cold spots on the stairs, no areas where his lantern flickered, no sounds—other than those he made himself—of creaking boards or shifting foundations. It was as if the house had done all its shifting years before, as if it were permanently settled and was now just waiting.

When darkness came, he did not go inside right away, but sat in the car and waited until the moon had moved through an hour of arc. At ten o'clock he entered the house and stood for some time in what he had guessed was the living-room before he decided how to proceed. By his lantern light he lit three candles and let them drip on the floor boards until the puddle of wax could hold them upright. Then he sat on the floor, back against the wall. He left the lantern burning for a few minutes more before he allowed himself to admit that it was fear that kept it lit. Finally he turned the knob and the white-hot light blinked out, leaving him in the pale yellow glow of the three candles.

Suddenly he felt unbearably alone, as if the house were in the center of some unpopulated continent, thousands of miles from the nearest living being. All the specters that had failed to haunt him in childhood returned, frightening him now that he knew what they meant, now that he knew what death entailed—its horror and finality. And he thought, quite rationally it seemed, that the ghosts in which he now believed were born of *will*, of a desire for immortality so strong as to transcend the mundane facts of worn-out cells and cold flesh—born of will and the energy that survived corporeal death. He looked down at the floor between his knees, not wanting to look up where the flickering candles made the shadows move on the rotted ceiling, the tattered walls.

The fear passed slowly, like a cloak of ice melting away: its weight lifted, but the feel of it, like cold water, remained all about him. He looked up and saw nothing but the candles, the bare walls, the dark doorway to the rooms beyond. Gazing into the flame, he waited longer, and then, thinking that what he sought and dreaded was not in this room, pried the candles loose from their bed of wax and moved through the next room into the kitchen at the back of the house. There he sat and watched and waited, and his candles burned down until he took new ones from his pocket and lit them from the stubs of the old.

Just as he had finished the process and was sitting down once more, something at the window caught his eye—a quick, small movement on the other side of its dusty surface. His insides grew cold. He did not turn his head, only his eyes, but saw no movement, only the dull reflection of the flames off the filthy glass. He watched a moment longer, then turned away quickly. Just as quickly the movement came again, and now he twisted his head toward the pane, giving a small squeak of terror, and saw what appeared to be three fingers twitching against the glass. He froze, his eyes locked on the three pale appendages beating a soft tattoo that he could now hear, hear and *recall*, not as the sound of fingers on glass, but rather——

The wings of a moth. He breathed, laughed, gulped down great drafts of air, laughed again. 'Moth,' he said aloud, watching the wings flutter, the thick thorax beat against the glass, forming traceries in the dust. 'Moth,' he said. A moth seeing the candles, seeking the light, and wasn't that what *he* was doing, seeking the light as well? 'Hello, little brother,' he said, smiling, feeling foolish, tapping gently on the pane. The moth stopped its fluttering, clung to the glass, moved its wings slowly in and out as though breathing, and disappeared into the darkness.

He was about to move into another room, perhaps upstairs, he thought, when he heard a new sound. It seemed to come from beneath him, and the first thing that came to mind was rats scrabbling about in the cellar. But after listening for a moment, he concluded that it did not have the intermittent rhythm that he would expect animals to make, but was rather a continuous rustling, crackling sound. The moth had put him into a kind of dulled ease, and he walked to the cellar stairs, two candles in one hand, and opened the door. The sound grew louder.

It *was* coming from below, he was sure of it—a noise of newspaper whirling over a sidewalk on a windy day. He wondered if he had not noticed that a window was open down below, and if now a breeze was stirring the old papers he'd left on the floor. He walked down the steps, waiting to feel a slight rush of air from below, but his candles did not flicker, his hair did not stir. Arriving at the bottom, he held the candles out and up, knowing that it must be mice making the papers rustle, no doubt taking bits and pieces for a nest. Of course—he could see the paper moving on the floor now, wiggling and twitching in places as though it were alive. He walked closer, intending to kick the fragile pile and watch the animals scuttle away, but two feet from it something made him stop. It was not the movement of several small rodents under the brittle sheets, but rather of the whole mass of paper shifting at once, bunching together, gathering toward the center, growing in height.

And as he watched, as he realized, very slowly, what was truly happening, the wads of newspaper coalesced, merged, took on form and shape and character, until there stood before him a snowman made of rotting paper, but with none of a snowman's roundness or levity. Instead it was gaunt, thin, composed of boluses of wadding. There were no legs, only layers joined together with no regard for anatomy. Torn strips of colored comics, now uniformly yellow, stuck out from the torso, a parody of arms, with even thinner ripped shreds for fingers.

The head and face formed last, as small clumps of mildewed paper rolled upward over the carcass and united on its top with a wet, slapping sound like that of papier-mâché being formed, sending off a sour odor that would have gagged Ormond had he been able to breathe. Then smaller pieces, dry and brittle, seemed to float into place, somehow sticking to the whole, and he found himself gazing into a face of torn and wrinkled paper, black print on yellow, its thin shadows deepened by the flames of his candles.

Ormond stood frozen, unable to move or speak. Even thought seemed to have retreated for his sanity's sake. The face looked into his, and his strength faded until the clenched fingers still holding the candles relaxed, opened, and the lights fell to the dirt floor and winked out. Though he could not close his eyes against what he saw, the darkness closed them for him.

He came to life then, letting some of the fear escape in a tense cry that stayed mostly within. He swung around and ran blindly toward where the stairs had been, tripped once, ran again, banged his shin into the first step, ignored the sharp pain, scrambled sobbing up the stairs on hands and knees, fell across the kitchen threshold, pulled himself to his feet, and bounced off walls and doorways, forging a madman's path to the front door, finding the knob, leaping off the porch, fumbling for keys as he ran to his car, the car turning over, then catching, starting, the clutch flying out, tires kicking up the stones of the lane, turning on the lights and not slowing down until he was out on the two-lane, not stopping until he saw up ahead the bright neon of the truck stop.

Finally, seated on the counter stool, he nestled in the diner's warmth, inhaled the smell of early morning bacon frying, let his fingers keep time to the country-western song on the jukebox. He did this for ten minutes, eating a donut and drinking coffee, before he allowed himself to think about what he had experienced. And when he did, all else faded. He could not hear the music, smell the bacon, feel the heat that stuck his shirt tight against his ribs. There was room for nothing in his mind but the thing he had seen.

He *had* seen it. Of that much he was certain. He knew that he did not possess the grim unpleasantness of imagination necessary to concoct a hallucination of such originality. A shrouded man or a shapeless white Halloween haunt were all he would have come up with. Thus it followed that what he had seen existed.

But how? Paper did not live, did not build itself into a mockery of humanity to frighten off interlopers. That meant, he concluded, that there must have been some animating force behind it, and what could that force have been if not a ghost?

He nearly laughed. Ghost, revenant, call it what he would, still it was a survivor, a remnant of life once lived. It was enough, wasn't it? It proved that there was something after, didn't it? *Didn't it?*

'Mister?'

Ormond looked up. The waitress was eyeing him from over the top of her glasses. 'Yes?'

'You okay?'

'Yes.' She offered more coffee and he refused, thinking that he had blown it after all. What had the books said, every single one of them? *Ask*. Ask it what it wants, why it has returned, where it is bound, where is the treasure, and it is impelled to answer. But he had asked nothing, when he could conceivably have bridged the abyss between life and death. Instead, he had run like a terrified schoolboy from a county-fair funhouse.

What else could I have done? he asked himself. The sight of the thing had literally frozen him, stopped his voice as well as everything else. He thought of returning, but knew that if he did there would be no change. One cannot grow used to the Inferno, and that, he felt, was what he had seen—a face and form from the deepest wells of, if not a literal Hell, then the Inferno of man's darkest fears. He could not accept it, could not bring himself to speak of it. No one could, no one who could see it.

No, he thought. *No one who could see it.*

Ormond reached down, rubbed the aching shin he had bumped on the cellar steps, then asked the waitress for more coffee. He sat there for over an hour before driving back to New York.

℘ ℘

'You want to make ten dollars?'

The blind man's head twitched birdlike toward Ormond. 'Who you?' His voice was suspicious, unfriendly. His dog raised its head from its paws and looked up, wary but without malice.

'My name's David Ormond. I want to buy you a cup of coffee. Talk to you about something. Ten dollars just to listen. Coffee's on me.'

'You try and mess with me, Mister, my dog'll bite your white ass.'

Ormond frowned. 'How do you know I'm white?'

'Shit, don't you try that, next you'll be throwin' a fist in my face to make me duck. You *sound* white, boy, you sound like a necktie and a briefcase's what you sound like.' The man chuckled. It was an unpleasant sound, deep and filled with phlegm. 'You gimme ten bucks first.' Ormond handed over two fives. '*Singles*, Jack, you think I was born fuckin' yesterday?' Ormond went into a luggage store, where a frowning clerk broke his fives.

'Here,' he said, rejoining the blind man and placing them in his hand.

The man counted the bills slowly, then pocketed them. 'Where we go?'

'Horn and Hardart,' Ormond replied. 'Should I . . . take your arm or anything?'

'Just walk, Jack. Shit, I could lead *you*.' Ormond had no idea how the man separated his footfalls from the hundreds of others around them, but when he sat down at a table, the man was there across from him, the dog at his feet giving a low whine. An assistant manager in a white shirt and string tie started over, but Ormond held up a hand and shook his head quickly, and the man stalked away, looking doubtful. 'Muhthuhfucker was gonna throw me out, wasn't he?'

'Maybe, not anymore. Look, are you really blind?'

'You look at these, man,' the old man said, opening his eyes wide and leaning toward Ormond, who drew back from the fetid breath. 'You think these is contact lenses or some shit?'

The eyes were red, full of lesions, the pupils a pale gray. Ormond had not previously noticed the puckered skin of the eyelids. 'Okay,' he said placatingly. 'Okay, I'm sorry. What's your name?'

'John.'

'John?'

'You expectin' a Leon or a Mustafa or a Willie? My mama named me John.'

'John what?'

'John Washington Wilson. That's more like it now, ain't it, *Mister* Ormond? Now what you want to talk to this poor old blind nigger about?'

Ormond got them coffee, and then he told Wilson as clearly and simply as he could, offering him three hundred dollars to come along and speak to the apparition when Ormond's voice froze in fear, with an extra two hundred if it responded. When Ormond had finished, he sipped his coffee, now only lukewarm, and watched Wilson's broad, black features. The man started to chuckle deep in his throat, then actually laughed in a loud, wet bark that turned half the heads in the room. Even the dog looked up.

'Dave, you is somethin'! This is a joke, right? You got boys watchin' me, right? Waitin' to see my eyes pop out 'n my hair stand up like Willie Best, huh?'

'No joke, Mr Wilson. I'm very serious.'

Wilson's smile faded, hiding the ruined teeth. 'Goddam,' he said softly. He finished his coffee in one gulp. 'You know, when I was a kid I *liked* Willie Best. Willie Best and Rochester. I didn't give a shit they was servants or nothin'. They made me laugh. They was funny. I could see back then.' His face swung toward Ormond's again, and had Ormond not been sure of the blindness, he would have sworn Wilson was glaring at him. 'How I know you be straight with me? How I know you not gonna kill me or nothin'?'

'Bring the dog along. Or we can tell your friends where we're going.'

'My daughter. We tell my daughter. When you wanta go?'

'Next weekend? Saturday?'

'Not weekends. Weekends I spend with my daughter.'

'Look, Mr Wilson, I'm paying you . . .'

'No weekends.'

The voice was like stone. Ormond decided to fake a sick day at the office. 'All right. This week then. Wednesday.'

'That be all right. Now I got one more question. How come me? Why didn't you go to the Blind Institute and get somebody classy?'

'Well . . . I . . .'

'Never mind, I know. They'd 'a' thrown you out on your ass. Guess I oughta be glad. I can use the money.'

'I thought you could. I heard you once . . . saying that everybody was a ghost. Because no one was buying any pencils.'

'I said that? Crazy nigger. Forget that shit. Sometimes I get pissed. Forget that shit.'

ꕤ

The following Wednesday Ormond picked up John Wilson on the corner of Fifth and Fiftieth at three in the afternoon. The signboard went in the trunk, the dog in the back seat, where he sat watching the street with a greater amount of interest than Ormond had ever seen him display. 'Lousy day,' Wilson said, lighting a Lucky. 'People damn cheap. Maybe in a few weeks when Christmas decorations start goin' up.'

'Your dog trained?' Ormond asked. 'Seeing-eye?'

'Nah, not really. He know when the lights is green or red, 'n what they mean. Won't let nobody hurt me neither. He's smart.' They got out of the city, headed north. 'What you wanta do this for anyway? You really see a ghost?'

'I saw something. Something that scared me so much I couldn't talk. I think anybody who saw it would've felt the same.'

'But I won't see it.'

'That's right. That's why you do the talking.'

'Jes' ask it what it wants.'

'That's right.'

'You still ain't said why.'

'Hell, Wilson, don't *you* want to know?'

'Know what?'

'Know what comes after. After you die.'

'What the fuck do I care? I be dead. Maybe I be with Jesus. I sure as shit ain't goin' to no hell, I up to here with that shit right here on earth. Like them boys who been in Vietnam. Like I hear their jackets say.'

'Well, maybe you'll find out anyway. Maybe tonight. That bother you?'

'We ain't gonna find nothin'. I gonna take your money, but you ain't gonna find nothin'.'

It was growing dark when they arrived at the house. Ormond had called Mal the previous Sunday and asked to keep the key for another week. Mal had hesitated, but agreed. Ormond and Wilson ate some sandwiches Ormond had brought, and drank some coffee from a Thermos. Wilson let the dog out of the car and fed him a sandwich. The old man swallowed the last of his food, washed it down with a final sip of coffee, then sniffed the air. 'Smells clean,' he said, 'but there's somethin' else.' As if he understood the words, the dog raised his head and sniffed too. 'Musty. Musty smell. That the house?'

'That's it.' Ormond could detect no smell, but there was nothing else around that it could have been. 'Let's go in.'

They walked into the house, Wilson holding Ormond's arm. Ormond watched the dog closely to see how he would react, if the supposed heightened sensitivity of animals to spirits would prove to be true. But the dog seemed at ease, following them steadily as they went through the door.

Ormond found the lantern where he had left it when he had fled the house, put more fuel into it, and lit it. Its mantles blazed brightly, bringing light and warmth to the dark, chilly room. 'The cold bother you?' Ormond asked the old man.

'Shit, I stand outside all winter with them winds tryin' to blow me down. This is nothin'.'

'All right. We'll go in the cellar now. That's where I saw it. Now remember . . .' Ormond heard his voice shaking and stopped talking for a moment, thinking, *Control. Get hold of it. You'll never make it if you're this scared this soon.*

'Remember what?'

'Remember I'll have hold of your arm. If I squeeze it hard, you'll know it's there. Or if I stop talking. Or if you feel me stiffen or freeze. That'll mean it's there. We'll go into the cellar. The steps are steep.'

Ormond led the way. Wilson's hand on his shoulder. The dog trailed behind. Near the bottom of the stairs, Ormond thought that if he'd have to run up them now, he'd have the blind man and the dog to go through first. Then he told himself he would not run. This time he would not run.

The cellar stank of foulness. Was it worse since he'd been there? Ormond wondered. The dog whined softly. 'Hush up,' Wilson said. 'You smelled worse'n this.' The old newspapers lay disordered on the dirty floor. The long strips and torn shreds told Ormond that he had not imagined it all. He felt vindicated, but at the same time more frightened now that the last natural explanation—hallucination—was gone. He kept walking until he was only a few feet away from the pile.

'We there?' Wilson asked.

'We're there.'

'Now what?'

'Now we wait.' Ormond set the lantern near the wall and went back to where Wilson and the dog stood. He took Wilson's arm and watched the mound of paper on the floor, alert for the slightest bit of movement.

The dog was the first to notice. His head twitched, his ears went up, his eyes opened wider, as if looking for what he had heard. 'What's 'at?' barked the old man.

'What?' Ormond asked, his voice thick.

'Noise. Somethin' rubbin'.'

It was several more seconds before Ormond heard it. Paper, wet and dry, moving against itself. 'Oh God. . . .' he said, less in awe than if to see if he could still speak.

'What's *happ*'nin'?'

'It's . . . coming,' Ormond whispered. 'Forming.' A large mass heaved up amidst the rest, and Ormond knew his voice was gone. He could only watch spellbound as the clumps of paper joined and grew, colliding wetly, rising higher, rolled papers lurching sluglike up the trunk, strips slithering behind them, the whole growing, growing, even more terrifying in the harsh beam of the lantern than in the candle's feeble glow, for there were no shadows now to soften and disguise, but only the blazing light, so that he could not deny what stood constantly higher before him.

He heard Wilson speak, but only understood the last few words, '. . . you think you're goin'? Git back down here, you . . .' and he realized the dog was gone. But the face formed, and then he couldn't remember the dog at all. It was worse this time, for the depressions, which had before been only empty sockets, were now filled with eyes, two egg-sized balls of paper whose *whiteness* stunned Ormond with their incongruity in that field of yellow. Two bits of black, torn from thick headline letters, drifted over the white balls and stopped dead center, ragged pupils that fixed him as no human eyes ever could. There was a sharp rip, and a mouth, wide and seeping, dropped open, a cloud of must bursting from it, reaching his own face in an instant and clogging his throat with its vileness. The jaw did not close, but hung sagging like a rotted limb as, just above, a wad pushed outward in which two dark holes were poked as by some invisible hand, forming nostrils which expelled two puffs of moist, sour air, along with tiny fragments of powdery paper. The face was complete.

Ormond had expected it, but the expectation in no way diminished the shock. He was stunned, immovable as rock, and only the irrevocable commands of his body kept him breathing. He thought later that he would have stood there forever, staring into the face, had Wilson not spoken, playing his part, doing as he'd been instructed. The blind man's voice intruded only dimly into Ormond's smothered consciousness, but he heard, and understood the words.

'*Who are you? What do you want?*'

The yellow, rotting head swiveled until the thing was looking at Wilson. Sweat coated the old man's face, giving him the sheen of onyx, and now Ormond could hear his breathing, heavy and labored. Suddenly Wilson groaned deep within, then grunted again and again, as though he were being repeatedly struck by blows, or wracked by tubercular coughing. The final grunt, instead of dropping away, began to soar in an ascending cry, and the blind man howled as he had that day when he'd shouted of ghosts on the streets of New York, howled so high and so long that Ormond, not seeing him, could imagine blood streaming upward from his throat, could almost see it splashing the horror in front of him, deep red drops on the yellow-gray paper.

The howl ceased, and Wilson sank to the earth as gently as if hands had lowered him. At the same time the upright tower of paper crumbled, falling upon itself layer by moldering layer, the face descending in lurches toward the floor, but turning, turning to once more face Ormond, keeping its newsprint eyes on him as it sank and dissolved into damp shreds, the jaw twisting as if in an effort to shape some expression prohibited by its very composition. As it fell, Ormond's fear fell with it, so that he detected in its dissolution a sense of purpose fulfilled, not from anything he saw, but rather from what he felt.

He didn't know how long he stood looking down at the pile of rubbish on the dirt floor, but after a while he heard low growls interspersed with high whinings. At last he looked away and saw that the dog had returned. It had Wilson's shirt collar in its mouth, and was slowly dragging him backward, away from the musty pile. The sight broke the spell that had been laid on Ormond, and he leaned down to help, the dog yielding when it realized that he meant no harm. Wilson's bubbling breathing told Ormond he was still alive, and when he had pulled him several more feet from the remnants of the apparition, he shook him gingerly until the blind eyes opened and the wide, trembling mouth could speak.

'Where are we? We still there?' The voice was cracked and shaking.

'In the cellar. Yes.' They were the first words Ormond had spoken since the thing's coming, and he was surprised to hear how calm he sounded.

'Get me outa here,' Wilson said, stumbling to his feet. 'For the luvva Jesus, get me outside. . . .'

They went up the stairs together, the dog trailing solicitously, Wilson muttering, 'Oh Jesus, oh Jesus,' in a litany as they went. At the top of the stairs Wilson turned to Ormond. 'Where is it?' he asked.

'It's gone. Fallen apart. Gone.' He tightened his grip on Wilson's arm. 'What happened?' he asked. 'What did it say? What did it tell you?'

'Get me outside. In the car. Outa here.'

They got to the car and climbed in. 'You want to go?' asked Ormond. 'Shall we leave now?'

'No. Let's just set a while.'

From somewhere in his voluminous coat Wilson drew a pint bottle of Kessler, took a long pull, and offered it to Ormond, who drank without wiping the neck. 'All right,' he said, handing it back, 'now tell me. Why did you pass out?'

Wilson hacked up phlegm, shook his head. 'It hit me too strong. Like all at once it just started comin'. And I couldn't hold it all, like it'd been keepin' it back for so long it just all poured out at once, and I couldn't hold it.'

'But did it *tell* you anything? Before you blacked out?'

Wilson's face seemed far away, and his eyes looked as if they could see again. 'It told me. All it wanted to. All I could hold.'

'Was it a ghost then?'

'Yeah.'

'Then . . .' He struggled to voice the thought, because now it was no longer theory, but truth. 'Then there *is* life after death.'

'But not for him.' Wilson sounded sad.

'What?'

'Not the life the rest of 'em have. Not that good life.'

'I don't understand . . .'

'There's a good life, but he don't got it. He stuck here. 'Cause he tried to come back.' Wilson shook his craggy head. 'They don't *want* us to know. And he tried to come back to tell. And they didn't like that. He told me. How'd he look anyway? Bad? Really ugly?'

Ormond nodded, remembered Wilson was blind, said, 'Yes.'

'I thought he felt bad. Couldn't help it. I think he was glad you brought me to ask. I don't think he coulda told nothin' if nobody'd asked.'

'We're too afraid to,' Ormond said softly.

'What?'

'We're too afraid to ask, so we never know.' He said nothing for a while, thinking it through. 'Even if there are some who *want* to tell us,' he went on, slowly, cautiously, 'who want to come back to comfort us, they can only come back as horrors. As things that frighten us away from the truth. And who wants to seek *that* out? So it stays a secret. Or becomes the stuff of legend.'

'I think we crazy, but I think you right. I was scared, scared as hell, but I felt sorry too. Sorry for that thing.'

'It's trapped,' Ormond said. 'Trapped between life and death for trying to tell the truth.' They sat in silence until Ormond finally spoke. 'Was there anything else?' he asked Wilson. 'Anything you can remember?'

'No. Just . . .' Wilson's face twisted, trying to recall. 'There was a song, like a little tune. I mean, he didn't sing it to me or nothin' like that, it's just like I remember that it was there. Now how did that go. . . ?' And Wilson hummed a snatch of melody that Ormond had not heard for many years, and only remembered one man ever singing. 'That's all,' Wilson said. 'That's all she wrote.'

He leaned back and rubbed his dog's head, and Ormond dug into his pocket for the car keys, filled with a new knowledge that he could never share and that no one would ever believe, filled with a new, burning lust to know what distant Zeus, so needful of faith, would chain an immortal to a rock on which the vulture of man's fear would gnaw forever at his generous, misunderstood soul.

'Wonder who it was,' Wilson said. 'Wonder just who that poor bastard was.'

'Prometheus,' said Ormond, turning the key to make the engine spark and start. 'My father. Prometheus.'

Miss Tuck and the Gingerbread Boy

MISS TUCK FROWNED AS SHE PICKED up the small balls and noodles of Play-Doh from under the chairs. She frowned as she tossed the wet paper towels into the dark green metal waste can, and put the milk carton back into the small refrigerator with the animal magnets all over it. She frowned at the thought of Don, her aide, home sick with a cold. And she frowned at Bobby Sullivan, sitting quietly in the corner.

'Did your mother say how late she was going to be?'

'No, Miss Tuck.'

'Hmph.' What did Linda Sullivan think she was, a baby-sitter? 11:45. The children were supposed to be picked up at 11:45 at the *latest*, and it was now 11:53. She'd barely have time enough to go down the block to the luncheonette in the drugstore for her usual soup and sandwich and get back in time to prepare for the 1:00 invasion.

Miss Tuck was straightening the final chair, frowning at it for being out of alignment, when Jenny Pierce came into the room. 'Dotty,' she said, 'do you have the Nutshell Library over here? I want to use it this after . . . Oh, hi, Bobby.'

The boy tentatively returned her smile. 'Hi, ma'am.'

'Bobby's mother's late,' Miss Tuck said. 'The Nutshell books are in the corner.' Her voice was brusque, but only a bit. Jenny Pierce was second in command to Marti Donohue, who ran the nursery school like a benevolent despot. It wouldn't do to offend either of them.

A knock on the door made them both turn, and Linda Sullivan, looking younger than any mother of a four-year-old had a right to do, appeared in the doorway. 'Hi, sweetie,' she said to her son, who ran to meet her. 'Hello, Jenny, Miss Tuck. Sorry I'm late.'

'It was no problem,' Miss Tuck said. 'Bobby's never any trouble.' Although her stiff smile belied the words, Linda Sullivan seemed not to notice. She bundled up her son and left with a friendly wave. Miss Tuck was putting on her own coat, when Jenny Pierce asked her about the gingerbread boy.

'I didn't think I would,' Miss Tuck replied.

'Oh Dotty. . . .' Jenny Pierce sounded genuinely pained. 'We *always* do it for the four-year-olds. Every classroom. They love it so.'

'Is it so much a tradition?' Miss Tuck asked through pinched lips.

Jenny Pierce nodded, and Miss Tuck frowned again. The gingerbread boy. Surely one of the most idiotic of the *many* idiotic tales for children—a baked gingerbread boy jumping out of the oven, running all over the place, spouting that inane, 'You can't catch *me*, I'm the *gingerbread* boy!' before finally being devoured by a clever fox. Just one more directionless fantasy. 'What do we have to do?' she asked.

'Oh, it's fun,' Jenny Pierce grinned. 'Tonight you make two big gingerbread boys, big enough for the whole class, and you cook one of them. Tomorrow you hide the cooked one before school starts, and when the kids come, you let them see you put the uncooked one in the oven. Then you have Don read the story while you sneak into the kitchen and hide the one that's baking so that they can't possibly find it. When it's time to open the oven, surprise, no gingerbread boy, and the kids go through the church looking for him.'

'And when they find him, they eat him?' Miss Tuck asked dryly.

'Sure.'

Miss Tuck shook her head. 'All right, Jenny, but it seems silly.'

It was Jenny Pierce's turn to frown. 'Why silly?'

Miss Tuck sighed. 'Kids get so *much* fantasy. Talking animals, fairies, elves, dragons . . . it seems that's all we give them. And now a gingerbread boy that jumps out of the oven. I mean, stories are one thing, but to pretend that gingerbread really comes to life is another.'

'Oh Dotty, the kids don't really believe it.'

'I don't know. They're not all mature enough to differentiate between what's real and what isn't. I bet that at least some of them will believe it's real. Just like they believe in Santa Claus.'

'And what's so bad about believing in Santa Claus?'

'When children believe in things that aren't true, sooner or later they're going to be disappointed, going to be hurt.'

'But that's part of growing up. Those are small hurts, Dotty, and when they're over, the child is older, and he knows it and feels good about leaving behind all those silly beliefs. They have to face reality soon enough. Why not let them hold on to their fantasies for a while?' Jenny Pierce smiled. 'Besides, if they believe enough, who knows but that they might come true?'

Miss Tuck had no answer for Jenny Pierce that morning, but that night, with two vodka and tonics inside her, she wished Jenny Pierce was there, so that she could tell her about what fantasies could do. Jenny didn't *have* to have fantasies, did she? She had it all—a husband, a child, a career—you don't *need* fantasies when you live them, do you?

Miss Tuck added more flour to the dough, and took another sip of her drink, leaving wide, white finger marks on the sweating glass. She went back to kneading the dough, thinking how stupid it all was, remembering the fantasies *she* had had. Not about Santa Claus or the Easter Bunny, but more recent fantasies, a fantasy of fifteen years before, when she imagined that Tom would come back from Vietnam and marry her. My, how she believed that one, looking at the ring with the tiny, tiny diamond bigger than the Ritz. He came back, all right, only in a bag.

Miss Tuck pounded the dough a final time, and reached for the cookie cutter Jenny Pierce had lent her. It was in the shape of a gingerbread boy, though one could have imagined it a snowman or a farmer or anything remotely humanoid. 'It's the extras that'll make it cute,' Jenny had said. 'Raisin eyes, cherry nose, maybe an orange slice for a mouth, buttons, a little tie—use your imagination.'

She pressed the cutter into the sheet of dough twice, lifted it, and cleared away the rest of the dough, rolling it up into a ball, and tossing it in the sink. There they lay, two foot-long gingerbread boys, each one capable of feeding ten children, who would tear it apart and wolf it down regardless of their belief that it had just been running through the room not a minute before.

It was an unpleasant thought, and Miss Tuck tried to drive it away by thinking what she could do to spark up the pastries, make them more than dull brown doughboys. She took raisins from the refrigerator and positioned them as eyes and buttons, then cut a slice of orange peel for the mouth, but she had no cherries for a nose. She tried a raisin, but it looked too much like the eyes. 'Come on, Dotty,' she said to herself. 'Use your *imagination. Fantasize.*'

Sure, she thought, fantasize. Just like you fantasized that all of those men you met, one of them, just *one*, would want to stay with you when they woke up in the morning, that just *one* would be like Tom.

'Don't tell *me*, Jenny Pierce,' she said aloud. 'Don't tell *me* that fantasies might come true; don't tell *me* that dreams don't hurt.'

There was nothing that hurt more, and she growled as she pressed a yellow M & M in the center of each pliant face, right above the orange-slice mouth.

This year she would do it, play the gingerbread game, because she had said she would. But not *next* year, oh no.

She was through with fantasy.

The next morning, however, when she wrapped the gingerbread boys, she had to admit that the cooked one looked quite handsome, and she stopped at the store for licorice whips to make a small string tie for each, feeling irritated at herself for doing so. *It's for the children*, she told herself. *If I'm to do it, I may as well do it right.*

She got to the church a half hour before the children were due to arrive, and began to look for a hiding place. After some consideration she decided on one of the closets in the Fellowship Hall, a large meeting-room downstairs with a small stage, institutionally green walls, and unused shuffleboard tiles in the floor. Two or three closets were filled with the leavings of the Cub Scout pack that met there every week, but the third closet, back behind the faded red curtains of the stage, was empty of everything but a broom, a mop, and two buckets. It was the perfect place.

She first put wax paper over the floor, then set the gingerbread boy down carefully on top of it. For a moment she wondered if the church had mice, but decided it was unlikely since Jenny Pierce hadn't cautioned her about it. She left the door ajar and went up to her room.

Don, her aide, was getting the room ready, and he smiled as she came in. 'Feeling better?' she asked.

He was, and except for her directions and his questions as to what the morning would hold, there was no further conversation between them. It was a polite silence, born of mutual disinterest rather than dislike. The children started to come in at ten minutes before nine, hanging their coats on the proper hooks, and playing quietly with the toys Don had set out for them.

The morning went smoothly, and at ten o'clock, Miss Tuck told the children that she had a surprise for them. Taking a tea towel off the plate that bore the unbaked gingerbread boy, Miss Tuck revealed it to the children, who ooohed and aaahed in excited anticipation, as if older brothers and sisters had told them about the tradition.

'All right, children, let's take the gingerbread boy into the kitchen . . . Billy, would you like to carry it? Be careful, don't drop it. Now, I'll turn up the oven . . . there we are . . . and who'd like to put him inside? Judy? That's right. Right on there. Don't worry, it's not hot yet. All right, now let's go back into the room, and Mr Reger will read a story to you about a gingerbread boy very much like this one, and the adventures he had. And while he does that, I'm going to pop in and out of the kitchen to make sure *our* gingerbread boy is baking just right. Okay?'

The children sat on the floor in a circle around Don, who began to read the story. Miss Tuck sat apart, lost in her own thoughts as the tale wound on, but still listening with half an ear so that she would know when to go into the kitchen, play Jenny Pierce's stupid game, lie to the children, pretend that flour and shortening and ginger and sugar had come to life and run away.

'"You can't catch *me*, I'm the *gingerbread* boy!"'

Don seemed into it, she thought sourly. Probably used to reading that kind of stuff to his own kids. She listened to the story for a moment.

'"And there before him sat a lean and lazy fox, licking a front paw and looking at the gingerbread boy with his head cocked to one side."'

The fox. That meant the story would be over soon. Time to hide the gingerbread boy on the top shelf where none of the children would see it, then take them out to the kitchen for the discovery. She thought Tricia Malone should be the one to open the oven and discover it was missing; she was the most excitable.

As Miss Tuck rose from her chair, she heard a harsh squeal of metal on metal, as though the oven door had been opened. Jenny Pierce, no doubt, putting *her* gingerbread boy in for *her* class. But a second later, when Miss

Tuck opened the door to the kitchen, she saw no Jenny Pierce, no other four-year-old class, only the open oven door, and the empty oven. A soft pattering sounded somewhere nearby, and a moment later a startled cry of excitement came from her room. Confused, she turned and went back to the children, who were standing now, smiles of thrilled amazement on their faces.

'He ran out there!' Tricia Malone cried.

'In the hall! In the hall!' added Bobby Sullivan.

Miss Tuck looked at Don for an explanation, but he was staring in fascination at the door to the hall. 'Who ran out?' barked Miss Tuck. 'Who are you talking about?' She did a quick count—all the children were there.

'The gingerbread boy! The gingerbread boy!' answered the high little voices in unison.

'We *saw* 'im!' cried Charlie Hockelman, grinning widely.

'Saw . . . Don, what's going on here?' Miss Tuck was frowning again. A tornado would have looked friendlier.

'I . . . I don't know,' said Don, shaking his head. '*I* didn't see anything, but I *heard* . . . something.'

'It was *real*!' crooned a wide-eyed Judy Manning. 'It was really *real*!'

Miss Tuck didn't know whom to be angry at first—Jenny Pierce (or whoever it was who had played this childish joke); Don, for going along with it; or the children, for believing in the reality of such obvious trickery. 'Real!' she boomed out. 'All right, I'll show you what's real!' And she stormed out the door and down the hall.

She'd show them, all right; she'd march right downstairs to the closet in the Fellowship Hall, take that gingerbread boy she'd put there, and tell the *truth* to all of them. She couldn't *believe* that anyone had had the effrontery to interfere with her class—*her class*—and had tried to make her look like a *fool* in the bargain. *We'll just see who looks foolish now!* she thought furiously, rounding a corner of the hall.

Miss Tuck didn't notice the crumbs until she started down the stairs. When she saw them, she stopped and looked behind her. They were there, too, all the way back to the corner she'd come around, and probably before that as well—red-brown crumbs nearly as fine as powder, in an unbroken trail that coincided with the route she'd taken.

So, into the basement, too, eh? She frowned even more deeply, taking the stairs two at a time. Instead of turning off into any one of half a dozen short halls that honeycombed the basement, the trail of crumbs led her to the Fellowship Hall, and it was not until she opened the door to the large, shuffleboard-floored room that she began to be surprised at the coincidence that the prankster should be heading straight for the room where she'd hidden the second gingerbread boy. She stopped in the doorway, fully expecting to confront the culprit, but the room was empty. She listened, and heard what she thought were light footfalls, but saw nothing except the trail of rusty crumbs that led up the side of the room, up the stairs to the small stage, and disappeared behind the curtain.

'All right!' she said, steel in her tone. 'The joke's *over*!'

There was no answer at first, only silence, but Miss Tuck fancied she heard a small giggle that sounded almost *crisp* in the big, empty room, followed by more light footfalls across the hollow boards of the stage.

A child? It must be, she thought bitterly. No one from *her* class; they had all been there. Some brat from Jenny Pierce's room, no doubt. *Relax, Dotty, relax, watch that temper, don't get mad*, she told herself as she followed the path of crumbs toward the stage. But it was no use. She wanted to wrench the child's arm out of its socket, smack his bottom until he screamed for mercy, drag him before her class, saying, *Here, here's your gingerbread boy!* That last she *would* do, that at least.

It was almost too easy. The trail led directly up the stairs, behind the curtain, across the dark backstage area, and right to the closet where she'd hidden the other gingerbread boy. And Miss Tuck stopped dead in front of the closed closet door, stopped and thought, *How did he know where I hid it?* She had told no one, and no one had seen her, or been with her.

No one but the other, unbaked, gingerbread boy.

There was no time for further thought or concern, for now a low laugh sounded from inside the closet, enraging Miss Tuck with its implied mockery. Savagely, she grabbed the knob and threw the door open.

It was on her so quickly she barely glimpsed it towering above her before it enveloped her in its warm sponginess, the fat, doughy arms wrapping about her, drawing her face against its chest, filling her nostrils with the sweet-spicy scent of ginger. It was a boy no longer, but a gingerbread man, holding her like a smothering lover, lowering its bald, round head toward hers so that, as with her last bit of strength she pulled up her own head, she could see the raisin eyes gleaming wetly with life, the orange-slice mouth split in a senseless grin. She was barely able to draw in a breath for a scream, when it embraced her again, forcing her eyes, nose, and mouth against its moist, suffocating softness.

ꟻ ꟻ

'Children,' said Miss Tuck, her smiling face framed in the door. 'I'm afraid that gingerbread boy's been leading me on quite a chase. I'm going to need your help. Let's see if we can find him.'

The children, delighted at the prospect of the hunt, leaped from their seats and streamed into the hall, searching for the elusive pastry. Miss Tuck smiled at Don, who looked at her with a puzzled expression. 'Come on, Don,' she said with a wink. 'He'll get away sure if we don't hurry.' And she turned and ran down the hall with the children.

No matter how hard they looked, they were unable to find the gingerbread boy. They were disappointed, but Miss Tuck only laughed. 'He escaped, children!' she cried gleefully. 'And isn't that the best thing that could have happened? He got away. He's free now, free and happy. Oh, I know you all wanted gingerbread, but I have a surprise that's even better.' And she took them down the street to the drugstore luncheonette, where they filled all the stools at the counter and ordered whatever they wanted—sundaes, shakes, or fudgeboats—while Miss Tuck paid the check. Then they walked back to the church, the children fighting for the privilege of walking next to Miss Tuck and holding her hand.

'I like her,' Tricia Malone confided to Judy Manning, ''cause she smells nice.'

'Your hand feels real warm, Miz Tuck,' said a grinning Charlie Hockelman, holding it like a trophy.

'Her eyes are so pretty,' Bobby Sullivan observed with wonder. 'Black and shiny . . .' He thought for a second, and his face beamed as he found the simile. 'Like big, bright raisins!'

And Don Reger nodded in agreement, wondering.

The Music of the Dark Time

I

THE FEAR TOOK HIM BY THE THROAT with the first chord. It was the violins and their high, piercing wail that caught him unaware, making the terror vibrate within him as the strings vibrated to their horsehair prod. Tortured, he thought. The bow tortured the strings to make them howl so.

The music grew in intensity and volume, and he knew he would have to leave before he *could not* leave, before the soaring, searing music immobilized him like a fly in amber, before the fear solidified and he was once more back in the years of darkness, where joy was a memory and music had become a cruel farce. His legs moved slowly, dream-thick, as he turned, and faces watched idly, uncaring, from the other side of the glass, where the red and orange lights shone like candles, the thousands of candles he had lit over the long years, the hundreds of times he had said Kaddish for those he had seen go to their deaths at Adlerkralle, while the Four Angels played and played on the strings that ground into his ears like gritty shards of glass.

Walk, Weissman, he told himself. *Walk, Jude!* And the feet rose and fell as he walked from the room, the vacuum cleaner lurching behind him like a balky dog. The music shrieked at him to stay, but he kept moving, and soon the sounds were lost behind the studio door. Karl Weissman remembered to breathe again, and leaned against the cool wall of the hall in exhaustion. He thanked God that he had escaped before he had heard more—the marching footsteps, the murmured remarks—before he had seen eyes that stared into his own with hatred and disgust, faces that had haunted him for over forty years.

He should find another job. One where there would be *no* music, none at all. He shook his head sadly. How could he? He knew no trade but one, and that one was out of the question. Unbearable. Unthinkable.

Unheard of.

II

Ron Talbot steepled his fingers, looked across the desk top, and shook his head slowly. 'I don't know, Bobby. It's so goddam downbeat.'

'Not if it's packaged right,' Bobby Goodman replied.

'Brummel said it wouldn't go in Germany.'

'They're too *close* to it in Germany. Hell, the camps are still standing—they don't need to be reminded of it anymore.' Goodman nervously fished his pack of cigarettes from a pocket.

'What I don't get,' Talbot said, 'is why Brummel offered it to you so cheap. He's no dummy.'

'He is where this is concerned. They don't realize the interest in it over here. Jesus, they sell *coffee table* books about the Holocaust now, and what about *Shoah* . . . and that miniseries a few years back . . . and what about that movie with what's her name—Vanessa Redgrave? That'd tie right in.'

'Too many years back—people don't remember TV movies.'

'There's an audience, Ron, I swear there is.'

'It's pretty sick.'

'It's all in how you *look* at it,' Goodman countered. 'We publicize it as a testament to survival, *dedicate* it to those who died.'

'Dedicate it?'

'Sure. Let me tell you how I see it—no quick and dirty pressing, no skinny album that gets lost in the documentary bin, but a two-record boxed set, with a nice booklet——'

'Two records?' Talbot interrupted. 'Is there enough material?'

'I've got that figured out. On the wire recording that Brummel got from the SS guy's widow, there are only two sides' worth—one is the Grosse Fugue, and the other is an earlier Beethoven quartet, one of the Rasumovskys. Now that's the only stuff we have that was actually recorded *in* the camps. *But*—there are tons of German recordings from the forties that we know were played on camp P.A. systems for the SS. I see maybe one side of vintage Wagner and another side of piano and vocals—Walter Gieseking, maybe a couple of others who sucked up to the Nazis. The rights would be dirt cheap, and we could still use the title.'

'*Music of the Holocaust*,' Talbot said.

'Right. Very classy package. Black and white print—or gold and silver. A lot of dignity.'

Talbot smiled thinly. 'The *contents* are sensational enough, huh?'

Goodman nodded. 'I've listened to it three or four times, once last night with Sam. It's effective as hell, obviously recorded outside—you can hear the wind whip the mike and at one pianissimo spot there's this voice that yells, "*Schnell, schnell, Juden!*"'

'Jesus,' Talbot whispered.

'Strong stuff. Another weird thing is that the last dozen or so measures, the cello drops out.'

'Can Sam engineer it?'

'Oh yeah, no problem. He can take most of the crap out, but we'll want to leave in all the background noises. I don't think we'd want to dub in the cello at the end—adds a little mystery.'

Talbot leaned back and stared at the ceiling. 'Christmas release?'

Goodman permitted himself a small smile of triumph. 'That's what I had in mind. Late October. I already talked to John Samuels at *Newsweek*, and he promises a paragraph in their gift record column.'

'You think of everything, Bobby. You got the book all laid out too?'

'Roughly. Lots of photographs, nothing too graphic, no piles of bodies. The focus should be more on dignity, like I said. Photos of faces, women, children, maybe some defiant-looking men. And a bonus record.'

'Bonus record?'

'Yeah. A twenty-minute seven-incher. Spoken word reactions to the music.'

'By survivors?'

'Sure. It'll be fantastic. What I'd like to do is track down some people who were really in Adlerkralle, see how much they remember about it, and record their reminiscences, then play them the tapes and tape their reactions.'

'Isn't that a little thick?'

Goodman shrugged. 'Since it's a bonus record you don't *have* to listen to it—but I know damn well anyone who buys the album in the first place will want to.'

Talbot's frown deepened. 'It could be perceived as insensitive.'

'Hardly.' Goodman shook his head. 'Remember *Bookends*?'

'Simon and Garfunkel, sure.'

'Remember the band that went into "Old Friends"? Recordings of people whining in an old folks' home. Two minutes of unrelieved misery, and everybody who heard it thought it was the most *sensitive* thing since Rod McKuen. Granted, that was the sixties, but they'll still eat this up.'

'How would you find these people?'

'They're around. Seems like every old Jew you meet was either in a death camp or had a relative there.' He smiled slightly. '*I* had an uncle at Bergen-Belsen.'

'No kidding.' Talbot's eyes widened. 'What would *he* have to say about this?'

'Nothing. He died there.'

Talbot pursed his lips as if he'd just tasted something sour. 'And what do *you* think about it? Personally?'

'It's history. It doesn't bother me. I wasn't even born then.'

Talbot sat silently for a moment. 'Okay. Let me think about it. Couple of days.'

'Fine. I've got enough to keep me busy. Sam and I've been working on the Philharmonic tapes. Haydn's done, but the Bartok still needs work.'

Talbot nodded dismissal. 'I'll get back to you.'

Sure you'll get back to me, Goodman thought, *after you try to sell it to*

Wildeboor, and he tries to sell it to Kearny, and when all three of you realize it'll sell like crack on the boulevard.

༄ ༅

It took a full week, but at the end of it Talbot called Goodman back into his office and told him that it was a go, with one reservation. 'The bonus record,' Talbot said. 'It makes me edgy. We've got a lot of Jewish stockholders. If they think we're exploiting this——'

'We're *not* exploiting,' Goodman interrupted. 'I promise you, this thing will be viewed as sympathetic and sensitive. Now we *can* do it without the bonus, but I really *want* it. I swear to God you won't be sorry.'

Talbot sighed through flared nostrils. 'Twenty minutes of whiny, crying people remembering all that shit would be awful. Like pulling wings off flies.'

'But it won't be like that! Sure, a few of them may cry or get mad, but that's real emotion, it's sincere, it's poignant. And besides, we can edit it so that we get exactly what we want.'

Talbot drummed his desk top with his fingers. 'There'll be extra expense involved—finding these people, the engineering, the vinyl cost. . . .'

'And worth every penny. Marketing guesses thirty percent increase in unit sales with the bonus disc. And even if they're only half right, figuring fifteen percent—on a nineteen dollar retail price, with expected sales of a hundred thousand units, that's an extra three hundred grand gross. I'm sure the stockholders won't fart at *that*.'

'Hmm. I don't know.'

'And no extra vinyl cost on the CDs.'

Talbot swiveled his chair to look out at the spiky skyline. 'All right,' he said finally, his back to Goodman. 'How about a trial run?'

'Trial run?'

'Yeah. Take a Nakamichi and find some of these people. Get their reactions and let me have them. If I like, you can go ahead with the bonus. If not, we release the record without it.'

And if Wildeboor likes it and if Kearny likes it and . . . 'You've got a deal.'

'So how are you going to find these people?'

'Start calling rabbis, I guess.'

Which was exactly what he did. Rabbi Robert Sakowicz's synagogue was only three blocks away from the Republic Records building. After setting up the appointment by phone, Goodman went to the rabbi's office the following morning.

'It's not something people talk about very much,' Rabbi Sakowicz said. 'Certain members of the synagogue were incarcerated in the Nazi camps, but it's not the kind of thing they want to remember. Why do you want to speak to them?'

Goodman smiled reassuringly. 'We're looking into the possibility of a recorded oral history of the Holocaust. It's not definite yet, and we're trying to get a feel as to whether or not it's workable.'

'Jumping on the bandwagon, then?' The rabbi did not smile.

'Rabbi,' Goodman said admonishingly, 'of course we're a profit-making outfit, but there are other reasons for doing this. As a Jew myself,' and he paused just a second too long, 'I think it's important that people *not* forget. Call it a pet project of my own.'

'I should hardly think the deaths of six million should be classified as a pet project.'

'Okay, an unfortunate choice of words. Let's just say I think it's important.'

'Other people want very much to forget, Mr Goodman, and I don't wish to intrude upon their privacy.'

'Well, could you contact them first, see if they'd be willing to talk to me? If not, no harm done.'

The rabbi thought for a moment, then opened a desk drawer and removed a Pendaflex file. 'Give me a minute.' He flipped through a sheaf of papers, paused briefly at each one, then glanced away as if recording it mentally, his youthful fingers stroking his thick brown beard. Suddenly the door opened, and the rabbi's secretary appeared.

'Excuse me, Rabbi. It's Mr Feldman calling. His grandson's bar mitzvah?'

'I'll call him back.'

'He's just about to go out of town on business for a week. He seems pretty insistent.'

Rabbi Sakowicz shook his head impatiently, excused himself, and left the room, letting the door stand ajar. Goodman thought it odd until he noticed the phone jack disconnected at the wall, and remembered the difficulty the secretary had had connecting him with the rabbi the day before. Then he looked at the file on the desk top and licked his lips. He could hear the dull tones of the rabbi on the telephone in the outer office; the secretary seemed to have disappeared. Leaning across the desk, he turned the folder so that he could read it, and saw the name, 'Weissman, Karl', at the top of a page.

He gave an astonished laugh. *It can't be. Jesus, what luck.* Goodman started to read on, but was only able to see '1943–44, Adlerkralle', before the rabbi's steely voice made him slap the folder shut guiltily.

'Find anything interesting?'

Goodman chuckled impotently, knowing full well that the rabbi would not be charmed out of his anger. 'Yeah, I did.'

'Don't impose on strangers, Mr Goodman. Please.'

'Not a stranger, Rabbi. A co-worker.'

A sadness crept into Rabbi Sakowicz's eyes. 'Weissman,' he said softly. 'You know Weissman.'

'I know all the custodians at Republic. I work late a lot.'

'I can believe that. And probably very hard, too. Do you go through other people's files as well?'

'I'm sorry about that, Rabbi.'

Sakowicz ignored the apology. 'Leave Karl Weissman alone, Mr Goodman. He can't help you and I'm sure you can't help him.'

'Why do you say that?'

'Karl Weissman is one of the few who still lives those days. Not only remembers them, but *lives* them. It would be . . . terribly cruel to ask him to tell you of those times.'

'Don't worry, Rabbi. I'm not a cruel man. And remember, I'm a Jew myself.'

The rabbi's smile was a thin line. 'And Benedict Arnold was an American.'

ꕥ ꕥ

Bobby Goodman had told Rabbi Sakowicz that he would wait to hear from him, but once he was sitting behind his own desk in his own office, he realized he wouldn't have the patience. Karl Weissman was a gift, a gift from the god of his fathers, Goodman thought wryly. If he cooled his heels waiting for Sakowicz, he could lose his momentum, Talbot could lose his interest, and Sakowicz might wind up a dead end anyway. No, Goodman wouldn't, couldn't wait. It was difficult enough to wait until the six o'clock shift, when old Karl came on.

Goodman had always thought of him as 'old' Karl, although Weissman couldn't have been over sixty-five, still the required retirement age for all Republic employees. Weissman *looked* far older, his brows crisscrossed with lines like a wartime map of Europe. His hair was a dirty yellow-white, and his eyes were constantly bloodshot, the whites appearing pinkish as a result. He looked, Goodman thought, like an albino with a hangover. He'd wondered more than once if Karl had a drinking problem. Now, knowing the man had been in Adlerkralle, he wondered how Karl could possibly have avoided one.

At 6:04 a soft knock sounded on the door of Goodman's office. 'Come in,' he said calmly.

Karl Weissman entered, drab to the point of invisibility in his janitor's grays. 'Mr Russell told me to come up here.' The voice was quiet, the accent Mid-western with only a hint of a Mittel-European comic opera precision. 'What needs to be done?' Weissman stood quietly, like a soldier awaiting orders.

'I need your help, Karl,' Goodman said. He didn't smile. He had the feeling that Karl Weissman had forgotten what smiles were for. 'We're whipping together a project on the Second World War.'

'Yes,' Weissman said. 'The rabbi told me of your visit to him.'

Goodman struggled to keep the angry surprise out of his face, but he felt his mouth twist nonetheless. 'The rabbi told you?'

'He told me what you might want. And I'm sorry, Mr Goodman, but I want nothing to do with it.'

'Karl, be fair,' Goodman said, damning the rabbi. 'You hardly know what this is all about.'

'Oh, I know. I know exactly what it *was* about.'

Goodman shook his head. 'That's not what I mean, Karl.' He stood up. 'Will you come with me? Just down the hall into Studio C. Let me explain the situation to you, that's all. You don't have to do anything you don't want to. This is just between you and me. You don't want to help, fine. Mr Russell doesn't have to know a thing.' The very use of Russell's name was an unspoken threat. The janitors hated the building superintendent, who ruled them like a petty tyrant.

'I don't care if Mr Russell knows or not,' Weissman said, his weak chin thrusting forward, 'but I . . .'

He hesitated, and Goodman dug into the silence. 'That's fine, fine,' he said, putting a hand on Weissman's shoulder. 'Five minutes. You don't have to say a word.' Goodman went out the door, not looking back to see if Weissman was following, knowing his confidence would pull the older man along.

As he opened the door of Studio C's control room, the awry chords of Bartok's *Concerto for Orchestra* came lancing out, piercing the hall with sound. He turned, saw Weissman behind him, saw the wrinkled face pale to a pasty grayness while veins bulged blue beneath the paper-thin skin of the man's temples. 'Karl?'

Weissman feebly raised a hand, gesturing for Goodman to close the studio door. Goodman let the thick door drift shut, and silence settled over the hall once more, broken only by Weissman's ragged, asthmatic breathing. 'What is it?' Goodman asked, though he was starting to suspect.

'Nothing,' Weissman said. 'I felt faint, that's all.'

Goodman stared heavily at him, but the older man would not meet his eyes. 'Wait here a minute, Karl,' he said, and stepped back into the control booth. When he reappeared, Sam Pearson, the sound engineer, was with him, and the room was now quiet, washed clean of music. Pearson glanced at Weissman, then walked away down the hall, while Goodman beckoned the janitor to join him inside. He did so obediently, and sat in one of the three high-backed padded chairs Goodman indicated.

'Karl,' Goodman said, still standing. 'You were in Adlerkralle, weren't you?'

'Yes.' The whisper was clear and distinct in the perfect aural environment of the shadowy control room.

'On this machine, Karl,' Goodman said, patting the gleaming surface of a Teac four-track, 'is a tape I'd like you to listen to.'

'No, I . . .'

'I don't want to tell you what it is,' Goodman went on, unheeding, 'because I think you'll know.'

Weissman looked up at the machine, from which the loaded reel and its take-up glared at him like sharp, pin-pointed eyes, the four VU-meters beneath shining like a row of yellow teeth. 'I must know,' he said, 'what it is. I must know before you play it.'

Goodman sat next to him, his mood swinging from stern disciplinarian to suddenly relaxed friend, his personality adapting itself chameleon-like to what he felt would affect Weissman most favorably. 'Music, Karl,' he smiled. 'Just some music.'

It would be unfair to Goodman not to say that something within him burned as he tried to persuade the janitor to do what he wanted, that no pain of betrayal gnawed at him even as he considered what his next method of coercion would be. But the sympathy he felt for the man before him was not so great as to smother the brighter urge, the demanding, overwhelming urge to fill a small cassette with memories of a hell where angels played, searing souvenirs so gripping that they would *sell unit after unit forever and ever . . . and maybe even a spot on the* Billboard *chart and I'm goddamn made and . . .*

'Just a little music.'

'No, no,' Weissman said, refusal giving his voice added strength. 'No music. I don't . . . want to listen to this music.'

Goodman pressed just a bit so as not to lose him. 'You don't like music, Karl? Everyone likes music.'

'No, I don't listen to music.'

'This is a record company, Karl. You've got to hear music around here.'

'I . . . I don't. I wait until it's done. . . .'

'No music at night, huh?' Goodman pushed now, hard and fast.

'Not at night. It's quiet.'

'You *scared* of music, Karl?'

'Not . . . scared, I just don't——'

'You *looked* scared just now, when the music came out of here. You looked scared as hell. What kind of music scares you, Karl?'

'I'm not . . .'

'I don't think *rock* scares you, does it? Or jazz? Maybe you don't like them, but there's one kind of music that *really* scares you, isn't there, Karl?'

'No . . .' There were tears in the voice. The jaw trembled, like a long-held tower about to fall.

'*Classical* music, right, Karl? *That's* what scares you shitless, isn't it? Huh?'

'Don't . . . talke to me like that. . . .' The accent was becoming more pronounced, guttural, and thick.

'Where did that happen, Karl? And when? I can guess. You want me to take a guess? Someplace you were locked up, wasn't it?'

'You have no *right*——'

'And you're still there, aren't you, Karl? You've kept yourself locked up for over forty years——'

'*No!*' Even in the perfect acoustics of the room, the voice echoed like a trumpet as the man leaped to his feet, his gaunt face towering above Goodman, who drew back involuntarily. '*Who are you?*' he cried. 'Who are you to talk to me this way, to pry into my life?'

'Hey, relax! Just relax now.' He'd pushed too far. He realized he'd been clumsy, careless, misreading the man, and he could have kicked himself. 'I'm sorry, Karl. I just got sort of carried away, you know?'

The older man went on as though he had never heard. 'You want to make your guesses? Then guess! Yes, I *hate* music. I cannot listen to it, it makes me *sick*!' Weissman's face twisted in trembling rage.

'Because of the camps . . .'

'Because of *Adlerkralle*, yes! But you knew that, didn't you? Oh yes, you're so smart, you knew that.'

'Well, the way you acted when you heard the music,' Goodman said smiling, trying to look open and careless. 'And then I remembered a couple of times before . . .'

'Before, when I would go elsewhere when you were playing your music, when I would clean a toilet rather than hear *this music*.'

'Karl, I'm sorry, really. All I want is——'

'What do to want me to listen to? Screams? People screaming? Isn't that what they call music now?'

'No, Karl. A string quartet.'

Weissman seemed to freeze in place. Then the set anger of his face melted into a kind of wondering fear. 'A string quartet?' The voice was far away, haunted, disembodied in the dimly lit room.

'Yes.' *Oh my God, I've got him now, will you just look at him.*

'What . . . is this quartet?'

'It played there, Karl. Where you were. At Adlerkralle.'

'The . . . the Angels?'

'That's what Commandant Hossler called them, wasn't it? The Angels that played the heavenly music while the condemned went to their deaths.'

'You have a recording of . . . the Angels?'

Goodman nodded slowly. 'A wire recording transferred to tape. It's on that machine right now.' He gestured around the room, at the hundreds of sliders and knobs and dials and meters. 'Everything is set to play it. All somebody has to do is push the *play* button on that machine.' Weissman, Goodman observed gratefully, was once more watching the Teac as he would a cobra, its hood spread, ready to strike. 'All it takes is a push, Karl. It's so easy. But I won't do it. I'd *like* you to hear it, I'd like you to tell me what you think of it, how it makes you feel. If you want to do it, Karl, all you have to do is press the play and record buttons on this smaller machine here, right next to the big one.'

Goodman felt vaguely absurd as he gave the instructions, as though he were advising a statue. But he had to make sure Weissman knew, knew and remembered. 'Just press both buttons at once and talk into the microphone, that's all there is to it. You understand me, Karl?'

He didn't answer right away, but finally a whispered '*Yes*' came out.

Goodman leaned toward the unwillingly fascinated man, and used all his wiles to sound like friend, brother, priest, father-confessor. 'All these years, Karl, you've kept yourself bound. Now, finally, you can be free. But it's got to be your choice, your decision.'

Goodman stood and went to the door. 'Nobody will come in here tonight. I'm leaving, and everyone else is gone. If you want to walk out, fine. Just leave things as they are, and we won't talk about it again. But if you want to listen, it's here. It's waiting for you, Karl. It's been waiting for a long time.'

He opened the door and stepped into the hall, his last glimpse of Weissman an unmoving, huddled figure whose head seemed buried halfway between his shoulders.

Goodman felt jubilant. He *would* have his tape now, he had no doubt, if there was enough left in Karl Weissman after listening to the Angels for him to articulate his thoughts and emotions. But after so many years of being bottled up, Goodman thought, they should flow out of him like blood in a slaughterhouse.

Goodman could have stood there all night waiting to hear the music from inside, waiting for Weissman to come out the door. But as much as he wanted to know whether or not Weissman would take the bait, he was hesitant about confronting the man again. Goodman generously interpreted it as decency on his part, and decided to go home and try to sleep. It was hard to turn and walk down the hall, but it would have been harder to face Weissman after that music had blasted his soul. Morning would come soon enough, and he honestly hoped it would come for Weissman too, that hearing the music might somewhat cleanse him of the terrors he'd borne for decades.

But only after he'd put those terrors on tape.

III

The eyes of the reels stared at Weissman. Time had stopped for him. 1988 was 1944 was 1988, and those years of horror and the empty years in between were all compressed into this hour, this moment in the dim room with the little lights like stars that expanded the time back into all the years again.

He felt as though he would sit there forever, waiting for his finger to push the button and see what happened, see what he would do when the dark time came again. The past forty-four years he had been waiting, been pressing it away from him like some black, cold gelatin that seeped through his fingers and around his wrists, forcing him backward into a shadowy corner, where at last it would envelop him.

And now the time was here, was all dark time, and the shadowy corner was this warm, softly glowing room where he sat and stared into the eyes and teeth of yesterday. An unexpected peace touched him then, and a sense of inevitability guided him forward, pushed the button so that the wheels began to turn.

There was no sound at first, and Weissman leaned back, taking his gaze away from the rolling eyes, looking upward to where the twin speakers hung. Then a hissing filled the room, and he stiffened, knowing what it was. Not the hiss of a speaker or of old tape, but the sly, teasing hiss of wind, the wind whose special voice had blown into his spirit. The wind that mocked them with its freedom, entering and escaping the camp a thousand times a day. The wind that tortured them with the odors of the burning, the olfactory evidence that *their* only escape would be on that same wind that would snatch them up as their smoke-wraiths fled from the pits.

Then he heard voices, faraway, low barks of orders that he wondered if he imagined rather than heard through the speakers. But no, they were there, followed by a harshly whispered imprecation that quieted them.

And the music began.

It nailed him to the chair as though a thick spike of ice had been driven through his heart and into the seat back. The volume was moderate, the tone was mellow, but the unison notes captured him between the octaves as though there were not nor had there ever been any other sound in the world. He would have screamed had he had the breath.

The music split into harmonies then, rocking and bouncing madly from the violins to viola to cello and back, while Weissman thought, *the Fugue, mein liebe Gott, die Grosse Fugue, die Engels, die verdammte Engels*! The wind added a fifth voice to the quartet, ethereal, pure, and taunting, higher than Saperstein could ever have played, Saperstein with his hollow eyes and bald, yellow head, scraping weakly at his violin with the split back, the violin Sturmbannfuhrer Hossler had batted from his hands after Saperstein had mangled a run in the Schumann.

Now the brief *overtura* was ended, and as the music grew more frenzied, he saw Saperstein in the gem-clear theater of memory the control room had become, Saperstein's bald head bouncing like a great, shapeless ball, trying to hold *die Engels* together in the chaotic labyrinth of the double fugue section. And there was Brendel sawing away on second, the poorest player of the four, a constant frown of fear on her cracked, gray lips. Dessauer on viola, consumptive, withered, brilliant, fingers clawed with cold and arthritis so that the simplest run became agony, and an extended trill a horror.

Oh, how they played, even with their infirmities and terrors, with the acrid wind in counterpoint and the moans of the dying as a constant *continuo*! playing because not to play was to die. And as the others passed by, the ones who would leave as smoke, whose dying music would turn to muffled cries of anguish as the gas stole all they had left, it was *their* eyes that burned, their sneers that accused, not the cruel eyes of the masters, the *Sturm und Drang*-headed fools who kept *die Engels* alive for their music, for the serenade sung to *their* master, Death.

The rollicking double fugue, clattering along like dead men's bones, slowed and shifted to the G-flat section, startlingly lyrical after the previous madness, and the slow, somber chords took Weissman back fully, adding to sight and sound and scent the sense of touch as well, so that he held the long horsehair bow in his right hand while his left palm pressed the sweat-polished smoothness of his cello's neck and his fingers trembled on the fingerboard. Oh, the faces were there, so real, so vivid, so full of pain and battered hope and envy as they looked at *die Engels*, and the thoughts were so loud he could hear them, saying——

—If *I* could play I would not be walking to death.

—I had my body to keep me alive, but it failed me at last.

—When your hands fail *you*, you will join *us*.

—Play your tunes, whores for the Nazis. You will play another soon enough.

They were the voices Karl Weissman had heard for over four decades, the voices that yammered at him in dreams, that spoke just below the surface of melody that lay in wait everywhere he turned, that made it impossible for him to have a radio, a television set, to go to movies or stores where always the music played, the remindful, ominipresent music that inflated the guilt within him like the bloated stomach of a corpse, until there was only one statement, one great truth:

You should have died.

It was what *all* the faces had told him as they passed, every day, every single face, even . . .

Anna.

Allegro molto! Now they were into it again, the notes galloping like war-maddened furies, weaving in and out of each other as Saperstein's head bobbed frantically, the fear of losing the beat clear in his eyes as the tempo increased, and now they were nearing the measure he had never forgotten, would never forget, when Anna . . .

There! His heart stopped, the shock was so great. Stopped, then started again in a frenzy as if to make up for its failure. The error, the false note he had played when he had seen her, the B-flat that had shrieked and twisted into a gratingly off-key natural before he could find his place in the fugue again. He had *heard* it on the tape, and its presence told him precisely what day it was, what day it had been ever since.

March 17, 1944.

The day when Anna, *his* Anna, Anna of the long, tapered fingers that had caressed a piano's keys like a baby's brows, had walked into the yard with the others, had turned to the left at the flick of the commandant's whip; Anna, whose fingers had been crushed by the cattle car's doors, whose *music* had been crushed by a young and careless Army guard too anxious to shut away the Jews from his sight; Anna who at last turned toward the path of death, of escape on the cruel wind.

His fingers had slipped then, the one time, the only time he had drawn disharmony into the air of Adlerkralle. But he had re-entered the tapestry of the fugue, playing as though sound alone could halt time, and reverse it, savaging the strings with the intensity of his grief. *No!* he had thought. *No! It is a mistake! Every time, every time she returns alive! They have made a mistake! They will see, she is still strong! They will see!'*

And now the fifth and final sub-movement began, a trembling, rapid pulse as he sawed and sawed, biting the notes off, back and forth, back and forth, while the melody soared leisurely above him as if two differing tempi warred above sublimely for predominance, he and Dessauer's unbridled ferocity against Brendel and Saperstein's patient and unhurried calm. The end approached, and he saw an SS *Obersturmfuhrer* cross to the women and look at Anna and he thought *Now! Now! They will see!* even though he knew that what had happened had happened and could never be changed. Nothing could ever be changed.

As the *Obersturmfuhrer* regarded the women coldly and turned from them, young Karl Weissman's last hope vanished like a *pianissimo* phrase on the wind, and all thoughts of music fled from him. His left hand slipped down the neck of the cello, and his right lowered the bow to his side while Saperstein's old eyes flared and blinked a panicked signal. But Weissman's full attention was on the young, fatally slim woman who walked past the quartet's platform with the others, others who looked at the musicians with a loathing that would survive them by a lifetime. And in the young Karl's eyes, the young woman stared at him with envy mixed with anguish, while her mouth opened pleadingly and formed words he took to be the muttered curses the others had voiced, and, perhaps worse, a call for help that he could not give.

But years later, in the old man's mind that looked in memory through the young man's eyes, Karl Weissman saw something else. To his surprise, and to the accompaniment of a startling joy that he told himself he must not feel even as it overwhelmed him, he saw not hate but love in the eyes, and hope. And he knew at last what she was saying, *knew*, not guessed or wished, for he *heard* her now above the whining, suddenly impotent wind and the other three trying to sound like four.

'*Play*,' she said. '*Play for me*.'

And while the young man in 1944 sat ignorant and powerless, deafened by guilt and grief and distance, Karl Weissman, hearing, grasped an unseen cello and an invisible bow, and, in a cracked voice that filled the darkened control room, sang for Anna, sang to its glorious end the great fugue he had begun so many years before.

As the notes poured out of him, so too did something else, something that eyes younger than Karl Weissman's might have detected as a veil of shadow, a sheet of darkness that unfolded from around Weissman like a cloak of the thinnest gossamer to hover just below the ceiling, into which it seemed to fade as the music ended.

IV

The halls were empty at five in the morning when an impatient Bobby Goodman arrived at the Republic Records building. The night janitors had finished their shifts hours ago, and it would be another three hours before anyone else showed up. Goodman wondered where Karl Wiessman was. He paused before opening the control room door, not knowing what his usually glib tongue would say if the old man were still there. But the room was vacant, at least of Karl Weissman.

From the instant he entered, Goodman felt oddly *unalone*, as if someone were watching from the shadows in the room's corners. He threw off the unexpected sensation long enough to look at the Teac, and grinned at what he saw. The take-up reel was full.

'He listened!' Goodman said, laughter in his voice. 'He heard it!' He shot his gaze to the Nakamichi's counter, which stood at 127. It had been at 000 when he'd left Weissman alone in the room. 'Oh, goddamn, goddamn!' he cried gleefully, rewinding the cassette on which Karl Weissman had offered up his reactions. 'Okay, baby,' he said, pushing the *play* button. 'Let's hear it.'

It seemed as though the voice belonged to a much younger man, as if years had been lifted from it and tossed away.

'*Thank you, Mr Goodman. I don't know what you want to hear me say, I don't know why you wanted me to hear the music, but I thank you for driving me to the point where I listened.*' The voice paused, then want on. '*I did not believe before. In anything. But now I do. I believe in God again, for how else can I explain how this has come back to me across all the miles and the years? Yet it has somehow. To give me peace. To give me back my music. Thank you for the part you played in this, whatever your reasons. I wish I could give you something in return.*'

Another pause, so long that Goodman looked at the machine to make sure it was still running. Only one word followed—'*Perhaps . . .*'; and then silence.

Goodman sat back, thinking. What the hell had Weissman meant? Goodman had expected almost anything but the cool, confident words that had come from the speakers. He rewound the tape and listened to Weissman again, but still could not unravel the mystery he had convinced himself must exist. Maybe the music would give him a clue, something he'd missed on previous listenings.

He rewound the tape on the Teac, started to play it, and listened as the cold wind swept into the room, chilling him through the heavy sweater he wore. As the first unison notes of music sounded, the lights of the room started to dim, and the darkness began to grow, creeping from the corners, melting from the ceiling until it encased him in a black, gelatinous shell of fear. And in the back of his mind he realized that some emotions do not die when their bearer deserts them, that when the nurturing of pain is strong and lifelong, then the pain, and the guilt and terror that feed it, live on, not destroyed, but waiting.

The music played on, rushing about his mind like waves on a blood-red sea, drowning him as he tried to float above the surface, pressing down upon him with gaunt, hate-filled faces, envious eyes, hands brittle and thin as sticks. The music cut and tore and burned and froze, every phrase more cruel than the last until he knew he could bear no more. But he did, unable to move, unable to retreat into unconsciousness, until the last few measures were ended, the final measures in which the cello, deep and sonorous, sang in triumph over its stringed fellows.

The fugue was ended.

Goodman sat in the chair, sick and shaking, his sole desire to run from the room when his legs would finally obey him. To run and run until he was far away from where the agonies of the music seared him.

He did not want to hear it ever again.

He did not want to hear the music.

Return of the Neon Fireball

'PICTURE IT,' MICHAEL PRICE SAID over chowder at Mario's, the chi-chi Italian restaurant that had once been Sam's Grill. 'Triple features—*It Came From Outer Space*, *Francis Joins The Navy*, *High Noon*, cartoon, old newsreels, and Jesus Christ the *clock*, remember the clock? "Only ten minutes until the next feature", and the dancing hot dogs—*da*-da-*dad-dah*!—and cups of soft drinks on little train cars? And don't forget the snack bar—quarter hot dogs, ten cent cups of Coke and popcorn, nickel Raisinets and Goobers——'

'Wait a minute,' Lenny Crane said. 'Who pays for *that* stuff?'

'*They* do—the patrons—when they come in. Lenny, the rental on those old films is diddley-squat. We'll sell the food at cost so we won't *lose* money, and we charge to get in—four bucks a person or twelve a car, whichever's cheaper. We'll make a good profit on that.'

'Mike, the friggin' place is closing in the first place due to lack of business, and you tell me people are going to pay four bucks a head to see stuff they can see on TV?'

'It's not the films—it's the *experience*. It's closing because they've been showing third-run crap you can rent on cassette. The snack bar sells expensive shit, they don't keep the place clean, they tore the old playground down—they tried to make an indoor theater outside, and that's where they screwed up. Now what *I* say is make it what it used to be, and you'll get people. We can use the line, "The Fireball Drive-In Theater—where it's always the fifties", or something.'

Lenny sucked his lower lip. 'And what stops people from filling their trunks with five cent Goobers?'

'Tickets they get when they come in that they have to turn in when they buy food. Maybe two or three items per person.'

'You got this worked out pretty fast.'

'I was up all night.'

And he had been. From the minute he had read of the closing in the paper, he had thought of nothing else but the Fireball. Though he hadn't been there in twenty years, Mike Price loved the Fireball, just as he loved everything he remembered about being young. Awake all night, he still dreamed. He dreamed about himself in high school—lean, muscular, with that thatch of white-blond hair the girls loved to ruffle. He dreamed about winning football games for the McKinley Marauders, pulling the ball magically out of the air and floating across the goal line on the light feet of youth. He dreamed of his '49 Merc, chopped and channelled, its seats filled with his friends, himself sitting tall behind the wheel, wearing his blue and white varsity sweater. But most of all, he dreamed of the Fireball.

It had blazed its way through his sleeping dreams at night for years, and now, as his life grew sad and empty, it began to light up his days as well, that bright, neon concoction of red and yellow and orange, with a tail of brilliant blue behind it, and the words in letters of fire: FIREBALL DRIVE-IN THEATER. It was huge and gaudy and high and beautiful, suspended twenty yards in the air above its cement base. Fall was the best season to see the sign, for it was dark when they started the show, and driving down Route 30 you saw its glow from a mile away, brightening as you drew nearer until you could finally see the comet itself streaking across the horizon.

But for real fun, summer had been the time—arriving at 8:00 when the gates opened, looking for a spot close to the screen, but not close enough for it to shine too brightly on you and your date. If you were with your pals, it was different. Then all you cared about was parking far enough away from the snack bar and from cars with families so that you could drink your bottle of beer and whoop and swear and make cracks at the love scenes without anybody calling the manager. You'd sit back, watch *The Blob*, *Five Guns West*, *Psycho*, *House Of Usher*, and feel the warm breeze, the bottle cool against your forehead, and want the screen, the white marquee, the neon fireball to shine forever.

But it wouldn't, not if it was sold to anyone but him. It would be stripped away, and a housing development would rise where the old speaker posts and snack bar used to be, or a factory would rear itself up upon the rows that rippled like the waves of the sea when you drive directly toward the screen after the movie. And that night he sat and thought about how another treasured chunk of his youth would be wiped out, just like the old high school, or the soda fountain down on Bainbridge Street where they had made the best goddam vanilla cokes on the planet. The next morning he had called Lenny Crane.

'How much they want for the thing?' Lenny asked.

Mike pulled out a slip of paper and slid it across the table. 'I checked this morning.'

'Jesus, that's a lot.'

'It's worth it.'

'Can you afford half of this?' Mike nodded. 'I don't believe you.'

'If I sell the store I can.'

'Sell the store?'

'It's a shitty store. I don't want it anymore.'

'Whatta you mean, you don't *want* it anymore? What's wanting got to do with it? For crissake, that was your old man's store, Mike. You don't piss away a family business like that.' Lenny shook his head. 'Sylvia was still alive, you wouldn't be acting like this. You're acting like a *kid*, Mike.'

'Don't lecture me, Lenny.'

'But why a drive-in theater?'

Mike puffed a sigh wreathed in age. 'I'm not having any fun, Lenny. I want to have fun again. The Fireball was always fun.'

'Yeah,' Lenny agreed. 'We had some good times there. But I don't know, I mean, can you really afford to take a chance like this? What if it flops?'

'So who am I saving my money for? Goddam it, Lenny, I got no kids, Sylvia's gone . . .'

'You might get married again.'

'Shit. Look at me.'

'What? You're forty-five, same as me.'

'Bullshit. You're good looking and rich. I'm bald and fat and . . . *not* rich.'

'Come on, knock it off.' Lenny waved his hands in the air. 'What about all the time it would take, Mike? After all, I got a finance business to run.'

'We'd only be open weekends. Friday through Sunday. I'd do all of the work needed doing during the week—advertising, maintenance, all that.'

'What, you wanta be a fuckin' janitor too?'

'Why not?'

Lenny sighed. 'Some guys with money buy model trains, or gliders, or expensive stamps. Me, I play racquetball and tennis and put it in the bank and get laid by pretty girls now and then, and that's about all. Maybe I need a hobby.' He gave a lopsided grin and shook his head. 'But, holy shit, a drive-in theater? You let me think about it, huh?'

'Remember, Lenny. Convertibles and summer nights. *Vertigo* and *The Deadly Mantis* and . . .'

'Okay, *okay*, go sell some clothes, all right?'

All the way back to his shop Mike Price thought *please God, let him do it, let him do it*, praying for the lost good times to come back again.

ꕤ

And somebody heard him. The next day Lenny called and told him that although it was a helluva time to start a new business in this deader'n shit town, he couldn't resist giving it a try. Besides, if it turned out to be a bust, it wouldn't have to be a complete loss—they could always sell the land.

They bought the theater and all the equipment the following week. Mike sold his store to come up with his half, but not for as much as he had hoped. He had to cash in his bonds and take a big chunk from the IRAs he'd set up for his retirement. He didn't tell Lenny about it.

But goddam it if it wasn't worth it several weeks later, on that warm, breezy Friday evening in mid-May when the neon fireball lit up again, and cars lined up for a quarter mile to get in. Lenny sold the tickets, and Mike ran the snack bar with the help of three giggly teenage girls. There was a double feature—*The Fireball*, a 1950 Mickey Rooney movie about roller derbies, and *It Conquered The World*—neither of them classics, but the names looked glorious on the marquee, and Mike had gotten photographers from the three local newspapers to come out and record it for posterity.

It was a great night. The weather cooperated, the three security men Lenny had hired arrested no one, children played in the well-lit playground, people mobbed the snack bar at intermission, and at the end of the show a winning ticket stub holder received a Dustbuster Plus vacuum cleaner, the first prize in a series of drawings to be held every Friday night.

After everyone else went home, and the Del-Vikings' last notes faded away on the P.A. system, Lenny and Mike remained to count the cash. 'Looks like you were right,' Lenny said, smiling. '*If* it keeps up.'

'It'll keep up,' Mike said quietly.

'Hey, what's wrong?'

'Wrong?'

'For a successful impresario, you don't seem too happy.'

Mike shook his head. 'I'm happy enough. It went fine.'

'It sure as hell did,' Lenny laughed, gesturing to the piles of bills.

'It's just that . . .'

'Just that what?

'It wasn't as much *fun* as I thought it would be,' Mike said with a sigh.

Lenny nodded. 'I know. I think I know what you mean. But it's *never* gonna be what it was. We were young then. But what it is now is pretty damn good. Hell, partner, we made the fifties live again.'

'Almost.'

'Yeah, almost.' Lenny looked down again at the money on the table, and with the tip of his finger shot a coin across to Mike. 'There. That's your souvenir. '51 Franklin half.'

Mike picked it up. 'You get this tonight?'

Lenny nodded. 'Car full of kids, really up for it. Came in an old car, all dressed up like the fifties. One of the girls had a *poodle* skirt on, for crissake.'

'And they gave you this?'

'Uh-huh. Bought tickets with it. I said hey, you know this is a valuable coin, but the kid just looked at me like I was crazy and said, yeah, it's worth a whole fifty cents. So I thought what the hell, if he didn't want it. Keep it if you want.' Lenny stretched, yawned, and stood up. 'Well, I'm going home. If you can take the stuff in to the bank tomorrow, I'd appreciate it. I got clients in the morning.'

After Lenny left, Mike sat for some time turning the half dollar over in his hands. It was bright and shiny, and showed little wear, and he began to go through the stacks of coins looking for other old ones. He found two, both quarters—the first a 1945 Standing Liberty, the other a 1953 Washington. With the fifty cent piece, they totalled a dollar.

Then he started on the bills. It was nearly two in the morning before he found them all—a five and six ones, all dated 1956 and before. Other than those, the oldest bills in the pile went back only to the mid-seventies.

One five, six ones, a dollar in change. Twelve dollars altogether, the admission price for one carful. A carful of kids, according to Lenny, who were really up for it.

That night Mike dreamed about double dating with Becky Geyer. They were watching the movie out of the corners of their eyes, most of their attention devoted to necking. Mike had his hand under Becky's sweater and on top of her bra, and from the panting in the back seat Phil Strickler, his class president, was doing pretty well with Crissy Medwick, the prettiest of the cheerleaders except for Becky. If Mike looked real hard out of his right eye, he could just make out Phil's hand losing its definition, becoming a lump that crept snakelike under the material of Crissy's skirt, higher and higher until the poodle embroidered on it seemed to shift in discomfort while Crissy moaned an insincere protest. . . .

The *poodle* . . .

Mike awoke sweating, felt his way to the refrigerator, and drank half a can of beer to cool himself off.

The next evening, Saturday, Mike sat in the ticket kiosk with Lenny, leaving the snack bar to the girls. Only one car of fifties vintage came through, a '55 T-bird with classic plates, occupied by a local real estate broker and his wife. The crowd was even larger that night, and afterwards, when the cars had gone and the two of them were counting the receipts, Mike asked casually if Lenny remembered what kind of car the kids with the old coin had been driving.

'Didn't look too close,' Lenny said. 'Ford, Merc, something like that.'

'Pretty old?'

'Shit, yeah. Had that clumsy round styling, y'know? Didn't look like a reconditioned one, though. Dull paint job, and the interior looked worn.'

'You think it might've been a Merc?'

'Maybe.' Lenny looked up from the piles of singles. 'Why?'

'Just wondered,' Mike said.

That night he dreamed about LaVern Baker wailing from the Merc's tinny speaker while he screamed down the back road playing chicken, swerving at the final moment, skidding off the blacktop into the field, corn shocks scattering like frightened birds and laughing while his heart beat so fast that it filled the car, buoyed it up, made it fly, with a fiery comet's tail dragging behind it that froze in the cold upper sky, hardening to thick bright tubes of neon.

There were fewer cars on Sunday, but the attendance was still respectable and highly profitable, and Mike thought with deep satisfaction that he was not the only one who needed to escape, to retreat into a bright and peaceful past.

Monday through Thursday, while Lenny worked in his office in town, Mike played janitor, accountant, and purchasing agent, faithfully recording income and expenses, buying the snack bar food for the next weekend, repairing the speakers that had been snapped from their wires, and walking down the softly curving rows, picking up the beer bottles, soda cans, popcorn boxes, candy wrappers (and yes, one used condom, by God), and dropping them into his wheeled cart under the warm May sun.

He didn't mind it. He had never worked beneath the sky before, and he liked the scent of approaching summer, the crunch of the loose stones under his feet, the sounds of birds roosting in the grove behind the last row of the theater. When he closed his eyes, the breeze brushed his face so lightly that he could almost believe it was once more smooth and beardless, young. He dreamed at night, imagined by day, and waited for Friday, when the Fireball would shine again.

ꕥ

Lenny frowned when he saw Mike approaching the kiosk. 'Hey,' he said, 'what's up?'

'I thought you might be lonely,' Mike answered.

'Don't you think you oughta be at the snack bar?'

'The girls can handle it.'

'They screwed up last Saturday. Not enough doggies out of the freezer, remember?' He looked pointedly at Mike. 'You wanta take tickets tonight, or what?'

'Would you mind? Just trading for tonight? I'm a little tired.'

Lenny sighed. 'Yeah, okay.' He climbed off the stool, then looked at Mike again. 'You feel sick or anything?'

'No.'

'Mike. Tell me. This place getting to you?'

'No,' he said defensively.

'Okay.' Lenny nodded, but there was doubt in his eyes. 'Just . . . don't take things too seriously, y'know? I mean, this is just fun, a fun way to make a buck, right? When we were kids it was fun too. But it wasn't all *that* great. It wasn't everything.' Lenny nodded again, agreeing with himself, and walked to the snack bar, leaving Mike alone in the ticket kiosk.

The cars started to arrive within a few minutes, and Mike took the money, counting heads and giving out change and food tickets automatically, waiting, watching for one special car.

It was nearly dark by the time it arrived, a '49 Merc, chopped and channeled. The color was a faded baby blue, accented by bright orange flames painted on the rear fenders. The front bumper bore a blue and white

McKinley High sticker. Mike recognized the car, and thought he recognized the people inside, four of them.

'Twelve dollars,' he said in a harsh whisper. The driver took out a light tan wallet with a western design on the leather and counted out some bills, then reached behind him to take the money the boy in the back seat was offering.

'There ya go, pardner,' the driver said, giving Mike the money and keeping his hand extended for the change.

'Do you . . .' Mike cleared his throat roughly. 'Do you kids go to McKinley?'

'Yeah.' The driver nodded. 'McKinley. Why?'

Mike shook his head. McKinley. It had been John F. Kennedy High for almost twenty years, one martyred president's name replacing another's in white metal letters above the tired entrance.

'Hey.' Mike looked at the driver. 'How 'bout the change?'

Mike handed the boy three singles and the snack bar tickets, which the boy looked at strangely. Then he shrugged. 'Thanks, daddio.'

The car pulled away from the kiosk fast, making loose gravel fly up in narrow twin geysers. Mike watched it go. It was not until he saw the car park in the center of the lot, five rows back from the screen, that he responded to the driver of the next car. 'Hey, buddy,' he finally heard the man say, 'are you okay?'

'Yes. Yes, fine.' He took money and made change, glancing every few seconds, his heart pounding and stomach churning, toward the middle of the fifth row where the Merc sat. Time and again he wiped the sweat from his forehead and prayed that the car wouldn't disappear, not before he got to it, not before he could talk to them again.

Night came, the screen glowed, the stream of cars became short and staggered groups, then a single car every minute or so. Mike thought he could still see the tubular, whale-like shape of the Merc, imagined he could see the four heads within. At last there were no more cars coming in, and he turned off the kiosk light, locked the door, and walked down and across the rows until he was behind the Mercury. The two heads in the back were together, kissing. Those in the front were together too, but watching the film, Kirk Douglas in *Indian Fighter*.

He didn't want to startle them, so he rapped on the left rear fender before coming to the window. The pairs of heads parted like a shadowy mitosis, and as Mike moved up the length of the car he saw, by the light of the screen, the white poodle on the skirt of the girl in the back seat. The driver looked at Mike and frowned. 'So what is it? Necking illegal?'

'No . . . no. I just . . .' Mike gave a short, brittle laugh. 'I just thought I recognized you.'

'You recognized us.' They were all looking at him now, questions on their dark faces, discomfort in the smoky air of the car. The boy in the back took a drag on his cigarette and blew in Mike's direction.

'Yes. I know you.' He looked at the girl in the passenger seat. 'Becky,' he said. 'Becky Geyer.' He turned his head toward the back seat. 'Phil Strickler. Crissy. Crissy Medwick.' Then he looked at the driver and could not speak.

'So far so good,' the boy said. 'What about me?' He smiled like a shark, showing white, even teeth that complemented his white-blond hair, as his hands tightened on the steering wheel, and the muscles of his arms and chest stood out tautly.

'I . . .' Mike could not say it. 'Tell me. You tell me. . . .'

'He's Mike Price,' grunted the boy in the back seat. 'You know who he is, you know who we all are, now what's your beef, dad? You wanta check us for beer or what?'

Mike shook his head, suddenly feeling very old, very tired, but very excited as well. 'No, no trouble. I just want to . . . to talk to you.'

'Why?' the driver asked.

'Becaue I'm *one* of you!'

The girl in the back seat laughed.

'One of us,' the driver said flatly.

'Yes!'

'You're not one of us.'

'But I *am*. Let me explain . . . let me talk to you.' He grasped the door handle. 'Let me in. . . .'

The boy pushed the cylinder down, locking the door. 'After the movies. When everyone's gone. We'll wait.' He put his arm around the girl and turned back toward the screen, away from the older man.

Michael Price walked back to the ticket kiosk and sat inside in the dark. When the first feature ended he did not go into the snack bar to help Lenny and the girls. He only waited.

Ten minutes into the second feature he head footsteps on the loose stones. 'Mike!' Lenny said beside him. 'What are you doing out here? You sick?'

'Just thinking.'

'We coulda used some help in there. Busy as hell.'

'I'm sorry.'

'You coming in?'

'Not right away.' Neither spoke for a moment. 'Lenny . . . do you think if you want things bad enough . . . they come to you?'

Lenny sucked his lower lip. 'Nothing comes to you. You get it for yourself. I'm going in. Why don't you come with me?'

'No. I'd rather stay here.'

'Come on in, Mike. Things look too different out here.' Lenny turned and walked back to the snack bar. Mike stayed in the kiosk.

The movie finally ended and the cars formed into a long procession, red and white lights gleaming as they left the presence of the darkened screen.

When all the cars but one had vanished, Mike walked across the empty lot to where the Mercury sat, its engine running, its lights on. The driver looked at him with a strangely blank expression.

'One of us,' he said again, as though no time had passed.

'Yes, I am.'

'If you want to be one of us,' the boy said, 'there's only one way.'

He raced the engine and patched out of the space, yanking the wheel around and roaring down the gentle curve of the fourth row. Mike threw up an arm against the barrage of stones that shot from beneath the tires. The Mercury slowed as it reached the row's end, then turned completely around so that it faced down the fifth row, its headlights shining directly into Mike's startled eyes.

He stood for a moment, pinned in the high-beams, before he understood. The Merc's engine roared out its challenge, and he turned and started toward his Buick, parked next to the snack bar.

Lenny met him halfway there. 'Mike, what the hell are those kids doing?'

'They're . . . it's okay. They're waiting for me.'

'For you?' He got into step beside Mike, moving toward the Buick. The Merc roared again, lurched like a caged beast. Stones flew. 'Jesus Christ,' Lenny swore. 'What's *with* them? They're acting like'—a dim memory moved within him—'play chicken.'

Mike put the Buick in reverse and started to back out, but Lenny shot an arm through the window and grabbed the wheel, making him brake.

'Let go!'

'What are you *doing*?'

'They're *waiting* for me, Lenny!'

'Who? Who are *they*?'

'Phil, Crissy, Becky . . . Becky Geyer . . .'

'In that car? You're nuts! Those're *kids*!'

'You remember, Lenny, you remember what they looked like, you saw them the other night!'

'I only saw the driver, for crissake . . .'

'That was *me*! Me and my friends.'

'You? Your *friends*?' Lenny shook his head, confused. 'Hell, Mike, they were never your friends, they didn't even *talk* to you. . . .'

'*Me*, Lenny! Me and my car! My Merc!'

'God *damn* it, what is *wrong* with you? You never had a car, Mike, you always came in *my* car, you and me . . .'

'But it was *me*,' Mike sobbed. 'You remember *me*!'

'The blond kid? That was never you,' Lenny said, near tears himself now, remembering the pudgy, unpopular junior he'd pitied and befriended, remembering Michael Price. 'That wasn't *you*. . . .'

'Let *go*!' shrieked Mike, slamming a fist down on Lenny's knuckles so that Lenny cried out and released the wheel. Mike hit the accelerator, and the

Buick surged backwards with a rattle of stones, then swung left, raced down the row, swerved, fishtailed, straightened out, moved toward the screen, turned again, and stopped.

The two cars faced down the hundred yards of gravel that defined the fifth row, the curve of it making the beams of their headlights cross several rows further back. Speaker posts marked the boundaries of their arena, the worn, metal surfaces gleaming dully in the beams of the headlights. The Merc roared, and the sound seemed louder than before. The Buick tried to respond, but its tone was ratchety, unskilled, its fuel-saving engine unable to issue screaming challenges in the night. At last Lenny realized what was going to happen.

'No!' he cried, running toward Mike's Buick. 'You can't! Mike, goddammit, stop it! *Stop!*'

'I've done it before!' Mike yelled through the open window. 'I know how!'

'Never!' answered Lenny. 'You never . . .!'

The Merc streaked forward like a sprinter from the blocks, and Mike slammed his foot to the floor. The cars rushed toward the center, the beams of their headlights straightening, meeting, driving the light before them until it met in the center of the row, a rising flare of whiteness.

Neither turned.

The impact shook the world.

'Oh Christ,' whispered Lenny. 'Oh Christ Jesus . . .' He started to walk toward the spot, then ran, then slowed, and walked again, stopped.

There was no Merc. There was only the Buick, its lights extinguished, crumpled as though it had run into an invisible wall, a dead beast lying in a pool of darkness.

They had to cut Mike out of the car with torches.

❧ ☙

In the office behind the snack bar Lenny told the troopers that he had heard the crash, run outside, and found the car.

'There must have been another vehicle,' a trooper said.

'I didn't see it.'

'He had to have hit *something*.'

Lenny shook his head and the troopers frowned. There hadn't been a sign of another car, no impressions in the stones, no shattered pieces from whatever it was the dead man hit at forty miles per hour. 'We'll check the body shops around here,' the trooper said. 'We'll find out who he hit, or who hit him.'

Lenny shook his head again. Again the troopers frowned.

The Fireball was closed the next week, but the following Friday it opened with an Abbott and Costello double bill. Lenny hired a ticket seller, and stayed with the high school girls in the snack bar. He didn't want to be alone.

Twenty minutes after the first film began, the new girl came in from the kiosk with the money. 'Look at this,' she said, dumping change into Lenny's hand.

He looked down at the forties and fifties coinage and felt ice on his spine. 'Who gave you these?' he asked so harshly that the girl's smile vanished.

'Some kids in an old car.'

'A Mercury?'

'I don't know. I don't know old cars.'

'Two guys, two girls?'

'I . . . I think so, yeah.'

Lenny walked out into the night and made his way through the maze of cars to the fifth row near the center. The Mercury sat there, undamaged. He made himself walk on until he stood by the left rear fender, until he could see the face of the driver reflected in the outside mirror.

Then he turned and walked back toward the safer light, wondering how much he could get for the land after he'd torn down the screen and dismantled and destroyed the neon fireball, trying desperately to forget the driver's face, that fleshy, forty-five year old face smiling at the movie, at the girl beside him, trying without success to forget Michael Price, happy, among his friends at last, and for the first time.

The House of Fear

a study in comparative religions

I
Wandering in the House of Fear

WHEN I WAS A CHILD, WE LIVED in a house my father called the House of Fear. It was an old house, thick with the presence of old women, though only one elderly lady lived there. The rooms were high-ceilinged, yet managed to give the impression of confinement nonetheless. The carpets were worn through in places, so that the light brown of the backing was visible. I used to pretend that they were brighter islands in a sea of reds so dark they became chocolate, and navigate small wooden boats around their faced surface. Every object in the rooms that was not our own (the apartments were furnished) was covered with a film of dust that had adhered to what it coated and would not be wiped off, so that all was seen in shadow of the deepest brown. Even the bulbs of the lamps were not immune, for though Father and Mother bought the bulbs, the lamps were of the house, and made the bulbs part of themselves. The windowpanes too were uncleanable past a certain point, and on the sunniest days the sash had to be raised to allow a direct ray of light to enter. When it did, one could feel its warmth, but the ray itself was invisible, for no motes twisted in the air, and now I fancy that the dust must have clung, mold-like, to the very perimeter of the ray. The furnishings were of another era, perhaps the turn of the last century, though my knowledge of antiques is inadequate and my memory of the pieces themselves dim, for I do not remember when my family came to the old house, and only fitfully recall the occasion of our leaving. There were, I am sure, antimacassars, their white laciness darkened with years, on the thick-boled arms of the sofas and chairs. Lamp shades, tasselled like mushrooms dripping with rain, towered above the child I was. Small, stumpy tables, their black woods nearly unseen in the permanent shadow, were conspicuous only by the specimens of glassware that littered their scarred surfaces. There was nothing of the ornamental in these items. They were indelicate and awkward, shapeless lumps of crystal, fist-sized and larger. One afternoon, left alone, I stared into the smallest of these and detected a movement, the suggestiveness of which prevented me from ever peering into their depths again. Pictures hung here and there on the walls, a few cloudy landscapes, several on classical themes, and two of Christ.

The house itself was in the shape of an octagon, three stories in height, and bisected twice in the center of the planes, like an 'X' on a stop sign. The result was four tall slices, each shaped like a keystone. The boundaries were therefore plain, the walls divided the apartments firmly. Yet it seemed that rooms often doubled back onto themselves, that doors led elsewhere than one expected, that on passing down a short hall to get to my parents' room, I would find myself at the edge of a staircase, familiar but forgotten, which led me to a windowless storage chamber in which my parents kept their trunks and suitcases. I would pass through another door and find myself in the parlor. But, days later, when I opened that door in the parlor, there was only a vacant closet with solid walls. At other times, the halls and staircases led me to rooms which, by all laws of geometry and logic that I knew in those early years, should have been within the boundaries of my family's keystone, but were instead inside the tenancies of the house's three other residents, from whence I would retreat in a panic more the result of prospective embarrassment than from any fear.

The main floor of our apartment consisted of a kitchen at the top of the keystone (so that its rectangle paralleled one of the eight sides of the house), a smaller dining-room to one side of the kitchen, and, on the other side, a parlor the mirror image of the dining-room. What remained was a smaller keystone still larger than the other three rooms combined, which we used as a living-room. Since there was no airshaft in the building's center, the vast living-room was windowless, and could only be occupied with electric lights burning, since the doors that opened into it from the parlor and dining-room supplied it with barely enough daylight to define the hulking forms within as furniture.

Our second floor I recall less distinctly. It seems that the higher I rose in the house, the more unsure I became as to whether or not I would reach my destination or be seduced by one or the other of the house's bewildering byways. I can still see my own room, of course, with a window that looked out upon some vague and indistinct landscape thick with evergreens that allowed little sunlight to pierce their canopy (as though in sympathy with the house), so that I seldom cared to play outside.

There was also my parents' room, which likewise had a window, and a bathroom, with windows that remained shuttered, and a tub whose feet were white porcelain claws, complete with nails. My mother told me, in later years, that the first time they placed me in it I screamed, crying that the great white beast would swallow me. I cannot recall that event in the slightest. Of the other rooms on the second floor, little remains in my memory. All were dark and windowless. Most had dressers and beds that were covered with dusty quilts. From some, staircases led up into attic halls that led only down again, sometimes to the same room and the same staircase, though such a thing seems impossible.

The attic itself was confusion, and when a distant cousin visited—once, and once only—we played up there until she felt herself lost and began to cry, and would not be quieted, even when I led her downstairs to her mother and father. I saw her again years later in a city, and she did not mention it.

As ethereal and multi-dimensional as the attic was, so was the cellar its antithesis. It was based firmly in the realities of stone and heavy timbers, which shored up the airy pile above it. One reached it from the kitchen, by opening a stout door and walking down a long, steep, and straight stairway which stood unsupported, as if carved from a single piece of wood. It was exorbitantly deep, a full thirty feet, and each of the four apartments had an equivalent stairway, the bottoms of which met on a twelve foot square slab of stone in what much have been the exact center of the house. In later years, when I read of the dungeons of the Inquisition, it was that cellar I pictured. As unsettling as it was to descend those steps alone, as my parents on occasion bade me do, it was all the more disconcerting, halfway down their length, to hear the dull pounding of old men's shoes, and, looking across the space from my own stairway to the one opposite, descry the form of another of the house's residents, crooked with age, looking across the abyss at me as if out of some subterranean glass that mirrored the future, turned my smooth, pink flesh to wrinkled white, predicting the mortality that stalks all children.

Now it is of that resident, and the others, that I must speak, for it was not the strangeness of the building itself that caused my father to christen it the House of Fear, but rather the peculiar properties of its denizens, my own family not excluded.

II
Dwellers in the House of Fear

Those who lived in the apartments into which the house was quartered were not fearsome, but rather fearful. It is only now, on looking back, that I can define their lives as ritualistic in the extreme. Once I knew their names, I am certain, but those unnecessary memories have long fled. As I recall, I hardly spoke to them aloud, and knew them only from overhearing the conversations of my parents, for the knowledge that I retain of those neighbors stems mainly from those quiet talks, which I often heard late at night through the wall which divided my parents' room from my own.

The occupant of the apartment directly opposite ours (with whom we shared no walls, only the point of a triangular closet) was an old man. My child's eyes were unable to gauge his years, but I do know that he seemed to me ineffably ancient. He was not tall—my father was larger, and he was only of average height—but perhaps his stoop was responsible for that impression.

He carried his head low, and seemed to be always peering downward, so that his chin was on a level with his sternum. I doubt that he would have been able to look upward even had he tried. Though his hair was still dark on top, the sides had worn to a yellow-gray, the shade of fireplace ashes, framing the deeply cut fissures that crossed his face. His eyes were set deep in lined pouches, and must have been invisible to an adult, but they were all too plain to my child's height, like wet raisins sunk deep in a pudding. He dressed darkly, never wearing anything brighter than a dusky gray. There was always a frayed sweater or suit jacket of unfashionable length, ending just above the black knees of his baggy trousers. These sweaters and jackets were always buttoned tightly, even in the humid summer months. He carried a plain walking stick, curved at the end, with no ornamentation of any sort. I never saw him without it, nor did I ever see him without a book.

His world was built upon and bordered by books. My father once told my mother (after he had helped the old man carry some heavy boxes up to his second floor) that the apartment was crammed with volumes of every description, and once, when I shone a flashlight through a crack in the door of the old man's storage closet in the cellar, I saw, in varying slices of light, hundreds of brown, gray, and black spines which, not yet being able to read, I could not specifically identify.

Although I saw him on rare occasions in the cellar, my contact with him was mainly limited to the porch, which was constructed outside our dining-room and the parlor of the adjoining apartment. It was covered by a roof, and several pieces of iron and wicker furniture were arranged against the wall, enough for all the tenants to gather there at once, though such was never the case in our years there. I saw him most often in late spring and early fall, when, just before evening and after our supper, he sat in the center of the iron glider, pushing himself gently from time to time, and read his book. My father or mother might come out as well and read the newspaper, while I sat on the porch steps and looked at the comics or a funny book my father might have brought home for me. After a while I noticed that when the old man neared the end of a book—say the last few pages—he placed his bookmark and carefully lay down the volume where he had been sitting, then went to his side of the house and returned within a few minutes bearing another book. He sat down once more, finished the first volume, and immediately, without a second's hesitation in which to digest the tale's conclusion, began to read the second book. Never did I see him finish a book without starting another instantly. At the time I did not think it odd. This, I supposed, was the way this man read his books, and there it ended. It was not until I heard my father speak of his practice to my mother that I was aware of the strangeness of the old man's actions. He was, my father had learned and so informed my mother, apprehensive of dying until he had read all the books he wished to, and at some time had decided (stemming, my father hazarded, from the myth that once one read all the thousand and one nights' tales of Arabia, one would die) that he would not perish while a volume remained unfinished, and for that reason got another book underway the moment he finished his previous one.

Naturally, this concept was quite foreign to me. I scarcely understood death, indeed only barely grasped the mystery of aging, which, as I have explained, had come upon me in a purely visceral manner when I glimpsed the old man on the cellar stairs. But, with my father's overheard explanation, his perception of the old man's oddity became my own, as the prejudices of the sire are passed to his offspring, and from that day on I gazed at the old man with pity, knowing his fear.

The old woman was the second tenant. Her part of the house was to the right of ours as one faced our door from the outside, and it was her parlor window that overlooked the porch. She was as tall as the old man was short, and thin to the point of emaciation. Her hair was the color of new snow in sunlight, and her eyes were the deepest and richest shade of blue, the gradation of blue that lay nearest the irises of the eyes of our Siamese cat, Jezreel. She moved smoothly and effortlessly, as though it were no task for even old legs to bear such a fragile and delicate body. Her clothing was delicate as well, soft-colored, pastels of green and pink and blue, all of which abetted the impression of gentleness and gentility. She lived alone, and though my father and mother spoke to her (as did I, in response to her pipingly voiced questions), I never heard her speak a word to the old man, nor he to her, nor either of them to the black man who occupied the final apartment. Not that there was often a possibility of such a verbal exchange. The three seemed to have some unspoken agreement that when one occupied the porch, the other two remained in their own rooms.

While the old man's time was spring and fall, the warm and clear summer evenings belonged to the old woman. She sat on a wicker rocker, a piece of sewing on her lap, needles darting in and out of the cloth to make petite and subtle patterns. Music came through her open parlor window, and she hummed to it constantly. She had three radios on her first floor, all of which were tuned to different stations that played only music, so that if an announcer's voice took the place of melody for a time, there was still music, soft but distinct, further back in the realm of hearing. These radios played all night and all day. She had none on her upper floors, for she did not occupy those, having turned her large living-room into a bed-sitting-room. I once heard her tell my mother that she did not need all that space, and when, on my errant rambles through the house, I came unexpectedly into her upper chambers, recognizing them as hers from the clarity of the music beneath, my apprehension at being discovered was greatly decreased since I knew she did not frequent those regions. She told my father one time that she simply had to have music playing constantly. My father, on hearing this, determined that she had fallen prey to the same type of delusion from which the old man suffered, namely believing that completion of one thing meant finality in all.

It was absurd, he said, a foolish superstition, to think that the continuation of one's life was in any way dependent upon the continuation of extraneous actions, and he laughed to my mother at the thought. There was no harm done, at any rate. The old woman's hearing was (mercifully, said my mother) excellent, so there was no need for her to play her music loudly enough to be heard in our rooms. I do not think we could have complained in any case, for the impression lingers that she was our landlady, the owner of the house. It may be merely that I have made that up to explain the vaguely old-ladylike furnishings of our apartment, but I fancy not. There was also about her an air of proprietorship, as of an extremely benign monarch, by whose grace we occupied our station.

I often wonder why she rented a quarter of the house to the black man, not because he was black, but because his spirit seemed so out of place there. He flashed like a Fourth of July rocket in the gray sky of the House of Fear. To begin with, he was younger. The only gray in his hair was at the temples, and the skin of his face was just beginning to crack apart into those deep, chocolate lines of character. His movements were lithe, though unhurried, and his flesh barely served to conceal the delineated strands of muscle beneath. His yellow eyes were alert and bright, and he took each step as if he were glad to leave the earth, yet not averse to coming down to it again.

He was the only resident, save for my father, who worked somewhere during the day, although he remained at the house in the summer, so he may have been a teacher, though what he might have taught I am unable to say. Dance springs most quickly to mind. He was a wonderful dancer, in my memory at least. On the hottest of summer noons, when the gnats had to keep stirring for fear of being crisped if they sat too long, he came out onto the grass behind the house and danced in the large area, free from pines, where sunlight struck. The music of drums accompanied him, played on a portable phonograph whose cord wound serpentlike up the side of the house and into his window. With the sun pouring down upon him like a spotlight, he danced until he was in shadow, prancing and leaping as if possessed, but with a grace and control madmen never have. Finally, the sunlight gone, the drums silenced, he stood trembling, his upper torso glowing as if with a sheen of black oil. Then he laughed delightedly, and smacked his chest with shovel hands, so that the sweat beads leapt from between his fingers into the air, as though part of him were still dancing. At the last, he picked up his scarlet or purple or orange shirt, threw it over his shoulder, and tied the sleeves in a single knot over his breastbone.

All seasons he danced, outside in the summer and inside in winter. Because of the thickness of our walls, we never heard his drums inside, but in the evenings I could feel the slight, rhythmic vibrations in the floorboards, the black man's dance, its ghost carried throughout the entire house on the silent wires of wood.

My father remarked on this as well, comparing the black man to the others, frowning at the dogged and mindless tenacity that led a soul to repeat the same meaningless patterns day after day, year after year. Despite the times, my father was not a racist, so he could have said more, but chose not to, and I remain thankful for that. He viewed the black man, the old man, and the old woman with a grudging good humor, finding them eccentric only, annoyed by their fears and rituals, and feeling superior to them, right up to the morning that Jezreel disappeared.

III
My Father's Truth Comes to the House of Fear

It was Father's habit every morning, before he went off to work, to kiss my mother and me goodbye and to pat Jezreel, our cat, on the head. Most of the time Jezreel, an indoor cat, sat in the kitchen between the radiator and the refrigerator, either of which might be counted on to provide a constant source of heat, depending on the season. Nine mornings in ten, Father would find her there. But occasionally she forsook her usual place, and sought comfort on or under my parents' or my own bed. At such times Father would go upstairs, muttering something about saying goodbye to the old girl, and come down within a minute. One morning, however, he went upstairs to look for her and came down frowning. He reported that she was in neither bedroom, indeed was not to be found upstairs at all. With unaccustomed desperation in his voice, he queried both my mother and me as to Jezreel's whereabouts, but neither of us had seen her. He then began a systematic search of the first floor, in which he induced the two of us to participate. We looked in corners, under furniture, behind shelves, but we could not find the cat. My mother cautioned my father that he would be late for work, but he waved the concern away in exasperation and continued to look for Jezreel. When we had scoured the downstairs, we went upstairs once more, but the search proved fruitless. Mother told Father that she was certain the cat was all right, that she couldn't have gotten outside, and must be somewhere in the house, but Father merely shook his head and went up into the perplexities of the attic. I started to follow, but Mother held me back. At last Father came down, his face pale. He remarked that he was sure she must be somewhere, but he had to get to work, and he damned the cat. It was the first time I had ever heard him swear. After he was gone, my mother told me that he was just upset, because he was so used to patting Jezreel goodbye. She found the cat an hour later, under the bed. It had crawled into a tear in the cloth that covered the bottom of the box spring, and had been sleeping there, as if in a hammock.

Father returned home that night smiling. When he saw Jezreel in her habitual place between radiator and refrigerator, he laughed and rubbed her roughly behind the ears, making her purr. Then he apologized for his behavior that morning, saying that he had been silly to let it matter so much, but that he had been so used to doing the same thing every morning—patting

Jezreel three times—that when the pattern was broken, he felt near panic, as though something dreadful would happen that day. But, he went on, here we all were, safe and sound. Nothing at all had occurred that could be considered out of the ordinary. It had made his ritual unimportant. Such things had no effect upon events whatsoever.

From that day on, my father was changed. In the morning, if the cat was there, he would pet her. If not, he did not bother to look for her. He still kissed my mother and me, as often as not. But he seemed more solemn. It was as if there was less of joy in him than there had been before. His attitudes toward the other tenants changed markedly, from a grudging acceptance to a barely suppressed anger when in their presence. One Sunday he asked the black man point blank why he danced every day, and the black man said that he didn't know, that it was just something he had to do. One cool evening he asked the old woman what she thought would happen if the music stopped for good, and she said she didn't know. When Father then asked if she was scared to find out, she grew very quiet and did not say any more. When he asked the old man why he did not simply pause upon finishing a book rather than starting another, the old man told him directly that if he did this he was afraid he would die.

To all of these responses my father reacted with derision, challenging the three to give up their obsessions, confessing that he had been a victim to such vague superstitions himself, and now that he had been forced to see their foolishness, found himself free and unencumbered as never before. The three tenants turned from Father's suggestions with discomfort, refusing to take his course, and continued to read, dance, and embrace musical harmonies with as much if not more fervor than before. My father decided that something had to be done. Mother tried to dissuade him, arguing that the tenants did harm to no one with their eccentric actions, but Father replied that they were harming themselves, and stated that such fantasies and delusions could eventually lead to hysteria and madness. He determined upon a course to cure his fellow tenants of what he now looked upon as their illness, and in only a few weeks was able to put it into effect.

Father was in charge of the fusebox in the cellar, taking care of any electrical repairs that were needed, or seeking out someone who could. Up to this time, his job had consisted of changing the fuses at regular intervals, to insure a steady and uninterrupted flow of voltage to all corners of the house. It was the end of the summer when his chance came, an electrical storm of great power that sent bright streaks of lightning ripping through the sky over the house. The night was windless, however, the rain falling straight and heavy, so that we were safe beneath the porch. I sat near the steps, my father beside me in the wicker rocker, the old man several yards away on the glider. By the illumination of the porch light, the old man was reading the last several pages of a book, his new volume close at hand, to be picked up when needed. My father was watching him, a look of disgust on his face. Then his expression changed, and he knelt by me, handing me a nickel and a quarter. He told me to lean over the porch railing and toss the coins so that they clicked against one of the recessed cellar windows just at the exact moment that the old man closed his first book and reached for the second. Then he disappeared into the house.

I was only a child, and I obeyed my father, watching until the old man slammed shut his book and reached for the next in his never ending chain of volumes. The coins rattled on the cellar window glass just as he picked up the book. But before he could open it, the porch light winked out, throwing us into the thick twilight of a stormy summer night, as the music coming from the old woman's window abruptly stopped. The old man was only a dark form in the shadows, and I suddenly felt very much afraid. He moaned slightly, and I heard the soft sound of paper rustling, as if he expected the words to illuminate themselves. Lightning flashed, and I saw him for only a split second, staring straight ahead, directly at me. Though I am sure the look was one of terror and supplication, it sank straight into the depths of my guilt. I knew that he hated me, and, for the first time in my young life, I was afraid of a fellow human being.

He called my name, but I could not answer. He called again, asking me in a pinched voice to see what was wrong with the light. Since he did not sound angry with me, I went to the switch mounted on the porch post and flicked it off and on with no result. I asked if he wanted a candle, but he said no, and muttered about it being too late for that now. In another minute, the old woman came onto the porch, her face whiter than ever, given a ghostly glow by the candle she carried in a silver stick. She asked what had happened, but neither one of us could answer. I knew that my father was in some way responsible, but it was only later that I learned he had removed the main fuse and replaced it with one that had burnt out, no doubt pulling the good one just as the coins clinked against the windowpane.

My mother was the next to arrive on the porch. She carried a flashlight whose ray she cast over our little group for recognition. The old woman, her head cocked in an attitude of listening, asked my mother if she thought the lightning had caused the power outage, but Mother said that she didn't know. She asked me where Father was, and I could tell by the look of anger in her eyes that she suspected him immediately. I was about to answer when he came up the porch steps, his shirt plastered to his back from the rain, which was now falling with crushing force. Mother asked him where he had been, and he told her he had gone into the cellar to see if he could do anything to bring back the power, but that a fuse had blown, and there were no new ones with which to replace it. He sat on the porch steps, and remarked that he had never seen such heavy rain, that it completely drowned out the sounds of the old woman's music. Her candles wavered as she said snappishly that that was because her radios had all stopped when the electricity had failed, and my father laughed and said that he was stupid not to have realized that. Then he turned to the old man and said how lucky it was that the blackout hadn't caught him between books, to which the old man gave a sigh of despair and clutched the unbegun volume to his breast. My father pretended surprise and concern, and offered the use of Mother's flashlight, but the old man only shook his head, his eyes vacant and far away, as if looking for something he fully expected and dreaded.

In another moment we heard the sound of large, bare feet slapping through the wet grass, and the black man appeared. He was shirtless, and in his yellow eyes was a superstitious fear. Trembling, he asked what had happened to the power. When Father told him, he said that there must be a fuse or two Father had overlooked, and ran into the cellar by way of the old woman's apartment. That she was upset may be seen by the fact that she made no protest as the man, dripping rainwater, crossed her rugs and wooden floor. A few minutes later he returned, saying that it was impossible, that we could not be out of fuses, and that he would go to the store to buy some more. But Father reminded him that the store was closed, and would not open until morning.

At this the black man began to sob, and when Father asked him why, he said it was because he could not dance. Dance without music then, my father suggested, but the black man said he could not, and wept louder. Then Father observed aloud that it seemed as if everyone's plans had gone awry—the old woman was to have no music, the old man had finished a book without beginning another, and the black man found himself unable to dance. But nonetheless, he added, they would all live through the night and in the morning all would see how absurd their rituals had been, and how foolish they had acted upon having them interrupted.

None of the three looked at him after this speech, but my mother drew him aside to the end of the porch where I still stood, leaning on the railing from whence I had caused the unhappiness that lay before me. She dug her fingers into his upper arm and asked, loudly enough for only the three of us to hear, where he had hidden the fuses. Father said that he had hidden nothing, indeed that he was the only one of the party not hiding anything, and he looked at the others with a grim smile. Then Mother asked him who he thought he was to deprive these people of their sole pleasures in life, and he replied that when one's pleasures became one's obsessions, it was time to deal with them most harshly. He had done what he had done, he said in rough whispers, to help, not to harm. The fools, he said, were living according to the dictates of lies, falsehoods—and then he smiled as the word came to him—*misapprehensions*.

My mother looked at him with mingled sadness and bitterness, and then turned to the others and invited them all to come to our ever-shadowed rooms, to gather all the candles they could, and, as she put it, keep the dark away. Father began to protest, but Mother stopped him with a glower, implicit in which was the threat to reveal his perfidy. He closed his mouth and sat on the porch floor, his back against the railing.

The others were hesitant to accept the invitation, but did, grudgingly, and the old woman went into her house and came out with two umbrellas, under whose protection we walked the few yards to our front door, the old man and the black man beneath the other. My father would not come. He remained on the porch.

Inside our living-room, Mother lit the candles we had in the house and those the others had brought. There must have been three dozen of varying thicknesses and heights, and they brought to the room a warmth and comfort it had never before possessed, but which did nothing to ease the troubled spirits illuminated by it, who sat stiffly as my mother and I brought in a tray of crackers and glasses of iced tea with lemon. My mother, smiling sympathetically, made a toast to the restoration of light, and they drank without speaking. Then it was time for me to go to bed.

Alone, I heard the muted drone of their voices downstairs, but could not make out, try as I might, what was said, and after a while I drifted off to sleep, dreaming of huge rooms with impossibly high ceilings, and white faces lit by small, yellow, flames.

IV
Exodus from the House of Fear

No one died in the night. The following morning my father went out and pretended to buy fuses, returned, and restored power to the house, then went off to work, not having said a word at the breakfast table. Though Jezreel was in her usual place by the refrigerator, he did not pet her when he left.

The storm of the night before had passed, and sunlight shone down onto the grassy patch at noon, but the black man did not come out to dance. In the afternoon I heard music from the old woman's window, but it lasted only a brief time before silence fell again. That evening the old man sat on the porch, finished reading a book, closed it, and walked through the darkness to his own door, from which he did not return that night. I do not recall my father ever speaking to any one of them again, nor they to him.

That winter my father found a better position in another town, and we moved away from the House of Fear into a house in which no one lived but our family. It had white walls, and sunlight shone unencumbered through the windows. The following year I went to school and quickly learned to read, an occupation which I have practiced assiduously, my primary field of interest being nineteenth century novels. My father died of a heart attack when I was in fourth grade, and after his death my mother gratified my wishes by financing and allowing me to take lessons in dance, from which I now make my own living by teaching. My wife is a musician. Our own house is filled with books, dearly loved and often read, and music which plays constantly and at its loudest volume when my mother, who is slightly hard of hearing, visits us. We have one son and one daughter, and I tell them, from time to time, the story of the House of Fear.

V
Author's Disclaimer

But the story, all of it, is from my earliest memory, and so may be false.

Blue Notes

WE WERE ALWAYS ARGUING about them, about blue notes. Hell, we had ever since we were kids. I guess it was to be expected. Even though we played together in the same band in high school, we came from two different musical worlds. Todd was headbanging 4/4 straight-ahead rock and roll, as dependable (and to me as dull) as clockwork. Jazz was where I came from, and it was as boring to Todd as his music was to me. Jesus, he could play that guitar, though. I have to give him that.

Or maybe I should say *had* to give him that. I just hope wherever he is he got his right hand back.

But blue notes. I love them and use them like a carpenter uses a hammer and nails. You play jazz, you have to, you want it to *sound* like jazz. But Todd thought they were bullshit.

'Man, a note's a note, Lute. I mean, you got C, you got C sharp, there's *nothin'* in between there.' And he hummed a note and went up a half step: 'Da-*dah*. See? Nothin' in the cracks of the piano keys except dust. And no magic invisible frets on my Rickenbacker either, you know?'

And I explained to him again about the notes, slightly flatted, called blue notes, told him one more time about the tribal singers in Africa who can sing eight different tones between a C and a C sharp, told him how his own sweet rock sprang from the blues, and that the blues were called the blues because . . .

'Okay, spare me the adventures in good music,' he said. 'We're living in America, man, not Africa. Land of the free, home of the brave. Rock and roll heaven. We descend from European musical ideas, not from your African ancestors, no slur intended.'

'None taken.' Say what you would for the heavy metal thickness of Todd's skull, there wasn't a racist bone in his body. He had kicked a lot of white boys' asses while we were growing up to save me from getting mine kicked.

'Now I'm not saying they don't exist. I mean, I know about quarter-tones and all that crap. But what I *am* sayin' is that nobody gives a shit. You go up to your average rock fan and start layin' quarter tones on him, you see how long he says around to listen. It'll just sound flat to him, like get it in *tune*, y'know? Sure, I bend a note now and then, but big fuckin' deal. You make it sound like blue notes are God's own truth or something.'

'It *is* God's own truth that there's always something between,' I said. 'It's not just black and white.'

'Yeah? Look at us.'

I grinned. 'I've got lots of white blood in me, Todd. And maybe there's a drop of Africa in you.'

'In the eyes of the world, ole bud, it's still black and white. Like everything else.'

Like everything else. That was the way life was for Todd. One-two-three-four, rock steady. I signaled to Tamara to get us two more beers and looked at my watch. I had another five minutes until the next set. 'How do you like the new drummer?' I asked Todd.

He swung his leonine head around, the long blond hair following a millisecond later, and looked toward the bandstand at the lustrous black Yamaha Power Series drums surrounded by the gleaming Zildjian cymbals, then back at me. 'He's okay, but there's sure no strong beat there. Does all those little riffs between the beats, don't know how the hell you can follow him.'

'It's jazz, Todd,' I said patiently. 'I don't know why the hell you come here if you don't like it.'

'Shit, you know why,' he said, taking his fresh beer from Tamara's tray as she set mine in front of me. 'You're my old bud, and I like to hear you play. You blow like nobody else, man. I just wish I could get you out of this jazz crap and over into rock.' His face lit up with the boyish glow that had lasted into his late twenties. 'With you behind me, I could be the new Boss, you could be my Big Man——'

'It's been done.' I took a sip of beer. 'Besides, I'm not big enough to be any Big Man.' It was true. Todd was only medium height and was taller than me by half a head. 'Besides, you're doing well enough without me.'

'Yeah, sure. You know where my album's stuck at on the *Billboard* charts?'

I nodded. 'The low sixties. You told me.'

'The past fuckin' month. Hit with a bullet, then goes from sixty-one to sixty-five, then to sixty-eight, and this week it's at sixty-nine.'

'Erogenous number,' I said. 'Maybe some people'll buy it because of that.'

Todd shook his head and drank half his beer. 'Shit.'

'What are you "shit"ing for? At least you're *on* the charts.' Five months before I had recorded an album with myself on alto and EWI, Fives Markham on keyboards, Tommy Aleet on bass, and Tweet Lewis on drums. The four of us had put up most of the money, and the album sank like a stone. The distributors treated it like musical AIDS, and as far as I know, the only place you can get it is the NMDS catalog. It didn't get one review, good or bad. 'Maybe I should change my name to Kenny G,' I told Todd.

'Number sixty-nine don't mean dick,' he said. 'If you're not in the top ten—hell, if you're not number *one*, you're nothing.'

'No blue notes?' I said.

'Huh?'

'No in-between. All or nothing.'

'You got it.'

'It's all black or white, up or down, huh?'

'That's right. No in-between.'

'How about good and bad?'

'That too.'

'And what are you, Todd?'

He thought for only a second. 'Bad.'

'Bull.'

'I'm a Savage, man. We scare little boys and threaten little girls. Tipper Gore wants to stick labels on our albums and our crotches.' He was grinning. I could see he was really into it, just the way he psyched himself up with the other Savages on stage. 'We sing about blood and death and guns and knives and pain and——'

'And you get past the phony image, you're a Boy Scout.'

The grin hung there on his face for another moment, then melted down into a soft, sad smile. 'No, man. I think I *am* bad. The Savage stuff is image, sure, but goddam it, Lute, I'd sell my mother to Libyans if I could hit number one. You know I'm not much for loyalty . . .'

'You keep coming to hear me in dumps like this.'

'I like dumps like this.' His face twisted in the little-boy sneer that had gotten him a quarter cover on *Tiger Beat*. 'It makes the dumps I play in look good.'

'Thanks.'

'No, really, I'm not a good person, ole bud. I'm really really selfish.'

'And because you're selfish, that makes you all bad.'

'Basically.'

'That's stupid. I'm not all bad, and I'm not all good. I'm in between, like everybody else.'

'Nah. You're good. You're a sweet little chocolate bunny who's true to his ideals, and who won't'—he thought about the words, finally came up with them—'compromise his art.'

How fucking wrong you are, my friend, I thought. But I didn't say it. 'Well, I won't give up my blue notes,' I said, and went back to the tiny stage, where Chip, the drummer, was warming up with his brushes.

As I took my alto off its stand, I felt the need inside me, and I wondered if good guys did blow. Christ knows I never wanted to get hooked on the shit, but people had offered, I had taken, and before too long people weren't offering as much as I wanted to take. Maybe the desire was more psychological than physical—I don't know, I never looked it up—but I couldn't play without it.

Couldn't play without it and couldn't live with it.

I was in hock to my balls for the stuff. I had two grams left of the twenty I had bought at the beginning of the month, and owed Mickey three thousand dollars. The grams had sat untouched now for four days, the same four day grace period Mickey had given me to come up with the money, come up with it or go down the tubes, over the bridge a block from the club, into the water of the bay.

I didn't have three grand. I didn't even have a hundred bucks, and I wouldn't until Saturday night, which was payday. Jim, the owner of the Purbright Jazz Club, wouldn't give me another advance, and I had already borrowed more from my friends than they could afford. I never borrowed anything from Todd, though. I could never bring myself to ask him. It was weird, but it seemed like Todd came to hear me play to recharge his batteries with our youth. Shit, neither of us was a kid any more—he was twenty-nine and I was only a year younger. But he still had this image of me as the shy little black boy who played the hot sax, and somehow I didn't want to destroy that. It sound stupid and probably was, since I'm sure Todd did his share of toot along with a helluva lot of other goodies, and wouldn't have held it against me, at least not overtly. But I was always afraid that it would disappoint him.

Of course, the alternative was disappointing Mickey, and that was the one thing I didn't want to do. Mickey was in his early forties, a veteran of at least a quarter century of mayhem and scuffling that had made him cocaine king of the section around the bay. The flake he handled was excellent, and the price was commensurate with its quality. Apparently people who Mickey offered credit to had been sticking him lately, and Mickey didn't like that at all. In fact, he told me when he gave me the four day ultimatum, 'It's high fucking time I made an example out of somebody. Like, see, people know you've been buying from me, and they know you haven't been paying on time, and so if you were found somewhere dead in an alley, or washed up at the docks with your balls sewn in your mouth, then other people who owe me might begin to pay on time, you see what I mean?'

I saw all too well, and had been around long enough to know that Mickey didn't make idle threats. He wasn't a big guy—even I was taller than him—but he could move as fast as the lightning and hit as hard. He must have had money out of his ass, but he looked as poor as dirt with his long, greasy hair and the faded jeans and worn cowboy boots he dressed in. He had rat eyes, and a mouth whose lip always lifted to show yellow teeth. It looked like a harelip, but I don't think it was. I think it was just a mean mouth.

After the last set was over, I sat down again with Todd and told him about Mickey. I was right about his being disappointed.

'I never had you pegged for a cokehead, old bud,' he said, smiling to make me think he wasn't taking it too hard.

'I'm going to kick it. I have to. I just can't afford it. And it's doing shit to my breath control.'

He nodded. 'Didn't think some of those rides of yours were as long as usual. Where you meetin' this guy tonight?'

'The bridge. Middle of the goddam bridge. That way if I don't have the money, he puts me over.'

'Well, you won't have the money tonight, but I can get it for you.' I didn't understand him. 'Tomorrow, I mean. Shit, I can't lay my hands on three grand tonight, banks got hours, y'know. But tomorrow.'

'I don't know if Mickey'll wait till tomorrow.'

I had running on my mind. I knew I couldn't run forever, but at least it would keep me alive a little longer. But if I ran, then Mickey would do for me automatically. There would be no explaining, no pleas for an extension. If I stayed, there was a slim chance I'd live, but a better one that I'd die tonight. If I ran, death was certain, if more distant. The situation sucked.

'The sonuvabitch'll have to wait, man,' Todd said. 'Hey, Lute, he doesn't want your ass, he'd much rather have your money. The guy's a businessman, right?'

'Right. And businessmen can't afford to extend credit indefinitely.'

'What indefinitely? Tomorrow morning when the bank opens.' He looked at his watch. 'Eight hours away, he can't wait that long?'

'I guess I'll have to ask him.'

'No, no,' he said quickly, 'I'll ask him.'

'*You'll* ask him,' I said. 'Todd, Mickey would eat you. He would take one look at you, see everything he hates, and fucking eat you.'

'Hey, I'm no pushover.'

'Mickey is never alone, man. He has friends—two big ugly friends that go everywhere with him. They will kill and cook you before Mickey eats you.'

'Look, if you go they'll eat *you*, because you don't have the money, and all the blue notes all the boogies in Africa sing won't do you an ant's fart worth of good. But if *I* go, I can tell him who I am, tell him you just told me about this little problem, and that I can take care of it if he'll be so kind as to wait till morning.' Todd paused for a second. 'You think he's heard of the Savages?'

'Mickey doesn't give a crap for music. I doubt he's heard of the Beatles.'

'Well, no sweat. I'll just tell him I'm on the *Billboard* charts.'

'He'll be thrilled. Probably ask for your autograph. Look, Todd, I appreciate the offer, and if Mickey lets me live I'll take you up on it, but I can't let you face *my* executioner.'

'Will you relax? I can handle this, I've handled drug guys before—been a long time since school, ole bud. Believe me, the guys I've owed money to would make your Mickey look like Mickey Mouse.'

'Todd . . .'

'Now get your ass home and into your nice warm bed and let me keep your appointment on the bridge. The voice of reason, music hath charms, all that other shit, okay? Mickey will fucking *love* me. Meet me at Chemical Bank on 14th tomorrow at ten, and everything will be copacetic, right?' He smiled boozily at me.

The thing is, even now I know why I said yes. I can't rationalize it. I said yes because I was afraid that Mickey would kill me. If Todd had been a little less drunk, he might have realized that the better way would have been for us both to go meet Mickey. Hell, I thought of it, but I didn't suggest it because I didn't *want* to meet Mickey. So I nodded, I agreed, I sent my scapegoat, the guy who was willing to put it on the line for me—his money or his life.

The sons of bitches took the latter.

I tried to call Todd beginning at four in the morning to ask him what happened, but there was no answer. I called every ten minutes until six o'clock, then got dressed and went back out on the street. I walked the seventeen blocks to the bridge and got there just as it was getting light.

There was no one on the bridge, and no one nearby, so I walked out on the cement sidewalk toward the middle. The bloodstain was on the other side, so I didn't see it until I was almost past it, and wouldn't have noticed it at all if a gull hadn't flown close to my head, so that I turned to watch it. The stain was partway up the four-foot wall. It looked like a patch of rust, but I knew that cement doesn't rust.

I also knew that the blood must have come from where Mickey and his friends cut off Todd's right hand. The stump must have spurted like a hose. There were droplets of dried blood everywhere. And I knew it was his *right* hand because it was lying there in the gutter.

I didn't go over to it right away. I just stood and looked for a while—at the dry blood, at the gray hunk of flesh with the rings still on the fingers—and I thought, those bastards weren't interested in the money at all. Jesus Christ, they didn't even take the rings. Or maybe they left them on the fingers so I'd be sure it was Todd. At any rate, they didn't want the money, they wanted blood, and they got it, and if I had gone it would have been mine.

I wished it would have been. I still do. I don't like living with a friend's blood on my hands, especially after he gave it up to save my worthless ass.

Finally I went over to the hand and knelt next to it. Most of the blood had drained out, and it took me a moment to convince myself that it was real and not some Taiwanese novelty. But as I looked closer I knew damn well it was Todd's. It was just too perfect to be fake. Hairs, pores, all that crosshatching on the knuckles, it wasn't a fucking joke at all.

Go to the police? It crossed my mind for only a minute. What was the point? There was no proof, no definite link between Mickey and Todd. And even if there were some sort of proof, Mickey had friends.

I felt totally lost, completely powerless. I felt like a dead man. Like Todd.

The hand was cool and dry when I picked it up, not at all like what I expected to feel. It made a small splash when it hit the water, and sank right away. The heavy rings must have pulled it down. 'Bye, Todd,' I whispered to the expanding circles of water, and watched until I couldn't see them any more. Then I walked back to my place, thinking about Todd.

Todd had said he was bad. The old black and white routine. He wasn't bad any more than Jesus was bad, and I thought—and think—about Todd and about Jesus and about the Southern Baptist church my parents took me to, and about the preacher talking about laying down your life for your friends.

Thank you, Todd, and thank you Jesus. Thank you and thank you again. And thank you for making me live the rest of my life in guilt.

But back then, on that morning, it was the kind of guilt I couldn't live with, and I was almost relieved when Mickey called me at noon. He didn't identify himself, but I knew it was him.

'Stupid,' was the first thing he said. 'Very very stupid, Luther. Sending your faggot friend in your place—that way two assholes get killed instead of one. That guy really play guitar in a rock group?'

'Y . . . yes,' I managed to get out.

'Well, he's gonna have a rough time playin' now. Like, he can use those fret-things, but he ain't gonna strum for shit.'

Mickey was using the present-tense, and something hot ran through me. I had assumed they had killed Todd—Mickey had said *killed*—but maybe . . . 'Mickey . . .' I said.

'Who's Mickey?' Just in case, he figured. Just in case the phone was tapped.

'He's dead?'

'Playin' guitar for the fish.' He laughed. 'Like in *The Godfather*, you know? You see that? Part about sleepin' with the fish? Only this is playin' *guitar* for the fish, huh?'

I didn't know what to say, so I didn't say anything.

'What's the matter, *ole bud*?' he said, and the words cut me like a knife made of ice. 'Cat got your tongue? Or maybe a fish, huh? A fish with those sharp little teeth you can hardly see, but shit you sure can feel, those little teeth nibblin' away on the soft parts, like your tongue and your eyeballs and your ball-balls? How much you think they've chewed off your long-haired buddy right now? Or maybe I oughta ask how much you think is *left*?'

He started chuckling then, and I blinked hard to get rid of both the tears and the pictures I was seeing. 'What now?' I finally said.

'Now you pay,' he answered, the humor gone from his voice. '*You* pay, Luther. Your *ole bud* was one day's interest, that's all. One day's interest on three grand. But I don't want anymore meat unless it's yours, see? No more babies you send to be butchered. Uh-uh. I want you. You or your money. You be on the bridge tonight. At midnight. Then we'll see what you got.'

Absurdly, the first thought that went through my head was that I didn't get off from the club until two. It's amazing how the tyrannical details of everyday life intrude at the most inappropriate times. Fortunately, I didn't say it. I just said, 'All right. Midnight', and hung up.

I expected to die. I wanted to. I couldn't pay the bastard any more today than I could have the night before, and I didn't want to run. I was tired and sad and beaten. I would meet him at midnight and he could do whatever the hell he wanted to. I didn't even have the energy to kill myself. Or maybe there was just too much of that Southern Baptist stuff left in me to do that. Mickey could do the dirty work and send my soul to heaven. Maybe I'd see Todd there. Maybe he'd be willing to play blue notes then.

I played damn fine that night. My solos were clean and sweet as a baby's ass. When you know that death's waiting, I guess you want to leave something behind, even if it's only the memory of some beautiful sounds. The wailing was full of blue notes, and a couple of times it threw Max, the piano player, who asked me at the first break what the fuck key I was playing 'Tenderly' in.

Midnight came partway through the second set, and I nodded to Max to take a solo and walked off the stage out of sight with my horn. It wasn't a surprise to him—we did it from time to time when we wanted to take a leak or when Buddy, the bass man, wanted a line.

But I didn't go to the john. Instead I walked out the back door into the alley, my sax still in my hands. I wanted to take it with me. I guess I was thinking about Sonny Rollins, about the sax on the bridge. Besides, it was the only thing I had. It was my tool, what I made my living with. If I was going to go, I was damned if I was going to leave my horn behind.

With that slim piece of metal in my hand, I felt a little like a gunslinger going out to take on the Clanton gang. But it wasn't a gun, it was just an alto sax, and I would much rather have faced the Clantons than Mickey and his boys.

There was a light fog hanging in the air, just enough so that the street lamps that lined the bridge were haloed. There was hardly any traffic, and as I neared the middle of the bridge I saw that I had beaten Mickey there. I was alone in the night as I walked up to where the bloodstain was, the place where I had tossed the hand over the side, and where Mickey had tossed the rest of Todd. I leaned back against the wall, hugged my horn to me, and shut my eyes.

Ole bud . . .

It sounded like Todd's voice, but faint and faraway. Still, it seemed real enough that I opened my eyes and looked around. No one was there.

Although I should have been spooked, I wasn't. Instead I felt suddenly calm. I'd been nervous as hell walking out on the bridge, but now that I was here I felt a lot better. Maybe, after it was all over, I really would meet Todd.

A rough laugh ripped through the mist, and I looked toward the city.

There were three of them, a short one flanked by two giants, and they were coming toward me. When they were fifty yards away, I started to play.

It was bravado, no doubt about it, that made me bring my horn to my lips and blow, bravado and maybe that voice that I thought I heard, the voice that said *Blow it, ole Bud. Play them blue notes . . .*

I did, and I didn't stop then to wonder why the hell that voice I thought was Todd's should be telling me to blow the blue notes. I just played. I played blue notes between blue notes between blue notes, and I was sorry that the only people there to hear it were three shitbrains who wouldn't know good sounds if the muses came down and sat on their heads.

'Hey!' No voice inside my head. This one was real. '*Hey*, asshole,' Mickey repeated. 'Knock that shit off, enough to wake the fuckin' dead. . . .'

I didn't listen to him. I just kept playing. They were twenty feet away now, and had slowed down. Mickey put his hands over his ears, made a face, and stopped.

'You oughta get that thing in tune, Luther.'

'He must think music hath charms, Mickey,' said one of Mickey's helpers. From the puzzled and pissed way Mickey looked at him, I could see that Mickey had never even heard the old saying before. Then Mickey turned back to me.

'You got the money, Luther?'

I just kept playing.

'Goddammit, cut that shit out!' Fast as a thought, Mickey moved to my side, knocked the sax out of my hands, and swatted me on the side of the head. I went down hard, feeling hot warmth on my lips where the mouthpiece had ripped them. Then everything seemed to swim around me, and when I looked up at Mickey and his goons, I was looking through water.

I don't mean that metaphorically—I mean it *literally*. The whole picture shimmered, rippled, and I could have sworn I was not lying on the sidewalk, but underwater, at the edge of a pool, looking up at Mickey like some crocodile eyeing its prey. And *that* isn't metaphorical either.

What happened next didn't take very long. All of a sudden someone else was there on the bridge with us, someone who grabbed Mickey's boys and shook them like a dog with a rat. Their heads began to shake more than heads should, and then something wet struck me in the face. When I wiped it away I saw that the stranger had Mickey, and was carrying him with one hand to the wall. They both tipped over and I lost them, but I heard Mickey scream for a long time. I hadn't realized before just how high the bridge really was.

The sensation of looking through water was gone now, and I could see that the wetness on my hands and face was blood. When I looked at Mickey's boys lying next to me I saw where it came from.

Mickey was nowhere to be seen, and I staggered to my feet, walked to the wall, and looked over, down to the bay below, through the mist to the water lit dimly by the street lamp so far above.

I saw Todd. He was floating face-down, but I recognized him by his clothes, by the long blond hair that lay fan-like on the surface of the water, and by something else—the rings sparkling on his right hand, the same right hand I had thrown into the water the night before. I didn't see Mickey anywhere at all.

It was time to leave this place, to find a phone and call the police and tell them there was a body floating in the bay beneath the bridge. That was what was important, to get Todd out of the water. They could find Mickey's boys on their own. And I didn't give a shit if they ever found Mickey.

My sax was lying where it had fallen. There was a big dent in the bell, and the neck was bent, but the keys all worked. I thought about playing it again, playing one last farewell, and maybe thank-you to Todd, but I decided not to. What if this time the blue notes brought back Mickey?

Because it was the blue notes that did it, whatever it was. Maybe life and death is like everything else—with an infinite number of spaces in between, a spectrum of grays between the black and white, a symphony of blue notes between C and C sharp. And what if certain needs, certain sympathies, empathies, memories, voices—even the blue notes themselves—can bring those *spiritual* blue notes back, just long enough to do . . . what happened on the bridge that night?

Blue notes. It's the right name for them. Because all I know is that whatever I saw in those few seconds, whether it was Todd or some part of me, when I blinked away the red, it was blue, a deep blue, the deep dark blue you hardly ever find in nature, not in the nature that most of us know. It was the blue that lies between the brightness of the sky at noon and the blackness of that same sky at night. Somewhere in between those. That dark, sad, somber blue.

The blue note of blue.

O Come Little Children

'IT EVEN *SMELLS* LIKE CHRISTMAS,' the boy told his mother, as they strolled down the narrow aisles of the farmer's market. That it looked and sounded like that happiest of holidays went without saying. Carols blared everywhere, from the tiniest of the stand-holder's transistor radios to the brass choir booming from the market's PA system. Meat cases were framed with strings of lights, a myriad of small trees adorned a myriad of counters across which bills the color of holly were pushed and goods and coins returned, and red and green predominated above all other hues. But it was the odors that entranced: the pungency of gingerbread, the sweet olfactory sting of fresh Christmas cookies. There were mince pies and pumpkin pudding, and a concoction of cranberry sauce and dried fruit in syrup whose aroma made the boy pucker and salivate as though a fresh lemon had brushed his tongue. The owner of the sandwich stall was selling small, one-dollar, Styrofoam plates of turkey and stuffing to those too rabid to wait until Christmas, three long days away. The smell was intoxicating, and the line was long.

The boy's mother, smiling and full of the spirit, bought many things that would find their way to their own Christmas table, and the sights and sounds and smells kept the boy from being bored, as he usually was at the Great Tri-County Farmer's and Flea Market.

It was on the way out, as he and his mother walked through the large passage that divided the freshness of the food and produce stands from the dusty tawdriness of the flea market, that the boy saw the man dressed as Santa Claus. At first glance he did not seem a very *good* Santa Claus. He was too thin, and instead of a full, white, cottony, fake beard, his own wispy mass of facial hair had been halfheartedly lightened, as though he'd dipped a comb in white shoe polish and given it a few quick strokes. 'There,' the boy's mother remarked, 'is one of Santa's *lesser* helpers.'

The boy was past the point where every Santa was the *real* Santa. In truth, he was just short of total disbelief. TV, comic books, and the remarks of older friends had all taken their toll, and he now thought that although the existence of the great man was conceivable, it was not likely, and to imagine that any of these kindly, red-suited men who smiled wearily in every department store and shopping mall was the genuine article was quite impossible.

Even if he had believed fully, he doubted if anyone under two would have accepted the legitimacy of the Santa he saw before him. Aside from the thinness of both beard and frame, the man's suit was threadbare in spots, the back vinyl boots scuffed and dull, and the white ruffs at collar and cuffs had yellowed to the color of old piano keys. His lap was empty. The only person nearby was a cowboy-hatted man sitting on a folding chair identical to that on which the Santa sat. A Polaroid Pronto hung from his neck, and next to him a card on an easel read YOUR PICTURE WITH SANTA—$3.00. The $3.00 part was printed much smaller than the words. The boy and his mother were nearly by the men when the one in the red suit looked at them.

The boy stopped. 'Mom,' he said, loud enough for only his mother to hear. 'May I sit on his lap?'

She gave an impatient sigh. 'Oh, Alan. . . .'

'Please?'

'Honey, do you really *want* your picture taken with . . .?'

'I don't want a picture. I just want to sit on his lap.'

'No, sweetie,' she said, looking at the man looking at the boy. 'I don't think so.'

They were in the parking lot by the time she looked at her son once more. To her amazement, huge tears were running down his face. 'What's wrong, honey?'

'I wanted to sit on his *lap*,' the boy choked out.

'Oh, Alan, he's not Santa, he's just a helper. And not a very good one either.'

'Can't I? Please? Just for a minute. . . .'

She sighed and smiled, thinking that it would do no harm, and that she was in no hurry. 'All right. But no picture.'

The boy shook his head, and they went back inside. The man in the red suit smiled as he saw the boy approach without hesitation, and patted his thigh in an unspoken invitation for the boy to sit. The man in the cowboy hat had stood up, but before he could bring the camera to eye level, the boy said, 'No picture, please', and the man, with a look of irritation directed at the boy's mother, sat down again.

The boy remained on the man's lap for less than a minute, talking so quietly that his mother could not hear. When he started to slide off, he stopped suddenly, as though caught, and his mother saw that the metal buckle of the boy's loose-hanging coat belt had become entangled in the white plush of the man's left cuff. The man tried unsuccessfully to extricate it with the fingers of his gloved right hand, then put the glove in his mouth and yanked his hand free. With his long, thin fingers he freed the boy, who hopped smiling onto the floor and waved a hand enclosed in his own varicolored mittens. When he rejoined his mother, he was surprised to find her scowling. 'What's wrong?'

'Nothing,' she answered. 'Let's go.'

But he knew something was wrong, and found out later at dinner. '*I* think he must have been *on* something.'

'Oh, come on,' his father said, taking a second baked potato. 'Why?'

His mother went on as though he were not there. 'He just *looked* it. He had these real hollow eyes, like he hadn't slept in days. Really thin. The suit just hung on him. And, uh . . .' She looked at the boy, who pretended to be interested in pushing an unmelted piece of margarine around on his peas.

'What?'

'His hand. He took off his glove and his hand was all bruised, like he'd been shooting into it or something.'

'Shooting what?' the boy asked.

'Drugs,' his father said, before his mother could make something up.

'What's that? Like what?'

His mother smiled sardonically at his father. 'Go ahead, Mr Rogers. Explain.'

'Well . . . *drugs*. Like your baby aspirin, only a lot stronger. People take some drugs just to make them feel good, but then later they feel real bad, so you shouldn't ever take them at all.'

'What's the shooting part?'

'Like a shot, when the doctor gives you a shot.'

'Like Mommy's diabetes.'

'Yeah, like that. Only people who take too many *bad* drugs have their veins'—he saw the question on the boys face—'their little blood hoses inside their skin collapse on them. So they might stick the needles in their legs, or in the veins in the backs of their hands, or even their feet or the inside of their mouth, or . . .'

'That's fine, thank you,' his mother said sharply. 'I think we've learned enough tonight.'

'He wouldn't do *that*,' the boy said. 'He was too *nice*.'

His father shook his head. 'Aw, honey, you never know. Nice people can have problems too.' And then his mother changed the subject.

The next day the boy told his mother that he wished he could see Santa Claus again. 'Santa Claus?' she asked.

'At the market. *You* know.'

'Oh, Alan, *him*? Honey, you saw him yesterday. You told him what you wanted then, didn't you?'

'I don't want to tell him what I want. I just want to see him because he's *nice*. I *liked* him.'

After the boy was in bed, his father and mother sat in the living-room, neither of them paying much attention to the movie on cable. 'He say anything to you about Santa today?' he asked her.

She nodded. 'Couple of times. You?'

'Yeah. He really went for this guy, huh?'

'I don't know why.'

'Oh, Alan can be so compassionate—probably felt sorry for the guy.'

She shook her head. 'No, it wasn't like that. He really seemed drawn by him, almost as though . . .' She paused.

'As though he really thought the guy was Santa Claus?' her husband finished.

'I don't know,' she answered, looking at the car crash on the TV screen but not really seeing it. 'Maybe.'

She turned off the movie with no complaints from her husband, and began to go over the final list of ingredients for their Christmas dinner. 'Uh-oh,' she murmured, and went out to the kitchen. In a minute she returned, frowning lovingly at her husband. 'Well, it's not that I don't appreciate your making dinner tonight, but I just realized your oyster stew used the oysters for the Christmas casserole.'

'You're kidding.'

'Nope.' She was amused to see that there was actually panic in his face.

'What'll we *do*?'

'Do without.'

'But . . . but oyster casserole's a tradition.'

'Some tradition—just because we had it last year.'

'I liked it.'

'And where are we going to find oysters on a Sunday?'

'It's not the day, it's the month. And December has an *R* in it.'

'Sure. But Sunday doesn't have *oysters* in it. The IGA's closed, Acme, Weis . . .'

His face brightened. 'The farmer's market! They have a fish stand, and they're open tomorrow. You could run out and . . .'

'Me? I didn't cook the oyster stew.'

'You ate it.'

She put her left hand over his head and pounded it gently with her right. 'Sometimes you are a real sleazoid.'

'Now, Mrs Scrooge,' he said, pulling her onto his lap, 'where's that Christmas spirit, that charity?'

'Good King Wenceslas I ain't.'

'How about if I vacuum while you're gone so my mother doesn't realize what a slob you are?'

'How many pounds of oysters do you want?'

It started to snow heavily just before midnight and stopped at dawn. The snow was light and powdery, easy for the early morning trucks to push from the roads. The family went to church, then came home for a simple lunch, as if afraid to ingest even a jot too much on the day before the great Christmas feast. 'Well,' the boy's mother said after they'd finished cleaning up the dishes, 'I'm off for oysters. Anyone want to come?'

'To the farm market?' asked the boy. His mother nodded. 'Can I see Santa?'

His father and mother exchanged looks. 'I don't think so,' she replied. 'Do you want to go anyway?'

He thought for a moment. 'Okay.'

The parking lot was still covered with snow, although the cars had mashed most of it down to a dirty gray film. Only the far end of the parking lot, where a small, gray trailer sat attached to an old, nondescript sedan, was pristine with whiteness. It was typical, the boy's mother thought, of the management not to pay to have the lot plowed—anyone who'd hire a bargain basement Santa like that one and then charge three bucks for a thirty-five cent picture with him.

The seafood stand was out of oysters, but its owner said that the small grocery shop at the market's other end might still have some. 'Could I see Santa?' the boy asked as they walked.

'Alan, I told you no. Besides, he's probably gone by now. He's got a busy night tonight.' She knew it sounded absurd even as she said it. If *that* Santa was going to be busy, it wouldn't be delivering toys—it would probably be looking for a fix. Repulsion crossed her face as she thought again of those hollow eyes, that pale skin, the telltale bruises on his bare hand, and she wondered what her son could possibly see in that haggard countenance.

She thought she would ask him, but when she looked down, he was gone. In a sharp, reflexive motion, she looked to the other side, then behind her, but the boy was not there. She strained to see him through the forest of people, then turned and retraced her steps, as her heart beat faster and beads of cold sweat touched her face. 'Alan!' she called, softly but high, to pierce the low, murmuring din around her. 'Alan!'

It took some time for the idea to occur that her son had disobeyed her and had set out to find the market's Santa Claus on his own. She had not thought him capable of such a thing, for he knew and understood the dangers that could face a small child alone in a public place, especially a place like a flea market that had more than its share of transients and lowlifes. She told herself that he would be all right, that nothing could happen to a little boy the day before Christmas, that someone she knew would see him and stop him and take care of him until she could find him, or that he would be there on Santa Claus's lap, smiling sheepishly and guiltily when he spotted her.

She was running now, jostling shoppers, their arms loaded with last-minute thoughts. Within a minute, she entered the large open area between the markets. The chairs and the sign were there, the Santa and his photographer were not. Neither was her son.

For a long moment she stood, wondering what to do next, and finally decided to find the manager and ask him to make an announcement on the PA system. But first she called her husband, for she could no longer bear to be alone.

By the time he met her in the manager's office, the announcement had been made four times without a response. The boy's father held his mother, who was by this time crying quietly, very much afraid. 'Where was he going?' the manager, a short, elderly man with a cigarette in one hand and a can of soda in the other, asked.

'I thought it was to see Santa, but he wasn't there when I got there.'

The manager nodded. 'Yeah, he quit at noon. I wanted him to work through five, but he wouldn't. Said he hadda meet somebody.'

The boy's father looked at the manager intently over his wife's head. 'Who is this guy?'

'Santa? Don't know his name. Just breezed in about a week ago and asked if I wanted a Santa cheap.'

'What do you mean you don't know his name? You *pay* him, don't you?'

'Cash. Off the books. You'll keep that quiet now. And Riley, my helper, he got a Polaroid, so we made enough to pay him outta the pictures.'

The boy's father took his arms from around his wife. 'Where is this guy?'

'He's got a trailer the other side of the lot.'

'All right,' the father nodded. 'We're going to talk to him. And if he can't give us any answers, we're calling the police.'

The manager started to protest, but the couple walked out of the office and down the aisles, trying hard not to run and so admit their panic to themselves. 'It'll be all right,' the boy's father kept saying. 'We'll find him. It'll be all right.'

And they did. When they walked into the open area where Santa had been, their son was standing beside the gold aluminum Christmas tree. He smiled when he saw them, and waved.

They ran to him, and his mother scooped him up and hugged him, crying. His father placed a hand on his head as if to be certain he was really there, then tousled his hair, swallowing heavily to rid his throat of the cold lump that had been there since his wife's call.

'Where *were* you?' the boy's mother said, holding him ferociously. 'Where did you *go*?'

'I wanted to see him,' he said, as if that were all the explanation necessary.

'But I told you *no*. You know better, Alan. Anything could've happened. We were worried sick.'

'I'm sorry, Mom. I just *had* to see him.'

'But you didn't,' his father said. 'So where *were* you? Why didn't you answer the announcements?'

'Oh, I saw him, Dad. I was *with* him.'

'You . . . *where*?'

'He was here. He said he was waiting for me, that he'd been hoping I'd come again. He looked really different, he didn't have on his red suit or anything.'

His mother shook her head. 'But . . . I *looked* here.'

'Oh, I *found* him here okay. But then we went to his place.'

'*What?*' they both asked at once.

'His trailer. It's sort of like the one Grandpa and Grandma have.'

'Why . . . did you go out there?' his mother asked, remembering the trailer and the car at the end of the lot.

'He asked me to.'

'Alan,' his father said, 'I've told you never, *never*, to go with anyone for *any* reason.'

'But it was all right with him, Dad. I knew I'd be safe with *him*. He told me when we were walking. Out to his trailer.'

'Told you *what*?'

'How he always looks for somebody.'

'Oh, my God . . .'

'What's the matter, Mom?'

'Nothing. Nothing. What else did this . . . man say?'

'He just said he always comes back this time of year, just to see if people still believe in him. He said lots of people *say* they do, but they don't, not really. He said they just say so because they want their *kids* to believe in him. But if he finds one person who really believes, and knows who he really is, then it's all gonna be okay. 'Til next Christmas. He said it's almost always kids, like me, but that that's okay. As long as there's somebody who believes in him and trusts him enough to go with him.'

The boy's father knelt beside him and put his big hands on the boy's thin shoulders. 'Alan. Did he touch you? Touch you anywhere at all?'

'Just here,' he held up his mitten-covered hands. 'My hands.'

'Alan, this man played a mean joke on you. He let you think that he's somebody that he really isn't.'

'Oh no, Dad, you're wrong.'

'Now listen. This man was *not* Santa Claus, Alan.'

The boy laughed. '*I* know *that*! I haven't believed in Santa Claus for almost a whole *month*!'

His mother barely got the words out. 'Then who . . .?'

'And you were wrong too, Mom. He didn't have any little needle holes in his hands. Just the big ones. Straight through. Just like he's supposed to.'

Her eyes widened, and she put her fist to her mouth to hold in a scream. Her husband leaped to his feet, his face even paler than before. 'Where's this trailer?' he asked in a voice whose coldness frightened the boy.

They strode out the door together into the late afternoon darkness. Street lights illuminated every part of the parking lot. 'It . . . was there,' she said, staring across at white emptiness.

'The *bastard*. Got out while the getting was good. He . . .' The father paused. 'There?' he said, pointing.

'Yes. It was right over there.' The boy nodded in agreement with his mother.

'It couldn't have been.' He started to walk toward the open space, and his family followed. 'There are no tracks. It hasn't snowed. And there's no wind.' He looked at the unbroken plain of powdered snow.

'Hey! Hey, you folks!' They turned and saw the manager laboring toward them, puffs of condensation roaring from his mouth. 'That your kid? He okay?'

The boy's father nodded. 'Yeah. He seems to be. We were trying to find that man. Your Santa Claus. But he's . . . gone.'

'Huh! You believe that? And I still owe him fourteen bucks.' He turned back toward the warmth of the market, shaking his head. 'Left without his money. Some people . . .'

'Never mind,' his wife said. 'He's all right. Let him believe.' She touched her husband's shoulder. 'Maybe we should all believe. It's almost easier that way.'

When they got home, the boy took off his mittens, and his father and mother saw the pale red marks, one in each palm, where he said the man's fingers had touched him. They were suffused with a rosy glow, as if the blood pulsed more strongly there. 'They'll go away,' the boy's father said. 'In time, they'll go away.'

But they did not. They did not.

Other Errors, Other Times

BUCKTON LOOKED OUT ACROSS the blue flatness of the lake, then down at the stone in his hand. He rubbed it with his thumb. It was a land stone, rough, its edges sharp, untouched by the smoothing lap of waters. He placed his index finger along its edge, drew back his arm, and skimmed the stone out over the placid surface. It struck the water, leaped, struck again, leaped; four times it skimmed before disappearing with a small splash. *I would have caught that*, Buckton thought. *I would have caught that because it didn't matter.*

He noticed the cut only when he sat down on the dock, when he placed his hand beneath him to ease his body down. It was an inch long, running from the first joint of his right index finger up to the tip. It was straight and thin, like a paper cut, not at all ragged. The stone had cut him when he'd thrown it. *Cut my throat*, he thought, sucking the blood and watching the still-widening circle of ripples the stone had made in the lake. *Should've cut my throat with it.* He thought about the stone at the bottom of the lake, how it would stay there for centuries, the icy water wearing it away, slowly rounding off its roughness, softening its definition. It would do that to a man, too, soften him up, wear away the flesh that the fish didn't take, dull the sharp bones that remained.

Buckton looked beyond the lake to the wall of muddy-green trees on the other side, and tried to stop thinking. He should have brought Sally. It was no good to be alone. But he had known that all the time, had known that he wanted to be by himself only to taste his defeat all the more cleanly, to brood in solitude like a whipped dog licks its wounds and grows angry in some hidden culvert. He hoped she understood. He couldn't bear to have her hate him, too.

'Only a game,' he said aloud, then smiled, wondering if the fish cared. To the fisherman, angling was a game, but it was life or death to the fish.

A missed baseball. A matter of an inch, the fragment of a second, but, oh Jesus, what a second. Why, he asked himself, couldn't it have happened in April, or in July? Why did it happen in October, in the last game? Couldn't it have happened with the bases empty, or in the first inning, or with his team ahead? But it hadn't. It had happened with the bases loaded, bottom of the ninth, and two out, that dream that every kid who ever pounded a fist into a glove has had over and over again. A hopper to short—and not even *fast*, dammit—his glove down—*there*! . . . he could even see it go in!—and the ball was past him, beyond him, lost forever between his glove and his ankle, a play he had made hundreds of times without an error, and now . . .

Had it been the cold, the pressure, a bad hop, a stone? He looked at his stone-cut finger. The bleeding had stopped. No, he couldn't blame it on pebbles, like Freddie Lindstrom could in 1924. There were no pebbles on artificial turf. He had booted it, pure and simple; and as the bodies of the home-team crowd washed over the diamond on a wave of green and gold and crimson, Buckton had realized that he was legend, that his error had joined the Snodgrass Muff of 1912, and the 1908 Merkle Boner. What would they call it, the Buckton Blunder? The .982 lifetime fielding average didn't matter, nor the .302 batting average, nor the nineteen home runs this past year. All that mattered was one ball on one play. That was all.

They'd been decent enough to him in the clubhouse. Tough break, it happened to everybody, we'll get them next year—but the thoughts of lost bonuses tugged the smiles from the corners of their mouths, and he noticed the way Rich Washington glanced down at his black, long-fingered right hand, as if mourning the absence of a Series ring.

The fans had been the worst. They wrote him letters; drunks called him on the phone until he had the number changed to an unlisted one. There was no talk of trading him the next year. After all, as both his manager and the owner had told him, it was a one-in-a-thousand mistake that he'd just have to try and forget.

But he couldn't forget, or even learn to live with it—not until he stood alone with it. That was why he had come to the lake, to Canada. Up here they knew, they had seen, but it didn't mean so much. The CBC Radio generally reported only the scores of the Toronto and Montreal games, and if neither was a division winner, their national pride and polite contempt for affairs Stateside made them seemingly indifferent to the outcome. Yet, even if they hadn't been, he's still have been alone. The skies of central Ontario threatened snow by early October, and it was late now, early November, although the snow had not yet fallen, and the lake was unfrozen.

There were twenty cabins around the main circle of the lake, and Buckton's was the only inhabited one. No one dared to water-ski or swim, and even the fishing became a challenge because of the chill temperature. The cabin owners, most of them business people from Toronto or Barrie, always closed up in early September and headed a few hours south, where the winters were only ten below.

So Buckton was alone, as he had wanted. The Franklin stove and the half cord of wood beneath the cabin would supply enough heat for a few days, and there was always the space heater. When the hydro had come in two years before, Buckton had felt betrayed by the tall poles and wires cutting back through the road, into his wilderness. But once it was in, he was glad for it. He had seldom been able to get up North in the past few years, but Sally and Janie Sullivan, Scoop's wife, had spent a few weeks each summer when he and Scoop were on the road with the team. It was Sally's place now, but when he retired, it would be his as well.

He tossed another stone into the cold lake, trying to decide what to do now that he was settled in, and looked across the water at the opening a half mile away linking the lake to the others in the district. On the map, Lake Osenawega looked like a loaf of French bread with a long, wide, slowly curving hook attached. The hook narrowed until it became only a thin line that eventually met another, smaller lake miles away. And there the map ended. What was ahead was mystery.

He would go down the lake, he decided, follow it down the stream and into the next lake, and then, who knew where?

The foldboat was under the cabin. He dragged it out, found the paddles leaning against the woodpile, and carried them down to his dock. As the tip of the boat entered the water, it splashed him slightly, and he shivered. The water was freezing. He would have to be very careful not to tip the boat. He went back to the cabin then, and put matches, some sandwiches, and a few pieces of fruit into a double-strength plastic bag, and changed into warmer clothes, paying special attention to his feet. Insulated socks went on first, then plastic bags, another pair of wool socks, then hiking boots. He added a third pair of socks to the food bag, thinking that if the boat sank and he had to walk back all the way around the lake, he'd damn well better do it with dry feet. He finished dressing, and took the food down to the boat.

The sun, half-hidden behind grayness, was only halfway up in the sky, and Buckton thought it might be near 10:00 or 10:30. He'd left his watch in the cabin's bedroom, hoping that living by instinct and bodily needs would break his summer habit of firmly adhering to schedules. He would watch the sun, he thought, and start back so that he could reach his dock before night came. He lowered himself into the boat, settling down onto the red flotation cushion with a groan. The pain in his back that had come in the fourth game on diving and making an impossible catch was still there. Buckton tucked the plastic bag of food behind him, screwed the handles of the oars together to make one long, two-bladed kayak paddle, and pushed himself out into the lake.

The steady stroke of the paddle, the ease with which the boat sheared the placid water, the drops falling from the upraised blades like strings of crystal beads—all relaxed him, gave him ease, and he found himself happy with the day, the lake, and his role in them.

It took thirty minutes to get to the hook's opening, and he saw instantly that the hook was wider than he had expected, two hundred yards (*meters*, he thought—*I'm in Canada now*) from one side to the other. He found that interesting, a discovery of sorts, and he smiled as he paddled down it, straining in quiet excitement to see around the next bend. It was all virgin timber here, thickly grown to the edge of the water so that the leaves of autumn lay on the hook's surface like other, smaller boats, drifted out upon the wind and brought by that same wind back safely to the shore, where the leaves floated in a thick mass that colored the water's edge, an immense flotilla of brown and red and yellow craft. From time to time, Buckton paddled in close to shore, and let the foldboat drift through the leaves, spreading them gently apart and watching as they closed together again behind him, as though determined, in their fragile ignorance, not to let him return.

The hook went on, and he began to fancy it, not as the arm of a greater lake, but as a river, a thing unto itself. Now, when he looked back, he could no longer see the lake with the cabins and docks comfortably dotting its perimeter. He saw only *the river* behind and ahead, only the trees and bushes on the shore. *Passed from the sight of men*, he thought calmly. Except for himself, it was as though men had never been, that the world belonged solely to the trees, and the birds that he occasionally saw drift above him. It seemed so like the end of the earth that it came as all the greater surprise to him when he saw the cabin on the water's edge.

It sat back twenty yards from the water, and the earth surrounding it bore nothing but high yellow weeds and a few bushes that had long since lost their leaves, leaving only bare branches, like scrabbling fingers petrified by the windless day. Buckton paddled up to the shoreline and stopped, the foldboat parallel to the front of the cabin. As ugly as was the land immediately surrounding it, the cabin was worse. It was small, sixteen feet from one side to the other; the roof was slanted; and here and there on its surface, shingles lay askew, bent up toward the gray sky, or dangled from the eaves, like flaking skin on a psoriatic victim. Enough paint remained on the rough boards of the cabin's sides so that Buckton could tell it had once been a bright, florid red, but now only patches remained, and sun and wind had faded those to a sickly carmine. A heavy wooden door with a white enamel knob stood directly in the center of the cabin's face, flanked on either side by two windows that had long been boarded over. Buckton could see, even from a distance, the thick and rusty nails that protruded, spikelike, from the protecting boards. It looked, he thought, not so much like a house as like a disease-riddled face—the gaping mouth of the closed door, the blinded eyes of the windows, the leprous surface of the faced boards, all topped by that Medusa's fright wig of rampant shingles. Even the ground on which it stood, he thought, had yielded to its creeping sickness. There was not a healthy tree or bush or flowering plant for yards around.

Buckton paddled on, looking over his shoulder as the cabin receded behind him. He had the absurd feeling that if he turned his back on it for too long a time, it would shadow him down the shoreline, leaving desolation in its path. But it did not move, and was soon lost to sight around the bend of the water. Buckton kept stroking until his arms grew tired, then looked up at the sky. The sun was past its zenith, its yellow ball so occluded by clouds that Buckton could look directly at it without blinking. His stomach growled its hunger, but he decided to keep on until he reached the mouth of the stream that led to the next lake.

A mile further on, he saw the railroad bridge. It was thirty feet high, and four pillars of rough-hewn and mortared stone held it above the water. As he drew closer, he saw, sitting on the base of the right-hand pillar, a man fishing, with a small tackle box beside him. When the man looked in his direction, Buckton waved, and the man waved back. Buckton paddled close enough to talk without shouting and disturbing the man's quarry. Now he could see that the man was old, in his mid-seventies, with a grizzled beard. An International Harvester cap sat perfectly level on his head, and he wore a brown canvas jacket, blue jeans, and worn but sturdy walking shoes. 'How they biting?' Buckton asked.

'Pretty good,' said the man, in a deep, vigorous voice. 'Rock bass, mostly.'

'Rock bass?' Buckton said, thinking of the dirty brown, hand-sized multitudes that made fishing from his dock such a nuisance. 'They worth the effort?'

'Well, not in spring or summer, but around this time they start gettin' big enough to pop in a pan.' He pulled out of the water a cage in which several dozen good-sized fish lay. 'Fillet 'em and freeze 'em. They taste pretty good come March.'

'You walk back in here?' Buckton saw no boat.

'Hell no,' the man smiled. 'There's a dirt road in, Railroad built it to fix the bridge every spring. Turns off 142 about five miles west of Studholme. Got a gas station there. Or my boy does. He does all the work now, and I go fishin'. Where you comin' from?'

'Lake Osenawega. I got a cabin there.'

The old man raised his eyebrows. 'Pretty late in the season.'

'Wanted to see what it was like before winter came.' Buckton gestured ahead. 'The stream mouth to the next lake much farther ahead?'

'Thinkin' of goin' down there?' Buckton nodded. 'You're gonna have to portage a fair distance.'

'I can't boat through?'

'Water's high enough for that in spring, no other time.'

'How long's the portage?'

'Good three kilometers, maybe more.'

'Well, forget that.' Buckton frowned. By the time the ice thawed, Buckton would be well into spring training, if they renewed his contract as they had promised. He looked back up at the old man. 'Mind if I eat my lunch here?'

'Sure, c'mon up. Just gonna eat a bite myself.'

The old man steadied the boat while Buckton climbed out onto the rock base of the pillar. They sat together and ate, the old man's sole item a huge sandwich of what looked like beef engulfed by two slabs of homemade brown bread. He accepted an apple when Buckton offered it, and stripped the meat off as neatly as a machine, until only core and stem were left, which he hurled into the bushes on the shore. He introduced himself as Dave Coker, and Buckton told him his name as well, relieved when Coker did not recognize it. They chatted about fishing and the weather as they ate, and finally Buckton thought to ask about the desolate cabin he had seen.

'That's the cabin Ralph Terwiliger built for his boy Ben,' the old man said with a frown.

'How'd they ever get back in there?'

'Boat. Took everything in by boat. Old Ralph didn't like people much—lived out pretty far. Figured his boy'd like the same thing. So when Ben went overseas, Ralph built that cabin for him as a surprise when Ben came home, only Ben never did. He got killed over there. So Ralph used it for a while, then finally boarded it up and left it. Died soon after that.

'Who owns it now?'

'Nobody I know of. It's probably still listed with realtors hereabouts, and I think there's relatives up in the Maritimes, but I never seen them down here. No one'll buy it—too hard to get to. Ugly place, too.' Coker changed the subject back to fishing again, and told Buckton about a spot filled with walleyes, several kilometers toward the lake.

When Buckton thought to look at the sky, the cloudy sun was halfway into its descent behind the hills. 'Jesus, what time is it?' he asked.

Coker tugged back his sleeve to reveal a yellow-faced Timex. '3:30.'

'I've got to get going. I'll be lucky to make it back before dark.'

'Be glad to drive you. Leave your boat here and come back and get it tomorrow.'

Buckton considered the offer, which would mean driving back the next day and trying to load the foldboat on his rackless BMW, or walking miles of unfamiliar shoreline, neither of which seemed especially appealing. 'Thanks,' he answered finally, 'but I'm rested now. I can probably make it.'

'You sure?' The old man looked up, spat downwind. 'Felt like rain all day. Maybe even snow. Cold enough.'

'I'll be O.K. I'll hug the shoreline.'

'Up to you.' Coker held out his hand and shook Buckton's in a surprisingly genteel manner. 'Pleasure to meet you. You get to Studholme, you stop by the Gulf garage and say hello. I'll give you a soda.'

By 4:30 Buckton realized that he should have driven back with Coker. The sky had become much darker, and even without the clouds, the day was dying far more quickly than he had guessed. The dim patch of gray light that was the sun had nearly fallen behind the western trees, leaving him in a damp and oppressive twilight. Buckton's thoughts were equally dim. The adventure of drifting down a tiny stream into the discovery of a new body of water—his Champlain fantasy—had been cruelly aborted by risen land, wet hummocks that he had seen as he sat and talked with Coker. *Even fuck up a boat ride*, he thought bitterly, paddling with tired arms, trying to beat the darkness.

Then it started to rain. He had hoped the gloom was only the result of the coming night, but the fat raindrops told him otherwise, bursting upon him with a cold insistence, scurrying beneath his collar so that he was forced to tug it tightly around his neck and press his chin down upon it. The rain increased until the surface of the lake was dancing madly, and he paddled blindly toward the left-hand shore, able to sense only its outline in the thundering rain and darkness. He wished only to land, to seek shelter beneath the trees, perhaps beneath the boat itself, and wait until the storm wore itself out, then try to paddle back to his dock by either moonlight or starlight.

He moved along the shore in near panic, searching for a place where trees did not reach out like thick-boled fingers to prevent his landing. He felt as though he were lost in a clinging gray sea that was coating his entire frame with its cold wetness. The light in the sky was nearly gone.

Then the clinging limbs of the trees withdrew, and Buckton saw ahead of him a thin strip of sand that shone dark gray in the deeper blackness. He gave a thin laugh, and pushed the boat toward the open sand until he heard the faint scrape of the bow gripping the tiny beach. Grabbing the plastic bag that now contained only a sandwich, the matches, and his dry socks, he straddled his way to the bow and vaulted out, landing gracefully on the wet sand. With a heave, he pulled the boat higher, until only its stern touched the gelid water of the lake. Then Buckton turned.

A face peered out of the storm, a huge face, larger than any beast's. Buckton gasped, breathing in rain that caught in his throat, so that he choked for a moment, long enough to recognize the wide, dark eyes, the gaping mouth, the dimly mottled skin. He laughed in relief and in gratitude at his luck.

It was the cabin. No windigo, no north woods monster out of Indian legend. It was only the cabin he had seen on the way up the hook, the one he'd asked Coker about.

Buckton hunched his body over the bag with his precious matches, and walked to the white-knobbed door. There was no need to run. He could not get any more soaked. The door was locked, as he had expected, so he drew back his foot and kicked beneath the knob. It held the first time, so he kicked harder, heard something snap, and the door moved inward to his next push. Buckton stepped into perfect blackness.

At first he thought it was merely an optical trick, but when he turned to look behind him, he could make out only a slightly lighter upright rectangle of darkness, like obsidian against black velvet. It was too dark, he thought. He should have been able to see something inside the cabin.

He turned again, and the motion made the rough boards of the cabin floor creak. It was not a sharp sound, but dull and heavy, as though the timbers were rotten with dampness, and Buckton wondered how high up the sand the lake rose in the spring when winter's snows had melted. The smell of it was rotten as well, a musty, sour odor that held more than wood rot and mildew. There were two reasons that Buckton did not immediately strike a match. The first was that creating a light would somehow commit him to the cabin, familiarize him with it so that it would be easier to remain, and he was not quite sure he wanted to. The second, and more irrational, was his fear that lighting the match would have no result whatever on the vacuum of ebony that filled the room, that the flame would cast its light outward only for a matter of inches, as if in some jellied, impenetrable fog.

He physically shook the thought from himself and felt droplets of rain leave his hair to fall into the depth of the cabin. After fumbling in the bag, he withdrew the watertight container that held the matches, then unscrewed the lid and drew one out, scratching it on the striker. It burst into life.

In the twenty seconds before the first match burned down, Buckton surveyed an interior of mundane and abandoned rusticity. A rough stone fireplace occupied the back wall. Beside it was a large woodbox with no top. Against the left wall stood a board table with thin, straight branches for legs, and a single wooden chair with a ladder back. Three shelves were hung near the left-hand window. All were empty but for a few yellowed candle stubs. Against the opposite wall was a metal cot with a heavily stained blue-and-white-striped mattress. Buckton saw large patches of mildew on its edges. Above the bed hung a cheaply framed picture of the head of Jesus, the only decoration in the room. A small cabinet of rusting white metal completed the room's contents.

Buckton closed the cabin door and struck another match, lighting one of the candle stubs with it, and let the hot wax form a small puddle on the table into which he pressed the stub. There was some wood in the woodbox, old and moldering, but it would burn. With his pocketknife he feathered some of the smaller pieces and stacked them carefully in the fireplace. As he lit them, he hoped that the chimney was not clogged with leaves, but the draft was sufficient, and the room was soon warm enough for him to take off his sodden jacket and shirt, which he laid on the boards to dry. He sat by the fire in his damp and slowly stiffening jeans, turning his head now and again to look at the picture of Jesus on the wall. Though Buckton had not been inside a church in nearly ten years, the picture comforted him, if for nothing more than the quiet serenity of the face.

After a while his buttocks began to ache, and he looked at the moldy mattress with a cautious longing. Finally he dragged it from the cot onto the floor in front of the fire, heaped a few more logs on top of the blaze, and lay down, his damp shirt keeping the pungent-smelling surface of the mattress from his face. He was asleep in minutes.

When he awoke, it was with the sense of not being alone, and in his semiconscious state, he wondered if owls lived in the cabin, coming in through holes where the stuff of the eaves had rotted wetly away, and if they returned with dawn. But it was not, he realized dully, the figure of a giant bird that stood dimly lit by the dying coals, but the figure of a man.

Buckton froze, unable and unwilling to move, thinking that it was a dream, no more, and that in another second he would wake and be alone. But he did not wake, and the figure in the doorway moved, shifted slightly as though in discomfort. A voice came, thin and tentative.

'Hello? . . . Are you awake?'

It sounded real, alive, and Buckton let out his held-in breath. 'Yeah,' he croaked, trying to hide the terror that even now had not totally left him. He sat up and squinted, but the man's figure remained indistinct. 'Um . . . I've got a candle here.' He found his matches and lit the stub so that the room blossomed with a pale yellow glow.

'Didn't mean to startle you,' the stranger said. Buckton watched him in the dimness, guessing him to be somewhere in his early thirties. He was dressed plainly, and not warmly enough, Buckton thought, for a northern November. His height was an inch under six feet, and he was stocky, carrying the weight effortlessly, as muscle rather than fat. His skin was pale and clear, his hair a reddish brown. He smiled, just a little.

'Didn't expect to find anybody here,' Buckton said a bit apologetically, wondering if the man had any business there, or if he, too, were an interloper.

'Neither did I,' the man said, closing the door behind him.

'Did you get caught by the rain, too?'

'No. I live here. Sometimes.'

'You *live* here?' Buckton said, looking around the cabin's desolate interior, feeling something cold start to grow deep in his stomach.

'Yeah.' The stranger crossed to the woodbox and threw some wood on the fire.

'Who are you?' Buckton asked, not sure if he wanted to know, expecting to hear a name, and knowing that if his expectations were realized, his sense of reality would be shattered beyond repair.

'My name's Ben Terwiliger.'

A wild, high-pitched laugh left Buckton's throat, and the stranger whirled about.

'What the hell's wrong with you, mister?'

Buckton thought that if he kept laughing, at least kept smiling, that maybe he wouldn't be scared. 'That's funny,' he said. 'Funny. But you're not Ben Terwiliger.'

'Hell I'm not.' The man straightened, but there was nothing threatening in his manner.

'Then the old man was lying.'

'What old man?'

'Coker.'

'Don't know him. Lying about what?'

'He said . . . you were dead.'

The man who called himself Ben Terwiliger smiled. 'That's what they think, is it? Well, that's all right. That's good.'

'Wait a minute, just wait. Are you saying you're really Ben Terwiliger? And this . . . this isn't a joke or anything?'

'Why would I joke you, mister? I don't even know you. But I know who I am. Now, if you want to spend the night here, you just go ahead. I'll go back out where I was.'

'No, wait, please. Look, I'm sorry. I didn't know anybody'd been using this place, and with the rain and all . . . well, I broke your door there, be glad to pay for it.' Buckton babbled on, still confused, uncertain as to what was dream and what was reality, though this undoubtedly felt like the latter. '. . . and it's raining so hard that . . .'

'It's not raining,' Terwiliger said, and sat on the rusty springs of the bed. He said no more, only sat and looked at Buckton, who began to feel uncomfortable in his seminudity, and put on his remaining clothes.

Buckton expected something to happen any second—for Terwiliger to disappear, to spring upon him, to start laughing at the joke he'd played upon the Yank tourist, to fall away into a puddle of slime. But Terwiliger only sat and watched him. 'Why,' Buckton said finally, 'do you want people to think you're dead?'

'It's easier. Then no one bothers me.'

'But why did you tell me who you were?'

'I'm not used to lying. Just to hiding.'

'Hiding,' Buckton repeated. 'Why?'

Terwiliger gave a sigh that spoke worlds.

'Coker—the old man—said you were killed in the war.'

Terwiliger shook his head. 'I came home.'

'Why? If you wanted to hide?'

'You hide in places you know best.' He got up, making the springs squeal, and placed another log on the fire. Then he drew the single chair over next to the hearth, and straddled it, facing Buckton so that his face was in shadow. 'I never told anyone before. Summers I stay back in the woods, away from here. Too many people around all the time. But in October I come back. To stay warm. It's hard to keep warm, especially in winter.' He paused for a long moment. 'There were eight in the squad, and I was their leader. I led them, all right. There was this minefield, and we went across it slow and careful, and found a few, and after a while we didn't find any more. And I asked Sooner if he thought it was all right, and he did, and so did I. And we got together for a smoke to celebrate getting across, and Gary pulled out his pack of Player's and stepped over the rest of us to share them.

'It was my fault. I was the leader. I should've known. They just disappeared, blew apart before my eyes. I had nothing. No squad, no more friends, nothing. So I came home. Back where I could hide.'

'Deserted?' said Buckton quickly, thinking about making a way through jungles, across paddies, over an ocean and a continent of these woods.

'I came home,' Terwiliger said. Then he rose and looked down at Buckton. 'You stay here tonight. I'll go back out.'

'No,' Buckton replied. 'We can both stay. Here, you want the mattress? I can sleep on the floor.'

Terwiliger shook his head. 'Keep the mattress.' He lay on his back on the bare springs of the cot and closed his eyes.

Buckton thought he looked like a dead man. He shivered and lay down on the mattress, unable to close his eyes, to stop watching the man reclining on the cot. Or was it a man at all? he thought. Do men hide from other men, live alone in the woods like animals? His own error seemed small and insignificant, next to the tragic mistake Terwiliger had made, and for a time he felt at peace, just time enough to let him go back to sleep.

When he awoke, the fire was only coals, but he could make out a thin slice of light underneath the cabin's door. He felt his way across to it and flung it open. The day was cold but clear, and a bright sun was partway up in the east. Buckton breathed in the biting wind, letting it disperse the musty aroma that coated his lungs, then, refreshed, turned once more into the cabin.

Terwiliger was gone. There was, as Buckton had expected, no sign he had ever been there. Buckton looked around the cabin again, this time opening the white metal cabinets only to find them empty. He put on the rest of his clothes, went down to the foldboat, eased it into the water, and paddled out to the middle of the stream.

In a few hours, he landed at his own dock and made himself a breakfast of eggs, sausage patties, potatoes, and thick slices of wheat toast. He finished packing and closing up the house by early afternoon, then drove out the dirt road to the macadam two-lane that would eventually put him on 495.

Buckton was not yet happy. The only lesson learned from his meeting with Terwiliger was that it was futile and destructive to withdraw from other men. Terwiliger's mistake did not expiate his own in any way. Nothing had changed. It was only chance that had led him to discover the truth about Terwiliger, coincidence that had brought them together. He could not be redeemed by a coincidence. Temporarily comforted perhaps, but not redeemed.

Just outside of Studholme, Buckton remembered what Dave Coker had said about having a Gulf station there, and glanced down at his gauge. The tank was half-full, but Buckton decided to stop anyway. There was just a bit more that he wanted to know.

When he pulled in, a sturdy man in his mid-fifties came out of the station, snapping an oily rag in the air. 'Fillerup?' he asked.

Buckton nodded. There was some resemblance to the old man, but he wasn't sure. 'Dave around?'

'Fishing,' said the man.

'You his son?'

'Yep. You know Dad?'

'Ran into him yesterday. Out at the railroad bridge.'

'Oh yeah,' the man nodded, 'he mentioned that. You the baseball player?'

Buckton nodded, made himself smile.

'Saw you play a couple years ago in Toronto.'

Buckton nodded again. 'Your dad was telling me,' he said, 'about a cabin on the hook off Osenawega?'

'Cabin? Oh, Terwiliger's place.'

'Yes. He said the son was killed in the war?'

'Uh-huh.' The younger Coker was cleaning the windshield now. 'Minefield.'

'Do you . . . happen to know where he's buried?'

The man shook his head. 'Oh, they never found the body.'

'Yeah,' Buckton said, certain now, only making conversation. 'Those Cong mines were bad.'

'Cong?' Coker snorted. 'Weren't any Cong in Germany.'

'Germany? But . . .'

'You give me one good reason why a Canadian boy'd go fight a Yank war, and your gas is free.' Coker scrubbed roughly at a hardened bit of bird dropping.

'But Germany . . . that means . . .'

'World War II. That's right. That's where Ben Terwiliger bought it.'

'Forty years,' Buckton whispered to himself, thinking of the man not out of his thirties whom he had seen the night before.

Coker had to repeat '$11.50' twice before Buckton took out his wallet. Something was storming inside his brain, a suspicion that sometimes, in odd places and on singular nights, things other than mere coincidence enter the web of life to shape and to teach.

He thought about it all the way to Barrie, all the way to Toronto, considered it without fear as he crossed the bridge at Niagara and went down past Buffalo, and ultimately exulted in it, as he drove straight on through the night.

By the time he arrived home, he was beginning to think about the green thickness of Florida grass, short sleeves, and white spheres against the sky.

Ex-Library

IT WAS NOT, KENDALL HARRIS thought, the ideal place for a family vacation, and he would damn well let Riggs know it when he got back to Boston. The SeaHarp Hotel, despite Riggs's paeans of praise, struck Harris as little cheerier than a mausoleum, and the town of Greystone Bay was not so much 'charmingly caught in time', as Riggs had put it, as it was embalmed, like a long-dead insect trapped in amber.

Every face Harris had seen in the hotel, including his own in the mirror, had a pale, sickly cast that unerringly reflected the pallor of the sky. Was it ever blue over Greystone Bay? Harris wondered. And was there any haven in this great pile of a building where you could not hear that damned surf? The pounding of each wave on the strand seemed to mock the pounding of each worry, every concern that beat against the rickety seawall that was all that was left of his relationship with Maureen and David.

His wife. His son. He said those words to himself over and over, trying to find in them something that moved him, some saving grace that would make things the way they had been before Deborah had come into his life, Deborah with her heart-shaped face, her willowy form, and her heart of oak that would brook no rival, not even a wife. She had refused to be a mistress, and for that Harris loved her all the more.

But his family was too important to him to give up, even for Deborah, and he told her that, and told her that it had to end between them. She had understood and had walked away, leaving his life emptier than it had been before, the memories of his happiness with her creating an abyss in which the small amount of affection he still had left for Maureen was totally swallowed up.

Maureen had known that he was having an affair. She was neither dumb nor blind, and her pain had lashed out at him, and he had returned word for word, curse for curse, until there was nothing left but legalities to bind them together. They had gone to a counselor, and the counselor had said to get away, go on a vacation together, escape the petty pressures of everyday life.

And so they had come to Greystone Bay, where the petty pressures vanished, making room for the huge and deeper pressures that Harris carried inescapably within him, the pressures that now boiled inside his brain as the foam boiled on the rocky strand.

They had arrived only that morning, and already the large, second-floor suite they occupied seemed tight and claustrophobic. Christ, Harris thought, the Superdome would have seemed claustrophobic if both he and Maureen had been in it. Her presence, smoldering with disgust toward him, filled the room, leaving him no air to breathe, and the way in which she sheltered David, as though his father were some brute who might devour him, both saddened and angered Harris. The worst of it was that the boy had begun to share his mother's aversion, and in the presence of his wife and child Harris now felt leprous, monstrous, murderous.

So much, he thought bitterly, for a fucking family vacation. And this was only the first evening. Ten more days to go. Jesus God, he wondered, grimacing inwardly at the absurd melodrama of the thought, will I be able to get through this vacation without killing somebody?

He shook his head at the idea, wondered if a third drink would be too many, decided that it would not, and ordered another Glenfiddich. He drank it in less time than he had taken with its two predecessors, and after it was gone he decided that he would drain his bladder before adding any more fluid to its contents. It was a long way to the door of the bar, but he made the trip easily, and just as easily found his way to the men's room beneath the staircase. No, he thought, not drunk yet. He sighed. Not drunk enough. Never drunk enough.

He urinated, washed his hands, splashed some water on his cheeks, and ran a comb through his graying hair, trying not to look at the haggard face that suddenly seemed so old and sad. Forty-two, he thought. Only forty-fucking-two and everything is over? He slipped the comb back into his pocket and listened for a moment.

It was there. The sound of the breakers. He had heard it in the bar, and could even now hear it in here, in a room with no windows. Maybe through the pipes, he thought. Jesus, was there any place you couldn't hear those goddamned waves crashing?

Harris went back into the hall and took a few steps toward the bar, but then stopped and looked to the right down the corridor. Was there someplace down there, he wondered, someplace quiet, where a man could stop thinking about those waves?

He crossed the corridor only to find a locked meeting room on the right, a locked ballroom on the left, and, further down the hall and to the right, a room with a closed door marked *Club*. 'Not a member,' Harris muttered to himself, and went back the way he had come. At the cross-corridor, he turned left, and heard the sharp sound of billiard balls striking one another. Not tonight, he thought. Not in the mood. Then he noticed the door with the words *Reading Room* lettered on it. It was closed, but Harris could see a light beneath the door. He walked up to it, turned the knob slowly, and pushed it open.

An old man was sitting in a leather armchair against the far wall, the only light in the room coming from the brass floor lamp whose green shade hung over him like a censer. When the man looked up, Harris thought for a moment that he was staring at an egg, not so much for the shape of the man's head as for its color—or lack of it. His hair was a brilliant white, as was the well-trimmed beard that wreathed his chin, and the pallor of his flesh was almost equal to that of his hair and whiskers. Harris, frozen in the doorway, was relieved as the apparition's face split in a friendly smile, and blue eyes observed him from behind shining bifocals.

'Come in,' the old man said warmly. 'I had the door closed to keep out the sounds of the billiards, not fellow readers. Make yourself at home. The chairs are comfortable, the ambience is pleasant, and the silence is delightful.'

Harris smiled back and closed the door behind him. Peace settled over the room like a shroud. He listened in pleased surprise. 'You can't hear the surf,' he said.

'You're glad of that?'

'Well . . . yes.'

The old man nodded and quoted:

> 'Sophocles long ago
> Heard it on the Aegean, and it brought
> Into his mind the turbid ebb and flow
> Of human misery . . .'

'"Dover Beach",' Harris said, happy to recognize the allusion.

'Ah!' the man said, delighted. 'You *are* a reader.'

'I, uh, remembered it from college, that's all.'

'You agree with Matthew Arnold? The ebb and flow of human misery—the surf reminds you of it?'

'I . . . guess so. Sometimes.'

'Well, you're safe from it for the little while you're here. But I'm being rude, I should introduce myself.' He pushed himself to his feet with surprising agility, and thrust out a hand. 'My name is Samuel. And you?'

Harris took the hand and shook it. It was warm and dry and gripped his own hand firmly and a bit longer than Harris thought necessary. 'Harris,' he said. 'Kendall Harris.'

'A pleasure, Mr Harris. And to what tastes does your reading run? I know this room and its holdings quite well. Perhaps I can help you to select a suitable volume?'

'Well . . . I don't know. I mean, I came in here mainly for a place to just sit and . . . and think,' Harris finished weakly.

'Ah, and here I am chattering away.' Samuel put his head to one side and frowned. 'But are you sure, Mr Harris,' he went on more softly, 'that you *want* to sit and think? You appear, if you don't mind my saying so, to be more than a little ill at ease. Perhaps some literary escapism would be more in order.'

Jesus, it shows, Harris thought. He didn't know why he just didn't tell the old man to be quiet and sit down and finish his damn book, but there was something that stopped him. Perhaps it was the air of occupancy that Samuel possessed, as though this reading room was his private suite, and Harris was only there at his indulgence. 'Look, I don't know . . .'

'Mr Harris, have you ever read M. R. James?'

The name struck a chord, and Harris remembered a Dover paperback that he had bought when he was in college. A roommate had turned him on to Le Fanu, and for several joyously chilly months he had immersed himself in English ghost stories whenever he was not doing the required reading for his classes. 'I have, yes.'

Samuel stepped up to one of the packed mahogany bookshelves that surrounded the room, and drew from it a small, thick volume bound in a dark red cloth which he handed to Harris. 'Please, take this. There's a certain story I'd like you to read, if you have a half hour or so?'

Harris looked at the book, *Collected Ghost Stories* by M. R. James. He opened it to the title and copyright pages and saw that it was a British edition published by Edward Arnold Ltd. in 1931. The volume was dog-eared, and the front hinge had broken. As Harris turned to the back, he noticed a paper library pocket pasted in, and in it a yellowed card, covered with several signatures. 'Greystone Bay Public Library,' Harris read aloud.

'Yes. Destroys its collectors' value, but it also brings . . . another dimension, shall we say, to the book. Now the story I'd like for you to read is "'Oh, Whistle, and I'll Come to You, My Lad'".'

Harris sighed in exasperation. 'Look, Mr Samuel——'

'Just Samuel.'

'All right, Samuel. Now I don't know why you want me to read this story, but——'

'An experiment,' Samuel said, never losing his soft smile.

'An experiment,' Harris repeated.

'To be explained when you finish the story.'

Harris smiled thinly. 'Samuel,' he said, 'what is it with you? Are you a retired high school English teacher who misses the old days or what?'

Samuel chuckled. 'I assure you I'm not, Mr Harris. What harm can it do? Do you have anything better to do with your time tonight?'

Harris thought of Maureen and David watching television in the cavernous living-room of their suite, and felt a hot flame of revulsion blaze through him. He shook his head. 'No. No, I don't.'

'Then make yourself comfortable. What better way to pass an evening than to sit comfortably and read a thrilling tale?'

While Samuel resumed his own seat and volume, Harris stepped over to a chair twenty feet away, turned on the floor lamp, sat, and began to read. He dimly remembered having read the story years before, but was soon caught up in it enough to forget both the odd circumstances under which he was now rereading it and the old man seated several yards away.

It was, he thought, a truly eerie story, with an effective and terrifying ghost, and he blinked quickly several times at the story's end until he felt free of the false yet chilling reality of the tale. He looked over at Samuel, and closed the book with a loud enough report to make the old man look up.

'I'm finished,' Harris said. 'Do you want me to do a book report for you?'

Samuel grinned, and Harris was not surprised to find that his teeth were as startlingly white as his hair. 'No, Mr Harris,' he said. 'All I want is to ask you a question about the story. A single question.'

'All right.'

The old man stood up and crossed the room until he was next to Harris's chair. 'What did you *see*?'

'What did I . . . see? What do you mean?'

'When the ghost . . . the malignant thing . . . forms itself out of the bedding.' He held out a hand for the book. 'Allow me.' Harris placed the book in Samuel's hand, and the man opened it and read: '"I gathered that what he chiefly remembers about it is a horrible, an intensely horrible, *face of crumpled linen*. What expression he read upon it he could not or would not tell, but that the fear of it went nigh to maddening him is certain."' Samuel closed the book. 'We all create mental images when we read. Now what I should like to know is what, specifically, was the image that you saw in your mind's eye when you just read that passage.'

Harris had no trouble remembering. For some reason the image had been extraordinarily vivid. Still, he was hesitant to allow the strange old man to share his thoughts.

'Well?' Samuel pressed.

Why not? Harris thought. It was certainly neither secret nor intimate. 'It was . . . kind of silly, I guess. The sheet that made the image of the ghost had these waves of hair parted in the middle . . . there were bulging eyes, and the mouth was wide open with'—Harris had to chuckle—'with linen teeth. Fangs, I suppose. And a beaked, pointy nose.' He shrugged. 'That's about it.'

'And does that surprise you?' Samuel asked. 'That you should create such a picture?'

Harris thought for a moment. 'Yes. Yes, it does,' he said slowly. 'When I was halfway through the story, I remembered reading it before, and I remembered that there was an illustration—I don't know by who—but it was of this, this *sheet*-thing rising up over its victim. But when I came to the part in the story where it happened, I didn't see that, but instead got this *other* image.'

Samuel reached into the pocket of his dark suit coat and withdrew a sealed envelope which he handed to Harris. It bore the return address of the SeaHarp Hotel. 'Open it,' Samuel said.

Harris tore it open and withdrew a sheet of hotel stationery on which was written in a spidery script, *Long wavy hair. Large eyes. Sharp nose. Fangs.* Harris read it twice, then looked up. 'What is this?'

'Evidence that our little experiment worked.'

Harris looked at the man, the book, the paper, and back at the man again. 'Experiment? In what, ESP? You read my mind?'

Samuel shook his head. 'No, no. That was in my pocket, sealed, before you even came in here. I would have to be precognitive to have done such a trick. No, Mr Harris, there was no thought transmission between you and I while you read that story. But there *was* something between you'—he held up the book—'and *this.*'

Harris was confused, almost frightened. 'Look, I don't know what you're trying to do, but——'

'Mr Harris, please be calm. You have done this much at my request, will you do one thing more?'

'Do . . . what?'

'Read the story one more time. To prove that this paper is no coincidence.'

'This is ridiculous,' Harris muttered, starting to get to his feet.

'Please,' Samuel said earnestly. 'It is important. More important than you may guess.'

Harris looked into the pale face and blue eyes for nearly a minute, then nodded curtly. 'All right. All right, one more time, but then I'm leaving.' He took the book, opened it once more, and reread the story. This time it took him only ten minutes, and when he had finished he looked up, puzzled.

'Yes?' Samuel said. 'You have read it, and what did you see?'

'I saw . . .' Harris swallowed heavily. 'I saw something different. It was more mature, more . . . fleshed out? The . . . contours of the face were lined and wrinkled, and there seemed to be traces of, of decay, or rotting on it.' He looked at Samuel. 'What is this all about? What is this book?'

'Look at the card in the back,' the man said. 'Read the first two names.'

Harris turned to the back of the book and slipped the card from the pocket. The first name, Donald Lorcaster, was written in a childish scrawl, the second, Richard Williams, in a firm, adult hand.

'Notice the handwriting,' Samuel said. 'A child, and an adult. Now, remember the two images that you saw in your mind—the first a child's cartoon horror, the second a more developed adult vision.'

'You're saying that this book is . . . a storage medium of some sort?'

Samuel nodded. 'A battery, if you will, that stores not power, but images. A single, strong mental image of each person who has read this particular story. In this particular volume.'

Harris barked a laugh that sounded unpleasantly loud in the quiet room. 'That's ridiculous! How could something like that happen?'

'I can't explain, Mr Harris. I can only tell you that it is so. And you can see for yourself. Read on, if you doubt me. There is a third borrower's name on the card.'

Harris looked down at the book in his lap as though it was a rattlesnake poised to strike. The third name was S. T. Plummer, and the script in which it was written was artistic, even florid. What had Plummer seen, Harris wondered, and did he really want to see it for himself? Despite his fear, Harris opened the book to the story, and began to read it again.

This time, when the apparition manifested itself, there was nothing of the supernatural about it. Instead, Harris saw the mental image of a young man's face, a face unmistakably human, but filled with inhuman hatred. It was a vicious, tortured mask, mindless and violent, with eyes that Harris knew would never close until whatever it saw was torn and destroyed, until the object of its fury and loathing lay dripping and lifeless on the floor.

'*Jesus* . . .' Harris whispered, and clapped the book shut. 'Oh, *Jesus*.'

'Plummer,' the old man said softly. 'His name was Plummer. And what you have just seen was his own face.'

Harris looked at the old man and shivered.

'He was a poet,' Samuel went on. 'It was over fifty years ago. One summer night he murdered his wife and child and slashed his own wrists. He was saved, only to enter a madhouse, where he most certainly deserved to be.' The old man stepped to Harris's side and took the card from the book. 'The deaths occurred three days before the due date stamped here. A terrible thing. Unforgivable. I knew the family, you see.' He sighed and shook his head. 'It is not often that we get to view the world through a madman's eyes. It can be . . . instructive.'

Harris sat, his gaze still on the book in front of him.

'Now. Since you have humored me with the gift of your time, might I repay you with a glass of sherry in the bar?'

Samuel strode to the door and opened it. Harris heard the sound of the waves. 'No. No thank you. I'd just like to stay here for a while.'

The old man nodded and walked through the door, which he left open. The billiard balls no longer clicked together, but Harris still heard the breakers on the shore. He picked up the book in his lap, weighed it in his hands, opened it, and read the tale.

This time, it was his own face that he saw.

He closed the book and sat trembling for several minutes. 'Instructive,' he whispered to himself.

Then he made up his mind, got up, walked out of the reading room and into the main lobby, where he asked the night clerk to call a taxicab for him. While he waited for it to arrive, he sat at one of the secretaries and wrote a brief letter:

> Maureen—
> There is no point to this. What we had has long been over,

> and any attempt to save it may lead to something far worse than divorce. I am leaving, and will have my attorney contact you when you return to Boston.
>
> Ken

In the cab, traveling toward the western hills and the highway beyond, Harris felt, for the first time in many months, at peace. He could no longer hear the waves crashing on the strand.

ꕥ

A week later, a red-cheeked and heavy-set man, dressed richly if not tastefully, burst through the doors of the SeaHarp Hotel's reading room. 'Now what the hell's this?' he loudly asked anyone who cared to listen.

Samuel looked up from his leather-bound volume of Milton and smiled. 'The reading room, sir. Please come in.'

'Reading room, huh? Great. You can't get dick on the TV, the bar is as dull as hell, and they won't let me in the goddam club room. I shoulda known the high point of this place'd be a library.' The man walked in and looked around, a belligerent set to his shoulders. It was obvious that he had been drinking, even without the evidence of the reek of bourbon that surrounded him like a cloud. 'So what've they got to read?'

'Well, they have a good many classics, and if you're interested in recent fiction, that shelf over there is filled with it. There are magazines and newspapers as well.' Samuel paused. 'But if I might make a suggestion?'

The man eyed him with bleary wariness. 'Like what?'

'Have you ever read M. R. James?'

'Pal, I never even *heard* of M. R. James. They got that new Tom Clancy in here?'

'I'm afraid not. M. R. James is considered the dean of English ghost story writers, and——'

'*Ghost* stories? I don't have time to waste reading that kinda crap, buddy.' The man swung his head back and forth one more time. 'Shit, the hotel's a mausoleum, and this place is the crypt. See ya around.'

'But, sir! . . .' said Samuel, rising to his feet. But it was too late. The man was gone.

Samuel sat down, the volume of Milton drifting closed as the memory came to his mind of the red-faced man, his timid, quiet wife, and their young daughter checking into the hotel that afternoon, of the man's quick, hot flare of temper when his wife did not remove the reservation confirmation swiftly enough from her purse, of his sharp and cruel command to his daughter to hurry up when she stopped to examine the oil painting of Captain Fletcher's ship that hung near the elevators.

Then Samuel closed his eyes and saw what the morning would bring, saw the sad-eyed woman and the shy little girl lying in their second-floor suite, lying and not moving, not even when the maid came in to make the beds, saw the red-faced man, exhausted and panting, his fury spent, his face far more red than before, with something more than his own blood coursing beneath his skin. . . .

'Sir?'

Samuel opened his teary eyes and looked up. Frederick and Noreen Montgomery were standing in the doorway of the reading room. He smiled, as he smiled at most people, but with the Montgomerys it was more heartfelt. They had always been kind to him, and had never asked him to leave the hotel before it was time to close the public areas. He felt at home at the SeaHarp.

'We have to close the reading room now,' Noreen said, her voice soft and apologetic.

'It's rather foggy,' Frederick added. 'Would you like me to call a cab for you?'

'No, thank you very much. I'll walk.'

Samuel stood, adjusted his suit coat, nodded at the pair, and walked past them into the hall, toward the main entrance. The thick carpet muffled his footfalls, and allowed him to hear snatches of the Montgomerys' conversation:

'. . . such a kind man . . .'

'. . . so gentle it's almost impossible to believe that . . .'

'. . . when he was young . . .'

The old man had just stepped onto the porch when he heard rapid footsteps and Frederick Montgomery's voice calling his name. Samuel paused, holding the door open, and Frederick came up to him. The younger man was holding a small, red, cloth-bound volume.

'This isn't from the SeaHarp's library,' Frederick said, slightly out of breath. 'I thought it might be yours.'

The old man nodded. 'Yes it is. I forgot it. Thank you, Mr Montgomery. I should hate to lose this book. I surely should.'

Frederick Montgomery held out the book, and Samuel reached out a hand to take it. His right coat sleeve inched itself up with the motion, and, in the glow of the large globe overhead, the thin and ancient scar on his wrist shone as white as his hair, whiter than the pallor of his mortified flesh, nearly as white as the bright fire of his atoning soul.

'Goodnight, Mr Plummer.'

'Goodnight, Mr Montgomery, ' the old man said, and walked off with his book into the fog and the night.

Jabbie Welsh

MARTIN FARADAY AND LINDA BEAUMONT had not heard any of the stories about Jabbie Welsh when they moved into the old farmhouse on Washburn Road, but even if they had they still would have bought it. Having lived in a succession of small New York City apartments for over a decade, and having lived in one of those apartments together for two years, they were ready to share a house, anxious to live in the city no longer. They both longed for privacy, and Linda welcomed the feeling of permanence a house would bring to their relationship.

They had first met backstage at the Beaumont. He was a set designer with a number of successful off-Broadway shows to his credit, and she designed costumes, so they hit it off quickly, and in a few months were living together in her loft on Christopher Street. The next two years were good ones, and when the opportunity came along to buy an old house upstate, they jumped at it.

A realtor in Albany had been scouting for them a few months, and called them immediately when the Welsh place became available. When they saw it standing alone across the field like a castle in a desert, they looked at each other and nodded in agreement. A walk through the old building confirmed their impression that it was right. It smelled damp, but was otherwise in good shape, and would need little restoration. After only a short round of haggling, they agreed on a price.

During the closing, Linda thought to ask about the house's history, and the realtor told them that it had been built in the 1850s by a wealthy farmer named Josiah Welsh for his wife Rachel. When the Civil War came, Josiah marched off as captain of a New York regiment, leaving his wife and a young daughter behind. He died two years later at Gettysburg. The daughter married, and the old woman lived there until her death, when the daughter and her husband took possession. Their family, the Washburns, had lived there ever since, until the last of the Washburn line, a widower who died childless, left the property to a friend who had put the house up for sale.

ꟷ ꟷ

Martin and Linda moved in in September. The month coincided with the busiest preparations for the New York theater season, so they found themselves commuting on an irregular basis. Martin drove down for a few days of concept, then returned to do his blueprints in an arboretum they had turned into a makeshift studio. While he worked, Linda drove down for fittings or to choose fabrics. To their dismay, they found that they only spent two or three days together each week, but somehow the house made it worth the trouble, and they made the most of the time they were able to share together.

They were just sitting down to a late dinner one evening at the beginning of October, when Linda mentioned the old woman. 'I had a funny one today. A visitor. It was the weirdest thing. I was upstairs, sitting in the rocker in the front window, doing some sketches for *Volpone*. I looked down at my pad for a few seconds, and when I looked back up, there was a woman walking down the drive. But the drive's so long I don't know why I didn't see her before. It was like she dropped out of the sky or something.'

'Maybe she was behind the trees.'

Linda shook her head. 'I don't think so. Oh, she could've been, but I don't think she was. No one would come that way.'

'What'd she want?'

'I . . . don't know.'

'Didn't she come to the door?'

'Yes, yes. And she knocked. But I didn't answer.'

'Why not? Was she selling something?'

'Well, she wasn't carrying anything. I thought at first she might be a religious nut—a Jehovah's Witness or a Mormon or something—so I didn't think I'd open the door. But then I figured since she walked all the way out here—I didn't see a car—I could at least see what she wanted. So when she knocked I went down to the front door with every intention of letting her in.

'But then I saw her shape through the sheers over the glass door, and . . . I just *couldn't*—I couldn't open the door. She seemed like a dark shadow, a bringer of bad news or something, so I went to one of the front windows for a closer look at her.

'She was in her late fifties maybe, and her clothes . . . well, they would have been perfect for *Mourning Becomes Electra*. I swear, Martin, it was a perfect post-Civil War ensemble, maybe 1870, 1880 at the latest. A fantastic recreation—buttons, hooks, everything looked authentic. I couldn't see her face too well at first—she wore a hat that covered it at the side. But then she turned, really slow, till she was looking at the window I was peeking out of. I don't know how, but I'm *sure* she knew I was watching her. It was like she could see right through the curtain, like she was playing a game with me. She was the cat and I was the mouse. I ran upstairs as quietly as I could, and when I went down later she was gone.'

'But you saw her face?'

Linda nodded. 'Grim. Like an old battle ax. Sort of beaky nose, and a real pale complexion. And her eyes. . . .'

'What about them?'

She shook her head in frustration. 'I don't know. There was something weird about them, but I can't . . . not like she was blind, but they were different somehow.'

'You mean different colors?'

The frustrated look vanished. 'That's it. One was dark, brown or hazel, and the other was a really pale blue.'

Martin sat back, his dinner forgotten. 'Sounds like a gem. Sorry I missed her.' He tried to make his tone light, but he was worried. He had lived in a small town until his late teens, and knew that not only cities bred crazies. 'Wonder if she'll come back.'

'God, I hope not.'

'You were really scared of her, weren't you?'

She laughed uncomfortably. 'Yeah. I was.'

He rose from the table, went over, and put his arms around her. 'Don't worry, babe. She was probably just a harmless old coot out to convert you to her particular denomination. If she comes back, don't answer the door.'

'She was just so damn *weird* looking.'

'That's great. Somebody who's lived in the Village ten years calling an up-stater weird.'

She laughed, and they started to talk of other things.

ꟸ ꟹ

But a week later, Martin found out just how weird the woman really was. Linda was in the city for fittings, leaving Martin with some plans for an O'Neill revival at Circle-in-the-Square. He had just tossed down his drawings in disgust, and stepped out on the porch with the intention of stalking through the maple grove fifty yards away and beating the bushes with a dead stick until they give him some inspiration, when he saw a strange woman at the bottom of the porch steps.

Her clothes were those of another century, and somehow her face was too. It looked as though it would have been right at home on any of the faded tintypes Martin had considered for set dressing on the O'Neill. Linda had been right. *Grim* was the operative word. And if he needed more proof that this was the same unwelcome visitor Linda had seen, he had only to look at the eyes, one a dark brown, the other a blue so pale that it looked like a white marble with a small black blot upon it.

He stood for a moment, looking down at what seemed an apparition from a long buried past, then said (rather stupidly, he thought later), 'Hello. Can I help you?'

Her jaw tightened. 'You can,' she said in a hard and grating voice.

That was all. He shrugged, and gave a little laugh. 'Okay, uh, how?'

'This is my house. You're in my house.' Her head moved in quick, peckish motions as she spoke, reminding Martin of the way a crow's head darts and jabs as it feeds on roadkill.

'Your house? I think you're mistaken. I own this house.'

The woman ripped out an oath that Martin had heard and said thousands of times, but this was the first time he had ever been shocked by it. It seemed so obscenely incongruous coming from this staid old specter of lost gentility, that he suspected she was truly a madwoman. '*Your* house,' she snarled in her gravel voice. 'This is a *Welsh* house. Are you a Welsh?'

'No, I'm not.'

'God damn you, at least you speak true there.'

'Look, who are you, anyway?' Martin spoke roughly, in response to the woman's remarkable rudeness, and to unwind the cold wire of fear that was twisting around his chest.

'A Welsh. Jabbie Welsh. And this is my house and has always been.'

'Listen, this house belongs to me, and I don't care if you're a Welsh or a Corleone. I bought it from a Mr Bryant, who it was left to by a Mr Washburn'—her eyes flared at the mention of Washburn's name—'and it's mine, mine and Miss Beaumont's, and if you want to see the deed, have your lawyer contact mine.'

'There are things older and stronger than deeds, you young bastard! As for Bryant, I never heard of him. And a Washburn shall *never* bide here! Now will you be gone from this house or not?'

Her eyes burned into his with a force that nearly staggered him, and he felt light-headed, as if in a dream. 'No,' he said weakly. 'I said this is my house, and I have no intention of leaving.'

'On your head then,' she said coldly, and from somewhere in her voluminous dress she took two long and tapered needles that shone blindingly in the midday sun. She held one in each bony hand, and slowly started up the porch steps.

Martin realized later that there was not a single, sudden moment when he knew what she meant to do with those sharp devices. Instead the knowledge came upon him like a murky image that sharpened with each step the woman took, until he finally saw her clearly, plunging the long needles into his face over and over until his blood blinded him. By the time he realized her intentions, she was nearly on him.

He barely had time to throw himself backwards into the house and slam the door behind him with an outstretched foot before he toppled onto the entrance hall carpet. From the other side of the door came a sound like fingernails on a blackboard, and he knew it was the needles sliding against the glass pane. A duller sound followed as they scraped across the wood underneath, then silence.

He lay there for a moment, heart leaping like a rabbit trapped in a pit. Then he sprang to the door to make sure the lock was snapped, that the insane old woman would not, in another second, burst through, needles raised above her head like the thunderbolts of Zeus. He thought of the gun in the den, and ran to get it. It was a .22 revolver, a present from his father when he had first moved to the city, that had lain untouched for years. Now he was glad for the comfortable feel of its cold metal in his palm, and the reassuring and businesslike click the chamber made as it snapped shut on half a dozen verdigris-coated cartridges.

When he returned to the front door, he pushed the curtains aside with an umbrella, then stepped around for a look.

There was nothing there, not a sign of a black-garbed bulk of female lunatic with knitting needles poised. He ran to the back door, gun held out in front of him like a crucifix warding off a vampire. The door squeaked slightly as he opened it, but there was no other sound, and he slipped out and circled the house, but there was no sign of the old woman. As he looked around, he realized that the grove was the only cover she could have taken. But the nearer he came to the densely packed trees and bushes, the less he relished the thought of entering their labyrinth. Dead leaves lay in thick piles underneath, and their crackling would announce his presence to anything standing in wait behind an overgrown bole.

Instead he turned back to the house, pulling out the key to open the front door he had locked from the inside. As he slipped it into the lock, he became aware that something was wrong, something was missing. Then he remembered the rasping scrape of the needles on glass and wood that should have made a scratch inches long in the dry and flaking white paint.

But there was nothing—no line of whiteness on the glass, no snakelike scratch in the wood of the door. Nothing. He stayed inside the locked house until Linda drove in late that evening. When he told her what had happened, she started to shake as if all the windows were open to the October chill.

'I knew it,' she said. 'I just knew there was something horrible about that woman.'

'You know,' said Martin, 'the thing that frightens me the most—in retrospect, that is—is that I was actually ready to kill her. I found myself hoping that she'd try to resist being held, that I'd be forced to fire. And goddammit, Linda, I wouldn't have tried to wound her. I think I would've aimed right at her chest.'

Linda put an arm around him. Now only her hands were trembling. "I know. I think I know how you felt.'

'I felt *violated*, dammit. Jesus, all those years in New York and never robbed, never burglarized. We move up here and a nut tries to stab me with needles! It doesn't make any sense.'

'There's another thing that's weird. Those needles. They must have marked the door. So why aren't there any scratches?'

He shook his head. 'I don't know. Now I think maybe I didn't hear the needles hit at all. Maybe I just *expected* to hear them, so I did.'

'What do we do now?'

'Go to the police. I'll tell them what happened. Who knows, there may be an escaped maniac running around here. With our information they may find her a little sooner.'

ꟾ ꟾ

But there was no escaped maniac, as Martin learned from the police the next day. The chief said he would send a man out to look the place over that afternoon, and told Martin he had received no other complaints concerning a woman named Jabbie Welsh, or anyone of her description. As far as he knew, no one named Welsh had lived in or near the town for a long time.

The deputy came out at three o'clock. Martin told him the story and walked him around the property, but they found nothing. The thick carpet of dead leaves in the grove was undisturbed, and the woman had left no footprints in the soft dust of the driveway. The deputy, a gaunt, older man named Joe Kready, looked at Martin oddly when Martin finished his story.

'Jabbie Welsh, Mr Faraday?' he asked. 'You're sure she said Jabbie Welsh?'

Martin nodded. 'Positive.'

'Now that's a queer one.' Kready rubbed the two-day stubble on his chin.

'Why?'

'Name's familiar. My daughter June, she went to Cornell and majored in history. Teaches at the NYU branch now, but anyway her thesis or whatever was a criminal history of the county, and she came across a court case—this was a few years back, mind, so I don't recall too much—but this case concerned someone named Jabbie, and I think it was Welsh. I remember it 'cause it's such a queer name, you see? Not her Christian name, but what other people called her.'

'A nickname?'

'Sort of. Anyway, this woman was widowed, and when her son, or it might have been a daughter, left her, she went crazy. People stayed away from her, but when a visitor came one time—it might have been a tax collector or such, *damn*, I wish I could remember—she killed him. Stabbed him with needles.'

'Jesus.'

'So it seems to me, Mr Faraday, that somebody's playing you a pretty sick joke.'

'You mean that someone might have been dressed up like this Jabbie Welsh?'

Kready shrugged. 'Don't know what else it would be.'

Martin laughed in disbelief. 'But why? Why would someone do that?'

'Christ, I don't know. But there's all kinds. You listen now. If that woman comes back again, just stay inside and give us a call. You got a gun?' Martin hesitated, then nodded. 'That's good. You use it if you have to.'

'Mr Kready, do you . . . or does your daughter still have the notes from that case?'

Kready licked his dry lips. 'June might have something. I'll call her. If I find out anything else, I'll get back to you.'

They talked a few minutes more until Linda came down from where she had been working in the studio. Kready seemed a bit put off when Martin introduced her as Linda Beaumont rather than Faraday, but didn't let his moral discomfort show for too long, and became positively ebullient when Linda asked him if he knew of a good carpenter in the area.

'Oh, yes, ma'am. My cousin Fred Pritchett. He's a great one for carpentry. Makes rocking chairs and other furniture and sells them to shops in Albany. What do you need done?'

Linda led him up to the master bedroom, where she showed him a built-in mahogany wardrobe that hung open like an idiot's mouth. 'It's a beautiful piece,' she said, 'but it needs refinishing and could stand a new door. The only thing is it can't be removed.'

'You think your cousin would be interested?' asked Martin.

'Oh sure. I'll have him give you a call about it.'

ᘓ ᘐ

Fred Pritchett called the next day. He sounded cheerful over the phone, and said he could get to it that week. Linda told him they would both be tied up in New York City most of the time, but promised to drop off the house key so that he could come out and work on it at his leisure.

'Do you think that's wise?' Martin asked when she told him about it. 'Letting a stranger in here after what's been happening with this crazy lady around?'

'He's not a stranger. He's the deputy's cousin.'

'I meant what if this Jabbie person would come when he's alone? She might hurt him.'

When they dropped off the key, Linda told Pritchett that they had had a little trouble with a stranger, and not to let anyone in while he was there.

'I know, Miss Beaumont. My cousin Joe told me about it. Don't worry, I'll be careful. Besides, my boy'll be with me. Thanks for the key, and you have yourself a good time in the city. We'll lock up good after we're done.'

Martin and Linda did have a good time. It was the first they had been in Manhattan together for almost two months, and in the evenings they ate at the old restaurants, visited friends, and caught some new shows.

'I'd forgotten,' said Martin one night as they were walking down Fifth Avenue, 'what this city's like when you're with someone you love.' Linda said nothing, only snuggled closer to him as if to banish the chill. They walked without speaking, turning at 44th Street toward the softly glowing marquee of the Algonquin a block away.

Linda had just started to recall to Martin a particularly clever line in the play they had just seen, when suddenly a squat, dark shape seemed to *roll* from a doorway onto the sidewalk in front of them. Linda gasped, clinging to

Martin's arm with a strength that made him wince.

It was an old woman, wrapped in so many layers of nondescript clothing that she looked like a ball of gray rags with a wizened face. One arm protruded tumor-like from the mass, thin, ungloved hands clutching a worn shopping bag filled with her life's debris. The other arm extended outward toward Martin while her voice rasped, 'A dollar, mister? You got a dollar?'

He stared at her for a few loud heartbeats, then fumbled for his wallet, from which he drew a bill. When the withered hand took it, he barely heard the mutter of thanks that followed him as he steered himself and Linda around the hag and toward the safety of the hotel. He looked back once, but the woman was gone.

They went to the Blue Bar as they had planned, and ordered their drinks. Martin drained his scotch in under a minute, and laughed hollowly. 'Christ, I've been panhandled a thousand times since I've lived in this town, and that is the *first* time I've ever felt *scared.*'

Linda kept nodding. 'I know. There was just something about her. She reminded me so much of . . .'

'Yeah. Jabbie Welsh.' He quickly signaled for another drink.

'It wasn't that she *looked* like her,' Linda said. 'It's just that . . . I thought she was going to attack us or something. God, that seems so crazy.'

Martin lit a cigarette. He had quit smoking when they moved up-state, but had bought a pack at dinner that night, to Linda's disappointment. 'We don't have to go back,' he said softly. 'We could live in the city again.'

'Are you kidding? I love that house, Martin.' She took a long pull from her glass. 'They'll catch this woman. She'll do something else crazy sooner or later.'

'We just better make sure that she doesn't do it to *us*.'

so cs

They drove back the next day, arriving just after noon. An impending storm had turned the sky to the color of dusk as they had traveled north, and light rain had just begun when they reached the end of their drive. A red mini-van was parked near the house, and a few lights glowed thinly through the sheer curtains, giving them a cloudy view of the house's interior.

'Must be Pritchett and his son,' said Linda, as Martin turned off the engine.

'Hope they haven't ruined the piece,' said Martin. 'They sure took their time getting to it.'

Linda started to walk toward the front door. 'I'm going to see how they're doing. Can you handle the bags?'

As she pushed open the door and stepped into the entrance, Linda immediately became aware of the smell. At first she thought she had left the milk on the counter to ripen for three days. But it wasn't that. It was deeper, richer than sour milk.

Then she listened, expecting to hear hammering upstairs, but the house was as silent as the empty theaters in which she had passed so much of her life.

'Mr Pritchett?' she called. There was no answer. She had just started up the stairs when Martin clattered through the door, a flight bag in each hand, an artist's case wedged under one arm.

'What's up? They're not here?'

'No one answers.' She called louder. 'Mr Pritchett?'

They waited a few seconds. Then Martin set down his bundles. 'Come on. Let's see.'

The way his voice shook alarmed Linda, but she followed him as he nearly ran up the stairs, and as they padded down the hall she was surprised to find the smell growing stronger.

It was at its height in the master bedroom, where Fred Pritchett and his son lay on the floor, their heads pillowed by velvet pools of blood, their eyes and faces pierced by innumerable puncture wounds that made them look as though they had been stricken by a disfiguring plague. Except for the riddled faces, the bodies were untouched.

Linda screamed and bit a knuckle to keep from gagging, while Martin turned away and vomited helplessly on the worn hall runner. When there was nothing left but dry, ragged gasps, he straightened up. 'The phone. We've got to call the police.'

Linda looked around in desperation. 'The gun. Let's get the gun first. She may still . . .'

Martin's voice cut at her. 'No, she's gone! They've been dead at least a day. Christ, can't you smell it?' And he lurched out of the room toward the phone in the studio. She followed, filled with the age-old terror of being alone with the dead.

Chief Montgomery and Joe Kready arrived in twenty minutes, an ambulance behind them. A state police car pulled in ten minutes later, and while the medical examiner and police photographers did their work upstairs, the two local officers talked with Linda and Martin. Kready had gone white when he saw the bodies, and the color had not returned to his face. He asked no questions, simply sat on a settee staring down at the old, patterned carpet. When the chief finished and left the room, Kready stood up and walked over to where Linda and Martin were sitting, as if he had a secret to share.

'I talked to my girl,' he said in a near-whisper, 'told her about the trouble you were havin' and asked if she knew any more about the Welsh place. . . .' He paused, and they could tell that the horrible picture upstairs was being played back in Kready's mind. 'Goddam,' he muttered. 'Sixteen years old. That boy was only sixteen. Who'd do that. Who'd want to do that? Oh, Fred . . . oh, Jesus H. Christ . . .'

'Mr Kready,' Linda said gently, 'I'm so sorry. Please, please sit down.'

Kready shook his head and blinked away tears. 'No. No thank you, miss,

I'm all right. . . . Anyways, June sounded real funny when I told her about this. She said to me to tell you to be careful, that there were other peculiar stories hooked up to your house. Well, I knew you were gonna be away for a few days, but I forgot about . . . about Fred and Terry comin' out. I just forgot.' His voice started to bubble again, but he cleared his throat and went on. 'She's comin' up to town tonight, June is. She said she wanted to meet you two, talk to you about all this. Could you come over?'

Martin nodded. 'I don't think we'll want to stay in the house anymore. Not while that maniac is loose. What time?'

They left the house and the corpses to the mercies of the police, packed their bags, and checked into the Holiday Inn south of town. After a quick shower and a scarcely touched dinner, they drove to the Kready's house and arrived at eight.

June Kready was a solemn, dark-haired girl, too buxom to be stylish. She wore the frank, unassuming expression of one who cares more for the company of books than of people. She came straight to the point.

'Your house has a bad history, Mr Faraday.' Linda lifted her head, wanting the girl to address her as well, but June's gaze remained on Martin. 'You might have heard a little about it, but not all, I imagine.'

Martin told her what he and Linda had learned from the realtor, as well as what Kready, seated uncomfortably in a fully erect lounger, had told them of Jabbie Welsh.

June nodded throughout the narrative. 'There's more to it,' she said, 'and a few mistakes as well. When her husband didn't come back from the war, Rachel Welsh went slowly mad. Paranoid, I suppose. She believed people were trying to take her house away, seduce her daughter, who knows what else. She knitted constantly, and was never without a skein of gray yarn and her needles. Her neighbors gave her the nickname Jabbie, in part because of her chattering conversation, but mostly because of the way she used her knitting needles to make a point, or to ward off her imaginary persecutors.

'One of those "persecutors" went a little too far and paid for it. He was a tax collector, name of Crane. The daughter, Eleanor, handled most of her mother's business affairs, but it got to the point where she couldn't bear to live with the old woman anymore, and didn't have the guts to have her committed. She left her mother and married a young man named Washburn who'd been trying to court her, much to her mother's displeasure. This supposed desertion sent her over the edge, and when this Crane came out to the house to inquire after the delinquent taxes, Jabbie Welsh killed him, stabbed him with those kitting needles.

'In the eye?' Martin asked. Linda thought he looked horrified, yet fascinated.

June Kready shook her head. 'The accounts don't say. They were pretty circumspect about such details back then. At any rate, Crane's wife reported him missing, and knew that he had been planning to go to the Welsh home, so the law came out to investigate. They found Crane dead on the front porch, and Jabbie Welsh inside the house, sitting and knitting by a cold fireside. When the sheriff and his men tried to take her, she attacked them, and one of them struck her in self-defense. She fell against the fireplace, her head hit the bricks, and she shattered her skull. Died instantly. A few weeks later Washburn and the daughter moved back in, and the house stayed in the Washburn family right up until you bought it.'

Martin nodded. 'Except for Jabbie Welsh's death, that pretty well jibes with what we've heard.'

'There's more,' said June, and her puritanically solemn face grew even more rigid. 'Supposedly, Jabbie Welsh appeared again. In 1895, one of a pair of tramps the household had turned away was found dead in a nearby grove of trees, his eyes and face pierced by some sharp object. His friend said they were going to sleep there that night when an old woman stepped from behind a tree and started to stab his companion with long needles. *He* was found guilty of the crime and hanged.

'Then in 1919, when the family returned from a short vacation, they found a traveling drummer dead on the lawn. He had been stabbed, the wounds centering on the head. The murder was unsolved.

'The most recent occurrence'—she looked sadly at her father—'not including what happened today, was in 1937. A young couple was parking in the driveway of the house, again at a time the family was away. The girl said that someone came up to the car and began stabbing her boyfriend through the open window. She didn't say whether she thought it was a man or a woman, since what happened affected her reason. She died a few years later in the state asylum. And that,' she concluded, 'has been the unpleasant history of the Welsh house.'

All four of them were quiet for a minute. Then Linda's high laugh broke the silence. 'You don't mean to tell me, Miss Kready, that a ghost has been responsible for what happened today?'

June looked at her with strangely cold eyes. 'Can you come up with a better explanation, Miss Beaumont?'

'But the *physical* aspects,' Martin said, 'the fact that people were actually killed, not by fright, but by stabbing—doesn't that rule out anything supernatural?'

June shrugged. 'Does it? If psychic research has any validity at all, there are some ghosts that transcend the merely ethereal. Poltergeists, for instance.'

'But that's broken crockery,' Linda said angrily. 'Pranks. We're talking about *murder*.'

'What's the difference?' said June. 'If a ghost can throw a dish, why not a knife or a spear? If it can turn a doorknob, why couldn't it pull a trigger?'

Martin cleared his throat. 'There's something else we're forgetting. Jabbie Welsh was mad. A lunatic. So wouldn't her . . . her ghost tend toward the same random violence?'

'It might,' June agreed, 'but I don't think those killings were random. The victims might have been seen by a paranoid mind as interlopers, threats to the family or the house.'

'All right!' Linda said. 'Assuming all this *bullshit* to be true, what do we do about it? Call the *National Enquirer* and try to get their cover?' She felt furious at both the bizarre turn the talk had taken, and the way in which June Kready had studiously ignored her.

'You can do two things,' said June, her calm irritating Linda all the more. 'You can leave the house, try and sell it, maybe burn it down, or——'

'Destroy her.'

They all turned, surprised to hear Joe Kready's deep voice. He had not spoken since they arrived, and Martin had almost forgotten he was there. But now he rose from the lounger, his tall form looking like some spirit-possessed evangelist in the dim light.

'Destroy her,' he repeated. 'It should have been done years ago. I should have known what she was when you first told me about her, Mr Faraday.' His eyes were hollow, and his expression begged forgiveness for whatever misplaced guilt he felt. 'I should've figured it out. If I had, Fred and Terry'd still be alive.'

June put her arm around Kready's shoulders. 'Daddy, there was no way to know.' She shook her head. 'We don't even know now for sure. It all sounds so crazy.'

'No,' said Martin quietly. 'On the contrary, it all makes sense.'

'Martin, are you——'

'Just a minute, Linda. June's right. There's no other explanation. We're dealing with a ghost here. A physical ghost, who's strong enough and solid enough . . . and mad enough to kill. Only we've got to finish her first before she kills again.'

'Oh, that's *great*, Martin,' Linda said. 'That's just fucking *great*! There's some wacko around here killing people *in our house*, and all you can do is leap on the lunatic fringe bandwagon. Well, not me, ace! You can take your crucifixes and wooden stakes and shove 'em! I'm going back to the city.' She snatched up her coat from the sofa and stormed to the door.

'Linda, I——'

'Miss Kready, will you give my . . . *friend* a ride back to the motel?' June nodded.

'Yeah, I'll just bet you will. I'll leave the key at the front desk, Martin. I'll be at Charlotte's if you . . .'

She didn't finish, merely opened the door and slammed it behind her. There was dead silence in the room.

'I'm . . . sorry. I apologize for her. She's been under a strain with everything, and——'

'Forget it, Mr Faraday,' June said. 'Even with all the facts it sounds crazy to me too.'

'It's crazy, but it's real,' said Joe Kready. 'And it's gotta be stopped. what do you say, Mr Faraday? It's your property, but that thing killed *m* cousin and his boy.'

Martin automatically dug into his pocket, only to realize he had smoked his last cigarette on the drive up from the city. June offered him a Winston and he took it. 'All right, Mr Kready. I'm willing on one condition. That's that before we try to destroy this . . . this *ghost*, we make sure, dead certain that it *is* what we think it is, and not just some crackbrained old woman. I don't want the police coming after us with a murder charge.

Kready smiled grimly. 'I *am* the police. But all right. What you say makes sense.'

Martin looked at June. 'What about you, Miss Kready? Are you coming with us?' He hoped she was. She seemed oddly confident, and made the lunacy sound real, the solution practical.

June Kready smiled for the first time and nodded. 'I'll be there. Folklore's a lot more interesting close-up.'

'Anyone else?'

'I got a brother Bob,' Kready said, 'and Fred had two, Cyrus and Frank. They'll help us out, along with Fred's older boy, Wyatt. That's seven of us.'

'Seven,' June said. 'Lucky number.'

'Yesterday I'd have laughed at that as a superstition,' Martin said. 'Today I'm not so sure. But are they going to go along with this ghost stuff?'

'They'll believe me,' nodded Kready, 'and if not me, June. They know she's no fool.'

'So . . . when do we do it?'

June shrugged. 'I don't think it matters. Jabbie Welsh has appeared both day and night. Why not tomorrow afternoon? That'll give us time to get ahold of the others.'

'All right. What shall I bring? I've got a gun out at the house.'

'I know,' said Kready. 'That'll be good. I'll bring a pistol for June and a shotgun for myself.'

'And something made of iron,' June said. 'A sword, an ax maybe.'

Martin felt a lump come into his throat. An ax, Jesus.

'Well, we'd better get back to your motel, Mr Faraday. We've got a strange day ahead of us.'

On the way to the Holiday Inn, June and Martin's conversation was more relaxed. It seemed to him that the battle plans had been made, and now the soldiers could talk about themselves and each other for a while. The first time she called him Mr Faraday, he told her to make it Martin, but her reaction was not what he'd hoped for. Instead of further loosening her up, the remark made her more distant, and she called him nothing at all.

It was not until he heard the sound of her car driving away that he realized he had been wanting to sleep with her, partly to get rid of the tension that was knotting his gut, and partly to strike back at Linda. He thought about calling her at Charlotte's, but remembered that she would still be on the road, so he had a drink in the bar, and went to sleep watching Arsenio Hall.

ꝏ ꝏ

June called him at ten the next morning and asked him if one o'clock was all right to start out. He agreed and tried to work the rest of the morning on some roughs, but found it useless, and ended up watching game shows. When June picked him up at one, Joe Kready was with her, along with a heavy-set, red-faced man of about fifty who Joe introduced as Bob, his brother. The others, Joe said, would meet them at the house.

The sky threatened snow. It was cold enough for it, and Martin wished he had worn something heavier than his wind-breaker. The Kready men both had on red wool hunting jackets, and the contrast made Martin feel all the colder in the poorly heated car.

The three Pritchetts were there when they arrived, huddled together in an old green pickup truck. Cyrus and Frank, Fred's brothers, seemed bluffly hearty, as if they were about to start on a deer hunt. But Fred's son Wyatt was as grim as death, and merely nodded when Joe introduced Martin. The seven of them looked, Martin thought, like a small army. Most of the men had a rifle or a shotgun, as well as a holstered pistol on their belts. Cyrus and Bob had hatchets dangling from loops in their poplin trousers.

'What kinda gun you got, Mr Faraday?' Frank asked.

'A .22 revolver. Only it's in the house.'

'Ah, screw that. Wait a minute.' He reached into the back of the pickup and withdrew a red canvas case. He unzipped it and took out a rifle. 'Here ya go. Thirty aught six. This'll stop whoever we find a helluva lot better than your popgun. She's already loaded, so be careful.'

'How we gonna do this?' asked Wyatt sullenly. 'Junie, what do we do?'

She answered while she stuck a clip into her pistol and chambered the first round. 'I hate to say this, but I think we ought to split up. Not alone, though. Pairs. I don't think she'll appear if there are so many of us together. She could be scared off.'

Cyrus laughed bitterly. 'If what you say's true, Junie, that one ain't scared of the devil.'

'What do we do if she shows?' asked Bob.

'Don't shoot first,' said June. 'Ask her to give herself up. She won't. She'll most likely come at you with the needles, so be ready. Do whatever you can. If you can kill her, do it.'

They were all silent for a moment. Then Frank said shyly, 'Should we say a few words first? A prayer?'

Joe Kready nodded and bowed his head. They all followed suit, and Martin looked down at the ground. 'Lord,' Joe intoned, 'help us to do Your will. We don't understand what's been happening here, but if there's evil, help us search it out and destroy it. Watch over us, and over the souls of Fred and Terry. We pray in Jesus' name, Amen.' He straightened up and looked at the others with a firm resolve. 'All right, June, you and Mr Faraday come with me, Bob with Wyatt, Cyrus with Frank. We'll take the house. Bob, just roam around outside. Cyrus, Frank, look to the grove. Stay together. You see anything funny, give a holler.'

They all moved cautiously away, as if expecting to kick a rabbit from the dry brush. Joe, June, and Martin walked up the porch steps and into the house. The smell still remained, and June wrinkled her nose at it. They went single file through the first floor, Joe leading, then June, with Martin securing the rear.

The second floor was next. Martin looked out the window of the large front room and saw Bob and Wyatt moving behind the woodshed. He could see the grove, but Cyrus and Frank were hidden by the thickly grown trees.

Suddenly he heard a gasp from June. He swung around and saw her standing in the hall, just outside the door. 'There!' she cried, and pointed toward the stairs. In a second Martin and Joe were by her side. Her hand dropped, and both men looked toward the top of the stairs. There was nothing.

'She was there,' said June, panic edging her voice. 'An old woman dressed in black, standing at the top of the stairs. Then she . . . she blanked out—just disappeared.'

A gun crashed outside, then another. A man's scream cut the air, and Kready dashed to the window. 'Cyrus!' he yelled.

Martin and June were beside him instantly. Through the window they saw Cyrus Pritchett running empty-handed from the grove of trees. Even at that distance they could see the terror on his face.

Then there burst from the thick trees a woman in black who Martin knew was Jabbie Welsh. Her speed belied her thick skirts, and she caught up with Cyrus long before he reached the doorway. As the man turned his head to look back in horror, she struck with the needle she wielded in her right hand.

Martin saw the sharp metal flash dully, piercing Cyrus's cheek as easily as if it had been dry parchment. He thought he saw the red point protrude from the underside of the man's chin, but couldn't be sure.

As he watched Cyrus fall, watched the old woman straddle his body and plunge her needles again and again into his upturned, screaming face which grew redder and wetter every moment, Martin felt that he watched in a dream and was powerless to move, be it to flee or to help the man who lay dying outside his house.

Joe Kready muttered a strangled curse and ran from the room, his voice growing louder as he careened down the stairs, until he was screaming in hate and rage. Then Martin heard June's voice soft beside him.

'But she was *here*. She was up *here*.' The girl seemed, like Martin, drugged by the sight of the drama below. As they watched, they saw Bob and Wyatt beat Joe Kready to the woman. Wyatt was in the lead, and when he was less than five yards from the woman, he pointed his .12 gauge at her and let fly with both barrels.

The shot caught her high in the chest, shoving her back and away from Cyrus, who had finally stopped moving. Martin saw the lead hit, saw the black satin and lace tear apart, saw skin and muscle and blood laid bare by that tremendous wad of shot.

And he saw too the woman quickly get to her hands and knees, stand, and run toward an unbelieving Wyatt Pritchett like a nightmare sprinter, leaving a stream of blood in her wake.

She dug the thin spikes into the boy's head, driving him to the ground, while Bob Kready pumped round after round into her from his rifle. Her body jerked as each slug hit, and she seemed disoriented for a moment after one bullet pierced the left side of her forehead, scattering pieces of her into the air like obscene confetti. But she merely shook herself and fell to with the needles once again.

'How? My God, how?' Martin heard June's voice through an aural fog that thickened each word.

Now Bob was swinging his rifle at Jabbie Welsh, slamming it against the sodden mass of flesh that his slug had exposed. But still she kept stabbing the slick, red face of Wyatt Pritchett.

'How can she do that? How can she be so strong?'

Joe Kready came into view, springing across the driveway with his hatchet raised like a crazed Indian in a western movie. Screaming, he buried it deep in the woman's back and fell upon her, bearing her to the ground. She twisted beneath him, and shot one of her needles out and up, catching Kready directly in the soft round cavity just above the breastbone. He gave a quick, bubbling gasp through the newly made hole, and folded into death.

'How?' June Kready whispered, gazing at the still body of her father on the ground below, not moving, both she and Martin trapped like a pair of deer in a headlight's beams. 'I don't believe it . . .'

Then it came to Martin, a needle of crystal driven into his own eyes, stabbing the wisdom deep into his brain. 'Belief,' he said, and then louder, '*belief.*'

Jabbie Welsh was after Bob now. He had thrown down his rifle when Joe had died, and stood helpless for a pair of heartbeats. Then he turned and ran toward the pickup truck. His weight made him slow, and with uncanny ease she caught him and bore him down, out of Martin and June's sight, on the other side of the truck. He screamed three times, while ribbons of blood coursed into the air like gay, red streamers, spattering the truck top.

'She's strong because we believe,' said Martin, and it suddenly seemed so simple, so elemental, that he knew he was right. When he turned to June, his face was alive again, his eyes glowing with the certainty of his knowledge. 'Stop!' he cried. 'Don't think of her, don't look at her——'

'She killed my father!'

'Forget it! She's not *there*, she's *not*! She doesn't——'

'She's real! She's there now! She killed them all!'

Martin shook her so roughly that her teeth snapped shut on her tongue, and she gasped with the pain. 'You're wrong! Look out there . . . look out, but *don't see her*!'

He turned back to the window and looked down. Bodies littered the yard, and Martin thought he saw, just for an instant, an old woman, pale and ethereal, whose name he made himself forget. Then she was gone: the image winked out like a candle, and disbelief poured its cooling waters on his mind.

'She's *there*!' June screamed. 'Oh my God, *look*! She's there!'

Martin looked, saw nothing. His fingernails bit into the heel of his hand as he struggled to maintain his self-imposed ignorance.

'She——' June stopped, then turned toward the door to the hall. Martin saw her eyes go wide, and she threw up her hand in front of her to ward off something only she saw.

Her right eye collapsed into a red ruin, and she shed tears of blood and fluid. Then her arms dropped, and she stood like a lamb accepting the slaughter.

Nothing there . . .

An indentation appeared in her cheek, deepened, and the flesh parted as if of its own accord. Her mouth fell open, the muscle holding it closed torn by . . .

Torn by fancy, torn by imagination . . .

She fell to her knees, and Martin watched as the red marks appeared, one after another, in open mouth, running eyes, fragile cheek, nose, forehead, chin, neck . . .

Nothing! Only her belief, her BELIEF!

And Martin Faraday closed his eyes to banish the crazy vision, the thing that could not be. He threw himself to the floor, blotting out his thoughts, pulling blackness into his brain to deaden his mind, to eclipse the belief that could bring him death. . . .

. . . to destroy himself before he could be destroyed.

That was how the chief and two state policemen found him that evening, after Cyrus Pritchett's wife and Mary called him and said that Cyrus and Frank had gone out to Martin Faraday's house and hadn't come back.

Cyrus, Wyatt, Bob, and Joe were all dead, scattered among the leaves on the lawn and driveway. They found Frank Pritchett in the grove of trees. June Kready's mutilated body lay less than a yard from where Martin Faraday cowered, drawn into a fetal position, open eyes seeing nothing. He did not respond even when the chief slapped him sharply in the face.

ᘐ ᘓ

Three weeks later Linda Beaumont handed Charlotte Peters a cup of instant coffee and sat down beside her on the sofa of the living-room of what had been the Welsh house. Charlotte, a hard-faced woman in her late thirties, was helping Linda, who did not want to be alone in the house, to pack. It was late afternoon, and they were nearly finished. They wanted to be away from the house before nightfall.

'Never?' asked Charlotte.

Linda shook her head. 'They don't think so. It's as if his mind just . . . just blacked out completely, like all his thought processes were switched off.'

Charlotte sipped her coffee. 'What's the hospital like?'

'Horrible.' Linda shivered. 'But it doesn't matter. He has no idea where he is. He probably never *will* know. And they'll never find out the truth.'

'The truth,' said Charlotte. 'Honey, we already know the truth.'

'I'm . . . not sure. . . .'

Charlotte sighed. 'Don't get on this Jabbie Welsh thing again—it'll drive you crazy too.'

'I've been trying to tell myself they're right,' Linda said. 'That after I told Martin about the old woman, he *imagined* Jabbie Welsh and the needles, and that's why there weren't any scratches on the door. Maybe it *was* a drifter who killed the two workmen. And then maybe the stories and the killings influenced Martin to . . .' Linda broke off. 'No. No. I can't believe it.'

She took another sip of coffee, and suddenly tears burst from her eyes. 'Oh God, Charlotte, Martin loved this place so . . . and he was so kind, so gentle, he couldn't have done it. . . .'

The older woman put her arms around Linda. 'Okay, baby, shh, it's okay.'

'How could he?'

'I don't know . . . I don't. But he did.'

Linda's eyes grew large as she blinked away tears. 'No, I *saw* her. I saw her that first time.' She looked up into her friend's face. 'The old woman.'

Charlotte shook her head. 'You saw an old woman, nothing more. She never came back, but when you told Martin about her, it triggered something in him, and——'

'No, Charlotte!' Linda's eyes were huge now, and alive with purpose. 'Martin didn't kill them!'

'Who did?' Charlotte demanded. 'Who did, Linda? Who else could have? Jabbie Welsh? A ghost?'

'*Yes!*'

The word hissed through the room, and Charlotte pushed herself back from Linda, frightened by the force and the secret meaning of the word.

'Yes,' Linda repeated, in a voice so soft that Charlotte had to strain to hear. 'I believe it now. I honestly——'

But the sharp knock at the door interrupted her.

The Cairnwell Horror

'A MONSTER, DO YOU SUPPOSE? A genetic freak that's remained alive for centuries?'

'Undoubtedly, Michael. With two heads, three sets of genitals, and a curse for those who mock.' George McCormack, sole heir to Cairnwell Castle, raised a three-by-five-inch card on which lay a line of cocaine. 'I propose a toast—of sorts—to it then. Old beast, old troll, nemesis of my old great-however-many-times-granddad, whom I shall finally meet next week.' A quick snort, and the powder was gone.

George smiled, relishing the rush, the coziness of his den, the company, and found himself thinking about asking Michael to spend the night. He was about to make the suggestion when Michael asked, 'Why twenty-one, do you suppose? If it's all that important, why not earlier?'

'Coming of age, Michael. As you well know, all males are virgins until that age, and no base liquors or, ahem, controlled substances have passed their pristine lips or nostrils. Other than that, I can't bloody well tell you until after next week, and even then, according to that same stifling and weary tradition, I must keep the deep, dark family secret all to my lonesome.'

'Yes, but if you don't pay any more attention to *that* tradition than you do to the others, well . . .'

'Ah, will I tell, you're thinking? In all likelihood, if there's a pound to be made on it, yes, I damned well will. I've thought the whole thing was asinine ever since I was a kid. And the five thousand pounds your little rag offers can pay for an awful lot of raped tradition.'

'So when'll you be leaving London for the bogs?'

'The *bogs*?' George snorted. 'Careful, mate. That's my castle you're speaking of.'

'I thought it was your father's.'

'Yes, well.' George frowned. 'It doesn't appear he'll be around much longer to take care of things.'

'You've asked him what the secret is, I suppose.'

'Christ, dozens of times. Always the same answer: "You're better off not knowing until the time comes." Yeah. Pardon me while I tremble with fear. Bunch of shit anyway. When I was a kid, I spent hours looking for secret panels, hidden crypts, all that rubbish, and not a thing did I find. After a while, I just got bored with it.'

'Ever see any ghosts?'

George gave Michael a withering glare. 'No,' he said flatly. 'Whatever plagues the McCormacks, it's not ghosts.' He hurled a soft pillow at his friend. '*Jesus*, will you stop jotting down those notes—it's driving me mad!'

'George, this *is* an interview, and you *are* being paid.'

'I'm just not used to being grilled.'

'You knew I was a journalist when we became . . . friends.'

'You were about to say lovers.' George smiled cheekily. 'And why not?'

'We haven't been lovers for months.'

'No fault of mine.'

Michael shook his head. 'I'm here to do a job, not . . . rekindle memories. I didn't suggest your bogey story to David because I wanted to start things up again.'

'And I didn't agree to talk to you because I wanted to start things up either,' George lied. 'I agreed to it because of the money. We're having a lovely little hundred-pound chat. And if I decide to spill the beans after next week, we'll have an even lovelier five-thousand-pound chat.' George stood and stretched, bending his neck back and around in a gesture that he hoped Michael would find erotic.

'And I'm happy to keep it on those terms,' Michael said.

George stopped twisting his neck. 'Bully for you. Do you want to go up to Cairnwell with me next week?'

'I didn't know I was invited.'

'Of course you are.' George grinned. 'And I'll tell them exactly what you're there for—to expose the secret of Cairnwell Castle, should I care to reveal it to the whole drooling world. That should make old Maxwell shit his britches. You'll come?'

'Wouldn't miss it. Thank you.'

'I assume then you'll foot my traveling expenses? My taste for the finer things has laid me low financially once again, and that damned Maxwell won't send a penny. Once I'm laird of the manor, let me tell you the first thing I'm doing is finding a new solicitor.'

ꕥ

Cairnwell Castle was as ungainly a pile of stones as was ever raised. Even though George had grown up there, he always felt intimidated by the formidable gray block that heaved itself out of the low Scottish landscape like a megalithic frowning head. Often when he was a child, he awoke in the middle of the night and, realizing what it was that he was within, would cry until his mother came and held him and sang to him until he fell asleep. His father had not approved of his behavior, but his mother always came when he cried, right up until the week that she died, and was no longer able. From then on, he cried himself back to sleep.

'Dear God, that's an ugly building,' Michael remarked.

'Isn't it. You see why I came down to London as quickly as my little adolescent legs would carry me.'

As they drove into the massive court, charmlessly formed by two blocky wings of dirty stone, they saw an older man dressed in tweeds standing at the front door. 'Maxwell,' George said. 'Richard Maxwell.'

The man looked every day of his sixty-odd years, and wore the constant look of mild disapproval with which George had always associated him. His eyebrows raised as he observed George's spiky blond hair and the small diamond twinkling in his left ear. They raised even higher when he learned Michael Spencer's profession, and he asked to speak to George alone.

Leaving Michael in the entryway, Maxwell led George into a huge, starkly furnished antechamber, and closed the massive door behind them. 'What do you think you're doing bringing a journalist with you?' he said.

'I think I'm doing the world a favor by sharing the secret of the lairds of Cairnwell, so we can stop living in some Gothic storybook, Maxwell, *that's* what I'm doing.'

Maxwell's ruddy complexion turned pale. 'You'd expose the secret?'

'If it turns out to be as absurd as I think it will.'

'You cannot. You *dare* not.'

'Spare me the histrionics, Maxwell. I'm sure you've been practicing your lines for months now, looking forward to my birthday tomorrow, but it's really getting a bit thick.'

'You don't understand, George. It's not the nature of the secret itself that will keep you from exposing it—though I daresay you'll want to keep it as quiet as all your ancestors have. Rather, it's the terms of the inheritance that will insure your silence.' Maxwell smiled smugly. 'If you ever reveal what you see tomorrow, you lose Cairnwell and all your family's holdings. All told, it comes to half a million.'

'Lose it! How the hell can I lose it? I'm sole heir.'

'You can lose it to charity, as stipulated in the document written and signed by the seventeenth laird of Cairnwell and extending into perpetuity. I've made you a copy, which you'll receive tomorrow. It further states that you're to spend nine months out of every year at Cairnwell, and, *if* you have a male heir'—here Maxwell curled his lip—'the secret's to be revealed to him on his twenty-first birthday. Any departure from these stipulations means that you forfeit the castle. Understood?'

George smiled grimly. 'Thought of everything, haven't you?'

'Not me. Your four-times, great-grandfather.'

'Sly old bastard.'

'Now,' Maxwell went on, ignoring the comment, 'I would like you to dismiss that journalist and come see your father. He's been waiting for you.'

George walked slowly out to the entryway, where Michael was waiting.

'I'm afraid I've rather bad news,' he said, and watched Michael's lips tighten. 'You can't stay. I'm sorry.'

'I can't *stay*?' The last word leapt, George thought, at least an octave.

'No. It's part of the . . . tradition, you see.'

'Oh, for Christ's sake, George, you mean I motored all the way up to this godforsaken pile for nothing?'

'I'll be in touch as soon as it's over,' George said quietly, fearing that Maxwell would overhear.

'Christ . . .'

'I didn't *know*. But I'll call you, I swear. I said I was sorry.'

Michael gave him the same look as when he had told George that he didn't think they should see each other anymore. 'All right then. Come and get your bloody bags.'

Michael opened the boot, roughly handed George his luggage, and drove away with no words of farewell. George watched the car disappear over the fields, then went to visit his father in the largest bedchamber of the castle.

The twenty-second laird of Cairnwell was propped up on an overstuffed chaise, and George was shocked at the change in his father since his last visit over six months before.

The cancer had been progressing merrily along. At least another thirty pounds had been sucked off the old man's frame. What was left of the muscles hung like doughy pouches on the massive skeleton. The skin was a wrapping of faded parchment, a lesion all of its own. There was no hope in the eyes, and the smell of death—of sour vomit and diseased bowels, of bloody mucus coughed from riddled lungs—was everywhere.

His father was the castle. What the man had become was nothing less than Cairnwell itself, a massive tumor of the soul that grew and festered like the lichen on the gray stone.

Then, just for a moment, trapped within the rotting hulk, George glimpsed his father as he had been when George was a boy and his father was young. But the moment passed, and, expressionless, he walked to his father's side, leaned over, and kissed the leathery cheek, nearly choking at the smell that rose from the fresh stains on the velvet dressing gown.

They talked, shortly and uncomfortably, saying nothing of the revelation of the secret the next day except for setting the time when the three of them should meet in the morning. Eight thirty-five was the appointed hour, the time of George's birth.

That night, George could not sleep, so he sat by the fireplace long past midnight, thinking about Cairnwell and its hold on his father, its unhealthy, even cancerous hold on all the McCormacks. He thought about the way the castle had sapped his father's strength, and, years before, his mother's. Although she had never known the secret, she nonetheless had shared the burden of it with her husband, and, being far weaker than he, she had been quickly consumed by it, just after George's eighth birthday.

Then he thought about his debts, about nine months of every year spent at Cairnwell, about the horror that he was to see tomorrow.

When sleep finally came, it was dreamless.

The next morning dawned gray and misty, with no sunlight to banish the shadows that hung in every cold, high-ceilinged room. George rose, showered, and put on a jacket and tie rather than one of the sweaters he usually wore. In spite of his anger over the hereditary charade, he felt the situation demanded a touch of formality. He even removed the diamond from his ear.

His father and Maxwell were already breakfasting when George arrived in the dining hall: Maxwell on rashers and eggs, his father on weak tea and toast cubes. George took the vacant chair.

'Good morning, George,' his father said in a thin, reedy tone. The old man wore a black suit that hung on him like a blanket on a scarecrow. The white shirtfront was already stained in several places. 'Have some breakfast?'

George shook his head. 'A cup of coffee, that's all,' he said, and poured himself some from a silver teapot.

Maxwell smiled. 'Off your feed today? Can't say I blame you. It's a difficult thing.'

'Enough, Richard,' said George's father. 'No need to upset him. He'll see soon enough.'

'I'm not upset, Father,' said George, with a cool glance at Maxwell. 'I'll wait to hear Mr Maxwell's bogey story. I hope he won't disappoint me.'

Maxwell flushed, and George hoped he was about to choke on a rasher, but he cleared his throat and smiled again. 'I don't think you'll be disappointed, *Master* George.'

'I said enough—both of you.' The elder McCormack looked at the pair with disapproval. 'This is not to be treated lightly. Indeed, Richard, this may be the most serious moment of George's life, so please conduct yourself as befits your position. You also, George. You shall soon be laird of Cairnwell, so start behaving as such.' The voice was pale and weak, but the underlying tone held a rigid intensity that wiped the sardonic smiles from the other two faces.

'Now,' McCormack went on, 'I think it's time.'

Maxwell rose. 'Are you sure you don't want the wheelchair?'

'What'll you do, carry it down the stairs? No, I'll walk today as my father walked in front of me nearly forty years ago.'

'But your health . . .'

'Life holds nothing more for me, Richard. If death comes as a result of what happens today, so much the better. I'm very tired. It's made me very tired.'

At first George thought that his father was referring to the cancer, but something told him this was not the case, and the implications made him shiver.

He rose and followed his father and Maxwell as they left the room, passed down the hall, through a small alcove, and into a little-used study. Maxwell drew back the curtains of the room, allowing a sickly light to enter through grimy beveled panes. Then he dragged a wooden chair over to a high bookcase, stepped up on it, removed several volumes from the top shelf, and turned what George assumed was a hidden knob. Then he descended, flipped back a corner of a faded Oriental rug, and scrabbled with his fingers for a near-invisible handhold. Finding it, he pulled the trap door up so easily that George assumed it must be counterweighted.

'Good Christ,' said George with a touch of awe. 'It's just like a thirties horror film. No wonder I never found it.'

'Don't feel stupid,' said Maxwell, not unkindly. 'No one has ever discovered it on their own.' He then opened a closet, inside which were three kerosene lamps.

'No flashlights?' asked George.

'Tradition,' said Maxwell, lighting the lamps with his Dunhill and handing one each to George and his father, keeping the third for himself. Looking at McCormack, he said in a voice that held just the hint of a tremor, 'Shall I lead the way?'

McCormack nodded. 'Please. I'll follow, and George, stay behind me.' There was no trembling in McCormack's voice, only a rugged tenacity.

Maxwell stepped gently into the abyss, as if fearing the steps would collapse beneath him, but George saw that they were stone, and realized that Maxwell, for all his previous bravado, was actually quite hesitant to confront whatever lay below.

They descended for a long time, and, although he did not count them, George guessed that the steps numbered well over two hundred. The walls of the stairway were stone, and appeared to be quite as old as the castle itself.

Halfway down, Maxwell explained briefly: 'This was built during the border wars. If the castle was stormed, the laird and retainers could hide down here with provisions to last six months. It was never used for that purpose, however.'

He said no more. By the time they reached the bottom of the stairs, the temperature had fallen ten degrees. The walls were green with damp mold, and George started as he heard a scuffling somewhere ahead of them.

'Rats,' his father said. 'Just rats.'

For another thirty meters they walked down a long passage that gradually grew in width from two meters to nearly five. George struggled to peer past Maxwell and his father, trying to make forms out of the shadows their lanterns cast. Then he saw the door.

It appeared to be made of one piece of massive oak, crisscrossed with wide iron bands like a giant's chessboard. Directly in the center of its vast expanse was a black-brown blotch of irregular shape, looking, in the dim light, like a huge squashed spider. Maxwell and McCormack stopped five meters away, and turned toward George.

'Now it begins,' said McCormack, and his eyes were sad. 'Go with your lantern to the door, George, and look at what is mounted there.'

George obeyed, walking slowly toward the door, the lantern held high in front of him protectively, almost ceremonially. For a moment he wished he had a crucifix.

At first he could not identify the thing that was nailed to the oaken door. But he suddenly realized that it was a skin of some kind, a deerskin perhaps, that centuries of dampness and decay had darkened to this dried and blackened parody before him.

But deer, he told himself, do not have pairs of breasts that sag like large, decayed mushrooms, or fingers that hang like rotted willow leaves. Or a face with a round, thick-lipped gap for a mouth, a broad flap of bulbous skin for a nose, twin pits of deep midnight in shriveled pouches for eyes. And he knew beyond doubt that mounted on that door with weary, rusting nails was the flayed skin of a woman.

He struggled to hold it back, but the bile came up instantly, and he bent over, closed his eyes, and let it rain down upon the stone floor. When it was over, he spit several times and blew his nose into a handkerchief, then looked at the two older men. 'I'm sorry.'

'Don't be,' his father said. 'I did the same thing the first time.' He looked at the skin. 'Now it's just like a wall-hanging.'

'What the hell is it?' asked George, repelled yet fascinated, hardly daring to look at the thing again.

'The mortal remains,' said Maxwell, 'of the first wife of the sixteenth laird of Cairnwell.' The words were mechanical, as if he had been practicing them for a long time.

'The wife . . .' George looked at the skin on the door. 'Was she a black? Or did the tanning——'

Maxwell interrupted. 'Yes, she was an African native the laird met as a young man on a trading voyage, the daughter of a priest of one of the tribes of Gambia. The ship traded with the tribe, and the laird, Brian McCormack, saw the woman dance. Apparently she was a great beauty as blacks go, and he became infatuated with her. Later he claimed she had put a spell on him.'

George was shaking his head in disbelief. 'A spell?' he asked, a confused and erratic half-smile on his lips. 'Are you serious, Maxwell? Father, is this for real?'

McCormack nodded. 'It's real. And under the circumstances, I believe that she *did* bewitch him. Let Maxwell continue.'

'Spell or no,' Maxwell went on smoothly, 'he brought her back with him, she posing as a servant he'd taken on. The captain of the ship—and Brian's employee—had secretly married them on board, and by the time they docked in Leith, she was, technically, Lady Cairnwell.'

A low, rich laugh of relief started to bubble out of George. 'My God,' he said, while his father and Maxwell stared at him like priests at a defiler of the

Host. 'That's the secret then? That's what kept this family shamed for over three hundred years, that we've some black blood in the line?' His laughter slowly faded. 'Back then I can understand. But now? This is the 1990s—no one cares about that anymore. Besides, whatever genetic effect she would have had is long gone, and this "Cairnwell Horror" isn't anything more than racial paranoia.'

'You're wrong, George,' said Maxwell. 'I've not yet told you of the horror. That was still to come. Will you simply listen while I finish?' His voice was angry, yet controlled, and George, taken aback, nodded acquiescence.

'Brian McCormack,' Maxwell went on, 'once back in Scotland, quickly realized his mistake. Whether through diminished lust or the failure of the spell, we can't know. At any rate, he wanted a quiet divorce, and the woman returned to Gambia. She refused to be divorced, but he made arrangements to have her transported back to Africa anyway. She overheard his plan and told him that if she was forced to leave him, she would expose their marriage to the world. Why he didn't have her killed immediately is a mystery, as it was well within his power. Perhaps he still felt a warped affection for her.

'So he locked her away down here, entrusting her secret to only one servant. The others, who had thought her Brian's mistress, were told she had been sent away, and were greatly relieved by the fact.

'Brian then wooed and married an earl's daughter, Fiona McTavish, and the world had no reason to suspect that it was his second wedding. There was a problem with the match, however. Fiona was barren, and no doctor could rectify the situation. After several years of trying to sire a son, Brian asked his first wife to help with her magic. She offered to do so with an eagerness that made him suspicious, and he warned her that if Fiona should suffer any ill consequences from the magic, he would not hesitate to painfully kill the woman. Then he brought her the things she asked for, and secretly gave Fiona the resulting potion.

'Within two months she was pregnant, and the laird was delirious with joy. But his happiness soured when Fiona became deathly ill in her fifth month. It was only then he realized that the black woman had increased his hopes so that they should be dashed all the harder by losing both mother and child.

'In a fury he beat the woman, demanding that she use her powers to reverse the magic and bring Fiona back to health. She told him that the magic had gone too far to save both—that he could have either the mother or the child. Brian continued to beat her, but she was adamant—one or the other.

'It must have been a hard choice, but he finally chose to let the child live.' Maxwell cleared his throat. 'There was a great deal of pressure on him, as on any nobleman, to leave an heir, so we can't criticize him too harshly for his decision. At any rate, the witch was true to her word. The child was born, but under rather . . . bizarre circumstances.'

Maxwell paused and looked at McCormack, as if for permission to proceed.

'Well?' said George, angry with himself for the way his voice shook in the sudden silence. 'Don't stop now, Maxwell, you're coming to the exciting part.' He had wanted the forced levity to relax him, but instead it made him feel impatient and foolish. He tried in vain to keep his gaze from the pelt fixed to the door. It had been difficult enough when it was simply the skin of a nonentity. But now that it had an identity, it was twice as horrifying, twice as fascinating. He wondered what her name was.

Maxwell went on, ignoring George's comment. 'Fiona McCormack died in her seventh month of pregnancy. But the child lived.'

'Born prematurely then? Convenient.'

'No,' answered the solicitor quietly. 'The child came to term. He was born in the ninth month.'

'But . . .' George felt disoriented, as if all the world was a step ahead of him. 'How?'

'The black woman. She kept Fiona alive.'

'I thought you said she was dead.'

'She was. It was an artificial life, preserved by sorcery, or, as we would think today, by some primitive form of science civilization has not yet discovered. Call it what you will, no heart beat, no breath stirred, but Fiona McCormack lived, and was somehow able to nourish her child *in utero*.'

'But that's *absurd*! A fetus needs . . . *life*, its respiratory and circulatory system depends on its mother's!' He laughed, a sharp, quick bark. 'You're having me on.'

'God damn you, George, shut *up*!' The old man's words exploded like a shell, and sent him into a fit of coughing blood-black phlegm, which he spat on the floor. He rested for a moment, breathing heavily, then raised his massive head to look into George's eyes. 'You be silent. And at the end of the story, at the *end*, then you laugh if you wish.'

'I don't know how it occurred, George,' said Maxwell, 'but it has been sworn to by the sixteenth laird and his servant, as has everything I've told you. You shall see further evidence later.' He took a deep breath and plunged on.

'She gave birth to the child, and it suckled at his dead mother's breast for nearly a year, drawing sustenance from a cup that was never filled. A short time after the birth, Brian McCormack, with his own hands, flayed his first wife alive, and tanned the hide himself. He must have been quite mad by then. As you can see, he worked with extreme care.'

He was right, George thought. For all of the abomination's hideousness, it was extraordinarily done, as if a surgeon had cut the body from head to toe in a neat cross section, like a plastic anatomical kit he had once seen. George looked at Maxwell and his father, who were both staring quietly at the mortal tapestry on the door. It seemed that the story was ended.

'That's it, then,' George said, with only a trace of mockery. 'That's the legend.' He turned to his father with pleading eyes. 'Is that all that's kept us in a state of fear from cradle to grave? That's become as legendary as the silkie or the banshee? Dear God, is the Cairnwell Horror only a black skin nailed to a cellar door?'

The expressions of the two men in the lantern light added years to their faces. For a second George thought his father was already dead, a living corpse like the sixteenth Lady Cairnwell, doomed to an eternity of haunting the dreams of McCormack children.

'There's more,' said Maxwell, in such a way that George knew immediately that they had not been looking at the door as much as what was behind it.

Maxwell fumbled in the pocket of his suit coat and withdrew a large iron key, which he handed to McCormack. The old man hobbled to the massive door and fitted the key into a keyhole barely visible in the dim light. It rattled, then turned slowly, and McCormack pressed against the iron-and-oak panel. The door did not move, and the dying man leaned tiredly against it. Maxwell added his weight to the task. Though George knew he should have helped, he could not bring himself to touch the tarry carcass the older men seemed to be obscenely caressing. The door began to move with a shriek of angry hinges, and George thought of a wide and hungry mouth with teeth of iron straps, and wondered what it had eaten and how long ago. Then the smell hit him, and he reeled back.

It was the worst smell he had ever known, worse than the sour tang of open sewers, the sulfur-rich fumes of rotten eggs, worse even than when he had been a boy and found that long-dead stag, swarming with maggots. He would have vomited, but there was nothing left in his stomach to bring up.

His father and Maxwell picked up their lanterns. 'Do you want to come with us,' Maxwell asked, 'or would you rather watch from here at first?'

George was impressed by Maxwell's objectivity. It was as if the man were viewing the situation far outside, watching a shocker on the telly. George wished he could have felt the same way. 'I'll come,' he said, and jutted his weak chin forth like a brittle lance.

Holding the lanterns high, the three entered the chamber. It was a small room six meters square. A rough-hewn round table with a single straight-backed chair was to their right as they entered, another chair, less stern in design, to their left. It was the bed, however, that dominated the room, a massive oaken piece with a huge carved headboard and high footboard, over which George could not see from the door. Maxwell and McCormack moved to either side of the bed, and the old man beckoned for his son to join him.

The woman in the bed reminded George of the mummies he had seen in the British Museum. The skin was the yellow of dirty chalk, furrowed with wrinkles so deep they would always remain in darkness. The same sickly shade sullied the hair, which spread over the pillow fanlike, a faded invitation to a lover now dust. She wore a night-gown of white lace, and her clawed fingers interlocked over her flattened breasts, bony pencils clad in gloves of the sheerest silk. She had been dead a long, long time.

'The Lady Fiona,' whispered McCormack huskily. 'Your five-times great-grandmother, George.'

Again George felt relief. If this was the ultimate, if this dried and preserved corpse was the final horror, then he could still laugh and walk in the world without bearing the invisible curse all McCormacks before him bore. He held his lantern higher to study the centuries-old face more closely. Then he saw the eyes.

He had expected to see either wrinkled flaps of skin that had once been eyelids, or shriveled gray raisins nesting loosely in open sockets. What he had not expected was two blue eyes that gazed at the smoke-blackened ceiling, insentient but alive.

'She's . . . alive,' he said half-wittedly, so overcome by horror that he no longer cared what impression he gave.

'Yes,' said his father. 'So she has been since the spell was put on her.' George felt the old man's arm drape itself around his shoulder. 'The sixteenth laird wanted her undead misery ended when the son was weaned, but the witch said it could not be done. He tortured her—in this very room—but she would not, possibly could not, relent. It was then that he killed her by skinning. He kept his wife upstairs as long as he could, but the . . . odor grew too strong, and the servants started to whisper. So he brought her down here, and here she has been ever since, caught in a prison between life and death.

'She neither speaks nor moves, nor has she since she died. Giving birth and feeding her child were her only acts, and even then, records the document, she was like an automaton.'

George's head felt stuffed with water, and his words came out as thick as a midnight dream. 'What . . . document?'

'The record Brian McCormack left,' answered his father, 'and that the servant signed as witness. The history of the event and the charge put on every laird of Cairnwell since—to preserve the tale from outside ears and to care for his poor wife "until such time as God sees fit to take her unto Him". It is the duty of the eldest son, such as I was, and such as you are, George.'

The liquid in his brain was nearly at a boil. 'Me?' He lurched away from his father's cloying embrace. 'You want me to mind *that* the rest of my life?'

'There is little to care for,' Maxwell said soothingly. 'She requires no food, only . . .'

'What? *What* does she require?'

'Care. A wash now and again . . .'

George laughed desperately, and knew he was approaching hysterics. 'A wash! Good Christ, and perhaps a permanent, and some nail clipping . . .!'

'Care!' bellowed McCormack. 'What you would do for *anyone* like this!'

'There *is* no one *like this*! She is . . . she is *dead*.' The word had stuck in his throat. 'I'm not going to have any part of this, nor of Cairnwell. *You* chose this, not me! I won't rot here like the rest of you did. *Keep* Cairnwell—give it away, burn it, *bury* it, for Christ's sake—that's what suits the dead!'

'No! She is *not* dead! She is alive, and she *needs* us! She needs . . .' McCormack paused, as if something had stolen his words. A pained look grasped his features, and before George or Maxwell could leap to his side, he toppled like a tree, and his head struck the stone floor with a leaden thud.

Maxwell swept around the bed, pushed George aside, and knelt by McCormack. 'The lantern!' he said, and George moved the flickering light so that he and Maxwell could see that his father's face wore the gray softness of death.

ꟷ

Much later, in the study, Maxwell poured George another glass of sherry. 'I shouldn't have let him go down there,' the older man said, almost to himself. He turned back to the cold fireplace. 'After the last operation . . . it left his heart so weak. . . .'

'It was better,' George said quietly. 'Better that way than for the cancer to finish him.'

'I suppose.'

They sat, sipping sherry and saying nothing. George rose and walked to the window. The sun, setting over the ridge of the western fields, slashed a thin blade of orange-red through the beveled panes. He looked at a flock of blackbirds pecking in the damp earth for grain.

'I shouldn't have upset him,' said George.

'He hadn't been down there for quite a while,' Maxwell said. 'I shouldn't have let him go.'

'You couldn't have stopped him,' George said, still gazing out of the window.

'I suppose not. He felt it . . .'

'His duty,' said George.

'Yes.' Maxwell turned from the dead fire toward George's tall figure, outlined in the sun's flame. 'Will you go then? Leave Cairnwell?'

George kept watching the birds.

'It's not . . . there's really very little to it,' said Maxwell, with the slightest trace of urgency. 'You don't have to see her at all, you know, not ever, if you wish it. Just so long as you stay here.'

In the field, the blackbirds rose in formation, turned in the wind like leaves, and settled once more. George looked at Maxwell. 'May I have the key?'

ꟷ

The door opened more easily this time, and George walked into the room, holding the lantern at his side without fear. He knew there were no ghosts. There was no need for ghosts.

His earlier exposure to the smell made it much more palatable, and he thought about fumigants and disinfectants. He pulled the straight-backed chair over to the bedside and looked at the woman's face.

Strange he hadn't noticed before. The resemblance to his father was so strong, particularly about the eyes. They were so sad, so sad and tired, open all these years, staring into darkness.

'Sleep,' he whispered. 'Sleep for a bit.' He hesitated only a moment, then pressed with his index finger upon the cool parchment of the eyelids, first one, then the other, drawing them down like tattered shades over twilight windows.

'There,' he said gently, 'that's better now, isn't it? Sleep a bit.' He started to hum a tune he had not thought of for years, an old cradle song his mother had crooned to him on the nights when the terrors of Cairnwell made sleep come hard. When the last notes died away, caught by the smooth fissures of the chamber walls, he rose, laid a hand of benediction on the wizened forehead, and started upstairs where his brandy waited.

The twenty-third laird of Cairnwell had come home.

His Two Wives

I HAVE ALWAYS HAD AN AFFINITY for Poe. It began when, as a child, I found on my father's shelves, amid the detritus of book club selections from the forties, a rather small, blue-green boxed volume that contained a great many of his tales. This was before my reading had progressed beyond the one-syllable stage, and the words of the stories, though rich with promise, were mostly unintelligible to me. The illustrations, however, impressed themselves upon my pre-elementary imagination, so much so that I saw them in my dreams, and even now they return to haunt me in my midnight visions.

I learned later that the artist was Eichenberg, and from that day to this I have believed that no one came closer to capturing in illustration the spirit of Poe; neither Clarke nor Wogel, nor, among the more contemporary artists, Saty, and certainly not Rackham, whose cartoonish attempts are laughable. Only Eichenberg, in his dark and cruel woodcuts, caught the tragic soul of the angelic Virginian, perhaps because he, unlike the others, created his art not with pens or brushes, but with knives.

Years passed before I could read and comprehend the tales, but until that blessed time came, I feasted my eyes upon the pictures, bathing my soul in the black, luminous orbs that were the eyes of Ligeia, wishing that I was the faceless man whose head she cradled in her lap. I shuddered at the ivory smile of Berenice, her huge, drawn face hanging in the darkness of what I would later learn was the narrator's library, he himself prostrate with sorrow, his face on the table before him. And though I did not know the stories, I sensed unerringly that these men grieved because their women had been, or would be, taken away.

There were other illustrations, of course—the Red Death revealing himself to Prospero and the revelers, the narrator of 'The Black Cat' warily eyeing the sinister feline perched atop a hogshead of ale, Montresor and Fortunato about to begin their search for the Amontillado—but it was the women who held me in thrall, and with great effort and over many months I deciphered their stories, with a dictionary beside me, like some latter-day Champollion working his way through a later, far more fascinating Rosetta stone.

Slowly the understanding of the stories came over me, the themes of death and parting and return, and in that volume and others I found and read more tales of lost loves—of Eleonora, Morella, Madeline Usher, the lady of the Oval Portrait. Discovering the poetry, I imbibed the liquorous lines of 'Ulalume', 'Annabel Lee', and 'The Raven', sighing along for the lost Lenore, and finally, when I was ten, read 'The Philosophy of Composition', in which I learned (perhaps 'had reaffirmed' is more to the point) that Poe felt 'the death of a beautiful woman' was the most fitting subject for poetry.

I leave it to those who toy with psychoanalyis to determine the source of my own fascination with this particular subject. As Marie Bonaparte dissected Poe, so those who some day read this may choose to do with me. May you be kinder in your judgments than she was in hers. It should benefit you greatly to know that my father and I were deprived of my mother's graces by her death when I was but three years of age. Of her I recall only warm embraces and gay laughter and rooms filled with flowers. After her death I cannot bring to mind a single flower in our house.

As I became enamored of Poe and his themes, so I became enamored of the written word, and sought to make it my field of study. Never did I attempt to write fiction, for how could I hope to equal even the poorest offerings of Poe, my master and my god of prose? But what I *could* do, and what I did, was to learn all I could about Poe—man, writer, and thinker—and dedicate what feeble powers I could bring to bear to propagate the seeds of his philosophy and art.

I majored in literature, of course, at the University of Pennsylvania, drawn there by the spirit and the scholarship of the late Arthur Hobson Quinn, whose Poe biography is yet unsurpassed. I remained at Penn long enough to earn a Master's degree in American Literature, and took my doctoral studies at Columbia. In both New York and Philadelphia I haunted the sites where Poe had lived and walked, taking frequent trips to both Baltimore and Richmond to immerse myself still more deeply in his presence. My dissertation was *The Lost Love: Eighteenth Century Roots of Poe's Principal Theme*, which saw publication from the press of the University of Illinois. Besides earning me a minor niche in Poe scholarship, it also introduced me to Joanna.

How do I begin to speak of her? By saying that her loveliness, like Eleonora's, 'was that of the Seraphim'? Or shall I use Poe's words to describe Ligeia: 'In stature she was tall, somewhat slender, and, in her latter days, even emaciated . . . She came and departed as a shadow.'

Oh, she was a Poe woman all right, and I knew some fate had brought us together. I met her when she typed my dissertation. I had chosen a typist at random from a list in the student newspaper, and Joanna was the first name that had leapt to my eyes. When I saw her I knew. Even the name was correct. I had sought in vain for a Ligeia to share my life, but Ligeias are non-existent these days, as are Eleonoras and Morellas. Even Madelines are hard to come by. While a senior at Penn I did chance upon a Berenice, but on our first date quickly discovered that she was *not* a 'Behr-a-nees', with all the grace that name suggests, but rather a 'Buhr-NEECE', in style as well as in pronunciation. I felt that the appellation of Joanna might be as close as I could come to finding a name similar to those of Poe's women. Surely in this world of unromantic harshness I could find a *soul* no nearer the mark.

Joanna was too pallid, too fragile for most to consider beautiful, but it was that very quality that most attracted me. It was the face of a flower so lovely and delicate that the first frost that touched it would bring it death.

She was only a sophomore of eighteen, I a romantic older man of twenty-five. Although she could not have understood all the subtleties of my work, she complimented it highly, and I, charmed and flattered, was quick to ask her to dinner. The following evening I discovered the source of her rare and seraphic pallor. She had, she told me, suffered from diabetes since early childhood. Her parents had been extremely protective of her, and as a result she had never known the experiences that other girls of her age had. She was young and sheltered and pure and, I surmised, somewhat sickly, and I looked into her wide, deep, black orbs over which 'hung jetty lashes of great length', and knew that I should never find her like again, and determined to make her my own.

It was not until I found a position that I asked her to be my wife, although the event was not long in coming. I chose to accept the offer of a small college in Central Virginia to teach several courses in American literature. Larger stipends were offered elsewhere, but mostly from schools in the western United States, and I was no Julius Rodman to dare the vicissitudes of travel over the mountains, beyond Poe's beloved eastern shore.

So I accepted the Virginian offer, met the cautious parents of my betrothed, and arranged to have her junior year continue at the college to which we would go as man and wife. Joanna had accepted my proposal with little time for reflection. I believe she saw in me both husband and protector, and, as sheltered as she had always been, had no confidence in herself concerning the finding of a better mate. This is not to say that she did not love me, for she did, worshipfully at times, and the gods alone know how I returned that love. Like Poe with his tubercular cousin-bride, Virginia, I learned all I could about her illness, even to the extent of administering to her the twice daily injections of insulin she required, that fluid, more precious than the gods' nectar, that preserved her sweet life.

So the years passed. I taught my classes, wrote my papers, and by my fourth year at the college I was permitted to teach a graduate course on Poe, which I did with great relish. Joanna by this time had taken her degree, and, half-fearful to search for any sort of occupation, remained in our little home (cottage, as I always called it, for it was indeed cottage-like, on a seldom-traveled side street fringed by trees) and cared for my husbandly needs, for my days were long and my nights often spent with my studies. Let no one think, however, that our relationship was one, like Mr and Mrs Poe's, in which manifestations of love had no place. I performed a husband's duty, and she a wife's. Our tender couplings were necessarily infrequent, owing to the frailty of Joanna's constitution, for her malady was what the physicians referred to as of a brittle nature, the balance between good health and ill quite tenuous, and apt to be overthrown by nothing more than a slight cold, or even a mild mental upset.

So we loved and lived, somewhat more reclusively than my more upwardly mobile colleagues, but happily and contentedly, until one day, week, month—the exact moment is obscure in my memory—when I detected a *change* in my dearly beloved wife.

Her dependency on me was slowly, insidiously diminishing. Her greetings upon my daily return were not as warmly concerned as they had been in times past; her acceptance of my administrations to her well-being were not as total (indeed, she seemed to be almost resentful as I carefully injected her every morn and evening!). She no longer cared to read my papers, and actually professed *boredom* upon my nightly readings aloud of Poe's verse. I was at last forced to conclude that I was losing the love of my deepest heart.

I am not by nature a jealous man, so the idea of any infidelity on Joanna's part was long in coming, but once it had made its presence known I determined once and for all to ascertain the truth of it. Unbeknownst to Joanna, I reported myself ill one morning, parked the car but a block from our cottage, and discreetly re-entered the house, where I secreted myself in one of the two closets (my own, of course) in the bedroom we shared. There amid my tweeds and broadcloths and corduroys I reposed quietly, infinitely patient. I had always been admiringly astounded by the narrator of 'The Tell-Tale Heart' and the remarkable *slowness* with which he opened the old man's chamber door and operated his bull's-eye lantern, fearing that I could *never* equal such supreme stealth. But never before had I a greater reason. So, like the nameless man whose insanity the presence of the old man's vulture eye had claimed, I sat, completely sane but equally still, and waited for what I might discover.

To equivalent amounts of relief and remorse, I discovered nothing. From my land-locked eyrie I heard only the sounds of a vacuum cleaner, the washing machine, the refrigerator door opening and closing several times, and the television (a device that I never watched, but had purchased at Joanna's request), upon which were shows that seemingly consisted solely of discussions of the need for women to express themselves in ever more forceful ways, a highly unromantic view of life that I found distasteful even from the few brief snatches of words and phrases I was able to discern. I must confess myself appalled that my lovingly sheltered wife should be exposing herself to such execrable opinions. But instead of bursting from my hiding place and declaiming against such rot (an urge that grew in me the more I listened), I maintained my aching posture, listening as Joanna made her lunch, scarcely daring to draw a breath as she came into our room for a brief nap.

But she slept purely, and alone. Neither the phone nor the doorbell disturbed the placidity of our cottage, and late that afternoon when I heard her descending steps on the cellar stairs, I left the closet and exited the house by the rear door, returning to my car where I sat deep in thought, immersed in disquietude. It was then that I came to the only natural conclusion. My wife, my Joanna, had lived for too long.

It had not been destined for her to ride on life's rough current as long as she already had. She would die, and I would know the innermost agonies of the soul, the identical agonies that had tortured Poe. Only mine would be far, far deeper, for besides experiencing the passing of my loved one, I would be responsible for it as well.

The act itself would not be cruel, for would I not in fact be saving her from the encroachment of a cruel world that seeks to bind the soul of woman even as it mouths the platitudes of liberation? And already Joanna was feeling the cold bite of the first of these chains: dissatisfaction, envy, disobedience.

I would, I considered, not allow such a blossom to be so blighted. It would be better that it should die first.

Resolving to put a plan into action that very evening, before my wife's independence grew to such a degree that she would deny me access to her medication, I thought long and hard, and ultimately devised what I felt to be a perfect solution. That evening, instead of filling her syringe with a small amount of fast-acting insulin and a large amount of long-term, as was prescribed, I reversed the bottles completely, so that a far larger dose of the more powerful fast-acting type would enter her bloodstream. As I prepared the injection site with alcohol, I inquired solicitously if she might care to inject herself for a change, thinking it convenient to have her own fingerprints on the instrument of her death.

Her large liquid eyes flared as if with a challenge, and the effect was like that of a strong light deep at the bottom of the sea. Without a word, she snatched the needle out of my hand, and, with courage born of anger, sank it deeply into her thigh and pressed the plunger home.

I passed most of the evening in my upstairs study, the dull hum of the television on the floor beneath me drawing my attention from my work. At eleven o'clock I closed my books, put away my pen, and listened, hearing no sound from beneath. I took from the shelf the poetry volume of the Arnheim Edition of the works, and walked downstairs.

Joanna was sitting in her chair, her eyes unnaturally wide, her face glistening with perspiration. 'My dear,' I said in mild alarm, 'what is the matter?'

She snarled at me then, using harsh, guttural words that I shall not commit to paper. I could plainly see that she was not herself, that the insulin was dulling her senses to a degree it never had before. Food was the only thing that could save her now, but of that her conscious mind had no idea, and such was her mental state that had I even suggested her eating anything, she would have refused on general principles.

So I made no such suggestion, but only smiled, sat on the other end of the room from her, and said, 'Perhaps some Poe will make you feel better.'

She shook her head roughly and seemed to be trying to spit, but there was no moisture in her mouth. I opened my volume and began to read:

> 'Thou wast that all to me, love,
> For which my soul did pine——'

When I had finished 'To One in Paradise', she seemed more slack-jawed, stupid-looking (to my dismay). I went on:

> 'Ah, broken is the golden bowl! The spirit flown for ever!'

'Leonore' ended, and I looked once again at Joanna, who was now as one in a never-ending dream, lost and dying. Oh yes, she was dying, that I could see, and somewhere in the middle of 'For Annie' her eyes closed, and she drifted into what I am certain the physicians would term a coma. Then it was that I felt safe to sit next to her, hold her cooling hand, and do for her what I always hoped would be done for me as my own silent death crept on.

I read her prose. I read all night, of Eleonora, and Morella, and Berenice, and the Marchesa Aphrodite, and the Ushers, and Ligeia—oh, particularly of Ligeia. And as I read I sorrowed, and finally wept, wept as my love, my life, grew cold and stiff beside me, as, just before dawn, her final sigh streamed from her, a vaporous offering to the gods of Hellas. And it seemed to me as I held her there, my warmth unable to restore her own, it seemed I heard her own sweet voice saying what Ligeia had said:

> 'Man doth not yield him to the angels, nor unto death utterly,
> save only through the weakness of his feeble will.'

I called the ambulance service when the clock struck seven. They were of course far too late, and I explained to them that I had awakened alone in bed just after sunrise, and had hurried downstairs to see what had happened to my wife, and had found her thus. They asked me other questions then and later, and I explained that my wife had, despite my cautions, lately desired to administer her own medications, and that she had apparently erred in the dosage. The post-mortem examination proved my 'theory' to be correct, and the death was officially ruled accidental, the investigation closed.

Then came the funeral, and the second, more private service. The first was a sham, for show only. The funeral director had proven susceptible to bribery, as most men will, though I confess it took me far more money to turn his head than I had hoped, and money was no small consideration. I had originally thought of building a new tomb, but found that the cost would have been equivalent to that of constructing a house, and my finances would not bear it.

So instead I turned from the new cemetery (say, rather, 'Memorial Park'), on the outskirts of town, and sought the caretaker of the ancient Roman Catholic cemetery several miles distant. I told him quite bluntly that I could not bear the thought of placing my wife's corporeal form into the rank dampness of the earth, but that the cost of a new tomb was prohibitive. Was there not, by chance, an old and forgotten crypt back in the deeper recesses of the graveyard, one whose family had long since perished, and where I might surreptitiously lay my beloved's casket? A vault to which I could gain access whenever I wished?

He was hesitant, but when I spoke of money he brightened, and led me to the rear of the cemetery where, amid tall obelisks and large stone and marble tombs, he showed me an ancient pile, whose mortar was crumbling in half a hundred places. I squinted to make out the name that the years and the elements had all but eroded from the slab over the portal, and as I read it, I nearly burst out in peals of wild laughter. The name was *Fortunato*, and inwardly I chuckled at both the connection to Poe and the *lack* of fortune that had brought the family to the sorry state in which a stranger could let their tomb.

The caretaker opened the heavy metal doors with a large and rusty key, and we entered. By the dying light of day I could see the empty bier in the center of the tomb, the slabs of stone that covered the wall, the small, stained glass window high at the rear of the edifice. No more could I determine—not the names engraved on the slabs, those who slumbered in the thick walls, nor the filth on the floor, the droppings of small animals who, through the decades, had found the chinks in the tomb's armor. I saw only the bier, and, in fancy, Joanna's casket lying atop it. It was ideal in both atmosphere and seclusion, and I hastily sealed the bargain with the caretaker, who gave me the only key.

The mock funeral over, Joanna's grieving and remarkably bitter parents departed, the empty casket lowered into the grave and buried, the funeral director and I proceeded to carry out my plan. At dead of night we loaded Joanna's true casket into a tradesman's van which I had rented to preserve our anonymity—a hearse arriving in darkness at a cemetery would be sure to draw idle stares. We drove it to the Catholic graveyard's gates, and the informed caretaker was prepared to admit us. The three of us bore the casket into the tomb, locked it, and returned to our homes.

I waited a week before I returned to her tomb, a week of anxiety and withheld joy, knowing that the expectation, the waiting, the longing should make that first visit all the more intense, my grief all the more heartfelt. For I did miss her. Oh, not the Joanna of the twentieth century that she had been becoming, but rather the Joanna-Ligeia-Annabel Lee of the nineteenth century that she had been. So when at dusk a week hence I turned the key, and it grated its decaying fragments against the lock, when I entered and lit the candles I had brought, placing a stick between the door and jamb so that I should not be made captive by a sudden gust of wind, when all this was done, I thought then that I had at last realized the depth and height of man's emotions. I felt I had fulfilled my destiny, that Poe and his dreams and his feelings still lived through me. True, 'a sepulchre there by the sea' would have been finer, but for a land-locked professor on a small stipend, I felt I had done quite well.

So the months passed, and I visited the tomb of my departed wife, bringing with me my volumes of Poe, reading the works to the enshrouded form within the casket—did I mention that she was enshrouded? Oh yes, wrapped from head to foot, only her face visible, precisely like Wogel's interpretation of Ligeia. I thought it only fitting. So I sat and read and grieved and spoke to her of times past. On occasion the thought crossed my mind of opening the coffin and gazing into the sleeping face of my beloved, but I did not. In the first place, I had had the lid nailed on, as had been done in the early times, and, in the second, I did not think I could bear to gaze upon the dissolution that must have begun upon my wife's corpse, fearing that it would send me into a paroxysm of recrimination I would find utterly unbearable.

It was six months after her interment that I heard the scratching. It seemed to come—nay, it *came*—from within the casket itself, and at the first sound of scraping, as of fingernails on satin, I leapt up and investigated, thinking that by chance a mouse or rat had gnawed its way within in the hopes of finding some unspeakable banquet. But the casket was flawless, intact, and I dismissed the sound as autumn leaves blowing on the mortar outside.

The following evening it occurred again, and this time I stiffened, listening, then arose very slowly and moved toward the sound. It *was* from within the casket, and the knowledge burst upon me like a thunderbolt that *Joanna moved within the grave*, that, impossible as it seemed, *life* lay within that nailed casket.

There was no 'weakness of feeble will' in my beloved, but a will so strong that it had kept her alive without air, without sustenance, even while decomposition had begun its evil work.

And then I knew what was needed—a new vessel into which the life force of my wife could flow, as Ligeia's life force had surged into and overwhelmed Rowena, the narrator's second bride, so that Ligeia could, through her strength of will, her *refusal* to die, come back and walk among the living. So would Joanna come back, and love me once again. Leaning next to the lid of the casket, I whispered to my love that I would return, then left the tomb, locking it securely.

I went then to a tavern that I frequented on occasion, and there fell into discourse with a coarse but pneumatically constructed female who waited upon the tables there. Her name was Mildred, though she desired to be addressed as Millie, and I had fancied in the past that she had always looked on me with a certain amount of interest, a supposition that proved to be true, so that it was with little difficulty that I persuaded her to accompany me when the tavern closed, urging her to keep our assignation a secret.

As we drove through the night, I spoke to her of love and death, quoting liberally from the master, so that by the time we arrived at the Catholic cemetery, the woman was already in a highly excitable state. She followed me eagerly through the labyrinth of graves and vaults, laughing vacuously and remarking over and over how 'kinky' the whole experience was. When at length we arrived at Joanna's tomb, and I unlocked the door, she began to mutter the words 'Oh my God' repeatedly, while grasping me in a most undecorous manner. We moved crab-like into the chamber, I lighting a candle, she moaning lasciviously as she descried the casket lying on the bier.

Then I grasped the woman, and she pressed herself against me, mistaking my action for a different kind of passion. I turned her about, held her by the elbows, and cried, 'Joanna! She is here! She, for whom you have been waiting!' and thrust the woman toward the casket. Then I whirled about and left the tomb, slamming the ponderous door behind me.

I could hear the startled cries of the woman, even through the massive portal. She shouted certain words that should never appear on paper. The cacophony continued for a short while, and then the harridan suddenly grew silent. I fancied I heard the screech of nails as the coffin lid broke free, and then a harsh thud. Then . . . nothing but the wind blowing through the black trees about me, whistling over the stones.

I shuddered at the thought of the metempsychosis that was taking place within the tomb, but at the same time I rejoiced in the thought that even the chains of death were not enough to keep my beloved from returning to me. With trembling hands I unlocked the door of the sepulchre and flung the portal wide. I nearly screamed at the sight that awaited me.

The lid of the casket was lying on the stone floor of the tomb, and there beside it were the rotting remains of what had been my Joanna. One moldering arm, swathed in the yellowing linen of the grave, reached out toward me, its desiccated fingers seemingly longer than ever they were in life. The face, upturned, was eyeless, those luminous orbs of onyx having long since sunk into the skull. The lips were shriveled and pulled back, showing the shocking whiteness of the perfect teeth. Her nose was nearly gone. Was this, I shrieked to myself, my beauteous Joanna, my child-bride fled before her time? The worms of agony gnawed within my bosom. I would have remained gazing at the riddled corpse until the seas turned dry, had not a slight movement out of the corner of my eye wrested my attention from the grim sight before me.

A figure stepped from the shadows, and with ice running down my backbone I recognized the form as that of the woman whom I had lured to the tomb and shut inside. Yet there was something different about her, something *changed.* She still wore her uniform, which hung loosely on her cow-like frame, her hair still hung long and lank, her large-lipped mouth still remained open, whether in excitement or in the age-old position of the mouth-breather I could not tell.

Then suddenly she turned her face upward so that it was lit from below by the sickly candle beam, and her eyes at last fell upon mine. My heart leapt to my throat, and the closing lines of 'Ligeia', slightly modified, leapt over it. 'Here then at last,' I shrieked aloud, 'can I never—can I never be mistaken—these are the full, and the black, and the wild eyes—of my lost love—of the Lady—of the LADY JOANNA!'

'You're right there, schmuck.'

I stiffened, not believing my own ears. 'What?' I quavered.

It was Mildred's voice that responded, but with *Joanna's* inflection. 'Part right anyway. We're both in here now.'

'Both . . .?' The worms of anxiety still nibbled at my breastbone.

'Millie and me,' the woman replied. 'And she knows the whole story now.'

'I sure do,' the woman went on, but with an abrupt change in the fluidity of tone. 'Always thought you were a nice guy, and now I find out you're nothing but a shitheel. Just goes to show you.' My jaw waggled as I tried to speak.

'Oh, calm down,' said the Joanna voice. 'Honestly, you look like a gaffed fish.'

'But the corpse . . .' I babbled, quite undone. 'What's . . . who's in there?'

'Nothing's in there. At least not anymore. I got out just in time, you know. You can survive in something like that only so long. At least Millie's in good shape.'

'I sure am,' the Millie voice said. 'A little saggy in the middle, maybe, but hell, there are guys who *like* that.'

I felt all at sea. Poe never said what happened after 'Ligeia' ended, and the narrator and his love were reunited. I was on my own now, in uncharted territories. 'But . . . I don't understand!'

The Joanna voice answered me. 'You *never* understood. And I wonder if even Poe did, though he certainly knew more than you.'

'Knew *what*?' I inquired.

'That women are *stronger.* Poe never brought a *man* back, not technically speaking, anyway. But he knew you couldn't keep a good woman down. *Will* can keep us alive . . . if we've got something to stay alive for.' She smirked at that.

'You mean . . . love?' I ventured.

'If you want to think that, go right ahead.'

My mind was churning. 'What, uh . . . what happens now?'

'Poor man. Don't know how the story ends, do you? Well, we can promise that things are going to be different. For one thing, you're going to have a new wife in a new body.'

I looked at the width of Millie's frame, at her massive curves, at her solid, unsylphlike *corporeality*, and choked back a sob.

'Tell him about the other thing,' the Millie voice said.

'I shall. Millie wants to make the best of this as well. The status of being a professor's wife is alluring—though I've told her things to the contrary—but she also has certain needs, needs which were not as great in me.'

'What Joanna's saying, honey, is that I'm gonna expect you to put in a lot of sack time. And don't you worry, Joanna, you'll get to like it too.'

'I may at that,' I heard the Joanna voice say as a soft smile creased Millie's coarse features.

'I shan't be a party to this!' I cried. 'You can't make me!'

'True, we can't *make* you,' said Joanna. 'But if you refuse to participate, Millie will find a letter in your late wife's handwriting stating that you were plotting to kill her by tampering with her insulin.'

'Your . . . handwriting?' I was barely able to stand. My legs had turned to jelly beneath me.

'I think it's time to go home, dear. Don't you?'

A violent firmness stole over me then, and murder came into my eyes as I stepped toward this slattern who made a mockery of my love. I had killed once, why not again?

'That's *enough*, Eddie!' she barked, and it stopped me dead. 'I'll have no more of your foolishness now!'

I could not move. In just such a way must Maria Clemm, Poe's mother-in-law, have spoken to him a thousand times, badgering him about his drinking, his inability to find work, his literary pride . . . and it came to me then that Poe had been *ruled* by women, not only Mrs Clemm, but by the more subtle presence of his wife Virginia, and by the dozens of literary lionesses with whom he had come in contact over the years.

And at last I knew the anticlimax of 'Ligeia'. At last I knew what my fate was to be.

I bowed my head before those fiery black eyes, bowed my body as if before a queen, and bowed my voice to a meek, submissive tone as I whispered, 'Yes, my dear. Whatever you say.'

I married Millie the barmaid, to the extreme surprise of my colleagues and acquaintances, and Joanna's letter naming me as her murderer rests in some safe deposit box unknown to me. It will, however, never be used. I have resigned myself to my lot, and it is easier knowing that it was Poe's as well. My one regret is that I have so little time for the master anymore. As for reading aloud at home, that is a thing forever of the past. Joanna shows no interest whatsoever, as her preoccupations have begun to resemble Millie's, and they have become the greatest of friends, talking to each other constantly (only in my hearing, of course), and giving new meaning to the word inseparable.

Ah well, at least I am busier than ever before. By day I teach, in the evenings I clean, do the laundry, plan the next day's meals, and at night (have I not said that Millie's interests have become Joanna's?) I . . .

But hold. Let me end with a line from Poe, to show that he is still foremost in my mind. One might say I spend my nights:

> Keeping time, time, time,
> In a sort of Runic rhyme . . .
> To the moaning and the groaning of the belles.

From the Papers of Helmut Hecker

Letter to World Fantasy Convention:

November 12, 1986

DEAR SIRS:

My agent, J. Arthur Pembroke, has notified me that you wish to give me an award for my novel, *The Dark Borders*. When I asked him to investigate the situation further before accepting said award, he told me of the nature of your organization and the titles of other nominated works.

I do not wish, nor have I ever wished, my work to be compared with commercially written tales of vampires, werewolves, elves, unicorns, fairies, and other ragtag pseudo-creations of hack writers, and I am utterly disgusted to have it in some tawdry competition with the same. Likewise, I am appalled at the insinuation that I would actually *welcome* such an award. I have been informed that Borges received this same 'honor', but, after seeing a photograph of the award itself (a staring, prognathous monster of some sort, I assume), if I were to learn that Borges's passing came only a short time after he received it, I would not be surprised.

In short, I have received numerous awards, including the Pulitzer Prize, the National Book Critics Circle Award, the Faulkner Award, and the National Book Award. I neither need nor desire your goggle-eyed ghoul.

Helmut Hecker

Journal entry (November 18, 1986):

I often wish it were possible to perpetrate some of the more savage activities in my tales upon these so-called 'fans' of my work. (REMINDER: inform Arthur to refuse any more offers of appearances on these absurd call-in shows, both television and radio.) It is annoying enough that I should be expected to go on one of these 'book tours', as if I need flaunt myself to become any more popular, but on top of it that I should be subjected to the ignorant commentary of ignorant readers who buy my works for their own ignorant purposes is beyond imagining.

For example, today in a B. Dalton here in (what god-awful town is this today? Ah yes—) Providence, Rhode Island, I signed a book for some fool in a baseball cap, who then asked me if I feel I've been influenced by Lovekraft. I looked at him like the dunce he was, and asked *who* or *what* was a Lovekraft, and he replied, with misplaced and feeble pride, that this Lovekraft was a 'horror writer' who had lived in the very city we were in. I responded that I have never been influenced by these dreadful, so-called 'horror writers' for the simple fact that I have never wasted my time or energy or intellect *reading* any of their formulaic and puerile work, that I knew only the names of a few with whom I have been forced to share the bestseller list, told this clod that their presence thereon was futher proof of the execrable taste of that portion of the American public who still read, and reiterated what I have proclaimed in every interview I have ever given in the so-called 'popular' press, that I am *not* a 'horror writer', but deal with the dark side of humanity in the tradition of Hesse, Mann, Borges, and others for whom this Lovekraft and others I could name would not be fit to sharpen pencils, and that if he wanted to understand my work and its influences (as much influence as can be had upon a writer of supreme originality such as myself), that he should read the articles and interviews with me that have appeared in *The New York Review of Books*, *The Antioch Review*, *The Yale Review*, *Sewanee Review*, and others that would in all likelihood be far too challenging for his limited mental capacity. I further told him that I abhorred the idea of being read by readers such as he, who would buy Picasso nudes in order to masturbate, and would never be able to understand the politically allegorical aspects of my work, and I deplored a marketing situation that made it possible for such pearls of mine to be thrown before the misunderstanding eyes of swine like himself.

The cretin stood there, nodding placidly at all this, as though I had merely complimented him on his baseball cap (it bore a 'B'—I assume for 'Boeotian') then said, and I quote his exact words, 'Yeah, I don't really get all that stuff, but, man, I love the way you carve up the bitches.'

I hurled the book I had just signed at his head, missing in my rage. The manager of the store ended the signing early, of course, but I have remained livid with fury for the remainder of the day. To bystanders, I am sure that my reaction must have been viewed as a simple and justified attack on a Philistine. But I am not certain that the verminous pig did not touch on the truth.

Ever since I was a child in Hamburg, I have felt an amount of pleasure in the sufferings of others, and——

My Freudian musings must cease now, for Heuer has just begun to rub against my legs. He is the newest addition to my small retinue, a poor replacement for Jenny, perhaps, but not nearly as difficult to care for. Yes, Heuer is content with a saucer of milk and some tinned food (chicken or beef only—he turned up his nose at the fish). But then cats, male or female, seem so much more easily pleased—and more intelligent—than females of the human species. Indeed, if women did not whimper so marvelously when in pain, I swear I should have nothing to do with them at all. Foolish Jenny. I always knew when to stop. I never *truly* hurt her, never beyond recovery.

But enough thoughts of her. I must remark on finding Heuer. While in Boston several days ago, I received a call from Fritz, who told me my old cat, Jorg, died in its sleep. I loved Jorg dearly, having brought him from Germany when I moved to America fifteen years ago, and the news of the animal's passing deeply saddened me.

So it was, I felt, fate that placed the pet shop next to the B. Dalton, and that placed Heuer, a handsome and fully grown cat, in its window. As I walked by, he looked at me with such wise and knowing eyes that I knew immediately that he would be Jorg's replacement. I marched into the shop, the publisher's representative who accompanied me howling that we were late for the signing (and indeed the line already wound out the door and down the block), paid the small amount required, and told the manager to hold Heuer until I returned.

Why Heuer? I must confess that the name struck me immediately upon seeing the cat. It was the name of one of my mother's lovers, the only one I ever liked. There was something about the eyes that reminded me of Heuer, I believe, so Heuer he is. . . .

Journal entry (January 14, 1987):

Heuer is such a glorious creature. His thick yellow fur glimmers like gold in the sun that pours through my study window. He seems to love this old city as much as I do now, and sits for hours at the window, looking at me and then at the peaceful skyline of Providence. Though its age pales before the long history of the town in which I grew up, there is at the same time a sense of great antiquity here. I did not realize how much I admired it before I had left it, gone back to New York with Heuer. He seemed to languish, poor beast, and it was not long before I realized that his soulsickness only reflected my own.

There had been something about Providence that had captured my spirit in the two short days I was there—the tang of the sea air coming up from the wharfs, the quaint gambrel roofs that line Benefit Street, the inspiring steeple of the First Baptist Church, St John's Churchyard—so much so that it is astonishing that it took as long as two weeks before I ordered Fritz to Rhode Island to secure us lodgings on College Hill. The house in which the three of us now reside dates back to the American Revolution. The yard is large, and filled with old shade trees. When spring comes, Heuer and I shall spend our afternoons out there when our writing mornings are ended, cozily ensconced behind the massive brick wall that encloses our estate and insures our privacy.

I say *our* writing, because Heuer sits near me all morning, never sleeping, merely watching the sky outside or watching me. What a fine comrade he is. Soon, I trust, all the disjointed thoughts I have concerning my next book shall coalesce into a magnificent whole. . . .

Journal entry (February 6, 1987):

The day has been a long one, but at last I have in mind my next book. It shall be a group of related stories, perhaps four or five of them, all long novelettes. The theme shall be the effects of huge, primal institutions upon modern man, allegorized by——

No. My working notes will reflect all the details. I have filled pages with them today, and tomorrow I begin the long work of actual writing. And it *shall* be long. I see the years stretching out before me. My mind is stuffed with ideas, and I burn to begin.

But Heuer, who rubs up against my leg, is correct. The time has come to rest. Schnapps for me, and a dish of ice cream for dear Heuer, then an early bedtime. I feel even too weary for a woman. Strange that my desires have not forced me to roam Providence's seamier streets. Perhaps the sedateness of this town is having an effect on me after all. . . .

Journal entry (July 24, 1987):

Five months after beginning it, the work is going splendidly. It is slow and painstaking, but the vision taking shape is one of both human and cosmic significance. I truly feel that it is the finest work I have yet done, and should firmly establish me as one of the great masters of world literature. This book shall insure my immortality.

I have begun working more and more by night, my faithful friend Heuer by my side. My mind seems clearer somehow, more receptive to the marvelous and terrifying visions that assail me on every side. My style, too, seems to be changing. Whereas before I have cut my phrases to the bone, creating a clean economy of prose, I have now become more verbose, grandiloquent even, as though my previous terse style was incapable of communicating the altogether *fantastic* and *bizarre sense of outsideness* and *cosmicism* that flows from my pen.

Ah yes, I have retired my trusty typewriter for the nonce. It was simply impossible to use the machine on this book. The clattering drove me insane, until I realized that, for the first time, the noise truly was disabling my cognitive processes. When I took up a pen, however, the words ran onto the paper with the speed of some jellyish ichor heated to mad liquidity. . . .

Letter to J. Arthur Pembroke:

From the Nethermose Wells of Hali Hour of the Dim Moaning of the Wailing Bells, in the year of F'Thagn

Dear T'chei-Ahrp-Ahmb:
Although you have not heard from me in many months, I have not been idle. Indeed, the work is nearly finished! And it is, with all my usual humility, a masterpiece. It consists of four long novelettes, and ends with a short novel. They are interconnected thematically, though no characters appear in more than one tale. No *human* characters, at any rate. Dear Gawd, Arthurius, the vistas of cosmic terror I have opened in this work dwarf all my previous puny attempts at showing my readers the truth about this world. I have done nothing less than create a *Weltanschauung* that contains the *universe*!

I expect to complete the final tale within a month. Revision should take several more. As you well know, this opus has taken me over three years to create, but had it taken twenty, it could be no greater a work.

Yrs. for the Black Testament of Thog,
Ait'ch-Ait'ch

Letter from J. Arthur Pembroke:

April 30, 1990

Dear Helmut:
You may wonder why I choose to respond to your manuscript by mail rather than by telephone or a personal visit. It's simply that I know that Teutonic temper of yours, and I wish to spare myself its lightning bolts. All this is leading up to the fact that my reaction to *The Night Testaments* is not at all positive.

I suppose there is a possibility, first of all, that this is all a gigantic and clever hoax on your part, done in order to give me a minor stroke. If so, you have nearly succeeded. Please congratulate yourself, laugh sadistically for several hours, and then send me ASAP the actual manuscript you have been working on these past forty months.

If this is *not* the case, if what I have on my desk is truly your next work that you expect me to market, I must confess that the task is impossible. I know you work in secrecy, that you prefer to say next to nothing about works in progress, even to me, and that you refuse to sell your work until it is completed to your satisfaction. I have accepted all these quirks, feeling confident that you would continue to produce not only marketable work, but work that will garner excellent reviews, spots on the bestseller lists, and prestigious awards (by the way, the Horror Writers of America wish to present you with a Life Achievement Award again—refuse as usual?). This time, however, you would have done well to take me into your confidence, so that I could have kept you from making such a terrible *faux pas*.

Helmut, I'll make this as quick and painless as possible. Neither the market, the editors, the public, nor the critics will accept plagiarized work, not even from a writer of the stature of Helmut Hecker. I admit, your reworking of H. P. Lovecraft is extraordinarily well done, but you surely must know that it is nothing more than a reworking, as if Lovecraft himself had revised his own pieces years later. In fact, that's *precisely* what it's like. I compared Lovecraft's stories to your versions, and your writing is indeed better than Lovecraft's. But I already knew that, and it is small compensation for over three years' work. What on earth were you trying to prove? I didn't even know you'd ever *read* Lovecraft, let alone were obsessed by him.

For the life of me, Helmut, I don't know what to do with this. I can not and will not present it to Knopf. It's all so obviously a swipe that I can't even suggest that it be published under a pseudonym. Even if we were to find a publisher ignorant of Lovecraft, Arkham House, the small house that publishes his works, would sue instantly.

So, I am entirely at a loss. If you wish to seek other representation, you're free to do so, but frankly, Helmut, I know of no agent, respectable or not, who would be willing to market this manuscript, which I reluctantly and sadly return. I am, as always, at your service.

Sincerely,
Arthur

Journal entry (April 6, 1990):

I have just gotten off the phone from talking to Arthur, the greatest liar on the face of the earth! How in God's name, I asked him, can a man plagiarize from a book he has never read, written by an author of whom he has never heard, except for the occasional idiot in a B. Dalton or a Waldenbooks asking if this Lovecraft influenced him? Be reasonable, I told Arthur. Three and a half years rewriting another man's work? It is impossible! I never would have done it, and told him that the joke had gone far enough. He tried to patronize me, of all things, and I fired him on the spot. All right, he said, all right, so you haven't read Lovecraft. But read him right now, he said, and you'll see. *Patronizing* me, as if I were a child! Bastard! He is lying to me somehow, lying about all of this, and I shall prove it. I am going out and batter my way into bookstores until I find a book by Lovecraft. Can such a volume be found in Providence, I wonder? No matter—I shall find it!

***Journal entry*:**

It is true.

I do not know how, but everything Arthur said is true. I went through the town, searching for bookstores until I found one open near Brown University.

There I demanded volumes of Lovecraft, and was given two thick books with absurdly juvenile illustrations on their jackets. I purchased them immediately, and stepped out onto the street, where I opened one of the volumes and began to peruse it by the light of a street lamp.

I found nothing in the first few stories to support Arthur's claim, as they were mere bagatelles, stories for little boys to frighten each other with around a campfire—one about a ghost who bites off a man's feet, another about a monster who poses for an artist—the stupidest things I have ever read. I clapped the book shut, carried it home, and began to go through the rest of the stories, reading only the first few lines of each, until I arrived at the seventh tale, the one entitled 'The Haunter of the Dark'. When I read the first paragraph I knew.

It was nothing less than a paraphrase of my own new tale, 'That Which Came by Darkness'.

I was stunned, and turned to look at the copyright page, thinking the only thing I *could* think, that this Lovecraft had somehow broken into my home, copied my manuscript, rewritten it, and had it published while I was working on related stories. But then I saw that the copyright for the volume was 1963, and that the *story* was copyrighted 1936.

I continued to look frenziedly through the volume, and found therein my allegory of thought control, 'Encased Minds', under the title of 'The Whisperer in Darkness', complete with nearly identical situations and characters. My 'Submersible God' was called 'The Call of Cthulhu', and my 'Of Deepest Knowledge' was now given the pulpish title 'The Shadow Out of Time'. With shaking hands, I opened the second volume, and learned that my crowning achievement, my short novel entitled *What We Have Inherited*, has already existed for sixty years as *At the Mountains of Madness*.

Madness indeed. What have I done? Or what has been done to me . . .?

Journal entry:

I know now. I know. I went back to that bookstore and found one more volume of Lovecraft's work, and bought a biography of the man as well. I have spent half the night reading as much as I can, and it has been enough. Still, I must write everything down so that I can examine the logic of it all, or what little logic there may be:

Facts about Hecker

1. I have never before read any work by or any books about H. P. Lovecraft.
2. I began to write *The Night Testaments* after coming to Providence to live.
3. Changes that have lately occurred in me are:
    A. I now write at night rather than in the day.

B. My style has changed tremendously, even my correspondence, as in my salutations and signatures (e.g. Ait'ch-Ait'ch).
C. As much as it pains me to write it down, I have been unconsciously plagiarizing the work of a dead writer.

Facts about Lovecraft

1. Lovecraft lived for most of his life in Providence, and loved the city deeply.
2. Lovecraft liked to write at night, and wrote in a style far more verbose than mine.
3. Lovecraft's letters were replete with tiresome 'in-jokes', such as signing himself E'ch-Pi-El.
4. Lovecraft loved cats.
5. Lovecraft loved ice cream and detested sea food.

Facts about Heuer

1. Heuer was bought in Providence, and seemed to blossom when we returned here.
2. Heuer is a cat.
3. Heuer loves ice cream, but, unlike most cats, detests fish.
4. Heuer was in my study with me whenever I worked on *The Night Testaments*.

It seems clear. But before I draw the logical conclusion, I must make one experiment. Leaving Heuer in the room, I shall try to begin a new story. Then, after a line or two, I shall take Heuer to the basement, shut him in, and try to write again. . . .

***Fragments** (on single crumpled page)*:

West of Fenton the hills rise wild, and there are valleys with deep woods no ax has cut. . . .

I have been asked before why I fear a draught of cool air. . . .

The most merciful thing in the world is the inability of the mind to correlate its contents. . . .

***Fragment** (on second page)*:

Blood the color of roses screens my vision.

Her blood, shed for my sin, for the sin of men, of man, of mandarin manipulators of manacles, maniac, mangel-wurzels, and yes, I said yes how I would mangle her wurzel. . . .

***Journal entry*:**

No doubt lingers. The first page bears slight rewrites of the beginnings of Lovecraft tales, while the second shows no trace of that simple-minded Puritan. It is Hecker, Hecker, pure Hecker and no one else.

My conclusion then? That cat who now is shut up in the basement is nothing less than the reincarnated spirit of Howard Phillips Lovecraft.

Does not Heuer sound like Howard? And the distaste for seafood, the love of Providence—it all fits, does it not? Of course! While in the presence of this reincarnate mind, I was telepathically affected by it to the point of revising its own blasted work. I know it sounds ridiculous—a reincarnate telepathic cat!—but no more so than some of these egregious and incestuous theme anthologies I am always being asked to participate in. If an entire book of tales about lesbian vampire dolphins is acceptable to the great unwashed, how much more easily can my own present situation be believed!

One thing remains—the death of that creature who has caused me to waste a great part of my creative life. To think that I, Hecker, have thrown away years of talent merely rewriting the work of a man whose idea of a climax was to have the narrator write down his screams as a monster destroys him! Whose idea of wordplay and alliteration was to write of ghouls and gugs and ghasts! Whose poetry was even more noxious than his prose, and whose work could only find publication in the shabby pages of *pulp magazines*!

I shall destroy that beast with orgasmic pleasure. I shall literally rend it apart with my hands, breaking its paws first of all so that it shall scratch me as little as possible. Then I shall pluck out its yellow fur in great lumps, revealing the skin beneath, sodden with blood; I shall pluck out its whiskers one by one, then its teeth, and finally its eyes, mashing them to jelly on the floor. Then I shall yank out its tongue, that demonic tongue that never meows. And then—then I shall have some *real* fun. . . .

***Journal entry*:**

It got away.

A cellar window was open, and the damned beast must have pushed the screen aside and squeezed through. What a disappointment! But no matter. It is gone from my life. All that remains of it is that chasm of desire for its destruction that still gapes within me. It must be filled and satiated, if not with that monster's guts, then with the whimpers of another victim. Tonight I shall find a woman, some whore who, for enough money, will acquiesce to my demands. There must be junkies in Providence, yes? And then, when I am finished, when she leaves, exhausted, terrified, bleeding, then I shall sleep, and when I awake I shall begin again with my work.

But first I shall pillory Lovecraft.

I shall write an attack on him that will rattle the teeth of his idiotic admirers, that will insure that his damned name will never appear within the pages of any learned journal, that will make it an intellectual *crime* even to admit to having *read* the man's tripe! I shall——

I don't know why I broke off just then. I felt as though—but no, that's impossible—as though I were being watched, not only by eyes, but by . . . another mind.

Absurd.

But then why do I write on? When everything within me wishes to fling down the pen, rise, shake off this feeling, go out and find a slut, why do I remain here scribbling these words? Get up, Hecker! Arise, I tell myself! But I cannot!

And now I turn my head toward the doorway while I write on, and I see the source of my scrivening——

There sits Heuer! His tail wrapped around him, staring at me with huge, green eyes! All within me rages—I would leap up, grasp my chair, and smash him into a shattered mass of bone, muscle, and fur—but instead I *sit* here! *Scribbling*, like one of that damned Lovecraft's narrators!

I shall not let this creature steal my mind! My will is stronger! For I am Hecker! Hecker!

Hecker!

Hecker

Heuer

Heuer

Howard.

No! I shall break this spell if I must die to do it! I shall thrown down the pen—now! And escape!

The beast comes closer—closer—it leaps up onto my desk, sits directly in front of me, its eyes blazing!

No! It shall not take me! I tear my eyes away from its gaze!

Now—if only I could drop this cursed pen from my paw. . . .

My *paw*?

***Letter to J. Arthur Pembroke*:**

The Ancient Hill
May 30th, 1990

Dear Arthurius,

Many thanks for your inquiry as to Heuer's health. His temperament, as you know from your last visit when he scratched you, had been gradually worsening, so it was with sorrow but no little surprise that I found his torn body in the back yard the other day. I assume that the other cats of the neighborhood had had quite enough of his bullying, and joined forces to end his violent career.

I am indeed glad that the most recent chapters of *The Night Testaments* were to your liking, and enclosed are several more for your perusal. Again, I render my deepest apologies for that abysmal first draft, and my unforgivable burst of temper when you recognized it as the grossly derivative work it was. It seems as though my humble scribblings had to find their proper voice. I'm only sorry that it took so long to establish it. I'm quite content now, working from the philosophical core of that, if you will, 'posthumously collaborative' effort, and am pleased that you find it not only marketable, but meritorious. I sincerely hope the editors will agree with your kindly opinion, as it is quite unlike my previously published work. Perhaps we can speak of any revisions you feel necessary when I visit those Cyclopean modern towers of Manhattan Island next month to attend the fête thrown by the Horror Writers of America, whom I have recently joined.

Which reminds me—I have written to those running the World Fantasy Convention to be held in Providence this fall, and have informed them that I would be delighted to assist in any way possible. I offered specifically to aid in the bus tour of 'Lovecraft's Providence', since I feel that I might be able to show them some associational sites in the city of which they may not have been otherwise aware.

Yr. obt. Servnt.—
E'ch-E'ch

The Bookman

BOOKS CAN HAVE A LIFE of their own. It's a cliché, usually conditional on the quality of the book, as in *good* books can have a life of their own. But any book can, and not only in a figurative sense. I didn't know that when I first saw Nevin Huber's collection, first explored his houseful of paper. When I found out the truth, I felt as though I was living one of those wild fantasies I used to love reading about. But living it wasn't as much fun. It was like being a brittle butterfly pinned to yellow and equally brittle pulp paper.

But dear God, what a wonderland that house was to me at first—thirty thousand books, five thousand of which were older paperbacks. Ten thousand magazines, nearly all of them fiction, and half of them pulps. The condition? The Pacific could have thrilled Balboa no more than the way the sight of all that fine to mint material thrilled me. I felt my blood tingle, my heart pound, and that little node on my brain marked 'collector' shoot hot enzymes like tiny needles into every extremity. It was better than sex.

Science fiction and fantasy is my favorite genre, and there were complete runs of *Astounding Stories* and *Amazing Stories* through the thirties, hundreds of first editions in hardcover (nearly all of which had dust jackets) and paperback, shelves full of Burroughs and Wells, Verne and Haggard. It was paradise, and nearly every volume was unread, unopened, untouched. There weren't even any eye tracks.

The auction was what first drew me to the house. I'd pretty much given up on trying to find pulp magazines at local estate auctions in my Bible belt county, because ninety-nine times out of a hundred, when the ad says 'old magazines', what's there is religious weeklies. But my wife Jenny and I took a chance, and found several piles of near mint *Fantastic Novels*, *Double Detective*, *Movie Action*, and others, all of which I bid on successfully and gathered in thankfully. By the end of the sale I had over two hundred pulps, for which I paid only about a quarter apiece.

Afterward a long, lanky gentleman in his sixties came up to us, and introduced himself as George Huber, the son of the late owner of the house. 'Like those old magazines, do you?' he asked me out of the corner of his mouth that wasn't occupied by a giant briar pipe.

'Sure do,' I said, trying not to appear too triumphant or too overjoyed.

'I got a lot more of 'em.' He dropped it casually, but it hit me like a grenade. I wanted to physically surge toward him, embrace him, shake him, but held it back.

'Really?' I felt about as suave as a drunken seventeen-year-old in a whorehouse. 'You didn't auction them?'

'No, just wanted to put a few out, see if there was much interest.' He sucked on the pipe for a moment. 'Guess there wasn't.' It was true. There had only been one other bidder, an antiques dealer who had little interest and even less knowledge of paper. 'You want to see the rest? Maybe make me an offer?'

Needless to say, I did, and we made an appointment for an evening of the following week. George Huber did indeed have 'a lot more of 'em', a whole roomful, to be exact. No *Weird Tales*, unfortunately, but damn near everything else—besides the science fiction magazines, there were *All-Story*, *Argosy*, *Adventure*, *Blue Book*, more titles than I can list or remember. After some brief but friendly haggling, we settled on a price, and Jenny and I began to fill the bed of my father's pickup truck. When we had finished, George Huber showed us the rest of the house.

It was a fire inspector's nightmare, a small one story structure that had been built during the 1910s and looked its age. Of the seven small rooms on ground level, all but the kitchen had floor to ceiling shelves solidly lined with dusty books. The largest room, in the back, was also edged with bookshelves, and huge cardboard boxes piled four high made it tricky to maneuver. When we went up to the attic, I saw why the ceiling below was bowed. Old boxes were stacked to the slanted roof, permitting only thin aisles between. 'All books?' I asked.

Huber nodded. 'All books.'

'Did he ever do anything but read?' Jenny asked.

A quick smile made Huber's pipe shake. 'He hardly read at all.' Our looks of disbelief made him explain further. 'God's truth, Dad wasn't much of a reader. He just bought books. I can hardly remember his reading of nights. Mostly he listened to the radio, watched TV later, but when TV came along I was long gone.'

I was puzzled. 'But why did he buy them if he didn't read them?' It wasn't an altogether fair question. I know collectors whose passion is *collecting*, not reading, and I've paid high prices for items I knew I would never want to read. But this particular collection was eclectic as hell. As far as I could tell, the only unifying element was that it was all fiction.

Huber shrugged. 'I guess it was what you'd call an obsession. It was just like he *had* to.' His sharp-featured face softened, and he actually removed the pipe from his mouth as he reminisced. 'When we went on vacations, he'd pass a used bookstore, he'd always stop. No questions asked, he'd just stop and go in and near always came out with a shopping bag full. Me and Mom, we'd just wait in the car. Then when those paperback books came along, he wrote to the companies and had them send all the books they brought out each month, had them list him as a library—the Victoria Library, he called it, but he never loaned out any books, none at all.

'In fact, a cousin of mine took a book home with her to read when Dad wasn't here, and when he got home, he *knew*. It was really something. He knew not less than a minute after he was in the house that a book was gone, and *which* book, and who had it! I remember, he walked through the door and looked like he had an awful headache, and he sat down and said to Mom, "Why'd you let Fran take that Brontë book home with her?" And Mom asked him how he knew, and he just said never mind how, just get it back. I never saw him so mad. So Mom sent me down to my uncle's for the book, and we never let anyone take one away since.'

'Until now,' I added.

'Until now,' he agreed, nodding, placing the pipe back between his white teeth. 'I loved the old guy,' he said, 'but he sure was strange.'

He didn't know the half of it.

I wanted to buy the collections of paperbacks—complete runs of early Pocket Books, Avons, Bantams, and more, but Huber was insistent upon selling all the books, hard and soft, as a lot. I practically begged him to consider selling the paperbacks alone, and offered a quarter each for the five thousand, which he accepted a few weeks later.

Only the hardcovers remained, and, although there was no way I could have bought (or stored) them, I had noticed more than a few that I'd have liked to grace my shelves. So I called Jim Brubaker, an antiquarian bookdealer, figuring that if Jim bought the lot, I might be able to get dibs on the books I wanted.

Jim wasn't your typical bookseller, being neither old, stoop shouldered, nor myopic. Instead he was in his early thirties, with a passion for the outdoors in general and rock climbing specifically. By turns he cursed the occupation that kept him cloistered in musty rooms and blessed it for the bibliographical beauties and treasures it brought to his life, with the emphasis on beauties. For Jim loved books more than profit, and it was this side of his personality that made spending a few minutes a day in his shop such a pleasant part of my life.

The night I went to pick up my paperbacks was the first time Jim saw the books. While I carefully tucked my babies into their boxes, Jim made a cursory examination of the hardcovers, Huber dogging his heels, answering the few questions Jim asked as well as a hundred more he didn't. Though they were in other rooms, I could tell by the tones of voice that they had hit it off, and I felt euphoric at the prospect of dipping into the hardcovers.

I think that's why I was so surprised when I heard that sound as I carried the first box of books through the door. I stepped out onto the porch, thinking of nothing in particular, just feeling good about the situation, when I heard a small cry. It was a *whimper*, but not like that of an animal. I remember thinking that it was more the cry a plant might make (if a plant could cry out) at having a leaf torn off, or a branch suddenly snapped away. I stopped and listened, but didn't hear it again.

I told Jim about it later over a beer at my house. 'Spooks,' he said, smiling. 'Just spooks.'

I laughed, but wondered. 'Well, if a place were haunted, that would be it. All those fictional characters running around loose. . . .'

'It was probably just a bat or a bird outside. Maybe a rabbit. They squeal sometimes.'

Jim spent nearly a week going through the collection, then made Huber an offer and a proposition. After he picked out what he wanted for his stock (and I followed in his wake), a weekend book sale would be held for the public in the house, and whatever remained would be donated to local libraries. Huber was agreeable, and the deal was struck.

'It's funny,' Huber told Jim as he picked out the cream, 'I can't help but think Dad wouldn't have much cared what happened to the books, that he really didn't care about them as *books*, but as a *library*, y'know? 'Course, there'd be no way to keep 'em together, even if I wanted to.'

There's always sadness when a collection is broken up, when something that someone has spent years putting together falls apart with no hope of reconstruction. But the breakup of *this* collection, patternless as it was, caused not only sadness but pain, a dull ache in the heart and mind that both Jim and I felt as we bore our paper and board burdens from the house. Neither of us mentioned the feeling until later, when Jim found the manuscript, but it was there. It affected George Huber too, for he grinned neither as easily nor as often as he had before any volumes left the house. By Sunday evening, after the sale, when the last pile of books was loaded onto the final truck for delivery to a library, Jim, Huber, and I stood on the darkened porch like three out of work masks of tragedy. I had never seen a house as empty.

'It's all gone,' Jim said softly, and I think all three of us read several levels of meaning there. But Jim was wrong. It wasn't all gone. Not now, maybe not ever.

Jim called me at my office a few days later, and told me he had found something in a box of old magazines he had bought from Huber in a separate deal. He wouldn't talk about it over the phone, but said only that it was something I should read. At first I thought it might be a rare pulp I had overlooked, but there was no thrill of discovery in Jim's voice. Instead he sounded solemn, a bit confused, and uneasy.

I visited the shop at lunch, and was surprised at how pale Jim looked. When the other customers left the store, he reached behind his work table and handed me a worn manilla envelope. Inside were three sheets of yellowed paper covered with small, crabbed handwriting. It was difficult to decipher, and looked as if it had been written in haste. Jim told me that he didn't want to tell me anything about it before I read it, and guided me into a small storage room, where I sat on a sturdy box of books, and, in the naked glare of an overhead bulb, read the following manuscript written by the late Nevin Huber:

> Im going to try this way of telling what happened, if it will let me. I dont know for sure if it will or not. I dont feel it now, but I never know. It can be in me and I dont even know it till it talks to me. It doesnt really talk aloud, I dont mean that, its like it talks in my head so only I can hear it, and I talk back to it that way too so we can talk when there are other people around, and its just like Im day dreaming. It never talks to me outside the house though. I think it cant leave the house, I dont know why not. But when Im out of the house I cant tell anyone about it because I know it dosnt want me to, so I cant even though I want to. I tried to write about it at work once but I coudnt. It was like a hand was grabbing mine when I tried to make the words on paper. It *wasnt* there but it *was* somehow. I dont know if its letting me write here now at home or if its sleeping, if it ever sleeps, I dont know. Even if it lets me write it all down, Ill be really surprised if it ever lets me show it to anybody, this writing I mean. Theres no way I could show *it* because I dont know what it looks like. I think its invisable, like that book by Wells that it told me about.
>
> Im no reader myself, so it tells me about the books it reads sometimes. It really likes that Wells and those other wierd science stories in the magazines I buy for it, maybe becuase its from another planet somewher itself if its telling me the truth. I dont know why it woudnt since I do what it wants. It owns me sort of.
>
> It told me it was here a couple years before it learned how to make me do what it wanted me to. I think thats what gave me those headaiches back in 24–25 when it was practicing on me. Then one day in 26 it was just there. It was real nice at first. Its always been nice because it dosnt ever hurt me, but I *have* to do what it wants, I dont have no choice, I just cant not do it.
>
> Anway it told me real gentle so as not to scare me with what it was and where it came from, which is from some other star, a planet around the star realy. The stars the one we call Talitha, and sometimes I can find it at night. It told me it was here looking at our country when it lost its power to go anywhere, but it never told me what that really means, if its from a plane or whatever way it traveled. Anyway it was

stuck here and it cant leave this house. This is where it told me it landed but I dont know how it landed without breaking through the roof. When I asked about that it just told me I wouldn't understand and it didn't matter anyway, that I allready knew enough.

It learned quick that it liked books, we only had a few in the house when it came and it read them pretty fast. I don't mean *read* them really, because it dosnt turn the pages or anything. Id just bring a book in the house and in a few minutes it knows everything about the book without the pages ever being open. Almost like it eats it and in a way I guess it does, becuase it dosnt like it when a book goes out. It told me it hurts it becuase its become part of it, so I dont let no one borrow the books becuase it hurts it so much. It never really hurt me yet but I dont want it to get mad becuase I don't know what it would do if it did. Once when it talked to me about the books being part of it, I told it it was like a library allmost, and it liked that. I coudnt see it smile or anything, and it dosnt laugh, but I could tell it liked that. It told me that since it was a library it ought to have a name like other librarys did, and it asked me to name it. So I thought Id name it after my mother who was named after the queen of England, Victoria, and I asked if that was allright, if it was a man or a woman, and it said both and neither which made me feel funny, and then it said the Victoria library was just fine with it, so the Victoria library it was though I cant ever think of it as Victoria, just as *it*.

I dont think theres any way now that I can get rid of it or stop it. Its too strong, it always was realy, but its stronger than it used to be. I think may be it gets stronger the more books it is. Its sure cost me alot to buy all those books. Id like to spend the money more on Sarah and the boy, spend more time with them too, but so much of my time goes to old book stores and such so I can get it the books I have to at low cost. If I bought it all new we woudnt have any money at all. These pulp magazines are good becuase they only cost a dime or so and theres a whole books worth and more a lot of times. I tryed to get it other magazines for a dime or quarter but it didnt like them and told me it likes stories best, that is made up stories instead of real ones, so I only buy the pulp magazines now which are almost all story. I asked it why it didnt like real stories and it didn't answer me. May be since it cant leave here its like somebody in the hospital wholl never get well so the real world dosnt matter to

That was all. The sentence was unfinished. I held the papers in my lap for a while, then reread them. Jim entered the storeroom as I finished.

'I closed the shop,' he said. 'We won't be disturbed. So?'

'So?'

He was impatient. 'What do you think?'

I shook my head. 'Delusion. Obsessive-compulsive personality.'

'Delusion?' He looked at me through narrowed eyes.

'Sure. He became obsessed with buying books, like some people save bottle caps, or balls of string. Since he didn't know why—because he obviously didn't *read* them—he made up that story, wrote it down. Maybe to explain it to himself.'

'You believe that?' Jim looked at me belligerently, as if I were a silverfish he'd found in a book.

'Yeah, I believe it. The alternative is that some monster from outer space is living in that house, and that's right out of *Amazing Stories*, which is probably where Huber got the idea in the first place.'

'What about the cry you heard?'

I shrugged. 'Like you said, an owl, a bat, a rabbit. Why? What's that got to do with this?' I held up the papers.

'I was just thinking,' Jim said, 'that if it *was* true, if Huber wrote the truth before it stopped . . . before *he* stopped, then maybe what you heard was a cry of pain.' His voice had sunk to a whisper, as though he didn't want the boxes of books surrounding us to overhear. 'And if it was—if your mind was somehow open to the thing so that you heard it cry when a part of it—that box of books you carried—was torn away . . . Jesus.'

In the stillness of the room I recalled the strange qualities of the sound I had heard, tried to remember it as the high shriek of an animal, and knowing that it was *not* an animal . . . or at least none I had ever heard before. Then I thought about the dozens of boxes we had taken from the house, of the hundreds of people who passed through the door with piles of books, minds in a thousand other places, locked tight against the screams of a living thing being slowly, inexorably ripped apart.

'No,' I said, half in denial, half in horror. 'It just can't be. Delusion, coincidence . . .'

'What about how we felt?' Jim asked. 'You and me and Huber's son afterward, acting like something died?'

'A collection died, that's all.'

'I think you're wrong. I've had time to think about this, more time than you, and it makes so damn much sense. The fiction—it only liked fiction, and when Huber wrote down why, it stopped him. It was sensitive to it, because Huber was right, he had it pegged, it was stuck there, it could never leave!'

I closed my eyes, shook my head, but Jim's words, crazy yet totally logical, kept coming.

'The paperbacks were perfect for it—mostly fiction, just a quarter apiece, and getting them by mail gave Huber time to spend with his family. And the book the cousin took? Huber knew as soon as he came in because the thing *told* him, and it was hurt and angry, and that was why Huber was angry, angry and scared. It all adds up!'

I looked up at him, scared myself. 'So what? Even if it's all true, what do we do about it?'

'I don't know.' He swallowed heavily. 'But I want to go back to the house.'

'Are you crazy too? If you think it's true, why the hell do you want to go back? Aren't you afraid the boogie man will get you? Or is it the *bookie* man?' He didn't laugh. I didn't expect him to.

'We were there before and it didn't hurt us. It'd be much weaker now, if it's even there at all.'

'So what'll you do when you get there?' I was mad now, because I didn't want to show I was frightened.

'I don't know. Maybe try and open myself, drop my thoughts, see if it can contact me.'

'Oh, bullshit, what's the point?'

'I've got to, man! Nevin Huber had to buy books, and *I've* got to find out what the hell's going on here! Now are you coming with me or not?'

'Me? Why?'

'I don't want to go alone. If I've underestimated this thing, I'll need someone to help me out.'

'Why don't you call Ghostbusters and leave me the hell alone?'

He was quieter now, pleading with me. 'Come on, help me out. Don't you want to know?'

'Not enough. You don't know what this thing . . . *if* it's real . . . can do. Maybe it'll gobble you up and make you buy Reader's Digest Condensed Books and piles of old *National Geographic*. Now that's scary.'

'I'm going whether you come along or not.'

'Christ, Jim, only the idiot whore walks the streets when Jack the Ripper's on the loose!'

'Fine, I'm an idiot.' He smiled, just a little. 'I still haven't given Huber the extra key back. We can go in broad daylight.'

'High noon or nothing.'

His smile widened. 'High noon it is.'

'*Two* idiot whores,' I muttered.

We went at high noon the next day, a warm, sunny Saturday as scary as a Pee-wee Herman movie. The thick trees that surrounded the house made it relatively dark inside, but since we didn't want to be noticed we left the lights off. It was still bright enough to see where we were walking, and now there were no piles of books to stumble over.

There was nothing, in fact, that we could see or sense in the house except the gray dust that swirled in the few pitiful beams of sunlight that slanted through the grimy windows, and the smell of mildew and damp rot that, left to ripen a few more years, would claim the house forever.

'Satisfied?' I asked Jim.

'No. Let's look around.'

'Feel like the goddam Hardy Boys,' I said, but followed him into each room, where we stood for a while, waiting and listening for something that couldn't speak, and that I, at least, didn't want to hear.

The attic was the only room that was not vacant. It was filled with the empty cardboard boxes that had housed thousands of Nevin Huber's volumes. They sat there in the overhead attic light like brown blocks in a giant's playpen. I knew they were empty, but I somehow dreaded the thought of looking into them, and paused near the top of the steps.

Jim looked down at me reproachfully, and I joined him, stepping onto the sagging boards as if onto a scaffold, glancing into the room's shadowy corners.

'All right,' I said, 'here's the attic. Nothing here. Can we leave?'

'Wait,' Jim said, and started to make his way through the maze of dry and curling cardboard. I stood waiting, listening to his footsteps as he slowly circumnavigated the room. Then they stopped, and I heard him say, 'Come here, look at this.'

I followed his voice, and found myself under an eave with a long slant, so that I had to duck my head to see what he pointed to. At first I thought it was a pile of newspapers, but as my eyes adapted to the dim light under the roof I saw that they were tabloid-sized novel condensations published in Sunday newspapers back in the thirties.

Jim's voice seemed to come from far away. 'I wonder if it's in there,' he said. I looked at him, and saw that he was staring at the pile like a man hypnotized. Then he knelt, and looked at the brittle mass with intense concentration.

Slowly his gaze softened, relaxed until his face was a blank canvas, empty of emotion. It remained that way for only a few seconds, then started to change, very rapidly.

Jim's eyes widened, the whites turning to the color of old newsprint, the pupils nearly lost beneath the rheumy yellow film. His nostrils flared, and his jaw snapped down, hanging like a rotting branch. The very pores of his skin exuded a musty, black-green powder that I later realized must have been mildew. I stood there stunned into immobility, not moving until breath, in an attempt to form words, hissed from his throat with the bitter odor of moldering paper. I winced at the pungency of it, but it brought me to my senses.

I think I might have screamed, but I know that I grabbed my friend, pulled him back and away from the pile of papers, and held him down. I wanted to release him so that I would no longer have to touch the damp, waxy surface of his skin, but I was afraid to let him go, afraid that he would keep changing into something even more monstrous than what, in a matter of seconds, he had already become. So I held him, closed my eyes, opened them again, and when I did, his face had taken on the rudiments of humanity once more.

Suddenly he looked at me as though I was insane for holding him so tightly. 'It's all right,' he said calmly. 'It didn't hurt me.'

The tranquility on his face shocked me even more deeply than had his initial transformation. I was speechless. Then he actually smiled. 'It was in me,' he said. 'But it didn't hurt me, and I don't think it wanted to. It wasn't'—he searched for the word—'malignant.'

'But your face,' I managed to say, 'it was terrible . . . like a . . . a monster.'

He shook his head. 'I don't know why. All I felt was a kind of peace.' Then he added, uncertainly, 'And a need.'

'A hunger,' I said, and when he looked at me again, I could see his doubt had grown.

'A hunger,' he repeated, and his voice shook slightly.

'What do we do now?' I said, gesturing to the tabloids. 'Burn them?'

'No!' he said quickly. 'It would . . . I think it would destroy it.'

'Why *not* destroy it?'

'No. It can't do any harm. It won't. No one'll live in this house. It'll be torn down, another one put up in its place. Or an Acme or a twin theater, or a McDonalds.'

'We can't just leave it here. Not after what happened to you.'

He thought for a minute. 'Let's bury it then. The cellar's got a dirt floor. Let's bury the papers in the cellar. It's in there now, and there it'll stay.'

It made as much sense to me as anything else. In a shed behind the house we found a shovel with a broken handle. As we hauled the pile of papers down the two flights of stairs, I kept a running conversation going with Jim—baseball playoffs, movies, anything to keep both our minds occupied so that there was no room for an outsider.

We took turns digging the hard packed earth of the cellar floor until the hole was three feet deep, then dropped the papers into it. I shoveled the dirt back over them rapidly, and methodically, slapping down the top layer of soil as if to secure forever what lay beneath.

When we were finally out in the sunlight, Jim took a deep breath and gave a shuddery laugh. 'Jesus,' he said, 'I guess it almost had me there.'

He smiled, I smiled back, and we drove over to my house and got half loaded on too much beer, and never mentioned the house or the Huber collection to each other again.

It wasn't difficult, for my interest in book collecting waned over the next few months, and my visits to Jim's shop fell from daily to weekly to infrequently to never. And one day last spring, I saw that the windows of the shop were empty, and the hanging wooden sign shaped like a book was gone. I never tried to find out what happened to Jim. He probably moved back to New England to open a shop there, like he always said he would. But I'm afraid that I'll learn that he went out of business because he couldn't bear to part with any of the books in his store.

My collection, like Jim's shop, is gone now, because of Nevin Huber and whatever lived in his house. Or his mind, possessed by his possessions. I truly believe that his books took on a life of their own. Maybe it was a life apart from him. Maybe a thing from another star did actually come down and steal his will, create his obsession. Or, far more frightening to me, maybe the thing, instead of creating Huber's obsession, *was created by it*.

What if he started buying books, not really knowing why, but just because he was drawn to them, liked the feel, liked the *idea* of what was in them (even if he never read them), liked the way they looked on the shelves, for God's sake. I don't know, something he couldn't explain to himself, let alone to his wife or his friends. And as time passed, he *had* to explain it to himself, had to find a rational way to deal with an obsession that was taking most of his money and his time.

So he made up a story for himself about a thing that lived in his house, a thing that *made* him buy books. And his obsession was so strong, his need to believe so overpowering, that his creature became real—his books, his collection, his *accumulation* lived, spoke to him, became him as much as he became it.

And when he died, he stayed with it.

Then what had screamed as it had been dismembered, and what tried to get into Jim Brubaker, hadn't been something from another world. It had been Nevin Huber, or what his obsession had turned him into, even after death.

I don't pretend to know which answer is correct, but I think that one of them is. All I know for sure is that I don't miss my own collection. The twenty-six foot sloop Jenny and I bought with the money I got from selling it keeps us busy, and when I want a good book I go to the library. Or I buy the book, read it, and give it to a friend. I've learned to prefer salt air to pulp dust, and the creatures in the sea, though as surely hidden as those in the mind, are ones that I know, and can name, and need not fear.

A Father's Dream

YOU HAVE TO UNDERSTAND, first of all, that it was a dream. At least I *think* it was. It may have been just *déjà vu*, but I don't really think so. The intensity of the experience, the ease with which I can draw it from my mind, convince me that my memory is correct, that it *must* have been a dream.

These stories are familiar enough. The one I best recall is that about the woman who goes to a friend's country house and sees, or *dreams* she sees, a coach in the drive and a cadaverous coachman who beckons to her. Back in the city, she meets him in the guise of an elevator operator who beckons her into a full car. She leaps back, the doors close, and of course the cable breaks. Thus the premonitory dream. And now mine:

We—that is, my wife, my son, myself—are visiting the summer house of my brother-in-law in Canada. It is a white frame house, two-storied but small, like a block, square, but taller than its width. It stands by the side of the road under a gray sky. Behind it is a lake, empty of boats. My wife, my son, and I are in the kitchen of the house, having been invited by my brother-in-law to come and vacation there for a few days while he and his wife (they are childless) are elsewhere. They will join us in several days.

The kitchen is a large room with a high ceiling that belies the size of the house as imagined from the outside. It holds a refrigerator, an old, white porcelain sink, webbed with filamented cracks, a white metal table with metal legs, six matching chairs with thinly padded black plastic seats and backs, and green and white wooden cabinets above the sink. Against the outside wall, just under a window, is a couch of worn green corduroy, and next to it an old cabinet that appears to once have been used as a wardrobe. The cabinet is neither green nor white, but a thick, muddy brown, a color whose source I guess to be that of the wood itself rather than paint, for I feel that no one could consciously choose such a color.

The situation, as I relate it now, is fully realized as I come into the consciousness of the dream. No exposition is necessary. Furthermore, I simply know that there is some connection between this cabinet, now used for storing pots, pans, and appliances, and the trundle bed that is in my son's room. The room, next to the one my wife and I occupy, holds a single bed in which my boy sleeps. But beneath that bed is another that rolls out on rusty casters, no more than a bedspring on four short legs with the thinnest of mattresses over it. And I know that this tiny mobile bed and that hulking dark wardrobe have something curiously in common, a property that is in no small way responsible for the pallor and listlessness which has come over the boy ever since our arrival a few days before. There is something in these two pieces of furniture that I find disturbing, even foul. My brother-in-law and his wife arrive, and as we chat I bring up, not very subtly, the bed and the cabinet, and ask them if they have ever connected either piece with 'soulsickness'—that is the very word I use. My brother-in-law's wife laughs honestly and without understanding. But his face clouds, and he gives his head one quick shake, like a dog shunting off water, and I know he knows. Then I turn and look for my son, but he is gone, and from out on the road in front of the house comes the sound of raised voices shouting commands. I go outside and see, thirty yards down the road, a police car and an ambulance, their red lights bright in the gray day. White-coated men haul canisters, canvas, and poles toward what lies on the gravel roadside—two children, one with hair the color of fresh hay under the sun, the other with hair of a flat, lusterless brown—my son.

I run toward him, thickly, my legs pumping through jelly, I think I see his chest move (or is it merely the ground as it shifts beneath me?), and I wake up.

Rather the sensation was one of going to sleep, of *losing* consciousness instead of coming to it, so intensely real were the experiences of the dream. It was only when I grew aware of the hot flesh of my wife that I stirred, groaned, realized that I had dreamed. I sat up in amazement. My wife woke.

'What?' she said.

'A dream.'

'Mmm,' she said, turning her head on the pillow to face away from me.

I didn't tell her what the dream had been. If I had, it would ease all my doubts about the dream being real, for those doubts still exist. Yet I remember making the conscious choice not to tell her the dream; how could I otherwise recall negation? It *must* have been true. I *must* have dreamed it. I remember too getting out of bed and drinking some milk in the kitchen, thinking that in the story of the dream that the cabinet, the bed, and the blond boy must fit together in this way: the boy slept in the bed and died in the cabinet (or under it?), and his malign spirit remained in both items, its presence felt primarily by my son, secondarily by me, until it manifested itself and lured my son into the path of a car.

I had to admit that the scenario made a great deal of sense, and put the lie to what I had always held to be the irrationality of dreams. Why, it seemed almost plotted. And though it ended with the injury, if not death, of someone dear to me, I found the novelty of its cohesiveness stimulating. I hadn't known I was liable to such flights of fancy. In my job as a marketing manager for a division of a farm equipment company, there is little opportunity for creating fantasy worlds. Oh, every now and then I daydream, perhaps a bit more than my colleagues, but they've always been of the I-wish-I-were variety, not a full-blown *story*, for God's sake.

The idea flashed through my mind that I should write it down, but I was already sleepy, and the milk only made me more so. If I *had* written it down, or if I had told my wife, then later I might have been able to speak of it without thinking that I would sound like an idiot. But instead I placed it only in my memory, that convoluted realm of doubt, and am now unsure, unsure, unsure as to whether I dreamed it or not.

Enough uncertainties. I know I did.

Three weeks later we drove to my brother-in-law's house in Canada. I'm sure it was the anticipation of that trip that had caused the dream in the first place. We had never been there before, since my brother-in-law had only bought it the previous August. So I was surprised to find myself feeling an easy familiarity with the worn, two-lane road that led unswervingly through a Turner landscape of trees, rocks, and lakes. Now we drove over a wide spit of land that separated two of those lakes, flanked more closely on either side by long rows of cabins and houses.

'It should be one of these,' my wife said, craning her neck as though a shift in her head would render her eyes telescopic. My son, in marked contrast, huddled in the back seat, his gaze directed only toward the contents of one of a huge pile of Little Golden Books, his sole voluntary source of literature. Then I saw the house.

I made no premonitory remarks for my wife to later recall. I could not; I think I was partially in shock. For there stood the house of which I had dreamed, white, plain, and square, just off the road and across the gravel shoulder. In the dream I had seen it shadowed by clouds, and now it was awash with sunlight, but that was the only difference.

'It must be that white one,' my wife said.

'How do you know?' I asked huskily.

'The picture. Oh yes, that's it.'

'What picture?'

'Will sent us a picture. I showed it to you.'

'Did you?'

'Sure I did. There's the drive. Pull in.'

I recalled no picture. I *did* recall the house, but not from a picture. 'I don't think you showed it to me,' I said, driving with a crunch across the loose stones of the shoulder. She seldom showed me the photos her brother often sent, and I never read the letters.

'Yes I did,' she replied, her eyes still on the house, examining, perhaps estimating. 'Bobby, look!'

'Huh?' came the grunt from the back seat. I turned off the ignition.

'We're here,' my wife said.

The head came up reluctantly, and the boy squinted at the house. 'Is that it? We gonna stay *there*?'

'Yes.'

'How long do we hafta?'

At long last I felt that the boy was perhaps more perceptive than I had thought him. 'Two weeks,' my wife said buoyantly. 'You'll love it. We're going to *swim*, and *fish*, and go out in Uncle Will's *boat*, it'll be *great*. Let's go.'

Her door opened and she climbed out, then looked back in. '*Hey*. Come *on*, huh?'

I made myself move. I had been trying to remember if she really *had* shown me a photo, and if that had caused my dream, the whole of which now came back to me more strongly than ever. It made sense. I had seen the picture and dreamed the dream, composing a fantasia upon the flat, bare theme of the house. Inside, there would be no trundle bed, no cabinet that had once been a wardrobe.

But the cabinet was there, along with the trundle bed in the room at the door of which my wife said, 'And this will be *perfect* for Bobby.'

'Did Will,' I asked, 'send any pictures of the *inside* of his place?'

She looked at me oddly. 'No.'

I nodded. Later, while my wife unpacked the clothes in the guest bedroom, I sat on the old couch in the kitchen, and looked across the faded gray and green linoleum floor to where the cabinet sat, heavy, stern, and imposing. In the evening we played Monopoly around the kitchen table. At first my son was sitting across from me with his back to the cabinet, but on the second or third time around the board, he got up and sat in the chair to my left.

'That supposed to change your luck?' my wife asked him. I knew full well it wouldn't. He was a poor Monopoly player, unable even to remember that one needed all of a color group before buying houses.

'I didn't like that seat,' he explained, his glance shifting to the cabinet.

'They're all the same,' my wife said. The boy did not respond, but rolled and landed on Pennsylvania Avenue, which he bought despite the fact that my wife and I each had one of the other two green properties.

It had been a long drive, and by the game's end (I won, as usual) we were all ready for sleep. Just after midnight I was awakened by a cry from my son's room. My wife did not wake, so I got up and felt my way down the strange, narrow hall to his room, the door of which was ajar, casting out the less dark wedge made by his night-light. I called his name softly, fearing to wake him if he had simply called out in a dream.

'Daddy . . .' he said, and his voice was shaking. 'I'm scared.'

'Scared of what?' I asked, sitting on his bed and smoothing his sleep-roughed hair.

'There's something under the bed.'

'Sure,' I said reassuringly, feeling a ball of cold deep in my throat. 'There's another bed under there.'

'But somebody's in it,' he told me, shivering.

'No there's not.'

'*Yes*, I *heard* him.' It was *him* he said, not *it*.

'No one's there.'

'Yes, *yes* . . .'

I turned on the light. The sheet of his bed hung down over the foot-and-a-half gap between bed and floor, and I hesitated a moment before I lifted it, but lift it I did. 'There,' I said. 'See? Nothing.'

He would not hang his head over the side to look.

'Go ahead,' I invited. 'See for yourself.'

He leapt from his bed as though a snake were under it, and scurried to the far wall, where he turned and looked back.

'You see?' I said cheerily.

His face soured. 'Pull it out.'

I pulled, and the bed rattled out on its rusty rollers. The mattress was bare, of course, but I imagined I could see an indentation, like a thin S, where a small body might have once lain. Suddenly my mouth was full of a bitter taste, and I seemed to sense rather than actually smell an odor of putrefaction, a scent I remembered from the time when I was a boy and had opened the storage cellar door after Trix, our cat, had gotten trapped and died in there. I crouched and sniffed at the mattress, but it only smelled old and slightly damp, and in another second the odor of rot had vanished. 'See?' I said, straightening. 'Just an old mattress, that's all.'

His usually dull eyes were bright with knowledge of my lie. 'Somebody was *sleeping* there.'

I looked at him for a moment. 'You're a big boy. Do you really believe that?'

He sucked his upper lip. 'No . . .'

'Well. Let's go back to bed then.'

'Take it out of the room. Please.'

'Could you sleep then?'

'Yes.'

So I did. It was surprisingly light. I put it in the kitchen, stood it up on end next to the cabinet, almost as a challenge. When I passed his room, he was asleep in a soft glow.

I walked into my room at a complete loss as to what to do. The rational man within me said that everything could be explained away—my memory of a dream was really *déjà vu*, my son's fears typical and easily understood. The whole situation was due to imagination, nothing more. But the *gut* feeling, the primal man, said run, take your family and protect them by fleeing this place. There is an evil here you can't understand, one that will hurt you.

But what explanation could I have given my wife? *I had a dream, you see, but nothing I thought important enough to mention. And if we stay here, our son will be run over by a car.*

That would have been wonderful. She thought I was flaky enough as it was, without handing her a story like that. I could not tell her. I chose to be rational, and the choice seemed to be the correct one. We had a pleasant few days until my brother-in-law and his wife returned. My son's interest was piqued by the atmosphere about him that stood in such high contrast to our nearly treeless suburban development back home. Although he would neither bait his own hook with worms or unhook the few small fish he caught (seemingly by accident), he enjoyed the trees, the lake, and let his hand trail in the wake of the canoe as though expecting at any moment to grasp one of the sun diamonds that glimmered on the shifting surface. There was a closet full of games, unfamiliar to him, and in the evenings, besides the Monopoly we had brought from home, we played Clue, Sorry, and Risk. He had trouble, of course, understanding all the rules, but my wife helped him. He tried, as he did at school; but the greater his attempt, the greater his confusion, and the more pronounced became his lack of facility. I must confess to an annoyance beyond what I would have normally felt, for in the back of my mind I was still recalling that enigmatic dream of his dying, or his injury. The first day there I had forbidden him to play outside the front of the house, the side that faced the road. It was no great loss, for the front yard was small, and topped with barren dirt with only a few sparse patches of thin grass with no shade at all. The heavily treed back yard was a paradise compared to it.

I feared the road. At night, after he was in bed, and my wife was dozing in front of the blurred images on the ancient black-and-white TV, I stood at the front window and waited for the infrequent cars to come out of the night, their lights' pale blades followed by the rumble of their approach, the growl of their passing, far too fast for the narrow two-lane road. One night at eleven o'clock, after my wife had gone to bed, I was reading one of the *Cossack Tales* of Gogol I had found on my brother-in-law's shelves. I heard a car approach swiftly, followed by a scream of brakes and a dull thud, like the sound of a full oil drum being struck with a tree limb. At once I went to the front door, expecting to see through the rusty screen the glow of headlights, and perhaps the doleful red blinking of emergency flashers.

But the road was dark, and when I turned on the front porch light that partially illuminated the road, there was no car visible, nor any sign of what the car might have hit. Taking a flashlight, I walked down the road, nearly expecting, with a low ache of horror, to see a huddled body that would be my son, and perhaps another with sun-blond hair.

I found nothing. There were no tire marks, no puddle of blood. Had I been hypnotized by the late hour and the book, hearing only in my mind what I had thought to someday hear from that house?

Back inside, my son was sleeping in his bed, his right arm hanging over the side, his hand hidden in shadow where another dark hand might have been holding it. I left it there, so as not to wake him. Then I went to the kitchen and looked at the cabinet for a long time. There was no place on it I left unexamined—the underside, tangled with dust and cobwebs; the back, of a wood lighter and thinner than the rest; the top, only an inch from the yellowed paper of the ceiling; and within, where I pushed aside the contents to inspect more closely.

There was nothing of consequence to be found. Aside from the sticking of the doors to the point where it required a solid tug to open them, there was nothing at all remarkable about the piece. Weary, puzzled, disappointed, I went to bed and took a long time to get to sleep.

My brother-in-law and his wife returned the next day, and late in the afternoon he and I went out in the small powerboat and trolled along the lakeshore, staying out far enough to avoid getting snagged in the numerous patches of reeds. We sipped lukewarm Labatt's, flicked away the fat and hungry horseflies, and chatted of nothing in particular.

'Nice little house,' I finally said, and he nodded. 'Furniture come with it?'

'Uh-huh.'

'Who lived there before?'

'Old man down in Toronto used it in the summers. Had to go into a home, so he sold it.'

I fished for a while. 'Know who owned it before that?'

'No.'

'That cabinet,' I said after another pause. 'The one in the kitchen? Looks like an old wardrobe?'

'Yeah?' He was fiddling with the engine. I couldn't see his face.

'I wonder where it came from.'

'Don't know.' He turned his back toward me, his face expressionless. The engine grew louder. 'Let's go up to the end,' he said. 'My neighbor caught a nice-sized bass up there last week.'

I could have asked him more—if he had had any strange feelings about the cabinet or the trundle bed—but he had seemed totally unconcerned when I had mentioned the former, and I'm sure the question would have brought only a look of suspicion, followed by a suggestion that we get in out of the sun. A pang of disappointment went through me as I realized that the conversation had not at all conformed to the other reality of my dream, and I decided that the next day I would meet this neighbor of his and learn if he knew anything of the history of the house.

That evening my brother-in-law and his wife went to bed shortly after sunset. They had had a long drive, and pleaded tiredness. My son went at the same time, and my wife and I read and played gin until eleven o'clock, when we both retired. I fell asleep quickly, and slept soundly until sometime in the early morning, when I was awakened by a dull, thudding sound. I recall thinking it may have been the generator beneath the house, and went back to sleep.

Just after dawn my bladder awoke me, and on the way back from the bathroom I looked into my son's room. His bed was empty. My breath caught sharply in my throat, and, in my underwear, I ran outside, across the sparse front lawn, and onto the stone shoulder of the road, where I looked to both sides and saw nothing. Running down the shoulder, I strained my eyes glaring into the still-dark woods on either side. Still I saw nothing. Not once during the whole search, I later realized, did I call my son's name. It could have been from a certainty that it would do no good, but I felt it was due more to a fear that he would not answer. The motives seem similar, but there is a subtle difference between the two that makes a far *greater* difference to me.

I walked wearily back to the house. The sun had just crept above the horizon when I pushed open the door, and as it thumped closed I remembered the thudding sound I had heard the night before, like a generator, yes, but also like . . .

Someone pounding on a thick door.

He was inside the cabinet. The door was stuck so tightly that I had to use both hands to open it, and when I did, he toppled out, his head striking the kitchen floor like a ball of hard rubber. I shouted my wife's name, then pulled my son out of the cabinet. His face was a sickly blue-purple, and his eyes, half-open, were yellow rather than white. His jaw hung like a ripe fruit.

Turning him on his back, I pinched his nostrils and blew my breath into his mouth. It was hopeless, for his skin was cold and his arms and legs moved stiffly, rigidly. I would later learn that he had been dead for hours at the time I breathed into his mouth. I kept breathing, harder and faster, in an attempt to make the little chest rise, and stopped only when I became aware of my wife screaming, and my brother-in-law and his wife standing ashen-faced in the doorway.

'The cabinet,' I said to them, panting for breath. 'He crawled into the cabinet, and . . .' I looked down at him, too exhausted, too empty to weep.

The death was, of course, ruled accidental. The boy had climbed inside (or been *lured* inside, though I mentioned this to no one), pulled the door closed, and had been unable to open it again. The tight fit of the door had allowed no air to enter, and the thickness of the wood held in the boy's screams, screams that must have used up the oxygen within at a terribly fast rate. Only the pounding of his fists had been audible, and I had ignored those, as I had ignored so much else.

It was not rationality that kept me from taking my family away from that place the first time I saw the cabinet and remembered my dream—it was vanity, the vanity of an unsure man who feared being laughed at and ridiculed. And that vanity, that refusal to heed the warnings, that desire to keep that door to wisdom closed, closed the door on my son's life. How could I not feel guilty? I was given a gift of prescience and disregarded it. I might just as well have closed the door on him myself.

My wife—*ex*-wife now—could not understand it, so I am alone with my grief and my guilt.

How fitting, I often think, that the cabinet should have originally been a wardrobe. Where we hang old clothes, outmoded ideas, ancient beliefs. Old rags of the mind. And when we try them on, it's surprising how well they still fit.

We should keep doors open, and I do, all the doors I can. Open doors let truth out. But every night, just before I fall asleep, I hear one close, so clear and sharp a sound that it seems to be in my room. Then I turn on the light and see that the closet door is still open. I walk through my open bedroom door into the other open rooms, and make sure the closets, the cupboards, all the doors are open, all open. Then I go back to my bed again.

But every night that single door closes, drifts shut as I try to drift into sleep, and I can find nothing with which to prop it open.

Coventry Carol

Lully, lulla, thou little tiny child,
By, by, lully, lullay.

I

AFTER IT HAPPENED, Richard was unable to eat grapes. He bought a bunch at a farmers' market, and set the bag on the car seat next to him, planning to munch on them as he drove home. But when his teeth pierced the resilient green skin and the juice burst tartly over his tongue, the image came immediately to mind of what had been floating there in the toilet bowl only a few weeks before. He pulled the car onto the shoulder, spit out the grape, and gagged, but was able to keep from vomiting. Then he hurled the grapes into the bushes for the rabbits, the groundhogs, the deer. For simpler animals, whose minds did not make such tenuous connections, such fine distinctions of taste.

For the primitive.

II

Both he and Donna had wanted the baby. It was time. They were in their mid-thirties, and the tales of complicated pregnancies haunted their age group as Hansel and Gretel's witch haunted young children. Hydrocephaly, brain damage, and worse, all because of the waiting. There was, Donna once joked, a price to be paid for living in the bygone Age of Me.

The timing was right in other ways too. Richard had just been made a full professor, and the market research firm where Donna had worked for the past six years was gearing down, so that her departure would save the necessity of firing a colleague, and odds were good, she was told, that in a year or two, when she was ready to return to a job, there would be a job to return to.

Two weeks after they discovered Donna was pregnant, they started on the nursery. Their farmhouse, which they had bought in their early twenties, had transformed over the years, changing as they grew older. In the first few years they had worked only on the kitchen, their bedroom, and their bath, leaving the rest of the building to its previous squalor, so that if, in one of the many parties of those early years, a joint fell burning and unnoticed to the floor, or a beer can spilled, or a bottle of Cribari shattered, it was of no account. The room would be redone someday.

And as they and their circle of friends aged and changed, left Cribari and Bud in cans to the closets of college memories, grew to be more careful with burning drugs of all kinds, started to marry and have children and divorce, to solidify and melt and rethicken, so did the parties and the house change. Carpets covered the planks too scarred to refinish, furniture of wood and glass and chrome replaced the overstuffed monstrosities that had sponged up little less beer than their occupants had drunk. Unframed film posters fell like dead leaves before the winter white walls, the stark muted graphics.

The farmhouse was different from when they had moved in, but it was, then and now, theirs. Only two rooms on the third floor and one on the second remained untouched, and it was that second floor room they worked on, sanding, scrubbing, cleaning, painting, preparing it for the child who would soon arrive.

They were painting the evening it happened, listening to an old Crosby, Stills, and Nash tape on the remote speaker. The music was punctuated by the slap of the rollers, and at times their motion fit the music's cadence, making Richard smile, then concentrate again on the rough plaster, putting his weight heavily against the roller so that the paint filled the crannies, lightened the dark tiny valleys.

He became aware that Donna's roller was silent, and turned to look at her. She was sitting on the floor, her back propped against an unpainted wall, her legs splayed out in front of her. She had pulled the sweatband from around her brow so that her ash blonde hair hung loose, and she was twisting the band in her hands. Her lip shook, and tears dropped from her cheeks onto the front of her old, faded blue work shirt. She looked like a handcuffed prisoner, alone and miserable.

'Donna?' he said. 'Honey, what's wrong?' He set his roller carefully in its tray, and knelt in front of her, hoping that it was anticipation and anxiety that had brought her down rather than pain.

She shook her head angrily, and he felt his stomach tense. These were not tears of joy.

'Donna?'

She opened her lips and took several deep, slow breaths through her teeth. At last she looked at him challengingly. 'I'll be all right.'

'What is it?'

'I'm *scared*. Okay?'

Her antagonism made him uncomfortable. 'Scared?' he muttered.

'Yes, scared. May I be scared?'

'Well . . . well, sure. I'm scared too, honey. Of the responsibility, the . . . the changes it's going to mean. . . .'

'You would be.' Her words were cold.

'What?'

'I'm scared for the baby,' she said quietly. 'And you're afraid you're going to have your life style cramped.'

'Donna, how can you say that? I *want* this baby, and you . . .'

She broke down then, and her arms went out to him, so that he gathered her in and held her tightly. 'I'm sorry, Rick,' she cried, 'but something's wrong, something *is*, I *know* it. . . .'

'Okay, relax, relax,' he crooned. 'Have you told the doctor?'

'Yes, yes, he says it's nothing, that nothing's wrong.'

'Have you been spotting?'

'No.'

'Cramps, pains?'

'No . . . twinges. It's just, oh God, a *feeling*. It sounds so stupid, so foolish, but it's *there*.'

He continued to hold her. 'You know,' he said slowly, 'you can't go through the whole pregnancy like this.'

'I don't think I can have a healthy baby,' she said with a sincerity that chilled him.

'That's ridiculous. Don't say that.'

'But all we did over the years. The grass, Christ, we did acid a couple of times, and the coke. . . .'

'We're not doing it *now*, and we won't any more, and that's what's important.'

'And the abortion,' she added desperately, 'when we couldn't afford . . .'

He cut her off. 'The doctor knows all about that, and it doesn't mean a thing. You heard him say that it would have no effect at all on this baby.'

'Yeah. I heard.'

'Donna, expectant mothers worry all the time. They worry if they drink coffee, they worry if they smoke, it's only natural.'

'I know all that, I just . . .' She paused, her eyes far away. 'I want this baby so much. I want to hold it and love it and watch it grow, and sing lullabies to it. I want everything I did in the past to stop, and to start everything over with this baby, have everything new, forget everything I did and was. . . .'

'Hey,' Richard interrupted, 'you don't have to feel guilty about a thing.'

She looked at him and smiled. 'If I don't, Richard, who will?'

'Donna . . .'

'You have to take responsibility sometime.'

'And we will. We *are*. But don't get upset before anything happens. Seven months is a long time, honey.'

'I know. All right. Forget it then. Let's get back to work.'

They started painting again. The CS&N tape ended, and after a while Richard heard Donna humming a tune. 'Pretty,' he said.

She stopped. 'Hmm?'

'The song. You were humming.'

'Was I?'

'Coventry Carol,' he said, renewing the supply of paint on his roller. He sang in a light baritone.

> '"Lully, lulla, thou little tiny child,
> By, by, lully, lullay."'

'Is that the name of it?' she asked. 'I must have heard it on the radio.' It was a month before Christmas, and the airwaves were filled with carols. Richard sang on.

> '"Oh sisters two, how may we do
> For to preserve this day
> This poor youngling for whom we do sing
> By, by, lully, lullay."'

She hummed as he sang, and when they'd finished the Coventry Carol, they sang others, sacred and secular—'Oh Come, All Ye Faithful', 'Up On the Housetop', 'What Child Is This?' and 'The First Noel'. Finally Donna set down her roller. 'Be right back,' she said.

'How about bringing me back a beer?' Richard asked.

'You got it.'

He heard her walking unhurriedly down the hall, heard the door to the bathroom close. He worked on, and found himself softly singing the Coventry Carol once more. It was no wonder, he thought. The tune was haunting, though melancholy for a Christmas song. There was sadness in it, as though its composer had kept in mind the ultimate destiny of the new-born child.

Then Donna screamed.

The sound froze him for a heartbeat, and he dropped the roller with a wet slap onto the floor, leaped from the ladder, and ran out the door, down the hall, where he threw open the door of the large guest bath.

His wife lay on the cold white tiles, her jeans and underwear in a tangle around her knees. Her body, shaking with sobs, was hunched embryonically, and her hands were buried between her thighs, as if striving to hold something in. A few watery drops of blood dotted the floor.

'I knew it, I told you,' she gasped. 'It's gone, I lost it, oh, Rick, I lost it. . . .'

He knelt beside her and smoothed the wet hair back from her hot forehead, whispering, 'Shh, shh,' not wanting to look into the toilet bowl, unable not to.

It was there. He could barely make it out, floating in a gelatinous cloud of blood and pus. The deep yellow urine darkened it further, a tiny, monstrous fish swimming in some underground sea.

My daughter. My son.

He wanted to vomit, but he kept it down, although the taste of bile was strong at the back of his throat. He started to reach for the flush handle automatically, as he would to flush down a spider, a wriggling centipede, a battered fly, then stopped, realizing that it was neither fly nor fish, but something that was to have been human, that was to have been—that *was*—his child. So he closed the lid, and turned his attention back to Donna.

'Come on, can you get to the bedroom?' His voice was thick with sorrow.

Hers was thinned by tears. 'I think . . . think so.'

'Ought to lie down,' he said, getting an arm beneath her. 'You lie down and I'll call the doctor.'

'Oh, Rick . . .'

'Now, it's all right, it's over . . .'

'I *lost* it.'

'It's done, it's over now, just relax.'

She leaned against him as they went down the hall into their room, her feet dragging, stumbling across the carpet.

'I knew it, *knew* it, all my fault . . .'

'Shh. It's not, Donna.'

'Oh yes, yes it is.'

He helped her take off her paint-spattered shirt and kick off her jeans. Tenderly he lowered her back against the pillow and stepped into the adjoining bath, where he took a lavender towel from a high, fluffy stack. When he came back into the bedroom a wave of love shook him as he saw her lying there clad only in an old t-shirt, her lower half bare and vulnerable as a child's. He tucked the towel beneath her hips and drew the sheet over her.

'Some water?' he asked. She looked at him strangely. 'Some water to drink?' he explained. She shook her head no. Tears pooled in her eyes as she stared at the ceiling. 'All right. You rest. You just rest now, and I'll call the doctor.' He could have used the phone by the bed, but he didn't want her to hear him say that she'd lost the baby.

Richard kissed her forehead, tucked in her sheet, and left the room. On his way to the downstairs telephone, he passed the open door of the guest bath and stopped, looking in at the stained tiles and grout, the closed lid of the toilet bowl, and wondered what he should do.

Then he knew, knew what the doctors and the laboratories would want, knew what they would want to see so that they could find out what went wrong, so that maybe he and Donna could try again and have a baby, a *real* baby, and not what floated, dead, in the cloudy water, not what he would now have to preserve, to save for study, dissection.

My child. Stained sections on a microscope slide.

'So be it,' he whispered aloud, remembering burying his first dog, scooping his dead goldfish from the smooth surface of the fish bowl. 'So be it.'

With a soft pop, he pulled a paper cup from the wall dispenser, then knelt and lifted the lid. It was there, as he knew and feared it would be, drifting against the white porcelain, still shrouded in its coverlet of thick blood and fluid, perhaps still dreaming that it was safely ensconced in its amniotic home.

Even now it was swimming, wasn't it, so unbelievably tiny, and yet a person. . . . *There*, did the little arms move? Arms or paddles, but yes, there were fingers, or the buds that would have been fingers, weren't there? Like a fly, oh certainly no bigger than a fly, and the limbs *did* move, yes, there *again*, and it *was* swimming, or trying to, wriggling like a tadpole, and wasn't it still alive, oh yes, of *course* it was, and he could save it now, and put it back where it could grow, couldn't he? Of course he could, he was the *father*, and he *could*, of course, of course . . .

Oh sisters two, how may we do
For to preserve this day
This poor youngling . . .

In a bottle, he thought suddenly, coldly, damning fantasies and accepting the real. *Preserved in a bottle*.

He dipped the cup into the water, pulled it against the side until what he wanted was surrounded by the paper, and then lifted it up out of the bowl, pressing the flush lever so that the urine and detritus whirled and sank away, and the water was fresh and clear again.

He carried the cup with the fetus down to the kitchen, put aluminum foil over the top, and placed it at the back of the refrigerator, next to the tray of baking soda, gray with age. As he dialed the doctor's number, he found that he was humming the Coventry Carol again.

III

'It's best that it happened,' Richard said.

'I can't believe that.'

'You know what he said—it would have been impossible to carry it to term, and if it *had* been born . . .' He left it unfinished and sipped his wine. It was the evening of the day Richard had thrown away the grapes. The fetus had disappeared into a laboratory, and was no doubt destroyed by now. Donna had recovered completely, at least physically. They had hardly spoken about it. He did not want to force her. The doctor told him in private not to push it, that she seemed extremely depressed (as if he couldn't tell), and that it would be best to let her come to terms with what had happened on her own schedule.

Tonight he had finally talked her into a glass of wine, which had loosened her tight facade enough for her to say, slowly and carefully, 'Well, I really did it, didn't I?'

Nature's way, Richard had replied, spoon-feeding the words the doctor had given him. Donna would not accept them, would accept nothing but the concept that her sins had found her out, and destroyed her child. 'I wouldn't have cared,' she said, 'if it *had* been a monster. I would've loved it.'

Richard could say nothing in response.

'Would you?' she asked him.

'What?'

'Have loved it? If it hadn't been right?'

'It still would have been my child,' he answered, too glibly.

'Until I killed it,' she said.

'You didn't do any such thing.'

'What I did killed it.'

'That's stupid. There's no way to know that,' he said.

'So there's no way to refute it,' she replied. 'Damned if I do, damned if I don't. And my poor little baby is damned forever.'

'Stop talking like that. It was a . . . a mistake, that's all, just a genetic fluke, Donna. It could have been as much *my* fault as yours, for Christ's sake. It *never* would've been a baby—odds are it couldn't have survived a minute out of the womb.'

She grew pale as he talked, but he couldn't stop. He had to tell her what he'd been thinking, what he'd been aching to say. 'You did *nothing*. Things *happen*, things like this *happen* to mothers who've never smoked a cigarette or had a beer. It could've been something that's been in you or me since we were *born*, something the goddam factories put into the air or water or food that just didn't *agree* with you, it could've been so goddam *many* things, Donna. So stop. Please. Just stop killing yourself over what you couldn't help. Let's just think ahead. To the next one.'

The look she gave him was cold, foreign, one he had never seen on her face. 'There isn't going to be a next one.'

'But . . . but there's no reason we . . .'

'No more,' she said. 'We can still fuck'—he blanched at the harshness of the word in her mouth—'but not for a baby. I won't do this again. I mean it.'

'But nothing says that this would happen again.'

'I won't take the chance.'

'Life's *full* of chances, Donna. From the minute . . .' He stopped.

'From the minute you're born,' she finished for him.

'Yes. From the minute you're born.'

'I'm sorry, Rick.'

'We should see someone.'

'No, there's no point.'

'A counselor, a . . .'

'A psychiatrist?'

'Maybe. Donna, I know, I know it was hard to lose it, it was hard for me too, but you can't let it rule your life.'

'It won't. Just maybe the one small part of it, that's all.'

Richard felt exhausted, unable to prolong their verbal skirmish. Her defenses seemed impregnable anyway, at least for now. In time, he thought, reason, the reason *he* possessed, might prevail. But not now. Not so soon.

That night, in bed, he put his arm around her and she moved into his warmth, but they did not make love, and he wondered if they ever would again.

Long after midnight, Richard awoke, conscious of Donna sitting up in bed next to him. Even in the dark, he could sense her tension, her attitude of expectant listening. 'Donna?'

'Shh.'

'What is it?'

'Listen.' Her voice shook with excitement. Slowly he began to be aware of an alien sound just on the edge of audibility, similar to the tiny cracks and pings of expanding and cooling heat ducts that he spent the evenings of October getting used to. But this new sound seemed non-metallic, liquid in nature. It was nothing so simple as a drip, but it *was* rhythmic, a steady, constant *surge* of sound, like waves on a shore, though they were five hundred miles from the nearest beach. It was haunting, soothing, restful, and Richard thought there was a familiarity to it. It was tantalizing, elusive, and he knew that if he could only think back, think back *far* enough . . .

The furnace kicked on, and its barreling *whoosh* swept the sound and the nearly grasped memory far away. 'Damn!' Donna cried. 'Oh *damn* it!' Beside her, Richard shook his head as though coming out of a dream. 'You heard it?' she said, switching on the lamp, barely blinking at its sudden glare.

'Yeah. Sure I did.'

'What *was* it?'

'I'm . . . not sure.'

'Where was it coming from?'

And he knew. Even though the sound seemed to lack any positive direction, he knew its source.

'The bath,' she whispered, saying what he would not. 'The guest bath.' She turned as he nodded agreement, and stepped onto the cold wooden floor. Without pausing for a robe, she left the room and moved down the hall. He followed her.

When he arrived at the guest bath, she was already inside. The bright fluorescents had flickered into life, but their hum and the muffled rush of the furnace could not quell the other sound, that deep roar of moving fluids, the ebb and flow of the thick, heavy juices of life, all the churning activity of the womb. It was impossible to remember it, but he knew it could be nothing else.

'Oh my God,' said Donna. 'It's the baby.'

The closed lid of the toilet started to rattle, lightly at first, then began to chatter like a giant bridgework, rising so high that he almost, but not quite, got a glimpse of what was inside. He walked past Donna and stood beside the clattering bowl, staring down at it, the surging sound all around him now.

'Open it,' she said hollowly.

He began to reach down, but before his fingers could touch the vibrating lid, it snapped open like a hungry mouth, startling him, making him stumble backwards into his wife. The lid stayed open, showing them the water inside.

It was as black as ink, the unrelieved black of midnight cellars. As they watched, it started to slowly swirl and sink soundlessly downward, and more water, just as black, entered from under the rim to pour down, dance and turn and sink, over and over again, the sound of it lost in the pulse of the thicker liquids, that cacophony which poured over them, drowning their senses.

'Stop,' Richard said, or thought he said, as he could not hear his voice. 'Stop!' he cried again, and this time it was thinly audible. Now he shrieked, '*Stop!*' and it cut the surging, parted the liquid waves of sound that deafened them, and the waters stopped pouring, the roar of fluid, of heartbeat, of life force quieted, leaving them in a flat, dead silence, a silence in which he *saw*.

It could have lasted only a split second, but in its brief space the bathroom winked from sight, and in its place was a face, huge and malformed. It was the face of a beast, yet a beast of *potential*. It was as primitive in form as a child's drawing, yet the texture of the flesh was rich, finely grained, highly defined, viewed with perfect clarity. It was crowned by a vast and fleshy dome, bisected by a line of demarcation that could only be there to divide the hemispheres of its massive brain. The lower half of the face was composed of folds and wrinkles, out of which Richard could define loops of flexed muscle parodying a nose, and, beneath it, a broad, mountainous ridge that split the face from side to side, sinking at the edges into a countenance-spanning frown. On those hummocky sides of the primitive face hung two pouches, with a pit in each, that Richard knew would be eyes. They were not now. The thing was blind, though he felt it saw nonetheless, and his fear at seeing the thing was dwarfed by the realization that he in turn was seen.

He gasped and drew back, and the vision vanished. Once again the whiteness of the bathroom was all around him, and he heard no sounds but his own ragged breathing, the rumble of the furnace, the voice of Donna beside him.

'Did you *see*?' she said, as though she still could.

'See what?' he asked, praying she'd say the water, or the lid jiggling, hoping against hope that she had not seen what he had. If so, it had to have been real. They could not both be mad.

She shattered his hopes forever. 'The face.' There was unimaginable awe in her words. 'It was the baby. I saw it.'

So simply, he realized that she must be right. The face of a fetus, unborn, undeveloped, primitive in the extreme, little different from the fetus of beast or fish or fowl. How long, he tried to recall, before a fetus shows traces of being mammalian? And how much longer after that until displaying signs of humanity? Longer, surely, than eight weeks.

Oh, dear Christ, what had happened here? What had died? And what still, impossibly, lived?

IV

When Richard and Donna looked at the water in the bowl, it was perfectly clear and still. Indeed, there was not a thing in the bathroom to ascertain the sounds and sights they had experienced. It was as though they had undergone the same delusion, though Richard found that theory so unlikely as to be impossible. He had seen what he had seen, heard what he had heard, and that it had been a delusion occurred to him only momentarily.

The later manifestations, though, were quick and short and sharp, like jabs of temper, angry releases of ghostly frustration. The first of them occurred when he and Donna sat at the kitchen table, drinking instant coffee, trying to determine what had happened in the guest bath and why.

'It was the baby,' Donna said with rigid certainty.

'It couldn't have been.'

'You saw it.'

'I saw *something*.'

'It *was* the baby.'

'Donna, the baby's dead. It *died*. I *don't* believe in ghosts.'

'How else can you explain it?'

'It can't . . .'

'*Listen*,' she said. 'I don't believe either . . . *didn't*, at least. But if ghosts are supposed to result from violent things that happen, from . . . from *traumatization*, well, *God*, can you imagine anything more traumatic than being stillborn? Being yanked out of the only place in the world where you can survive?'

'So what are you saying? That . . . that somehow this thing that wasn't even *born*, that was never even alive, that never had'—he felt absurd saying it—'a *soul*, has come back as a ghost to flush our goddam *toilet*?'

He laughed at his words, and as he did his untouched coffee mug tipped over, pouring a half-cup of scalding liquid onto his stomach, groin, and thighs. The thin robe he wore offered no protection, and he gasped and stood up, letting the steaming brew drip off of him, trying not to cry out.

Donna, shocked, leaned toward him as if wanting to help but not knowing how. In a few seconds, after the first searing pains were over, he opened the robe. The flesh of his loins was bright red, but there were no blisters. He took a jar of cold water from the refrigerator, poured some into his cupped hand, and patted it on his skin. 'Bastard,' he whispered fervently.

'How the . . .' He stopped, knowing the only answer.

'*It* did it,' Donna said. 'Because you laughed.'

It took Richard a moment to speak again. 'I'm going to bed,' he said, wrapping the wet robe around him. 'We'll talk about this in the morning.'

The morning came slowly. Richard lay awake, listening for noises, his eyes staring at the false lights of the darkness, seeing that bulbous face in his memory. When daylight came, they did not speak of the night before, and Richard kept one hand firmly on his coffee mug.

Nothing happened for a week. Donna seemed exhausted and slept well, but Richard took a long time to get to sleep, and when he did, his night was haunted by disquieting dreams he could not remember in the morning.

Donna had said nothing about going back to work, and Richard brought it up only once. She dismissed it rather flippantly, which annoyed him. Mortgage payments were not small, and it seemed to him a waste to have her idle at home. Still, he remembered what the doctor had said, and did not press her.

A heavy snow storm blew up the following Thursday, and rapid changes in temperature crusted the white-covered roof with ice. A warm front came into the area on Saturday, and the snow beneath the ice melted. Unable to drip off the roof because of the ice dam above the spoutings, the chill water trickled beneath the eaves, down into the walls, and ultimately dripped from beneath the interior window sills. It had happened one previous winter, and Richard and Donna grudgingly packed towels beneath the sills, bundled up, and went outside. Richard took a hatchet and ladder from one of the outbuildings, wedged the ladder into the snow, and climbed up to the edge of the two-storey high roof, where he began to hack long chunks of ice from above the rusty spouting. Donna stood below, watching from a distance of a few yards, her booted feet wedged firmly in eighteen inches of snow.

Richard was leaning far to his left, trying to minimize the number of times he had to descend and shift the ladder, when the house suddenly seemed to slew to his left. The sensation lasted only a moment, and he knew he was falling, the ladder with him. He pushed back and away, thinking only that he must not smash into the house. He felt his body leave the ladder, float dizzily, and fall. The impact as he hit the ice made a sharp *crack*, and he was still, lying on his side in the snow beneath the icy crust.

'Richard!' Donna cried, wading toward him. 'Richard! Don't move!'

He had no intention of doing so until he knew he was capable of it. His heart was ratcheting, yet he felt curiously alive, as though he had just stepped from a particularly invigorating roller coaster ride. 'I'm . . . I'm all right. I think I'm all right.' He tried a few tentative movements. There was no pain. 'I'm okay.' He struggled through the thick snow to his feet. 'What the hell happened?'

The ladder lay where it had fallen, the base at least twenty feet from where it had been solidly rooted in the snow.

'My God,' he whispered. 'What on earth . . .'

'It didn't fall,' Donna said. 'It was just like it . . . like it was pulled out of the snow and thrown away. Like some invisible hand.'

'That's impossible,' he said thickly.

'Look. Look for yourself.'

He saw that she was right. Had he merely overbalanced, the ladder's base would have been next to the holes in the snow. As it was . . .

'This is crazy,' he said. 'Some freak, that's all. The way it hit, it bounced or something. Just some freak.'

'Don't do any more. Let's go inside.'

He looked at the ladder, then up at the roof, from which he had chipped well over half of the ice. There should be space for the melting water to drain off now. Yes, he told himself, there *should* be.

'Please, Richard.' Donna took his arm. 'I love you. I don't want you hurt.'

He let her lead him into the house.

The next evening he was taking a shower when Donna came into the bathroom to get a pair of tweezers. As she opened the door to leave, the shower caddy, laden with several pounds of soaps, shampoos, and rinses, tore loose from the tile and fell, hitting Richard sharply in the back of the neck. When they looked, they found the adhesive had not dried out.

On Sunday, Richard was in the den writing a letter at the roll-top desk, and Donna was standing by the bookcase. The heavy roll-top, contrary to all the laws of physics, came crashing down, striking the typewriter that Richard had pulled toward the desk's edge. It was all that kept his wrists from being crushed.

Donna held him while he trembled and laughed simultaneously, but neither one of them said anything about the baby that had been lost. For Richard to suggest it would have meant admitting that something totally inexplicable and irrational was intruding into their lives. He could not admit to that, not after the night he had laughed at Donna for suggesting what he had considered to be the fantasy of a semi-hysterical woman. Now, he was unsure enough that he could not speak of it.

V

When Richard returned from his classes Monday afternoon, Donna was gone. She had taken the Accord, a great many of her clothes, and several thousand dollars, he later learned, from her personal savings account. She had left behind a letter, written in her sharp, slanting script:

> Dear Rick,
>
> I'm sorry that I have to do this, but I think it's for the best for everybody. For you, for me, for the baby.

> Maybe you'll think I'm crazy, but the baby's still alive, I know. Somehow, somewhere, and it's still bound to me. It's got to be. It's too small to survive on its own. So I'm leaving, and I think it will come with me, and then you'll be safe. It can *do* things, Rick. It can make things happen, and I'm afraid it will hurt you. Going away is the only answer. I owe it to you, and I owe it to the baby.
>
> I didn't tell you before, because I thought you'd laugh at me, but I honestly feel as though I've never lost it. After the miscarriage, I still felt (and feel) as though I was still pregnant, still carrying it inside me. So I'm taking it away. Please try to understand and try to forgive me. And please don't look for me. I'll be all right. I'm *not* crazy, Rick, and I say that knowing that that's what crazy people always say. I'm not crazy, but I *am* special, and if that's delusions of grandeur, so be it, but there's *got* to be some purpose behind all this. I don't know when I'll come back, but I *will* come back, Rick. I love you, darling. Merry Christmas.
>
> Donna

He put down the letter, poured himself a scotch, sat down, and listened to the silence. The house felt empty, lifeless. Had there been any kind of entity there, it was gone now. Gone with Donna.

He stood, encased by quiet, and turned on the amplifier, hitting the scan switch and letting the first station click in. It was a choir singing Christmas music, and he half-moaned, half-laughed as he identified it as the Coventry Carol. So fitting, he thought. His *soul* felt like Coventry, the latter-day Coventry, bombed, a shambles, wooden skeletons poking their fingers up through smoky rubble.

He listened. They were singing the final verse.

> That woe is me, poor child, for thee,
> And ever mourn and say:
> For thy parting, neither say nor sing
> By, by, lully lullay.

He kept listening until he fell asleep. He did not dream.

VI

Parsons finished reading the letter. He stuck out his lower lip, tapped the paper with the knuckles of his right hand, set it down, and looked at Richard. 'She's disturbed,' he said.

'No shit, Sherlock,' Richard responded bitterly.

'What did you expect me to say? You want a complete case history neatly labeled and explained?'

'You're the psychiatrist.'

'I'm not a goddam psychiatrist, I'm a goddam psychologist.'

'So what the hell does the psychologist have to say?'

'Little more than you can figure out with common sense. Donna was very upset by the miscarriage, and when these incidents began happening, she interpreted it as a sign that the baby—or the life force, call it, that had been the baby—had somehow survived. Isn't that what *you* think?'

'I suppose so.'

Parsons was silent for a moment. He eyed Richard carefully. 'Now what do you *believe*?'

'There's a difference?'

'You bet.'

Richard sighed. 'Everything seems *too* coincidental. Why did these things all start to happen at once? And what about that thing . . . those noises and everything in the guest bath? We *both* saw it.'

'You *thought* you both saw it.'

'Oh, come on, John, I know when . . .'

'Hold it. I didn't say you *didn't* see it. I think maybe you did.'

'What?'

'You want an answer. Okay. I'll give you an answer that isn't completely rational, but one that has nothing to do with ghosts. You're not going to find it in any textbook, but that doesn't mean it's not possible. It just means it's not proven. Hell, it's not even seriously proposed.'

'What are you talking about?'

'Look, when these things happened, the coffee cup, the ladder, the desk, where was Donna?'

Richard thought for a second. 'There with me.'

'Each time?'

'Yes. Why?'

'All right. This may be hard. Do you think that Donna felt angry with you? I mean about losing the baby?'

'I . . . I don't know. She may have.'

'You said you argued about responsibility.'

'Well, yes . . .'

'Isn't it possible that she may have blamed you for the things she feared? The side effects, and what might have caused them?'

'I don't know.'

'You think she may have wanted you to *share* that responsibility? And when you didn't, when you said that there was nothing to feel guilty about, she thought you were trying to cop out, leaving her to take the consequences?'

'Look, John!' Richard half rose to his feet.

'Relax, Richard, I'm not saying that it's true, I'm just asking if Donna might not have seen it that way.' Richard sat back, slowly. 'Well? Could she have?'

'I suppose . . . it's possible.'

'So then,' Parsons went on, 'she loses the baby, blames herself, but blames you as well, and then strikes out at you.'

'Strikes out? How?'

'Call it telekinesis if you like. Everything's got to have a name, doesn't it? What happened in the bathroom was something she projected. From her mind to yours. *She* knocked over the ladder, spilled the coffee, slammed the desk.'

'Jesus Christ, John, you're supposed to be a *scientist*. How can you spout this shit?'

'Richard, the more I study the mind, the more I learn I don't know. Now, I *do* have limits. Ghosts are out, as are demons. No magic spells. Astrology is crap. Lumps on heads, crystals, channeling, ouija boards, it's all bullshit. But what the mind can do isn't.'

'You mean you think that Donna made me see and hear it all? That she . . . she attacked me with her mind? Knocked over that ladder without touching it?'

'I think it's possible. Highly improbable, but possible.'

'All right, look. Assuming she could, *why* would she? Why try to hurt me? She *loves* me, John. She says so in the letter, and I believe it. I know she does.'

'If she's behind all this, Richard, it isn't her conscious mind that's doing it. It's her subconscious. And there, deep down in that pit of primitive irrationality, she may very well hate your guts. And instead of accepting her own hostility toward you, she projects it into the baby. The *fetus*, I guess I should say.'

Richard barked a laugh. 'But how can she do that? Turn her baby—what she *thinks* is her baby—into a . . . a monster?'

'Maybe it just gives her more to take responsibility for.'

Richard stood up, walked to the window, and looked out at the snow-covered quadrangle, where the down- and wool-wrapped students passed like purposeful bears. 'So what do I do?' he wondered aloud.

'Do you know where she could have gone?'

Richard shook his head. 'Her parents are dead. She was an only child. John,' he said, turning to Parsons, 'what do I do?'

'The only thing you can. Wait. Leave her alone.'

'. . . and she'll come home.'

'Probably. When she finds there *is* no baby. That she isn't still pregnant.'

'Do you think . . . when she has a period?'

'Maybe that soon. Or maybe she'll ignore it. Could be a full seven months. Or more. Whenever she realizes that there's nothing there to come to term.'

Richard swallowed heavily. 'What you said about the mind. Do you think . . . could it be possible that . . .'

'I know what you're thinking. And no, it's *not* possible. You can't get around biology, Richard. Donna lost her baby. That's all there is to it. She'll be back. And she'll come back alone.'

VII

Donna came back in July, in the middle of a summer so hot and dry that the grass around the farmhouse had yellowed, then browned to the color of dead leaves, crackling like melting ice when Richard walked on it.

He was sitting on the front porch, drifting back and forth on the rusty metal glider, a vodka and tonic dripping condensation onto his bare leg, when she drove down the driveway in the Accord. She parked, but didn't get out of the car right away. She sat there for a minute, watching him watching her. Then she opened the door, walked up the path, and stood at the bottom of the porch steps. He noticed her hands were empty, her belly flat. She looked as though she had lost weight. Her color was bad, her eyes tired, her cheeks as hollow as his stomach felt. 'Hi,' she said, with barely a trace of emotion.

He looked at her and nodded. Twice.

'Aren't you glad to see me?' Now there was, he thought, just a touch of pleading.

'You didn't write,' he said. 'Or call. Seven months and not a word from you.'

She tried to smile. 'I thought you'd try to find me. I didn't want you to.'

'I didn't try. If I would have, I could have. A detective could have traced the car, followed you.'

'Thank you.'

'For what?'

'For not trying. For leaving me alone.' She stepped onto the porch and sat next to him on the glider. 'Aren't you going to hug me?'

Slowly, he set down his drink and embraced her. His arms felt stiff and heavy as they touched her, but the contact changed his mood immediately, as a spark of power lights a dusty and long extinguished lamp. He held her tightly, buried his face against her shoulder, and began to cry.

'Oh, Rick,' she said, putting her arms around him and hugging him tightly. 'Oh, Richard.' Her eyes teared. Her nose began to run. 'I did miss you.'

'I didn't know,' Richard said through his crying. 'I just didn't know. You could have been dead. I didn't know if you'd ever come back.'

'I'd always come back. You knew I'd come back.'

'You were so upset,' he went on. 'I thought you might even . . . hurt yourself.'

'Oh no. Never that. Never that. Shh. Shh, darling. I'm home now. I'm home and I love you, and everything's all right. More than all right.'

He cried some more, and Donna kept holding him, lightly crying as well.

'Where were you?' he finally asked. 'Where did you go?'

'Ohio. A small town near Akron. I just drove until I found a place that felt right. A boarding house. An older lady had it. She was very nice. I helped her with the housework and things until . . .'

She paused. In the heat, Richard felt very cold. 'Until . . . you came home.'

'Yes.' Donna nodded. 'Until then.' She took her arms from around him, stood up, leaned on the porch railing. 'Rick, remember my letter?' she asked quietly. 'What I said I thought was happening?'

He nodded, smiling to drive away the specters.

'I was right, Richard. What I thought was happening? It happened.'

He would not stop smiling. If he stopped smiling, he would let the monsters in. 'No, Donna. The baby died. We *lost* the baby.' He smiled, being rational.

Donna smiled back. 'It's in the car.'

He shook his head. He smiled. How he smiled. 'No.'

'Come look. See for yourself.' She reached out her hand and took his, drawing him to his feet. Together they walked down the chipped and flaking wooden steps, down the path to the Accord. 'It was sleeping on the way in,' she said.

'It,' Richard parroted.

'I don't know whether it's a boy or a girl. I can't really tell. Not yet.'

'Donna . . .'

'Shh.' They were at the car, and Donna leaned over and looked into the back seat. 'Look,' she said.

Richard looked.

He did not see it at first, but as Donna's grip tightened on his hand, something swam into view, hiding the faded blue vinyl. Its outline was a pair of joined ovals, one larger than the other, with four protuberances he tentatively identified as arms and legs. They were round and fat, and, like the trunk and head, pink in color. His breath locked in his throat as he heard her ask gently, 'There, do you see it?'

'Donna . . . no . . .'

'Yes you do. I can see you do.'

'Donna . . .'

'It's very quiet. Very good. It doesn't eat, but it loves to be sung to, talked to.'

'Donna, it's . . . it's not there. Not really. You created it.'

'Of course, Richard. *We* created it. Together. It's our baby.'

'It is not there, Donna.'

'You can't say that. You can't believe it. You see it. It's what we did. It's *us*, Richard, it's part of us. It's who we are, and what we've done.' She looked down at the shadowy form, which was growing ever more distinct. 'So we have to take care of it.' She rested a hand on Richard's shoulder.

'Let's go inside now. Into our house.'

She turned and started to walk up the path. When she saw him hesitate, looking at her and then at what lay in the back seat, she gave a little bell of a laugh. 'We don't have to take it,' she said. 'It'll be inside before we are.'

She was right. When they entered the living-room, it was lying on the sofa, half-seen, like some plump fruit shrouded by leaves and branches. Donna looked down at it lovingly, then walked around the room, touching familiar things. 'You've kept the house nice, Rick. Everything looks so clean. We'll be happy now.' She smiled at him. 'I think I'll get my bags. I won't really feel at home until I'm unpacked.'

Richard continued to gaze at the shape, seeing it float on the brown brocade as he'd seen a similar shape float in water, dark and lambent. 'I'll . . . I'll help you,' he said huskily.

'No. You stay here.' She embraced him from behind. 'Sing to it, Richard. It loves that.'

He felt her kiss his hair, then listened to her retreating footsteps, the screen door slamming shut on its weary spring, the boards of the porch creaking under her weight.

It did not disappear, did not vanish in her absence as he had thought it might. It remained on the couch, its outline firm. *How strong can she be, how strong*?

And then the other thought intruded:

How strong have I become?

Parsons's mysteries of mind swept through him, and he wondered what cancer had clamped his brain, what sickness, what maleficent suggestion had given him the power to conjure this thing that shared his house, his wife's love, and, ultimately, his own affections.

The plumpness on the sofa moved as if trying to give an answer, and the appendages twitched, stroked through unseen waves, extended toward him as if to say:

Love me. I am here, am yours. Love me.

He looked at his baby, and found himself humming, very gently, very quietly. It was a carol, a carol and a lullaby.

I am yours. Love me, it said to him.

He would. Helpless, bound, he knew he would.

A Place Where a Head Would Rest

The following piece was written for Dancing with the Dark, *an anthology of stories about writers' actual experiences with the supernatural.*

THERE WAS A TIME, over a quarter of a century ago, one dark summer night away from my home, when something happened to me that was subtle, yet disquieting enough to make me leave that house and never go back.

I had just graduated from high school, and had gotten an apprenticeship at a summer theater connected with a college in New Jersey. My parents had helped me find lodgings in a house across the river in Bucks County, Pennsylvania. The house was a large three-story dwelling, the oldest parts of which were built before the Revolutionary War. It had a barn, a duck pond, a great many trees, and a name, which I will not print here, but the fact that it had a single appellation rather than a boring address impressed me greatly.

I was given a room on the third floor. Supposedly there was another roomer on that floor, but I did not meet him when I moved in, nor at any time thereafter, though in the week I lived there I did once or twice hear his footsteps as they came up the stairs to the third floor, and then moved into his room, into the shared bathroom, and back again.

My room was located in the front right corner of the house, and, though large, was furnished Spartanly. There was a bed against one of the inner walls, with a small table and lamp next to it, a high-backed easy chair, a chest of drawers, and a hall tree near the door. Several throw carpets were placed over the rough-hewn boards of the floor. The two windows, one looking out on the front of the house and the other giving a view of the side, were recessed so that, with the tall, encroaching trees all about, the room was fairly dark even with the sun shining.

Several nights after my tenancy began, I went downstairs to the kitchen to write a letter home, since there was no desk in my room. I fell into a conversation with the woman who owned the house, and she told me about its history, including the interesting fact that the money for the revolution's arms had been hidden under the wooden floorboards. When I said, chuckling, that a house this old must surely have a ghost, she smiled and said, 'Yes, it does.'

'Really? Where?' I asked.

'Right next to you.'

I turned, filled with a delightful *frisson*, to find a small, hand-painted wooden chair standing against the wall.

'That was Mr Picard's chair,' the woman told me, and went on to explain that Mr Picard was the man who had owned the house before she and her husband had moved in. He had done a great deal of restoration, and had bought period furniture for the house as well, but when he died, nearly everything was auctioned. When the woman and her husband moved in, they found that this chair had been overlooked in a back room, and brought it into the kitchen.

The first week they were living in the house, a neighbor brought over some groceries and set the bag on the chair. It fell over almost immediately, and my landlady swore that the bag had not *tipped* over, but had slid sideways and fallen straight down. After that, they dubbed it Mr Picard's Chair, and never sat in it nor set anything on it. She told me that I might hear Mr Picard moving through the house at night, but that he was a very kind and gentle ghost, and would do no harm. They even, she added, got him a present every Christmas. I neglected to ask how he went about opening it.

Naturally I felt a little creepy when I went to bed that night. I was also uncomfortable about my theater apprenticeship, since I had been told that I would be able to act in small parts, but instead found myself manning the ticket-booth phones. I comforted myself with Jules Verne's *Carpathian Castle*, and finally turned out the light around 11:30 p.m.

I drifted between sleep and wakefulness for some time, and remember looking over toward the easy chair. Though I had not heard the door to my room open—indeed it could not have, since I bolted it at night—I thought I saw a shape in the chair. Naturally, I looked for the easiest explanation, which was that I had tossed my bathrobe onto the chair and it had landed there in such a way that it approximated a human figure, nothing more. I did not even feel alarmed enough to switch on the light and reassure myself, but simply rolled over and went to sleep, wishing my bathrobe pleasant dreams.

When I awoke the next morning, I lay in bed for a while before recalling the shape in the chair the previous night. When I glanced toward it, I was surprised to discover that there was nothing whatsoever in the chair, and that my bathrobe was hanging on the hall tree. At first I put it down to imagination and got out of bed, but then I noticed something on the gray fabric of the easy chair.

It was a dark, round spot, and it was on the high back of the chair where a sitter might have rested his head. It was not wet, merely damp, for when I pressed my fingers to it they came away with hardly any trace of moisture.

I looked up at the ceiling, but saw no signs of a leak, and a glance out of the window told me that it had not rained the night before. The thought occurred to me that perhaps my mysterious fellow-boarder might have come into my room after his shower, and sat in my chair, either by mistake or through a dark design, but the fact that the small bolt on the door of my room was still thrown shut demolished that theory.

I showered quickly and headed over to Jersey, feeling slightly sick and very confused. At the theater, the situation had worsened, and I realized that I had been gulled. Neither I nor any of the apprentices would even be able to audition for the plays—we were nothing more than free help, and that realization led me to turn in my resignation.

After a less than amicable parting, I drove back to the house, where I met my landlady in the kitchen. I had simply intended to tell her that I would be leaving the next day, but I did not. To this day, I don't know why I asked her, but after saying hello, the next words out of my mouth were the question of how Mr Picard had died.

She looked at me oddly, but answered quickly enough. 'It was a heart attack,' she said, and I relaxed a bit, only to feel the tension come surging back as she added, 'They found him at the edge of the pond, partly in the water.'

That was enough. I didn't need to ask if his head was in the pond or not. I immediately gave up my idea of staying another night, and told her that things hadn't worked out at the theater and I would be leaving for home as soon as I could pack. Needless to say, I packed in record time. The spot on the chair had now vanished, the cloth bone dry. I said goodbye and drove home, never having seen the woman's husband nor the other roomer during the week that I stayed there.

So was it a ghost? I think not. I regret not. There must have been some other explanation. Perhaps I had somehow caused the spot myself, and imagined the shape in the chair. In all honesty, I would like to think that it *was* Mr Picard's ghost come to pay me a visit. The logical conclusion to that visitation—that life exists after death—would be a great comfort.

But rationality persists, whispering its dry and sandy explanations in my ear, turning me from beloved and kindly superstition. Sadly, this experience is the closest I have ever come to breathing the sweet air of eternity. So far.

Still, there are times when I silently beg Mr Picard to come again, and this time to let me see the other side of the wall through his ghostly face. I wait, and I hope, for some glimpse of light before the darkness.

The Blood-Red Sea

BLOOD-RED. YES, THAT WAS what he should have called it. But he had not seen blood before. He had tasted it, of course, just as he had tasted wine, but the taste of blood had no beauty in it, while the taste of wine did. Thus, the sea, what should be the most beautiful sight of all, as he thought then and knew now, had become wine-red as the sun rose and set upon it.

Red. That was all his pupils had told the singer.

—It's red, master. The setting sun makes the clouds red, and then the sea turns red as well.

Even Timaeus could say little more:

—It is the red of apples, master, and sometimes the pink of the inside of shells, and sometimes the red of the stone of certain cliffs.

Well, that was certainly edifying. Though blind, the singer knew that stone could be of many different colors.

And yet Timaeus had been the most promising pupil he had ever had. Though the youth had no gifts of song himself, he could nigh perfectly commit the singer's words to memory. Timaeus knew the two great songs, the first of war and the second of wandering, as surely as the singer did. And he had committed the new song to memory as well, the song of aspiration, the song on which the singer had worked for many years, his song of songs, his masterpiece. Only Timaeus and the singer knew that song. And it had died with them both.

That was how the singer finally knew the color of blood, by awakening next to Timaeus's body, with the great black bird sitting in the branches of the tree near him. In one moment, he was senseless, dwelling in the land of death, bereft not only of sight, as he had been all his life, but of touch and breath and life itself. And in the next moment, sensation had flooded back into his gashed and hacked body.

His eye sockets, their dead fruit plucked by the sword points of the renegades who had killed him, were filled anew, burning with the fire of the great golden orb whose light he had felt on his flesh but never before seen. He pressed his eyelids shut, but the burning ball remained glowing on the inside of them, a bright circle in the blackness, sending straight rays outward, blinding him with light rather than darkness.

Pressing his hand over his eyes, he turned his head away from the sun, and felt his bearded cheek rubbing against blades of grass. High grass surrounded him, embracing him on all sides, and he shielded his new, sighted eyes from the sun and opened them again.

—*Green.*

This was green, had to be green, for what grew all about him felt like grass, smelled like grass, and he knew that grass was what men called green, and though he expected the green of grass to be cool, it seemed hot to his unlearned eyes, as hot as the sun's touch upon him.

But there were other colors in the grass. The long, wide blades seemed touched by something else, by droplets that had clung and dried to the green. They were darker, a color the singer could not name, ignorant of what liquid, wine or water or milk or some exudation from tree or sky, had dropped thereon.

There were trees about him, too, but he had only a vague idea as to how close they were to him. He knew how big around trees were, and thought that perhaps that big oak might be thrice again the length of a man away. Then he heard the caw of a crow, and gazed upon his first living creature.

This was assuredly a crow, for he had touched both living and dead birds. He had been told that a crow was black, and black was the only color that he knew well, for it was what was seen when the eyes were closed or blinded. But he did not expect blackness to have this sheen to it. As the crow spread wide its wings, it seemed that blackness was many colors thrown over darkness.

Then the singer looked at his arm lying on the ground next to his body. The hand was still attached, and wasn't that wrong? Hadn't the renegades cut off his hands? Of course they had, because after the great pain in his left arm, he had felt upon it with his right hand, and discovered that there was nothing after the wrist, only hot blood that jetted against his right palm as he strove to hold it within his body.

And then they had laughed again, and cut off his right hand. They had done this, he recalled, but dimly, as of some other time and place, amidst the towers of the long-ago cities of which he had sung. They had killed him because he had tried to save Timaeus. He had heard the youth's screams, and cried out:

—No! I am only a singer, and he is my pupil! Don't harm him! I beg you!

But Timaeus shrieked all the louder, and from the renegades' bawdy oaths he knew that they were having the boy. The singer swung his staff toward where he guessed them to be, and connected with a hearty thud that made one of the attackers grunt with pain. It was then that he felt the sword sever his hand that held the staff. After they had cut off both hands, he had fallen to his knees, the weight of his body resting for a moment upon his stumps until the agony of the contact knocked him on his side. It was then that they had spitted his blind eyes, and stabbed at him with their swords, over and over, until the life left his body and all his senses were as dead as his sight.

As he was drifting into the land of the dead, he could only think of two things—the pity of Timaeus's dying, and the loss of the song of aspiration, the great song that could never now be sung, and he hated these men, these renegades, these cowards who attacked a youth and a blind man rather than their lord's enemies. He hated these creatures who took away, not only his life, but the greatest of his songs from the world.

Hate flooded through him as he died, and all he could think was:

—*This is not right. This is* not right!

Even as he was thinking it, he felt that it seemed a simple and childlike thought to be having, and wondered if the brave and swift Achilles would have had such a thought when he went down to death. Then, in the middle of that thought, the singer died.

And awoke.

It seemed to take only a moment, but now all was quiet, and it was day. The sun was shining brightly, too brightly for his new eyes, and the grass, green grass, was dappled with the strange, dark-colored drops. The singer turned, shielding his gaze from the sun with his hands, which Zeus had restored as well as his sight, and when he looked at what lay next to him, he knew at last what liquid had bathed the green grass.

It was the blood of the youth who lay only a few handbreadths away. The singer had never before seen flesh or blood, and it took a moment for him to realize that this thing next to him had been human. In his mind, he connected the spatial features that he saw with what he had known of the human form from feeling of it with his hands, and knew it for what it was. It was not, however, until he had crawled across to the body and placed his hand upon its face and hair that he whispered:

—Timaeus . . .

Timaeus had not come back from the land of the dead. His throat had been cut, and the swords had played about in his bowels. This then was blood, thought the singer. This then was red. It looked darker than he thought red would look. It was not the red of his rose-fingered dawn:

—*It is red, master, red like roses.*

He could smell roses, but the smell of their redness was not like the smell of the redness of blood. This was a briny, sour smell, a smell of death and loss and sorrow and stupidity, the smell of a song stopped in a throat opened by iron.

The singer heard the cry of the crow again, and he turned to look at it, but it came streaking over his head—his first sight of quick motion, unexpected and unique in his memory. He gasped and pressed his face down into the grass, felt the stickiness of Timaeus's blood against his cheek and forehead.

The crow screamed again, and he looked up to see it perching on

Timaeus's face, its claws clinging to his lips and jaws. It looked at him with sharp eyes, and the singer felt as though it were somehow challenging him, telling him about something he must do.

The crow's head bobbed as its eyes looked at the singer's hands, first one, and then the other, and then the singer knew that his rebirth, the regaining of his hands, and most miraculously, his eyes, were due to this crow, and he knew beyond doubt who it was. He spoke the name:

—Zeus.

Of course. It was Zeus, king of all gods, come down to the world in the form of a crow, as he had come down so many other times in the shapes of beast or bird, to interpose himself and his justice in the realm of men. He had given the poet his hands and eyes. He had brought him back from the everlasting blackness of Hades and given him life so that he could . . .

What? Sing his song, the great epic of aspiration and striving and triumph that had died when he and Timaeus had drunk of the renegades' iron? Or something else, something darker?

The crow's beak descended to the side of Timaeus's mouth, and it seemed to drink from the dark red blood that had dried on the boy's lip. Then the bird, Zeus, king of gods, lifted its head again and looked at the singer, and now its gaze was implacable. The singer knew its purpose and his own. The knowledge surged into his mind of what he should do, what he *must* do, for Zeus had brought him back from the dead, him, a simple singer, to take what was wrong, as boldly as Heracles had grasped the horns of the Cretan bull, and make it right once again.

The three men who had killed him and Timaeus, those who had silenced his song, must die. Only then could the singer rest in peace among the quiet dead.

He knew that it was true. He felt the torment of his and the youth's deaths in the taut sinews of his body, in the cold fire of the blood rushing through him, and the only thing that would assuage his torment, Zeus told him with the bird's beady eyes, was the sword, used against those who had slain him.

The god-crow startled him then by rising from Timaeus's body and flying into the air, flapping his dark wings across the sea of grass and descending some distance away. The singer followed.

The claws of the king of gods grasped a large bush, and beneath, the singer found a short sword, its leather hilt rotted until its green was lighter than that of the grass, its edge rusted to the color of Timaeus's blood. The singer reached for it, and was surprised when his hand grasped it so quickly. He had always been used to fumbling for things, and it was an unexpected delight to see his hand move to something and close upon it so easily, particularly this hand that had been severed. When the singer looked closely at his wrist, he could see a light, thin line where Zeus had reattached it.

The sword felt foreign in his hand, however, and he swung it through the air at the unspoken behest of Zeus. Immediately the god-crow arose and skimmed through the air, upward out of the bowl of land in which the singer stood, and in which he and Timaeus had met their deaths. The singer followed, holding the sword loosely at his side.

If this was what he had to do, then so be it. He truly hated the renegades, and wished their deaths. Perhaps if he accomplished this, if he fulfilled the will of Zeus, the god would allow him to remain on the earth long enough to teach his final song to another, or, better yet, to have the words written down by a scribe, as had been done with his other two songs, though unfaithfully, if the fragments of them that had been read to him were indicative. He had orally corrected the written texts whenever he could, but he could not know how many error-laden copies, twisted as rope and rotten as aged meat, existed.

—Oh Zeus, grant that, if I do your will and shed the blood of these men, I may sing my song one final time and leave it behind for men to hear, before I go down to Hades. Grant me this, mighty Zeus.

He followed the bird, his heart heavy with the thought of killing, but buoyed by hope as the sailor adrift on a roaring sea.

The heart of the singer lightened as he walked toward the rim of the hill. All about him were trees and weeds and flowers blooming in such colors whose names he could only guess. Some he had touched, and so recognized by their names, and remembered the colors that he had been told they possessed. So there was purple, there yellow, and that was pink. He paused to kneel down next to them as at shrines, and admire the hues that changed subtly, delicately on a single petal.

The god-crow called again. He looked up and saw it circling impatiently above his head. It seemed to want the singer to follow it, to go on and not stop to look at flowers. But when the singer looked at it, he could not help but stand amazed, marveling at the grace of the bird drifting through the sky, outlined against what he now knew to be blue, a pure color that seemed radiant, lit by itself as much as by the bright yellow ball of the sun. Clouds, *white* clouds, hung in the sky, round and puffy like great piles of cloths, and the singer laughed at the sight, at the sheer beauty of the sky.

Zeus cried angrily, and swept about toward the rim of the hill. The singer followed, moving his legs faster and faster until he realized that he was running for the first time in his life, not feeling his way, but tirelessly barreling up the hill, which ended in a sharp line across the sky.

Had he been wrong? Was Zeus taking him to Olympus itself? Would he run off the very edge of the earth and soar into the sky with the god?

But as he arrived at the edge of sky and earth, he saw that his road went downward. Spread out below him was a vista that stopped him dead in his tracks, so that he tottered and almost fell, unused to such strength in his limbs.

It was the sea. The sea lay before him, its waves sparkling and glinting with new light. The entire surface of it, as far as he could see, was moving, shifting constantly, and though he had sailed on the sea, to see it at last was awesome and terrifying. It seemed a living thing, ready to swallow up any creature bold or foolish enough to set out upon it. He heard the familiar sound of the waves crashing upon the rocks, but now he *saw* them, white-tongued claws of water ripping at the shore.

But the longer he stared at it, the less fearful he grew, and the more beauty he saw in this seemingly infinite creation of which he had sung, this sea on which his greatest hero had wandered. How much more might he have said in his song had he only been able to first view the majesty of these waters?

At last the raucous cawing of Zeus tore his gaze away from the sea, and he looked at the land below. A small harbor town lay as if between sea and earth. Several small boats, tied at the dock and a pier jutting into the water, moved constantly above and with the swelling of the waves. The singer saw men passing along the narrow dock and in the street, and even from a distance he could admire the supple fluidity of their limbs as they walked and raised their hands in greeting to others. There was so much movement and color and life that his mind could scarcely comprehend it all.

He walked down the road toward the village, the sword in his hand forgotten. Children were playing on the hillside, and birds flew from tree to tree. An animal ran with the children, and when it barked, the singer was sure that it was a dog, as he had first suspected. The animal came bounding in his direction, and he did what he had always done when there was a dog present. He fell to his knees and embraced it, his hands still responding to the tactile contact, but his eyes now able to see it as well, its hairy face and wide, friendly eyes, its red, drooling tongue. The singer laughed as the dog licked him. It was such a funny-looking creature, so happy and eager to please.

The god-crow screamed, angry and impatient, and the dog, startled, ran back to the children.

—Yes, my lord, I'm coming . . . but there is so much to see. . . .

The singer followed, wishing he had known how jolly dogs could look when he sang of old and faithful Argos. Perhaps, when his mission for Zeus was completed, he could sing some new lines about the dog, so that it not only wagged its tail and ears, but laughed to see its old master returned.

The huge black bird flew far ahead of the singer, and he saw its form drift down upon a post at the end of the narrow pier. The singer allowed himself to run again, down the hill toward the town. It was, he thought, like flying.

The wind rushed through his hair and made the cloth of his garment flap against his sides, as the trees and brush blurred past. But near the bottom he realized that he was running too fast to stop himself, and he tripped and fell, rolling over and over until he came sliding and scraping to a halt on the loose dirt.

He had fallen before, but, amazingly enough, this time he felt no pain. The flesh of his knees and elbows was not, as he had feared, ripped open, and he only laughed and pushed himself to his feet again. He felt invulnerable, almost like a god himself.

A young boy had seen the singer's tumble, and asked him if he was all right. He assured the boy that he was, then asked him what town this was. When the boy told him, the singer knew that he had been there several times before with Timaeus and his other pupils. He thanked the boy and walked on.

He saw several different people as he passed through the street. Some walked by without glancing toward him, but those who did looked at him for a long time as he smiled at them, nodded a greeting, and then strode on. He wondered if they recognized him, and were confused to see him strolling through their streets, able to see at last.

Then his smile faded, as he thought about what it was that had finally given him his sight—his own slow and painful death, and the death of Timaeus. It had been a terrible price to pay.

He was at the harbor at last, and the sun was sinking. Had he held out his arm and brought up his hand, its heel would have rested on the sea and his fingertips would have touched the fiery ball that had now darkened to a red orange. Great Zeus, the god-crow, perched on a piling halfway down the pier. At its end sat a man, his back to the singer. His hair was black and shining greasily, as if it had not been washed in many days. There was a short sword stuck through a leather strip that was tied tightly about his waist.

The great bird looked at the singer, and then at the man on the pier. The singer looked about, but saw no one else. The figures that he had seen moving earlier were all gone, perhaps, thought the singer, at the desire of Zeus. He walked slowly down the pier, sword in hand, looking at the waves slapping against the timbers of the pier and the planking of the small boats.

There, on the pier, the sea seemed to be all around him. He smelled its salt, tasted the air in his open mouth, felt the ocean breezes play at his hair and ripple his garment. But now, for the first time in his life, he *saw* it, and all his senses reeled at his proximity to something so huge and powerful. The might of Zeus seemed as nothing compared to the natural power of this kingdom of Poseidon.

As the wind whirled about the singer, the man at the end of the pier seemed to sense that someone was standing behind him. He straightened, and then slowly turned until he was looking at the singer. His mouth opened, dully and stupidly, as though he could not believe what he was seeing, and he staggered to his feet, his gaze still fixed on the singer.

—Have you come back from Hades to torment me? Isn't it enough that my comrades have stolen what we were to share and sailed away? Must the gods now send *ghosts* against me?

The singer felt an icy chill as he heard the man's voice. This was the one who had taken Timaeus, and who had laughed and grunted like a pig in the taking. He felt rage surge within him, waves of it, like the waves that he saw crashing on the nearby rocks. He knew what he was to do and yet he could not. He told himself that he had to be sure, that it would displease Zeus to make a mistake, ignoring the fact that it was the god-crow himself who had brought the singer to this place, this man.

—Do you know me?

—Yes, I know you. You have your hands back, and you see! What trickery is this? Are you a twin?

The greasy-haired man tugged his sword from his belt.

—If you are, I can kill you as I killed your brother!

He ran toward the singer, the fall of his feet making the pier tremble even more than the lash of the sea. His sword was raised above his head, and the singer looked on in wonder, seeing for the first time a man charging into battle, ready to slay and feed Ares. He could not help but admire the man's economy of motion, the way he held his weapon and balanced his body and closed the gap between them. The singer imagined thousands of men like this, closing the gap between the Trojans and his countrymen hundreds of years before. But not even Zeus could grant him *that* sight.

The greasy-haired renegade brought down his sword, hacking at the spot where the singer's neck met his shoulder. He felt a sudden pain that shivered through his entire body, and then the man wrenched away the sword. The singer saw a streaming trail of his own blood, dark red in the dying light, follow the sword blade.

Suddenly the pain was gone, and when the singer put his hand to his shoulder he felt no wound. He was whole and unharmed, just as he had been when Zeus had brought him back from Hades.

The renegade gawked at him in disbelief, but started to raise his sword again. Then he hesitated, as though considering where to strike next. But the singer could not allow another blow. He did not want to bear the pain again.

Before he even knew what he was doing, he had brought up his own rusted weapon, swinging it so that the blade bit from underneath into the man's ribs, ripping the flesh and cracking the bones, and knocking the renegade off the pier and into the sea. Great gouts of blood and bowel trailed behind the man, and he struck the water with a heavy splash. The singer, dripping sword in hand, walked numbly to the edge and looked into the water.

The renegade was floating on his back, rocking on the surface of the water. The current had spun him about, and his head was knocking rhythmically against one of the posts of the pier. His bowels, still attached to the cavity that the singer's sword had opened, were drifting next to him, thick and ropy.

But what struck the singer most was the blood on the water. It was spreading outward from the body of the dead man like a red cloud, and had even turned to pink the bits of white froth on the edge of the waves.

He looked outward, to where the sun, now red, was sinking still, half of its rondure beneath the waters of the sea, so that all appeared blood-red, the same hue as that surrounding the body of the man the singer had killed, the man who had killed him. Oh yes, it was not a wine-red sea, but a blood-red one.

The singer looked at the corpse again and shuddered. It was ugly. All that he had seen that day, save for Timaeus's body and now the body of this man, had been beautiful.

But this was ugly, this death, this blood, this unnatural taking of life, stopping of hearts, blinding of eyes. For the man's eyes were surely blind now, staring without blinking as the sea's stinging salt washed over them.

And he, a singer of songs, teller of tales, had created this present ugliness.

The call of the crow came from behind him, and he turned and looked at it. Then he asked of it:

—Is this your will?

Zeus did not answer, neither with words nor with a grating caw. Instead it looked at him, unmoving, stared and stared with its shiny black eyes so that he moved closer to it as though it were commanding him to do so, close enough so that the faces of man and bird were only a breath away, and he could see his own reflection in the dark depths of its eyes.

And in those twin mirrors of black glass, he saw his own face, the face of a man who had lost a friend, a song, a life. He saw the face of an angry and bitter man from whom fools had taken all. He saw the face of a man who, as he had entered the land of death, had wanted vengeance more than anything else a god could give. Then the singer realized the truth, and spoke it:

—It was *my* will.

He looked away from the god-crow, back out to the darkening sea, and felt tears course over his wrinkled cheeks. They were as cold as the air, as though the eyes from which they had come had not the heat of the living. He knew then that although he saw, he saw with dead eyes, for *he* was dead, a dead man who walked, brought back to the world for the purposes for which he had wished, the dark purposes for which he must have cried out for Zeus to grant him.

—It was for this, oh lord, wasn't it?

He looked at the crow and pointed down to the dead man floating in the sea. But the crow gave no answer. It did not have to.

Then it rose lazily and flapped into the air, flying along the coast heading north, seeking, the singer knew, the other men, the two who still lived and walked. The singer followed. He had no choice.

He walked through the night, feeling no need to stop to rest or drink or eat. Other roads turned off the one he was on, but whenever there was a fork, he would see the god-crow flying ahead of him, black against the starry sky, and follow it.

The singer moved slowly, so slowly that the bird often grew impatient, and would come flying about his ears, screeching at him to quicken his pace. But the beauties of the night were as new to him as were those of the day, and he hastened reluctantly.

The sky was a constant source of marvels. There was only a crescent moon far down against the horizon, a yellow sliver that allowed the countless stars to gleam brightly. There were patterns of which he had been told, and which Timaeus had once set out for him with pebbles, so that he might, by feeling the relative distance between them, know what lay overhead. He found the great bear and the warrior and the bull, and behind him he thought he could see, on the southern horizon, the great dog leaping out of the sea.

The golden curve of the moon held his attention most strongly, however. Though his new eyes were sharp enough to behold the hazy jewel in the dagger at the warrior's hip, he could not follow the stars as they slowly passed between the horns of the moon. One by one they winked out, and the singer wondered if the moon ate them, and then spat them out again behind him.

There were many such questions he would have liked to contemplate, but the god-crow hurried him on. Instead of sitting on a rock and watching how the sea mirrored the moon in its waters, he was forced to rush toward the fate of this first choosing, that fate for which Zeus had returned him.

He walked tirelessly all night, the sword in his hand, watching in fascination as the moon rose higher in the sky and then vanished beneath the sea, and the stars slowly wheeled through their arcs against the great sphere of blackness overhead. At last the darkness began to brighten in the east over the hills, and for the first time in his life he beheld the rose-fingered dawn of which he had sung for years, and was overjoyed to see that his words were true, free of hyperbole.

The growing light brought more and more to the singer's eyes, and he rejoiced in the sights of field and forest, of the rocks between land and sea, of the birds flitting and creatures scurrying about to begin their day. The world seemed filled with glory, until the sight of the man made him remember his errand.

The man sat on a fallen tree, far ahead. At first the singer thought that he was one of the two remaining renegades, but as he drew nearer he could see that the man was young, his aspect was gentle, and he bore no sword. The god-crow flew past him, continuing down the road, but the singer paused, looking into the youth's smiling face.

The youth greeted him and said that his name was Creophylus. The singer told him his name, and Creophylus stood, his smile replaced by a look which the singer could not identify, even though he was fascinated by the way the youth's face moved as he spoke, the play of flesh and muscles and eyes.

—I too am a singer. I have heard of you. And your songs. They are like no other's.

The singer smiled at this unexpected praise.

—But I had heard that you were without sight.

—The gods . . . are good.

So at least he hoped. Creophylus then spoke with ardor.

—May I go with you?

—I don't know where I'm going. I'm following that great crow.

—It doesn't matter. I only wish to walk and speak with you, if you will allow me.

So they walked on, the young Creophylus keeping up handily with the singer's rapid stride.

—Why are you following the crow?

—Because he is divine, and he takes me to my fate. I know little more than that.

He would not tell the youth of his death and rebirth. He did not know how he would act were he to know he was walking with a living dead man.

So they spoke of the singer's songs, and Creophylus recited parts of them. The singer was, as always, glad to know that his words would live after him. At least *some* of his words, he corrected himself. The song of striving had died.

Or had it?

—I have composed a new song, of aspiration and striving, on the life of Heracles. May I sing it for you as we walk?

From the way Creophylus's face beamed, the singer knew he was about to answer yes, but he did not have the chance. The god-crow darted back toward them, at first, the singer supposed, to harry him onward, but instead Zeus's incarnation drifted away from the road, toward the sea.

The singer turned off the path and trotted down toward the water, Creophylus at his heels. The first thing he saw was the wreckage of a small boat that must have been broken on the many rocks lying off the shore. The next was the bodies of two men lying on the strand.

They were still alive, pulling themselves up the strand and away from the lapping water, moving slowly and sinuously, like snakes in the cold. The rocks had torn their flesh, and they were leaving trails of blood upon the pebbles of the shore. If they had had swords, they must have tossed them away when they entered the water, lest the weight of the iron help to drag them down.

The first thing that came into the singer's mind was to aid them, and he ran to the closest man with the intention of pulling him up the strand and then seeing to his injuries. But when the nearly drowned man looked up and saw the singer, he gave a squeal and cried out:

—I am drowned after all and in Hades! And here is a ghost to torture me!

The singer knew the voice, and knew why the man said what he did. These were the other two men who had slain him and Timaeus. The god-crow had not led him on an errand of mercy, but on one of death.

The second man looked up at the singer then and said nothing, only whimpered, stopped crawling, and let his head fall heavily onto the pebbles of the strand. He was sobbing, his salt tears the heavy tide of his guilt.

The sword felt huge and unwieldy in the singer's hands. But the time had come, the time to kill again, to destroy, to make more ugliness in this beautiful world.

And was that not just? He had sung, and gloried in the singing, of the great battlefields where men threw away their lives for vanity, or for the motives of kings that meant nothing to them. His most terrible songs had been of the scores of dead and their hacked-off heads and limbs, of rivers of blood pouring across the plains of war. And having sung all these death-songs, could he not take the lives of two swine who robbed and killed, not understanding the great gifts they had been given, those gifts of life and eyes with which to see the world? He had justly slain once, so could he not do so twice and thrice? Could he not butcher these pigs, destroy these unworthy lives?

The god-crow circled overhead, cawing, cawing, its cries a shriek riding above the roar of the sea.

And the singer took the sword and drew it back, and flung it out, out over the waters, farther than the strength of any living man could have thrown it, and it entered the blood-red sea and sank beneath its waves.

The god-crow hovered in the air close to him, as if floating on the wind, and although the singer did not speak aloud, he knew that Zeus heard his thoughts:

—I am a creator, not a destroyer. I have sung the songs of shed blood, but I will shed no more. If I must suffer pain and loss throughout eternity among the shades in Hades, or in some far more terrible place intended for those who disobey the gods, then so be it. But I will not destroy. I will not defile this world.

And without waiting to see what the great black bird might do, he turned away from it and from the struggling and fearful men, and put an arm on Creophylus's shoulder, and led him away from the beach, up the hill, and into a place where the sun's rays could touch them. Then he bade the young man to join him as he sat upon a rock, and said to him:

—Now, while I still have life, I would sing to you.

And he began to sing to Creophylus the song of yearning and striving and triumph, the song of Heracles. He sang on even as the light began to fade from his eyes, and his voice began to weaken. He sang on as the cold possessed him and he no longer heard the wind among the leaves above them, and all the colors of the world darkened to a blood-red, and slowly to the blackness he had known for all his days, save for this single day and night of glory.

As death took him again, he hoped that Creophylus could remember the small portion of the song that he had sung to him, and his last thought was of how glad he was that Zeus had given him the chance to live again, and to die again.

To die singing. Creating.

ꕥ ꕥ

The Taking of Oechalia (Οἰχαλίας Αλωσις), a poem concerning one of the exploits of Heracles, has passed to this age under the name of Creophylus. Some consider it, however, to have been the work of Homer, who was said to have been Creophylus's friend and possibly his father-in-law. The true provenance of the work, and whether it was part of a larger epic, will probably never be known.

Excerpts from the Records of the New Zodiac and the Diaries of Henry Watson Fairfax

(Note: The Zodiac was a New York City dining club established in 1868, and consisted of twelve gentlemen active in New York society. At least two volumes of the collected minutes of the meetings were privately published.)

September 18th, 20—:

BEFORE I RETIRED LAST NIGHT, I read a column which suggested that many of the outrages perpetrated by both children and adults might be due to the lack of civility in society. I cannot help but agree.

The final decades of the previous century witnessed a dreadful decline in civility, and this new century promises to be no more refined. We are on every side beset by adversarial imagery. The media poses everything in terms of battles, wars, and combat, and I find myself falling into this modern-day vernacular.

I recall (with chagrin) speaking before the board of our computer company just yesterday, and telling them that we should not rest until we have thoroughly crushed Tom Chambers's company, which is all that stands between us and a virtual legal monopoly on network servers. I described our position quite accurately, as 'outnumbered and outgunned', but suggested that sheer courage and resourcefulness could yet win the war, though I would also be willing to shift some cash from other Fairfax corporations into the fray. I went on to demonize Chambers as the head of an evil empire who would be content with nothing less than total domination of the world's computers.

Although that representation is certainly true, I am ashamed of my martial hyperbole, and my forebears would be ashamed of me as well. For a hundred and fifty years the Fairfaxes have conducted their many enterprises with restraint and even temper, and I feel the ghostly censure of my father, my grandfather, and my great-grandfather for betraying that tradition.

Therefore, in order to assuage my guilt, I plan to institute—or rather, reinstate—a tradition which, I believe, has long been neglected and which will, I trust, add a touch of civility and goodwill to the practices of at least a dozen businessmen, myself and my most powerful competitors among them. . . . .

CONSTITUTION

Article I. This Club shall be known as the New Zodiac, modelled after the original Zodiac dining club founded in 1868.

Article II. It shall be made up of twelve members, or *Signs*, who shall be addressed by the zodiacal sign assigned to them by lot.

Article III. The New Zodiac shall meet for dinner on the final Saturday evening of every month, the place to be selected by that month's host, or *caterer*, who shall make all arrangements for the dinner, the cost of which shall be equally shared by the Signs. The cost of wines and spirits shall be borne by the caterer.

CHARTER MEMBERS

Aquarius............Mr Frank Reynolds
Pisces............Mr Todd Arnold
Aries............Mr Jeff Condelli
Taurus............Mr Richard Rank
Gemini............Mr Thomas Chambers
Cancer............Mr Edward Devore
Leo............Mr John Thornton
Virgo............Mr Clark Taylor
Libra............Mr Bruce Levine
Scorpio............Mr Cary Black
Sagittarius............Mr David Walsh
Capricorn............Mr Henry Fairfax

November 25th:

I fear that I may have made a mistake in selecting the charter members of the New Zodiac. Only Ed Devore and John Thornton come, like myself, from old money, while the rest are all nouveau. *The strength of the original Zodiac may have come from the fact that the Signs were all members of New York Society in a time when society meant something. Through its history, the Zodiac boasted both J. P. Morgans, Senior and Junior, the Revd Henry Van Dyke, Joseph H. Coate and John William Davis, both Ambassadors to the Court of St James, Senator Nelson W. Aldrich, and other wealthy and powerful, and, above all,* dignified, *men who knew the importance of civility. In my effort to make the club more democratic, I simply selected the wealthiest and most powerful men, hoping to bring civility to those who most needed it, myself included.*

But the first meeting was not as I had anticipated, even though I tried to recreate as best I could the original menu served at the very first dinner of the original Zodiac on February 29th, 1868 . . .

Minutes of the First Meeting of the New Zodiac

THE HOUGHTON CLUB, NEW YORK
NOVEMBER 24TH 20—
Present at table: All signs. Capricorn, caterer.

MENU:

Oysters	*Selle de mouton*
Potage à la Bagration	*Haricots vert*
Bouchées à la Reine	*Salade—laitue—fromage*
Terrapin à la Maryland	*Poudin glacé*
Suprême de volaille	*Gâteau*
Asperges	*Fruits*
Roman punch	*Café*

WINES:
Krug 1982
Lafitte 1969
Chambertin 1947
Old brandy vintage 1895

It was moved by Brother Gemini to make Brother Capricorn, the member who initiated this series of dinners, the Secretary of the New Zodiac. A unanimous voice vote followed, after which Bro. Gemini observed that perhaps the extra work would keep Bro. Capricorn so busy that he would find no time 'to f— over my business.' Much pleasant laughter followed, and Bro. Capricorn accepted his new post.

Dinner seemed to be received well, although Bro. Aries had to be reminded that fruit was not to be thrown at his fellow Signs. 'We are, after all,' said Bro. Capricorn, 'the New Zodiac and not the Drones' Club.'

'What the hell's the Drones' Club?' Bro. Aries asked, and when informed stated that he had never heard of P. G. Wodehouse. 'F— this Woodhead, whoever he is,' he said, and tossed a strawberry, which hit Bro. Capricorn in the left eye, to the merriment of the company.

When the party was asked who would volunteer to cater the following month's dinner, Bro. Gemini offered to do so, upon receiving assurances in the form of each Sign's solemn word that whatever went on at the dinners would remain confidential. Bro. Gemini then made a vow of his own, that he would serve the Signs a feast at the next dinner, 'like no billionaire has ever tasted before, but which we all f—ing well deserve. It'll make what we had tonight seem like sh—t in comparison—as far as scarcity goes, anyway.'

Bro. Gemini then inquired of Bro. Capricorn if he might borrow the two volumes of the original *Records of the Zodiac*, which he wished to consult for further menu ideas, and Bro. Capricorn happily agreed.

The evening was concluded by the relating of several humorous stories by Bros. Taurus, Libra, and Cancer concerning African-Americans, and some ribald anecdotes told by Bros. Virgo and Sagittarius about women who have worked under them.

Adjourned.

Capricorn, *Secretary*

. . . Most of them seemed to be Philistines, but I confess that I was not surprised to find Ed Devore joining in with the ethnic jokes. He's long had a prejudice against blacks, all the more so since his company was barred from doing any more business in South Africa, after nearly a century of high profits there. And though John Thornton didn't make a fool of himself as most of the others did, he seemed ready to join in at the slightest provocation, and I expect him to be equally frivolous at the next dinner.

At least they all seemed to be civil to each other, which is a start. And Condelli didn't throw any more food after my reprimand, except of course for the face-saving strawberry to show that my billions held no greater sway than his. Perhaps they will calm down in time. And perhaps Chambers's attention to the dinner he's catering will help to take his eye off his business long enough for us to make further inroads into his market share. I wonder, though, just what it is that he's planning to serve. . . .

Second Meeting

THE MEDIA MANSE, PORTLAND, OREGON
DECEMBER 29th, 20—
Present at table: All Signs. Gemini, caterer.

MENU

Sea Tag oysters
Potage crème d'orge régence
Timbale de crab
Cubicle Steak à la Pompadour
Champion de Virginie, sauce champagne
Soufflé aux épinards
Pommes Mont d'Or
Medaillon de foie gras
Salade Arlesienne
Asperges, sauce Hollandaise
Omelette Norwegienne

WINES:
Convent sherry 1894
Moët-Chandon 1969
Château Latour 1957
Musigny 1954
Hôtel de Paris
Blue Pipe Madeira
Holmes Rainwater Madeira 1879
Cognac Napoleon 1890

The sumptuous meal was a near-complete recreation, Brother Gemini so informed us, of a dinner put together in 1925 by J. P. Morgan Jr., the differences being the years of the vintages and the meat utilized in two of the entrées, of which he would say more later.

In further emulation of J. P. Morgan's magnanimity, Bro. Gemini presented the Signs with a linen tablecloth woven in Venice upon which were embossed all the signs of the zodiac, similar to the one Morgan had given to the original Zodiac.

As superb as was the meal (and its setting—Bro. Gemini's newly completed mansion that overlooks the Pacific), even more extraordinary were the wines and spirits. It was not until everyone had made their way through every vintage and was well fortified with the extraordinary Cognac that Bro. Gemini revealed to us the secret ingredient of the Cubicle Steak à la Pompadour and the Champion de Virginie, sauce champagne. Morgan Jr. had originally served Cotelettes de pigeouaux à la Pompadour and Jambon de Virginie, and all the Signs were curious as to with what meats Bro. Gemini had improved the recipes.

He informed us in a manner true to his personal style, transforming the dining-room into a multimedia presentation area with a few spoken words. Screens dropped into place in response to the voice recognition technology, the room darkened, and Bro. Gemini then told us that although he would bear the cost of the wines and spirits, which amounted to well over a quarter million dollars (a bargain, he claimed, considering the short time in which his staff had to gather them), the shared cost of the dinner itself amounted to eight hundred and fifty thousand dollars each.

At the gasp from the Signs, Bro. Gemini inquired of Bro. Capricorn the cost of the previous dinner, which he had solely borne, and was told the amount was seventeen thousand dollars, not including the wines. Bro. Gemini admitted that there was quite a difference between seventeen thousand dollars and over ten million, but that his fellow Signs would understand when they realized just what it was of which they had partaken.

The presentation began then, a combination of video and still photography that showed in detail the process of harvesting the meat, with sections entitled 'On the Hoof', 'Making the Purchase', 'The Butchering

Process', and finally 'In the Kitchen'. Much of the material was more graphic than several of the Signs cared to see, your secretary included, and Bro. Cancer and Bro. Libra wasted both the meal and the wines by disgorging the entire contents of their stomachs into thoughtfully provided plastic-lined silk bags.

Still, no one left their seats, and at the end of the presentation, Bro. Gemini gave an eloquent defense and rationale for his menu selections, by the end of which nearly all the Signs were in agreement with him, and checks for each Sign's share were promised.

Bro. Aries was named the caterer for the next dinner, and assured his brother Signs that he would continue in the tradition established by Bro. Gemini.

Adjourned.

Capricorn, *Secretary*

. . . Cubicle steak. Ed Devore and John Thornton, my old friends, actually laughed at the ghastly pun. Perhaps New England inbreeding has softened their brains so that they can find such a thing funny. Although Devore vomited at first, along with Levine, I think it was because of the graphic elements of the presentation rather than the knowledge of what they had ingested. They probably would have gotten sick at the sight of a steer being butchered, let alone a human being.

Cubicle Steak and Champion de Virginie, Chambers's dreadful wordplay. Champion for Jambon, *and it happens that Kevin Dupree, a purchasing agent in Chambers's company, was indeed the Virginia state spelling bee champion when he was in middle school, as his projected résumé told us.*

And what awful detail Chambers went into to carry out his parallels to the raising and purchasing of stock. We saw footage of Dupree 'on the hoof', both at his job and with his family; we saw the chilling purchase, Chambers himself offering the man ten million dollars for his family if he would vanish forever; then Dupree's slow breaking down as the realization dawned that he was Chambers's body and soul, and that if he refused he and his family would be ruined, both financially and in other ways that only a man with a vast fortune might accomplish.

The butchering itself was numbing, nearly as deadening to me as it must have been to poor Dupree; then seeing the meat cooked and prepared for serving, and most coldhearted of all, seeing us eating it in footage that had been shot by hidden cameras only an hour before and then assembled by Chambers's flunkies.

By the end, some Signs looked sick, some merely uncomfortable, and some were smiling as though they were boys who had been caught stealing candy. But when Chambers began to speak, their faces changed. Though the man can be as coarse as a line worker, he can be as eloquently silver-tongued as the devil when required. He talked about the twelve of us as the true leaders of the country, the new lords of the world, and how our employees, from the humblest we never see to the executives who work closely with us, are all commodities, material to be bought and sold and used as needed. 'Our intelligence and foresight and energy have given us the power,' he said, 'to enrich them or impoverish them . . . or devour them, if we will it.'

And God help me, I could not tell the others that he was wrong. He had already proven himself right. He has seduced them, my friends along with my competitors. I could see their minds churning, thinking of how they might top Chambers's feast. Condelli is next month's caterer, and he seemed thrilled beyond measure at the prospect.

My desire to spread civility has set something quite the opposite into motion, and I do not see how I can stop it. Honor compels me to remain silent, but also to end what I have unwillingly begun. I would do so immediately, but if that is not possible, I have nearly a year until it is once again my turn to serve as caterer, and many things can happen in a year. . . .

Third Meeting

THE HAVENS, BALTIMORE, MARYLAND
JANUARY 26TH 20—
Present at table: All Signs. Aries, caterer.

MENU:

Minestrone *Small eggplant*
Roast leg of Philip Lamb,
mint sauce . . .

January 27th:

. . . Lamb was Condelli's Director of European Operations. At first I thought it possible that he simply might have contributed his leg and survived, since the cost was far less than for Chambers's dinner, but my investigations show that Philip Lamb has disappeared.

Such an act boldly throws down the gauntlet for the other Signs. Lamb had been quite important to the success of Condelli's overseas ventures. It was as though Condelli was saying that anyone can lose an anonymous office drone, but he *was willing to make a real* sacrifice. . . .

Fourth Meeting

DOUBLE R RANCH, DALLAS, TEXAS
FEBRUARY 23RD, 20—
Present at table: All Signs. Taurus, caterer.

MENU:

Shysters Rockefeller	*Hot wings*
Double R Chili with beaners	*Texas fries*
Bar-B-Q Veep . . .	

February 24th:

. . . bad enough that Rank would discard his two top drilling men from his Mexican offshore rigs, but to further weaken himself by barbecuing his distribution Vice-President for that terrible beef/veep pun was utterly foolish. But far worse was his disposal of his entire legal team as a mere appetizer. Of course, he'll put together another, but still it seems insane. . . .

Fifth Meeting

THE DEVORE HOUSE, BOSTON, MA
MARCH 30TH, 20—
Present at table: All Signs. Cancer, caterer

MENU:

Caviar	*Dinde sauvage rôtie Parie aux marrons*
Potage velouté Chantilly	*Gelée d'Airelles*
Roast breast of Mindy, sauce Nautun . . .	

March 31st:

. . . a return to fine dining after Rank's reprehensible Texas barbecue. But Devore has taken the whole thing to a new plateau—or an even lower depth. Perhaps he felt the only way to top Rank was to make more than just a business sacrifice. I have no doubt that he loved Mindy. She had been his mistress for seven years. Psychologically, a loss like that can be far more devastating to a man and his business than the loss of personnel alone can be, and I could see that Devore was feeling the loss deeply. It will be interesting to see the progress of his holdings over the next few months. Rank's growth has certainly been curtailed in the wake of his dinner. Perhaps after Chambers is dealt with, I might try a silent run at Double-R industries. . . .

Seventh Meeting

CEO de lait, rôti . . .

Ninth Meeting

Directeurs à la crème . . .

Eleventh Meeting

Père à l'organe . . .

Twelfth Meeting

THE TAYLOR HOUSE, MIAMI, FLORIDA
NOVEMBER 30TH, 20—
Present at table: All Signs. Virgo, caterer.

MENU:

Huitres
Potage botsch polonais
Vol-au-vent of very young virgin sweetbread
Baron d'agneau Beauharnais
Pommes noisettes
Salade Nicoise
Asperges en branches, sauce mousseline
Bombe Alhambra
Petis pois au beurre

WINES:

Krug 1978
Château Latour 1946—Magnum
Clos de Vougeot 1948
Madeira, rainwater 1886
Napoleon brandy 1873

Most of the Signs seemed in somber mood this evening, in spite of Brother Virgo's splendid repast. Though Bro. Virgo himself seemed a bit glum, possibly over the business misfortunes that have adversely affected nearly all of the Signs, and possibly over the provenance of the sweetbreads, spirits seemed to lift as more and more spirits were consumed.

Several of the Signs joshed Bro. Gemini concerning the successful takeover of his company by Bro. Capricorn, who protested that in spite of the technical terminology he felt no hostility toward Bro. Gemini at all, and hoped that Bro. Gemini reciprocated his goodwill. Bro. Capricorn concluded by telling Bro. Gemini that despite the tides of fortune there would always be a place for him at this table.

A full year now having passed since the first meeting of the New Zodiac, it falls to Bro. Capricorn once again to perform the function of caterer at next month's dinner, which, he informed his brother Signs, he expected them all to attend.

Adjourned.

Capricorn, *Secretary*

December 1st:

. . . his own daughter. They've become monsters, but at a woeful cost. No matter how tough and ruthless you may be, you cannot remain unmoved when serving up your own flesh and blood.

And your business *cannot remain unmoved when your guilt interferes with your attention to it, and you leave gaping holes in your corporate charts by butchering those who made it what it is.*

Nor can that business remain unshaken when your surviving employees are individually informed of what has happened, by messages that remain on screen just long enough to read and then vanish forever from Fairfax Technologies' now universally used network servers.

December 9th:

The Signs are all, save one, ruined, victims of their own hunger and the things that hunger brought. With my inside knowledge of their troubles, it has been easy to buy them out and swallow them up in their weakened condition. The last one fell just this morning.

The companies of the Signs of the New Zodiac have been devoured

Minutes of the Thirteenth and Final Meeting of the New Zodiac

THE FAIRFAX CLUB, NEW YORK
DECEMBER 28TH, 20—
Present at table: All Signs. Capricorn, caterer.
Absent from their seats: Aquarius, Pisces, Aries, Taurus, Gemini, Cancer, Leo, Virgo, Libra, Scorpio, Sagittarius.

MENU:

Hors d'oeuvres à la Aquarius
Pisces jardinière
Potage queue de Aries
Taurus rôtis
Gemini pâté
Cancer à la crème
Leo d'agneau—mint sauce
Roast suckling Virgo
Libra Parmentière
Scorpio à la casserole
Sagittarius de lait farci au marrons

WINES:

Pol Roger extra dry 1956
Château Latour 1947
Tichner Madeira 1868
Café Anglais 1854

Discussion following the dinner was succinct. Brother Capricorn observed that sometimes there is no remedy for incivility in society but removal of the uncivil elements. No one spoke in opposition to this remark.

After a brief period of silence, it was moved by Brother Capricorn that the New Zodiac be dissolved due to lack of members. The motion carried 1–0.

Bro. Capricorn, having dined alone, offered to bear the entire cost of the dinner, and there were no objections.

The other Signs rested most comfortably, and most civilly.

Adjourned.

Capricorn, *Secretary*

A Collector of Magic

Annals of Entertainment

*(from the pages of The N*w Y*rk*r)*

WE NEVER WOULD HAVE IMAGINED, when we met Dwayne Orgel (pronounced with a hard G), that he would have been the kind of person to inspire visions. Most obsessive collectors are not. Those we have known are, for the most part, unprepossessing people, the type for whom you would not spare a second glance. Dwayne Orgel is one of these; bald, with a fringe of gray hair, overweight by at least fifty pounds, medium height, a rather doughy, Steve Forbes-like face, and eyes that seem always on the verge of tearing.

He was wearing, when he opened his door for us, a rather loud, Kelly green blazer and a paisley tie several years out of fashion in New York, though perhaps not in Juniata County, Pennsylvania, where Orgel's home and collection may be found. A blue shirt with a white collar, a cream colored pair of slacks, and cordovan penny loafers completed the *ensemble*, and he shook our hand and smiled without showing his teeth, then welcomed us into this large house built into the side of a mountain, a house expressly designed to hold, if not the most comprehensive or valuable, one of the most *distinctive* collections of magical apparatus and memorabilia.

Here you will not find the usual posters of Thurston and Houdini. There is no art on the walls because there is no room. Wooden shelves cover every wall from floor to ceiling, so that one is never able to gauge the true size of any room, since one never knows how deep those shelves may be. And on every shelf are magic tricks, for that is all that Dwayne Orgel, with the fifty-three million dollars he won four years ago in the Pennsylvania Powerball lottery, has purchased for his collection, one that began decades ago.

'I was always buying stuff,' he says in a flute-like timbre as he leads us from one room to the next. There are a total of forty-three rooms, many of them thirty or forty feet long, and several with twenty-foot high ceilings and library ladders on tracks to take Orgel to the highest shelves. 'In fact,' he goes on, 'most of the things on these shelves right here I bought before I really had money.'

He gestures to an eye-level shelf in a theatrical manner, twirling his fingers like a magician revealing a rabbit, but the pudgy hand and lack of grace doom the effect. Orgel reaches back into the darkness of the wooden shelf and pulls out what looks like a battered fur hat. It turns out to be what is called a 'Perfection Rabbit', an item sold by the National Magic Company in the 1940s for magicians too poor to afford or too timid to handle a real animal. This specimen appears to be well-used.

'It's made from real rabbit skin,' Orgel says, slipping a hand inside it and demonstrating the arrangement of threads that make the artificial beast twitch its head and kick its feet. Whether due to Orgel's lack of skill or the object's faulty construction, the resemblance to a real rabbit is only superficial. Orgel shrugs, looks sheepish, and hands us the device, inviting us to try it out. The hide on the inside is worn and smooth against our skin, and we quickly grasp the uses of the thread. The 'rabbit' unconvincingly kicks its hind feet, and Orgel laughs in approval and tells us that we're already better than he is at manipulating it.

'I really wanted to be a magician,' he says as we continue through the rooms. Dwayne Orgel grew up watching magicians on *The Ed Sullivan Show* and other TV variety programs. He recalls sneaking downstairs at night to watch *Tonight* whenever he read in *TV Guide* that Jack Paar had a magician as a guest. In the 1950s, when he was in elementary school, he sent for magic tricks from novelty catalogues, seldom paying more than fifty cents each, including postage, but claims he was never able to make them work. 'Even when they didn't need any real sleight of hand,' he says, 'I'd still screw up.'

Though Orgel's interest in magic never waned, his attempted participation in it did. Because of his inability to perform even the simplest tricks, as well as the demands of school, work, and family as the years passed, Orgel's desire to collect tricks lay dormant for decades. Then, ten years ago, that desire was reborn.

'I just had an epiphany,' he says, after we suggest the proper word. 'I just knew that I had to collect tricks again—not just any tricks, but ones that had been used by professional magicians, tricks they performed over and over again, and that lots of people saw, and *thought* were magic.'

Apparently the magicians didn't have to be top artists, although Orgel has his share of truly valuable and rare items, including cabinets and illusion devices used by the most famous nineteenth and twentieth century magicians. His interest stops short, however, at the new breed of magicians, and there is no memorabilia from David Copperfield, Siegfried and Roy, or Penn and Teller among his prizes. 'Everybody knows they're tricks now, even kids. But back forty, fifty years ago, I think a lot of people still believed that magic was *magic*.'

The collecting mania that overcame Dwayne Orgel in his mid-forties was not shared by his wife, Sherry. 'We were married about seven years. It was my first, her second—I waited pretty long. I never wanted children, and

Sherry felt the same way. But it turned out she didn't want magic either.'

Sherry Orgel abandoned her husband seven years ago, after experiencing three years of his tireless collecting. 'I don't blame her,' Orgel says. 'Other than collecting, I really wasn't interested in much of anything.' For a time, authorities were suspicious, since Sherry Orgel vanished as completely as an assistant in a magic box. Although a thorough search was made of Dwayne Orgel's property, nothing was found that was inconsistent with Orgel's account of her desertion.

Four years ago, after winning the lottery, Orgel made a public appeal to Sherry to return and share in his good fortune, but there was no response except for a small legion of imposters requesting travel money to return to Pennsylvania from as far away as Germany. Orgel remains a man alone.

It takes us several hours to go through all the rooms. Orgel seems as proud of the most modest tricks as he does of the most renowned. He points with pride to 'The Vanishing Bird Cage', a device that, he informs us, The Great Condolli bought for $17.50 in 1944. 'Condolli worked for thirty-five years,' he tells us. 'He was just a working magician, never became well known, but he did this very trick at every show. Can you imagine all the people that saw this cage vanish over the years? Can you even begin to count all the children—and not just children—who saw this trick and believed it was magic?' He speaks more softly now, touching the metal cage as though it is a holy relic. 'Can you imagine all the magic in this trick?'

For a full minute Dwayne Orgel stands there, looking down at the trick in his pudgy hands. We say nothing, unwilling to break the spell, or to keep him from what he might next reveal. At last he looks up and smiles, his teeth hidden by his full lips, and leads us to other marvels. He repeatedly discusses the history of seemingly inconsequential items, and his focus seems always to be on the lengthy career of the tricks he shows us, of the thousands, even millions of people who have seen a particular trick performed, a specific device in operation, and marveled at it.

Dwayne, as we have begun to think of him, since his personal feelings become more apparent with every item he examines, is enigmatically becoming more single-minded and thus less communicative, and this concerns us. After many representatives of the press have solicited him for interviews, ours is the first he has actually granted, and that after two years of requests, so we don't wish to see him grow more diffident, particularly since he has told us that he has a major announcement to make.

We follow as he moves on, picking up various sets of linking rings, stuffed birds, tubes from whose ends colored scarves trail like vines, a plethora of magic wands, most of them terribly worn, their nicked black paint showing bare wood beneath, revealing them to be nothing more than dowels with brass caps on the ends; handcuffs for escape tricks, decks of cards in abundance, many with edges shaved, other full decks of aces or kings or queens, some with cut out faces like pasteboard picture frames. And all of these items he hefts in his hands, and of them he speaks reverently, and talks of years and audiences, and how many seats the Palladium held, and how many times the magician who used this deck or this wand or these scarves played there, and to how many souls these objects spoke of magic.

At last we come to the top hats. There are hundreds of them, made of silk and beaver and rayon, all of them black, many of them worn, a few still shining. Dwayne picks them up, muttering the names of the magicians to whom they once belonged, most of them long dead and forgotten, though a few are familiar to us. He does not, however, demonstrate any false bottoms or hidden pockets in the hats, and we begin to sense that it is not the trickery, not the illusion that interests Dwayne, but the *magic* itself that may somehow exist within the objects he collects and touches.

'What is it?' we finally ask when the tour is finished and we are sitting at opposite ends of a large sofa facing a picture window. 'What makes you collect these things?' The view is extraordinary. We look out over the treetops down the side of the mountain to the Juniata River below. On the other side, there are trees and more mountains as far as the eye can see.

For a long time, Dwayne sits staring out the window. Finally he speaks. 'Because I knew that I'd been doing it all wrong.' His voice is soft, yet filled with a fierce intensity. 'I'd been trying all those years to do it by myself, and I couldn't. Some people are born for it, and some aren't.'

When we ask born for what, though we strongly suspect, he answers born for magic. 'I couldn't do sleight of hand,' he goes on. 'My fingers are too thick and short. And I'm not graceful. I'm fat. Whenever I tried to palm anything, I'd get it stuck in the folds of my hand.' He laughs, and we smile in sympathy. 'But finally I knew that if I wanted to do magic, the only way would be for me to do it . . . real.' He says the last word so quietly that we are barely able to understand it.

We gently protest that magic isn't real, that no matter how well done, it consists of trickery and illusion.

'Oh no,' he replies. 'There's real magic. Magic can *become* magic. Magic can make magic on its own.' We are starting to feel that we've wandered into an oddly Carrollian brand of logic here, but allow him to explain. 'It's belief, you see. Belief has great power. If people believe something is real, it eventually becomes real . . . like that story of the Velveteen Rabbit . . . or Jesus.'

It wasn't a connection that we would have made, but we remain silent.

'It's the same with magic,' Dwayne says, looking at us now. 'One day the idea came into my head that all these things that had created magic, that had made people believe, might slowly take on magic themselves. The more I thought about this theory, the more sure of it I got. You know how when magicians do the same trick for a long, long time, and it gets so they don't even have to make an effort to do it anymore?' We nod in affirmation. 'That's not just because it gets easier the more times they do it—it's because the magic starts forming in it. It's like energy. All these tricks, they soak up the psychic energy of the people who observe them, and of the magician too. And I knew that if I only got enough of these tricks . . . these, like, *batteries* of magic . . . then it would rub off on me. And *I* could do magic. Not tricks, but magic.'

It strikes us as a classic example of superstitious thinking, the idea of a child, something becoming magic simply because we so badly want it to be. Still, we can't help but be won over by Dwayne Orgel's enthusiasm and sincerity, by his apparent belief in the absurdities he is mouthing, and if we have not yet begun to believe him, we at least *want* to believe him.

'When I figured it out, I started buying used tricks. I had to find ones that had been used a lot, because that was the whole point. But those were the most expensive, because they were from magicians who had long careers, and most of them were pretty well known in the magic community, and when their stuff was available, it sold at a premium. Sherry didn't like it. Why was I buying all this junk, that's what she called it, junk. I had to let her think that I was just collecting it. I couldn't tell her the truth, she'd have thought I was nuts.'

We instantly wonder why he has decided to tell *us* the truth, but don't ask. It seems an indelicate moment to interrupt, as the thought of his wife has somewhat distracted him.

'I could feel it starting. I could feel the magic, but there wasn't nearly enough yet. It was just a thimble full, and I needed the ocean. Once I knew, there was no turning back, no stopping, and she tried to stop me. But I couldn't let her, and that's why . . . that's why she left.'

Dwayne is looking at us now, and his expression is that of a hopeful little boy begging us to believe that breaking some precious object was an accident that could have happened to anyone. We venture a comment that dedication like his might have been difficult to live with.

'It was,' he agrees. 'I thought she might understand, might even, in time, become my assistant—"my lovely assistant Sherry", you know. But she didn't. She was right about one thing, though. I was crazy if I thought I could reach my goal on the little money I had to spend. If it hadn't been for winning the lottery, it never would have happened. You can't imagine how much stuff I needed, how much it took, how *little* energy there is in one trick, even one that's been done over and over again in front of huge audiences for years. You can't imagine anything quite that small and insignificant. You've seen everything I have? Well, it took *all* of that before I finally did it.'

Unable to resist, we ask what it is that he has done.

'Collected enough magic to *do* magic,' he says with a satisfied smile. 'That's why you're here. That's why I invited you. To see what it is that I can do. I've bought my dream, and now I want to prove it.'

We nod politely, realizing that this piece will not be a mere casual, a collector profile one or two columns long in 'Talk of the Town', as originally intended, but something longer and certainly more serious.

'What would you like to see?' He stands up and suddenly appears to be taller than before. Despite the bulbous shape and the off-the-rack clothing, there is something commanding and dignified about Dwayne Orgel at this moment.

The radical change leaves us nearly speechless. All we can think of is the stock trick of pulling a rabbit out of a hat, and that is what we suggest that he do.

He is amused. For the first time since we have met him, he really laughs, a shrill, squeaking sound that makes us wince in spite of our best efforts to do otherwise. 'A rabbit out of a hat?' he asks, the words trilling along with his laughter as it subsides. 'I think I can do that.' Dwayne takes a few steps toward the window, then turns to us, beckoning us to join him. We push ourselves up out of the couch and stand several feet away from him.

Then he points out the window toward the trees on the other side of the river. In the distance, the sky is turning a light gray, as though rain is on the horizon. Closer, it is beginning to darken with the advent of sunset, but is still blue, dotted with high, white, wispy clouds. 'Watch,' Dwayne Orgel says.

At first we watch him rather than the landscape. He turns toward the window and closes his eyes. The furrows of his brow deepen, his lips press tightly shut, and his jaw juts forward. He curls his thick fingers into fists that look like pink, creased balls which he raises to the level of his waist. His knees are slightly bent. His head bows lower, and the fat neck seems to suck it down into his shoulders. Though we try to dismiss the thought, he appears to be in the throes of extreme constipation rather than concentration.

Then he relaxes. In less than a second, all the tension leaves him. His arms fall to his side and his eyes open. His face appears placid and calm, but his eyes are alight as he looks outside, across the river to the woods beyond. His expression sharpens, and we follow his gaze.

There, far away among the trees, something begins to rise. It looks like a shining black bowl many hundreds of yards across, with a wide, curved rim. We scarcely breathe, and we know, even as we see it push higher, as though growing from the forest, that this is impossible, that we are seeing, not reality, but an illusion, the result of pure suggestibility.

That thought, however, does not stop the black bowl from growing larger and rising higher above the tops of the trees. It moves slowly, as if on an hydraulic lift. Now we see something beneath it, as though it is supported by a pedestal, equally black and shining. The pedestal is banded vertically, but the banding ceases as more of it presents itself, and at last we realize what we are seeing or imagining or hallucinating.

It is a hat, a shiny black top hat with a black ribbon band growing upside down from the forest floor, a hat that must be a half mile high by the time it stops moving, its inverted top far below, hidden by the trees.

Though we are unable to remove our gaze from the titanic hat, from the corner of our eye we see Dwayne Orgel raise his hand and make a gesture. In spite of his previous imperfect effort, there is a strange grace to the motion. Then, from the opening of the hat, something white and pointed appears. In another second, the rabbit's entire head pokes out of the hat. It looks back at us, its nose wiggling, pink eyes sparkling. Its head retracts for a moment, and it leaps from the hat, a massive blur of white, leaps so high that it vanishes beyond the top frame of the window and is lost to our sight.

'Rabbits,' Dwayne Orgel says with a trace of contempt. 'Rabbits are nothing. You want tricks—here are tricks!'

His hands move again, darting and weaving in what, as far as we know, may be cabalistic patterns or simply random motions. Whatever they are, they are effective, as we now see the things that pour in rapid succession from the hat.

A dove bursts forth, as big as an airliner, and soars into the sky. It is quickly followed by many of the trappings and accoutrements of magic, all grown ridiculously large: multi-colored scarves flutter into the air, curving and falling to the ground like pink and yellow and lavender waterfalls, rushing down into the trees; a pair of linking rings are thrown from the recesses of the hat, each one large enough to hold a stadium within its circumference, and clatter away amidst the greenery; a pair of handcuffs (a nod to Houdini?) flop over the brim, their weight preventing them from being airborne, and the first cuff drags the other, by the massive chain that connects them, over the brim and out of sight; playing cards, each big enough to cover a city block, burst out of the hat with a sound of flapping celluloid heard easily through the thick glass behind which we stand; and finally a magic wand, gold-tipped and black and miles high, thrusts itself from the abyss and begins to grow, lengthening and thickening until it becomes as wide as the hat it fills, and its gold tip is lost in the clouds.

And then it all vanishes, vanishes with an intake of breath from its creator, leaving only the forest, the river, and the sky, leaving only the truth that always remains after illusion's bubble is burst. Or so we think, until we turn and look at what Dwayne Orgel is staring at so fixedly, his face white, his eyes wide.

In the doorway that leads to the collection rooms, those high-ceilinged chambers with tall and deep wooden shelves where almost anything could be stored unseen, in that doorway there stands what must be another illusion, another trick, not only of Dwayne Orgel's, but of our full and by now highly suggestible mind. It is a figure about five feet high, and it resembles a woman. Her skin is as dry as parchment, and there are no eyes in the sockets. Neither tongue nor teeth are visible in the cavity above the open, lolling jaw, which hangs like a pouch of yellow flesh from her face.

The woman we see has no body inside her skin. She is a framework of flesh over what might be a system of sticks, held together and controlled by threads. She wears a thigh-length skirt of purple satin, decorated with bright sequins, and a crimson silk vest embroidered with geometric designs. Pinned to the vest, a silken rose shivers over her left breast.

We look at her in horror and fascination and amazement that we are imagining such a creature, for rationality insists that another illusion is all she can be. Then she moves, with an unnatural precision, like a puppet controlled from within, and we realize that what we are seeing is a human version of the 'Perfection Rabbit' sold by the National Magic Company, a construction of skin and thread and whatever else holds it together and gives it shape. It would seem that Dwayne Orgel is a master illusionist after all.

'*Go back!*' we hear him say, and are somewhat concerned at the fear in his eyes. Or is it, we wonder, all part of the act? If so, his acting is impeccable, and we ourselves feel a *frisson* of fear as we look at what we have now come to think of as the 'Perfection Assistant', though not at all a 'lovely' one.

This current illusion does not vanish as did the giant hat and its contents. On the contrary, it continues its jerky walk, drawing nearer to us and to Dwayne, who once again goes into what seems to be his concentration/constipation mode. We would close our eyes too, but can't help but think that if we did, we might open them again to find the face of the empty yet terribly alive 'Perfection Assistant' only inches from our own, certainly an unpleasant prospect.

So we watch as Dwayne Orgel grimaces and clenches his fists, and after what may be a minute or an hour (for we seem to have lost track of time, and cannot look away from the construct before us to check our watch), the creature moves slowly backward toward the doorway through which it came. It passes through, its wrinkled, flapping face still toward us, and finally backs out of our view into the next room.

Dwayne remains tense for another few minutes, and then slowly relaxes. Now there is none of the assurance and sense of mastery that had come upon him during his 'hat trick', but rather a deep relief, we assume, that his astounding performance is over.

'Brav-*O!*' we manage to breathe out, then cross to the door through which Dwayne Orgel's second and more modest, but yet somehow more effective, illusion has passed. It is a splendid trick: there is no trace of the creature's presence. It has vanished utterly.

We cross once more to the window, look out at the empty forest and the darkening sky. There is not a trace of anything else. The hat, its contents, and the 'Perfection Assistant' are all gone. And how clever of the magician to set the stage so well with the Perfection Rabbit, so that we might all the more appreciate his climactic illusion.

For Dwayne Orgel *is* a magician, the best we have ever seen. Whether he has created his illusions out of thin air or pulled them from somewhere deep within our psyche, he has shown us things we have never seen before. He is peerless, a true genius of magic.

We tell him this as we leave, but he hardly seems to hear it. Undoubtedly the great effort he has put forth in our behalf has wearied him, and he collapses onto the sofa. We endeavor to ask several more questions, but he simply waves a hand of dismissal, and we see ourselves to the door.

As we drive our rental car back to the airport, we wonder if this annunciation of Dwayne Orgel's talents to the world through our magazine will be enough for him, or if, like most entertainers, he will feel the need for a larger audience. We suspect the latter. His constant attention to the number of spectators commanded by his predecessors indicates his desire for an audience greater than one. And his skill demands it.

Orgel has not only created a series of illusions without equal, he has also created one of the most believable personae on or off the stage. Never have we seen insecurity and inferiority so vividly rendered by a performer so obviously at the pinnacle of his craft. What makes his art all the more remarkable is that it springs from the mind of one who seems to be, at the very least, a few aces short of a trick deck.

Sherry Orgel did not reappear when her husband won his fortune, but now that he stands on the brink of international stardom, we feel certain that she will complete his dream. Nothing seems impossible for Dwayne Orgel now. As he told us so sincerely, 'There's real magic. Magic can *become* magic. Magic can make magic on its own.' And it is just that magic that may make Sherry Orgel, the lovely assistant with whom he has always wanted to share his life and art, come out of the woodwork and embrace him once again. With magic, anything is possible.

Subtle Knowing

ON ALL THE FACES, he saw only masks. People wore masks to hide all the things they didn't want others to see.

There was a high school boy looking with adoring eyes at the girl next to him in line for the carousel. He looked honest and frank and open and happy, but Spencer Brady suspected what that mask hid. The kid wanted in her pants, wanted to slide those designer jeans down over her hips and slip that sweater up over her breasts.

And there was the hawker offering three balls for a dollar, his face wreathed with smiles, saying in his loud, hearty voice how it was the easiest thing in the world to knock over three milk bottles. But Spencer thought he could see behind the mask, could glimpse that cunning, greedy face, as scarred and grimy and ugly as those fake wooden bottles, with a lead weight in the base of each. Despite his ebullience, the hawker had a heart of lead, just like the fraud he peddled.

Too many frauds, too many masks, Spencer thought. It had probably been a mistake to come to this travelling carnival, but Gina had wanted to, and had already made plans with Frank and Melissa. 'It'll cheer you up,' Gina had said, and he had agreed, though he didn't know how a goddamned cheesy carnival was going to make him forget the way Todd had screwed him yesterday when, during the Friday staff meeting, he had made the announcement that the marketing manager job was going to Kyle McAleer.

Spencer had worked his ass off for that job, and Todd had never given him any reason to believe that he wasn't going to get it. The sonovabitch had smiled at Spencer for months, patting him on the shoulder and complimenting him on his work, telling him that nobody did the job the way he did, and by God that was true. Spencer had busted his balls, staying late, coming in early, working at home nights, and his sole reward was to get pissed on. Oh, Todd had never actually *promised* Spencer the job, but anybody with half a fucking brain could see the way the land lay. The job belonged to Spencer by *right*, goddammit, and instead Todd had given it to a little ass-kisser ten years younger than Spencer, and when he had announced it, he had smiled at all of them just the way he had smiled at Spencer all those months, wearing that lying mask.

Spencer had wanted to jump up and smash Todd's mask, bust that smiling face in, but he didn't. It made him feel the same way he had felt when Susan's mask had finally dropped away, when his wife of twenty-four years had told him that she wanted a divorce because she had fallen in love with the bastard she had met at the health club. Christ, there had never been a *clue* that he could have seen, never so much as a whiff of after-shave or a scratch mark on her ass, or a phone call with someone hanging up when he answered. Susan had played her part to perfection. The mask hadn't slipped once, not until the night she told him she would be gone the following day.

He hadn't seen the truth then, and he hadn't seen it earlier when his son Robbie first went on drugs. The boy had seemed perfectly normal to Spencer, not a sign that anything was wrong. And then, almost before he realized what was happening, came the accident, the rehab, and Robbie walking out of the hospital and out of Spencer and Susan's lives. It had crushed him, but he didn't know how it had affected Susan. He had thought he did, but that might have been a lie too, just another mask she wore, this one of tears and sorrow.

Masks. Fucking masks.

And Todd's was about the last he could take. He didn't know who to trust anymore. Could he even trust Gina?

That was stupid. Of course he could trust her. She was the kindest and sweetest woman he had ever known. She had just about saved his life after the Susan debacle. He had felt comfortable with her from the start, because she had been through the same kind of hurt that was grinding away at Spencer. Her husband of twenty-two years had left her just a year before.

It was true, however, that Spencer and Gina didn't have much in common except for a similar brand of misery. She was a bank teller with only a high school education, and pretty naïve when it came to the arts, but Spencer had enjoyed exposing her to the things he loved, jazz and classical music, foreign films, and folk arts, and she seemed to enjoy them too.

All told, he was lucky to have her. She was warm, attractive, responsive when they made love, and, except maybe for Frank, the best friend he had ever had. He thought he would ask her to marry him before too long. There would be no hassles, since her two children were grown and lived on the other side of the country.

As if in answer to his thoughts, Gina squeezed his hand gently and asked if they could ride the Ferris wheel. He agreed, smiling at her enthusiasm, and they bought tickets and got into the short line with Frank and Melissa.

'Looks pretty creaky,' Spencer said with a grin. 'Sure we can trust it?' He was only joking, but in truth the Ferris wheel did look as if it were on its last legs. The bolts that held it together were brown with rust, and the sound it made as it moved was as harsh as the scraping of nails against a blackboard. As it turned, there seemed to be one place where every car lurched as it descended, bouncing its occupants for a second, making the girls squeal and even the boys hold on to the crossbar more tightly. Maybe it was intended, Spencer thought, built in for a cheap thrill.

The current ride ended, the wheel ground to a halt, and the boarding process began, with each car stopping at the base to evict its occupants and take on new ones. Soon Spencer and Gina were aloft, and the ride began. She clung to him with one arm and gripped the crossbar with the other.

Though he put an arm around her, he would much sooner have had both hands on the cool metal. The ride, he thought, was terrifying. The car shook continually, like a plane going through flak, and sounded as though it might fall apart at any moment. Despite his concern, he made himself laugh as Gina pressed closer against him, and he tried to think less about the wheel and concentrate on the view.

It was a good one. They seemed much higher than he had imagined they would be, and he could see the town in the distance, with all the lights of the carnival spread out below them. There was the field that was doubling as a parking lot; there the single road out to the carnival; and there, in the opposite direction, was the last carnival structure, a small tent that marked the boundary between festive light and the darkness of the fields beyond.

The tent seemed to be placed oddly, twenty yards behind the large trailer that housed a mirror maze, and Spencer wondered who would even see it from the midway. His eyes were good enough to make out the writing on a sign staked into the ground by the tent: *LUXOR*, it read, and then in smaller letters, *The Amazing!* Whoever Luxor was, Spencer thought, he mustn't pull in too many suckers. Maybe that was why they gave him such lousy placement.

At last the ride ended, and Spencer stepped out of the car with relief. Gina still had her arm through his, and didn't release the pressure until they were off the ramp and on the ground. Even then she glanced back at the wheel as though suspecting it might topple over on them.

'We paid for thrills and we got 'em,' Frank said, grinning, as he and Melissa joined them. Then he pointed to a large tent on the midway. 'How about there next?'

Although the banner stated, 'Scientific Oddities of Humanity', it was obviously a freak show, with what appeared to be ancient painted representations of the Chicken Boy, Alligator Man, and other strange folk who waited within. Both women immediately said that there was no way they would go in, and although the thought of it repelled Spencer, to admit it would have made him seem less macho. So he good-naturedly sided with Frank, and they reached a compromise in which Gina and Melissa would get sno-cones while the men checked out the freaks.

It didn't take long for Spencer to wish that he had gone for the sno-cones. The exhibits inside depressed and sickened him. He rushed through as quickly as possible, while Frank slowly inspected each variety of 'oddity', the dead ones preserved in jars, or the living with severe birth defects. As a result of his haste, Spencer found himself outside while Frank was still looking at only the fourth of the two dozen exhibits.

Feeling slightly sick from what he had just seen, he decided neither to wait for Frank nor to join the women, but to walk about and clear his head. He was certain Frank would remain in the show for at least another fifteen minutes or so.

He walked away from the food stands, down the midway to the end where the mirror maze stood. It was then that he remembered the small tent behind it, and, out of curiosity, he walked around the large trailer into the comparative darkness behind it.

The tent seemed even smaller on the ground than it had from above, and was ripped and torn in dozens of places, so that the light from within made the brown canvas look like a sky filled with streaking comets and exploding suns. Beneath *Luxor The Amazing*, there were words in smaller type that he had not been able to read from above:

Knows All—Sees All—Master Of The Truth

'Just what I need,' Spencer whispered to himself, but as he started to turn away, he heard a voice.

'More than you know,' it said. It was an aged, cracking voice, and the timbre of it froze Spencer. He looked at the front of the tent, and saw pale yellow fingers with ragged nails curl around the entrance flap. The fingers slowly pushed it back, and a dim light shone from inside, silhouetting the man who stood there smiling at Spencer. The flesh of his long face was fissured and wrinkled like a relief map of a fjord, and gray-yellow hair covered his forehead and entwined about his ears. Though stooped, his build was lean and rangy, like that of a tall man, but Spencer guessed that he was barely five feet high. He looked, Spencer thought, like some ancient fairy king.

'You want the truth,' the man said. 'Come inside and have it.' He let the tent flap fall back into place, hiding him from Spencer's view.

Only for a moment did Spencer hesitate. Then, absurd as he knew it was, he walked up to the tent, pushed back the flap, and entered.

He had been expecting something theatrical, possibly some worn, leather-bound books on a shelf, a few prop alembics, maybe a crystal ball and a skull. But inside the tent, whose only floor was the grass and weeds of the meadow upon which the carnival had been erected, there were only two folding chairs and a card table, whose gray leatherette top was as worn and tattered as the tent itself.

'Sit down,' said the old man, who was already seated in one of the chairs, hunched forward, his forearms resting on his thighs. Spencer sat across from him, and thought of leaning his arms on the table, but changed his mind when he saw the mildew, gray against the gray leatherette. 'I was right, wasn't I?' asked the old man. 'When I said you want truth.'

Spencer smiled, trying to make himself at least *look* comfortable. 'Isn't that why anyone would visit you . . . Luxor?' he said.

'Don't call me that,' the old man said easily. 'It's not my name, since it's truth we're after.' He licked his dried and wrinkled lips quickly, with a tongue that looked like a red sponge left out too long in the rain. Then he looked sharply at Spencer, who was surprised to see how vital and piercing were the old man's eyes, not at all yellow and rheumy, but sharp black pupils against cornflower blue irises, and whites the hue of arctic sunlight. 'What do you want to know . . . Spencer?'

Hearing his name come from between those raddled lips hit Spencer like an ax handle between the eyes. For a moment he couldn't speak. Then, finally, he managed to get out, 'How . . . do you . . .'

'I know all, Spencer Brady. I know about Susan and about your son, I know what happened at your office too. I know that you're tired to the death of lies. I know that you hunger for the truth—about everyone and everything.'

Spencer didn't know how it had happened, but he had stumbled upon one of those places and one of those people you read about only in stories, and, absurdly enough, all that he could suddenly think about was how desperately he had to go to the bathroom.

'I think you can manage to hold your water until we've finished talking, don't you?' the old man said.

Then Spencer got it. It wasn't real, none of it. It was a dream, or some sort of hallucination. He wasn't in this tent. He might not even be at any carnival, for that matter. He was probably home in bed dreaming.

'No, you're not home in bed, you're here,' said the man.

Spencer laughed, and thought he heard a touch of hysteria in it. 'No, you're wrong!' he said. 'The only way you could see inside my head is if I created you—if you were *already* in my head.'

The old man shrugged. 'If it gives you comfort to believe that, then do it.'

'There's no other explanation,' Spencer said, feeling more secure now that he had reasoned things out.

'Then . . .' the old man said slowly, as if trying to work it out. Spencer was amazed at the depth of detail he had created within his dream. He could see the man's individual gray whiskers. 'Then there would be nothing for you to lose were we to make a bargain.' The man smiled again, this time showing his teeth. Unfortunately they were not as clear and white as his eyes. 'Would you like to know the truth then, Spencer? Even in a dream?'

The thought appealed to Spencer, along with some pride that he had produced this vivid setting, even though his creativity hadn't extended to skulls and alembics. 'Yes,' he said, feeling in control at last. 'Yeah, I think I would.'

'I'll give it to you then—the gift—the ability to look inside people and see what they really think, to hear beyond the words that they speak to you, if you're really sure that you want it. Not many people would, you know.'

'*I* want it. I'm sick of lies, sick of looking at the devious masks everyone wears. I want to see what's underneath, so I don't have to guess anymore.'

'So you don't have to trust.'

'Maybe.'

The old man rubbed his stubbled chin with his knuckles. 'There's a price. You know that's always a part of any bargain like this. If you have extra sight, then you have to compensate in other ways.' He nodded toward Spencer. 'The sight in your left eye.'

Involuntarily, Spencer's hand went to his face. 'What do you mean?'

'Oh, don't worry, I won't pluck it out. You'll just lose the sight in it. It'll still appear normal, it'll move along with your right eye. Might make your peripheral vision less acute—you'll have to be careful when you drive a car—but that's your weak eye anyway, isn't it?'

That much was true. Of course the old man that he had made up would know about the strabismus in his left eye. He might as well make the bargain. After all, it was only in his head anyway, and if it wasn't, it was bullshit, and if it *wasn't* bullshit, then he would have the power the old man had promised him. Hell, even if he had the power in a dream, it would be better than nothing, and he'd still have his full sight when he woke up.

'All right,' Spencer said. 'It's a deal. So . . . what do we do?'

'It's done,' the old man said, and the sight in Spencer's left eye went black, as though he had closed it. He put his hand up to it immediately, and winced at the touch of his finger upon his naked eyeball. 'I told you,' the man said. 'We make our trade-offs in life, and you just made a choice, Spencer Brady. I hope you can live with it.'

Spencer looked around desperately. Suddenly this all felt very real, and he knew overwhelmingly that he was not dreaming or hallucinating any of this. He knew as surely as if it were God's own truth.

'It is, Spencer,' said the old man, truly reading his mind. 'When . . . *if* you grow tired of the truth, you can return here to the carnival. Anytime.'

The man looked away with an unmistakable sense of dismissal, and Spencer slowly got to his feet and moved backward until his back brushed the canvas flap that served as a door. He pushed through it, looked away from the man, and stepped out into the garishly lit night.

He looked at the lights of the midway, blinked several times as if to clear his vision, or bring it back again, but the left eye registered no light at all. He knew that it would not. He knew that was the truth.

Spencer walked around the mirror maze, back toward the midway, his head turned to the left to compensate for his lack of vision on that side. When he entered the shining avenue of stalls, Gina, Melissa, and Frank were nowhere in sight. He was glad. He didn't want to see them yet, not until he'd worked out in his head just what this meeting with that old man had been all about.

So he walked away from where they had been, and stopped at a stand where a woman was selling, for a dollar, a chance to toss three softballs into a box in which wooden slats formed a tic-tac-toe pattern. 'Line up three in a row and win a prize,' she called.

Spencer walked to the rail that separated the rubes from their target, and the woman stepped up to him, holding the three balls in her large, spider-like hand. 'Give it a try, buddy?' she asked.

With his single eye, he looked at her, concentrating intently on her pouchy cheeks, the deep wrinkles at the corners of her drooping eyes, the slightly twisted mouth on which she had slathered too much lipstick. And then that face, that mask that hid her true self, seemed to melt away, and Spencer saw what lay underneath.

He gasped and shrank back, scarcely able to absorb the psychic force pushing against him, the sudden knowledge, the *truth* battering its way into his mind. This woman was a monster, and the ugly mask she wore was a thing of utter beauty compared to the true face that Spencer saw. It was ravaged by greed, eaten away by envy, gnawed by hatred.

Spencer knew instantly that this woman hated him for what he was, for her assumption that, because of the way he was dressed and groomed, he had a permanent home, perhaps a family, a good job, all the things she lacked. He saw that she would, had she had the opportunity, have killed him, both for what he might have had in his pockets, and because he was what he was, something that she simultaneously loathed and desired.

It was a terrible knowledge, and he pushed her back, making her stumble so that she dropped the softballs she was offering, and they bounced off the rail with a hollow sound like ripe, falling fruit. Spencer turned away, shutting off his mind, not hearing her curses as they followed him down the midway.

He kept his remaining eye fixed on the ground. He wanted darkness, deep and comforting, far from the presence of any person. He particularly did not want to see Gina or Frank or Melissa tonight. He could not explain what had happened to him. They wouldn't believe it, just as he himself would not have believed it had he not *known* it was the truth, just as he had known the truth behind that woman's mask just by looking at her.

Both he and Frank had driven to the carnival, so he got a pen and paper from his car, wrote a note saying that he had gotten terribly ill and would Frank please take Gina home, and put it under Frank's windshield wiper, then drove back to his apartment. He realized that his disappearance was totally uncavalier, but he could think of no alternative to avoid confronting his friends.

An hour later, Gina called him, as he had thought she would, and he told her that he had gotten sick over himself, and thought it best to disappear. Her voice was filled with sympathy, and she offered to come over, but he told her that he would be all right, and all he needed was some sleep.

That weekend, Spencer stayed inside his apartment. He left a message on his answering machine that he had been called out of town, and moved his car around the block so that neither Frank nor Gina would think he was in if they dropped by. Then he sat and thought about what he would do with his new knowledge, his new way of seeing the truth.

He sat and thought for the entire weekend, sleeping in his chair, getting up only to eat and go to the bathroom. Gina called three times, and Frank twice, but Spencer didn't answer. By Monday morning he had made up his mind about what he would do with his strange new gift, and he showered, shaved, and dressed, and went to work.

At the office, he tried to avoid looking directly at people, and only glanced at them from the corner of his eye. The sole exception was his secretary, Anne, an average looking woman in her forties who had been divorced five years earlier and never remarried. Anne was so dedicated to her work that she had never even mentioned the breakup to him, and Spencer hadn't even known about it until he heard from a co-worker a few months after the split.

His impression of Anne had always been that she was quiet, dedicated, and basically a good person. He had never heard her make any negative comments about her colleagues, and had never even had any indication that she had a social life outside of the company, so he felt that she would be relatively safe to practice his new skills upon.

He was wrong.

He hung around the secretary station, chatting with Anne, waiting until her phone rang. When it did, and her attention was on the notes she was taking, he looked at her closely, trying to peer behind whatever mask she might be wearing. It took no effort whatsoever.

Anne's clean, pleasant face had been replaced by a thickly painted mask of lust. It was the face of an ancient whore, the flesh pocked by disease, the lesions artlessly covered by blobs of makeup that only accentuated them further. Behind that makeup, amid the convolutions of the woman's brain, Spencer saw the hundreds of liaisons, the unprotected sex, the weekends spent with multiple partners, the humiliations to which she had submitted. The debasements revealed sickened him. He thought he could even see the viruses teeming within her, pressing outward against her decaying flesh, as though something deadly bubbled within her.

With a ragged breath, he tore his gaze away and looked out the broad window at the blue sky, with just a few wisps of cloud high on the horizon. 'Mr Brady?' he heard Anne say. 'Are you okay?'

Spencer turned his head back toward her, but kept his eyes on the window. 'Fine. Thanks,' he said, and hurried to the safety of his office, thinking, with an understatement that nearly made him laugh in spite of his horror, *Still waters run deep.*

When he shut the door, he giggled, thinking of Anne's face. A whore. She was a goddamned whore, wasn't she? God only knew how many men she'd fucked in how many different ways in how many cheap hotels, and God only knew how many diseases she was carrying and spreading. Christ, and she acts like the biggest lady you'd ever want to know.

Spencer shook his head, and the smile left his lips. Was everybody like this? he wondered. Was everybody a liar under their masks?

He knew at least one more person who was—that sonovabitch Todd. And if there was one person whose true face he really wanted to see, it was that of his boss. Spencer punched the four digits of Todd's extension and smiled as he waited for the shit to answer. When he did, Spencer asked if he could see him for a few minutes about a current project, and Todd said sure, in that lying, hearty voice of his. Spencer took a deep breath and walked toward Todd's corner office, being careful to keep his eyes on the floor as he passed Anne's desk.

When he walked into Todd's office, he closed the door behind him, and then, without any hesitation, looked full into Todd's quizzical face. The features expanded from razor slim to a ravenous corpulence, the usually sharp jaw-line sagging, the thin lips plumping and lolling, revealing a fat and hungry tongue, the eyes shrinking, small and beady, into the pouches of plump flesh that grew up around them, until the whole face was given over completely to gluttony and avarice, and the man before him became the living embodiment of two of the deadly sins.

But it wasn't the change in Todd's features that affected Spencer as much as it was the ugly knowledge that simultaneously came upon him, the knowledge that in three more weeks, Spencer Brady was going to be let go, fired just two months before he could have received a partial pension, fired, not because he wasn't doing his job well, but because firing him would save Todd's department more money than firing anyone else who worked in it.

Fired because of the bottom line.

Spencer nearly choked with rage at the thought, and he picked up a small golf trophy with a heavy marble base from Todd's desk and raised it over his head, and was delighted to see that fat, jowly face quiver with fear. But then reason took him, and he realized that if he did what his anger demanded of him, there would be no chance to dig out of this hole, to make something better for himself. There would be no freedom, no life, no Gina. No, he would not do this thing that he so much wanted to do, because of Gina.

His hand trembling, he set down the trophy and looked into the true and porcine face of his manager. 'You son of a bitch,' he whispered. 'You're not firing me, you fucker. I quit.'

The cliché felt good on his tongue, and he walked out of the office, leaving the door open instead of slamming it. That way the bastard would have to get up and close it himself.

In his office, Spencer gathered the accumulation of twenty years of work and put it into a cardboard box. He pulled the files of his current projects, took them down on the freight elevator, carried them outside, and threw them in a dumpster. Then he went back upstairs, and the last thing he did before he left was order his computer to completely reformat the hard drive.

In his car, he wondered what to do next. He wanted desperately to talk to Gina, but she worked at the bank until 4:00, so he decided to go to Frank's sporting goods store at the strip mall. Frank would understand. He called Gina first, and asked her to meet him at his place after work, and then called Frank with the news.

'You *quit*?' Frank asked on the phone. 'Oh man, oh Christ, Spence, that's rough. Sure I'll meet you. How about O'Halloran's? We'll have a drink and talk this out, huh?'

Frank was in the usual booth near the back of the tavern, but when Spencer saw him, he didn't recognize him at first. Frank looked different, meaner somehow, his eyebrows arching, his teeth bared, and before either of them could say a word to each other, Spencer let the gates of his mind open fully, let the true face of his longtime friend come forth into his view.

It was the face of a lecher, a satyr, a man who lived to fuck. It was the face of a man who had slept with Susan for a full year before she had even met the lover she had run away with. His wife and his best friend. It would have been as funny as the dirty joke it was if it hadn't broken his heart.

He saw that truth and more. He saw, with a clarity that twisted his stomach, how much Frank wanted Gina, just the way he wanted any woman he found moderately attractive. Loyalty, fidelity, friendship were nothing compared to the demands that ran red and thick within him.

'What's up, Spence? What's the matter?' said the voice that came from the twisted, grinning mouth, the mouth that had kissed his wife in places he never had. A hand came out to offer succor and sustenance, but Spencer saw that it was covered with a white, viscous fluid in which pink threads drifted, and he drew back from the former friend who, he knew now, had never been his friend.

Then Spencer Brady turned and ran out of O'Halloran's, ran to his car, sped to his apartment, tears in sighted eye and blind eye alike, tears in his soul, thinking *Gina*, *Gina* . . .

He ran up the stairs to his apartment, wishing he could will time to pass as easily as he willed the truth to be visible. He waited, sobbing, his mind spinning, passing the hours by thinking of how much he had to see her, had to look at her face and know that there was one person in this world who was real, was true, and wore no mask.

But he saw it the moment she came through the door. There was a look of exhaustion, resignation, and disgust on the face behind her mask, and that face was sickly and sallow, with dark hollows under the accusing eyes, and creased with wrinkles dug by bitterness and resentment.

Gina didn't love him. She hated him. He disgusted her. She went out with him and stayed in with him and kissed him and spread her legs for him and made sounds for him and did all she did for him because she thought he could give her security. She had little money, and he had more, and she wasn't getting any younger and didn't have that many choices, and if she married him at least that part of her life would be secure, in spite of the fact that she didn't like the things he said or the way he touched her or the music he listened to or the movies he watched or the smell of his breath or the taste of his tongue or the feel of his cock or his hands or his flesh against hers or anything, anything about him or of him or on him or in him . . .

And before she could say a word, he knew all of that and much more, more than she had ever admitted to herself, all the things that she kept buried deep inside, *all* her secrets. And before she could raise a hand, he raked his fingers across her cheek, trying to obliterate that face that lay behind her mask. But it didn't work, and the sneering mouth of that face screamed out something that he couldn't understand, so he struck it again, this time with his fist, and it fell to the floor.

He followed it down, grabbing the nearest hard object he could find, a bronze American eagle bookend from the foyer shelf. He smashed it into the horrible face beneath him again and again, until the screams stopped and the face vanished and another mask covered it, a new mask, this one red and white, wet and dripping. There were other sounds for a while, bubbling sounds, but they quickly stopped, as did the movement of the liar's hands and feet and chest.

Spencer Brady got to his feet, looked down at what he had done, and felt strangely ambivalent about it. He knew that he had murdered the woman he had loved, but he knew too that she had not loved him, but hated him, and not even actively, but with a dull tolerance. That was what had inflamed him, that was what he could not accept.

His mind felt like his chest, as though a cold, gaping hole had been dug in both places. There was nothing left now, nothing, except the one place he knew he had to go, and he stepped out of his apartment, closed the door behind him, and went to his car.

On his way, he passed a Catholic church and stopped and went inside, wondering wildly and not altogether sanely if he might be able to see God's true face behind his mask. It was one last chance before he reached his final destination, one last attempt at . . . what? Redemption? He didn't know.

The church was empty, and he walked down the center aisle to the altar. But before he could even concentrate on it, a voice from behind him asked, 'May I help you?' It was a middle-aged priest who walked comfortably down the aisle toward him, but when he was a few feet away, he saw the blood on Spencer's suit and shirt and stopped. 'Is something wrong, my son?'

Spencer looked only indifferently at the priest, but the man's mask melted away instantly, leaving Spencer gazing at what came as close to a totally blank face as any he had ever seen. The countenance was that of a child, not sweet and innocent, but inbred and ignorant, the result of generations of genes grown ever more enfeebled by a steadily unenlightening diet of piety and platitudes.

Then Spencer turned back to the altar and looked at the carved wooden face of the man suspended from the cross. Spencer couldn't be sure, but he thought that for a moment he saw the face darken, until he was looking into nothing but blackness, eternal dark, an abyss.

Nothing at all.

Nothing at all. Then the wooden face again. But it might have been his imagination, a trick of the light. It might, came a thought that added even more chill to his cold soul, have *all* been imagination, a play of the light upon the masks, delusion upon illusion. But after a moment's consideration, he knew that could not be so.

'My son?' asked the bland, blanched priest from his face of unquestioning thoughtlessness.

He didn't deserve an answer, nor the appellation of *Father*. He deserved only the truth. 'I'm not your son,' Spencer said flatly. 'And that,' he said, looking at the crucifix, 'is not your father or your God. That's a piece of wood, and death is death, and you are a fool.'

He walked quickly past the priest, careful not to touch him, up the aisle, and out of the church of lies, not looking back at the building, thinking that if he did he would see its windows and façades fall away until all that remained was the mouth of a dark cave.

Spencer Brady drove outside of the town to the darkening fields and meadows where the carnival had been held, but when he arrived, there was nothing there but trodden grass and ruts in the earth to give evidence of the passing show. Still, this was where the old man had told him to come. He had said Spencer could return anytime, so here he was and here he would wait. He wanted neither this truth nor this life any more.

As the darkness came on, Spencer, sitting in his car parked in the middle of the field, occasionally thought that he glimpsed shapes against the sky, but could make out nothing solid. Soon the planets and stars began to appear, and the moon hung low over the woods in the east. Spencer watched the moon for a few minutes, and when he turned back to look at where the carnival had been, there was one structure standing alone in the middle of the field. It was a small tent, lit from within, and he could see a sign staked in front of it. Though it was too dark to read, he was certain that it said *Luxor The Amazing.*

And below: *Knows All—Sees All—Master Of The Truth*

Master Of The Truth. That was what Spencer had become, all right, and what he wanted to be no longer.

He got out of the car and walked over to the tent. The old man's voice invited him within by name even before Spencer had made a sound outside. He entered and found the interior just as it had been before, and sat in the folding chair across from the man.

'I don't want the truth,' Spencer said.

'I know that,' the old man told him.

'You said that . . . if I got tired of it, that I could come back here. Well, here I am.'

'And so you are. But the truth is already yours. You can't be free of it now. You've already learned too much, and that knowledge will never leave you.' He leaned across the table on his elbows, bringing his face closer to Spencer's. 'You can never believe again. You can never trust again. You can never love again. And now you know the reasons for the masks people wear—they're worn because people could never bear to know the whole truth about each other.'

A sudden fury swept over Spencer, but not the rage that had made him smash Gina's face. It was a different kind of anger, cold and defiant, and he looked full into the old man's bright, clear eyes. 'And what about the mask *you* wear?' he said. 'What's behind that?'

'Look,' the old man answered simply, and Spencer did.

He looked and saw, not another face, but the truth. He saw the truth about what his life would have been: he and Gina, happy together, their relationship growing over the years; his friendship with Frank deepening as they grew older; a new position in a new company in a new city, a manager at last. He saw all the things that would have been, had he been content with lies and embraced them, had he believed, as most do, that lies could someday become truths.

The vision faded, and Spencer thought now that he finally knew the whole truth. He smiled brokenly, and felt tears in his eyes, one dead, one living. 'Ignorance,' he said in a tone of self-mockery, 'is bliss.' The old man said nothing. What can you say, Spencer wondered, to a cliché so obviously true.

'I can't go back,' Spencer said, his throat choked.

'No. So you must stay here.' The old man stood up with a grace that belied his years, his movement as young as his eyes. 'Come.'

The old man led Spencer outside, where he saw that one other structure beside the tent had appeared in the field. Standing alone and unmoving, it was the Ferris wheel that had been there the previous weekend. But when they walked closer, he saw that it was a different wheel, far older and far stranger than the first, and that nearly all the seats were occupied. Standing there in the darkness, he could see some of the faces of the occupants, and the sight made him look quickly away.

'You look away from them,' said the old man, 'but most of them could not bear to rest their gaze on *you*, on the face of one who has looked on truth, for a face such as that is too terrible to see, even for such as these.' The old man reached into the darkness and held something out to Spencer. 'Wear this,' he said, and Spencer took from him a long dark robe with a hood. If it had a color, Spencer could not discern it in the dim light. He put it on and closed the front, hiding the stains of Gina's blood, and the old man raised the hood so that it covered Spencer's head.

'Now,' said the old man, 'this.' And he handed Spencer a pale mask on a stick. It was nearly featureless, with depressions where the eyes should be and the suggestion of something small and round for a mouth. It was an ignorant face, Spencer thought, like the face behind the priest's mask, an ignorant moon face with which others could be comfortable.

He didn't need to be told what to do with it. He held it up in front of his own face, and knew that he would never take it down again.

Then the old man led him to the wheel, and bade him sit in the only accessible and empty seat. He did, expecting the wheel to creak and groan with the additional weight, but there was no sound. Next to him on the wide seat, the old man set one final object, and Spencer turned and looked at it, seeing right through the mask he wore with no effort at all.

The thing on the seat next to him was small and red and hideous. Its surface seemed moist, and Spencer thought it moved slowly, but couldn't be sure. 'What is it?' he asked the old man in a hollow, lost voice that surprised him when he heard it.

'This is your truth made flesh,' said the old man. 'The truth of what you are. And you will bear the knowledge of it all the nights that you turn upon this wheel.'

Then the wheel gave a slight lurch, and started slowly to move. Spencer felt his seat moving backwards, away from the old man, whose face vanished in the darkness as Spencer was swept up and away. He thought he could hear distant music, but wasn't sure.

Was this then where he would spend the rest of his life, or even longer? He looked again at the thing on the seat beside him, and saw that it had indeed moved, had crept closer to him. As he watched, it slithered toward his thigh until he could feel it, both hot and cold at once, against him, and then it stopped, seemingly content.

At the top of the wheel, Spencer looked up at the black sky, and then down at the other riders, and at the things that clung to the wheel. The darkness made him think of what he had seen in the church, the abyss behind the hanging man's wooden face, and he wondered, if there was nothing afterwards, then how had he come here, and who were these creature companions? If the magic of religion was a lie, then what other magic turned this wheel?

He looked behind him then, and the question was blotted out by a new one:

If the dead were dead and God a lie, then why was Gina, her unmarred, liar's face filled with love, sitting in the car right behind him, rising over him as he slowly began his descent, falling and falling until he reached the bottom and started up once more?

Figures in Rain

THERE WERE ONLY TWO other people waiting in the reception area of The King's Arms Tavern when we arrived. It was 9:30, the last seating time, and when Caitlin and I entered the dimly lit room we spent several seconds folding the umbrella and shaking the droplets from our coats. It was raining furiously, drenching the stones of Williamsburg, plunging the already dark streets into even greater darkness.

The weather did little to improve either our mood or the looks of the town. Colonial Williamsburg was far less picturesque in late February than in the seasons in which we had previously visited it. Caitlin and I had both come here as children, dutifully brought by our parents, and we had done the same with Robert, making the Williamsburg/Jamestown/Monticello circuit the summer when he was between sixth and seventh grades. Too old to wear a tricorn and carry a wooden gun, and too young to appreciate the painstaking care with which the colonial community had been recreated, he found little enjoyment in the two days we spent there. Caitlin and I, however, had been taken with the totality of the experience—the crafts, the buildings, the food, and the people who recreated so vividly what it must have been like to live in English America.

We had found ourselves guiltily wishing that we had been there alone, and had returned to the place one long Easter weekend when Robert was in college. We found that Williamsburg in spring was even more exquisite than in summer. The gardens were a brilliantly hued profusion of lilies, daffodils, and tulips, and the trees were either blossoming or newly greening. It was a glorious time to be there, and there was the further benefit that Caitlin and I were rediscovering, after eighteen years of parenthood, what it was like to be lovers once more. With no duties to Robert beyond the financial and distantly (in space, at least) supportive, we had more time for each other. The empty nest proved, at first, to be as great a blessing for us as independence proved to be for Robert.

Then other concerns replaced those we had had for our son. A series of financial setbacks in my business required my spending more time at my office, and a restructuring of the staff which Caitlin oversaw meant that she brought home far more work than before. We were both at least a decade away from retirement, and every day were being made more aware of the necessity of storing up nuts against the long winter. A series of annoying if non-life threatening health problems did little to ease our commercial burdens, and the deaths of my mother and father further increased my depression. Dad went only a few months after my mother died of cancer. They loved each other deeply, and each had depended on the other. I think he willed himself into death when she died, and when it came he welcomed it.

I honestly believe that we went to Williamsburg in late February in desperation. We had grown apart, but not from choice. Both Caitlin and I knew that at this time in our lives more than any other we needed the other's strength and love to help buttress ourselves against the unpredictability of the world and of our own flesh.

Let's get away, we said to each other. We would leave everything behind, go somewhere we loved, and just be together. Our batteries were dead, and maybe several days alone together would give us a jump start. Maybe the world could become remarkable again.

Even before we arrived, it felt wrong. We had overslept and had to pack in haste, not even taking the time to remove from the trunk several boxes of my parents' personal things that I had finally been clearing out of their house. The sky was overcast, and it started raining by mid-afternoon when we crossed the Virginia border.

We arrived at the Williamsburg Visitors' Center just before it closed, and bought multi-day passes, then made reservations at Christiana Campbell's Tavern the following evening and King's Arms Tavern the next. We had seafood that evening at a restaurant in Merchants' Square, a collection of shops outside the colonial area, and then walked down Duke of Gloucester Street in a light, cold rain that grew heavier as we went. We gave it up, turned around, and went back to the car and drove to our motel. Although we were both tired from the drive, we felt duty-bound to make love. It was done without much passion, as are most deeds inspired by duty.

There followed two more days of intermittent cold rain, during which we spent most of our time indoors. Exteriors offered little: the gardens were brown and yellow, and the trees glistened only with the rainwater on their bark. The streets were dotted with puddles, and the vast, grassy areas were sodden.

The rain and the gray season brought out few tourists, and those who braved the elements seemed more sternly determined to see what they had to see than enchanted with the near-perfect recreation of the past. The costumed re-enactors at each occupied site maintained their good spirits, and energetically tried to brighten the fatally dull day by their interaction with the sparse crowds, but succeeded only fitfully.

Caitlin and I found none of the magic we had sought and so needed. The days were flat and gray. We took little joy in them or in each other's company. The sole pleasure of the first day was the meal at Campbell's Tavern. Though there were a few empty tables, there was still a sense of warmth and conviviality in the candlelit rooms. We were seated away from any windows, so the weather was of no concern, and the food was hearty and abundant.

Still, as soon as we stepped outside into the rain, the gray mood returned. Back at the motel, Caitlin soaked in the tub with a novel, while I, in spite of my promise to myself to do no work, cheated slightly. I brought up a small box of my parents' photo albums and scrapbooks from the trunk of the car, planning to see if there was anything my surviving aunts and uncles might want as a keepsake.

Caitlin gave me a *you promised* look when she came out of the bathroom and saw what I was doing. I closed the books and took a shower. She was sleeping when I climbed into bed.

The second and last full day held more of the same. We spent several hours in the well-lit Rockefeller Folk Art Center, but the proliferation of flat, two-dimensional primitive work did little to assuage our hunger for the deep and rich and unexpected. The shock that our systems required was not to be found there.

It was highly unlikely that we would experience it that night either. The King's Arms Tavern was slightly more formal—and more expensive—than Christiana Campbell's. We checked our wet coats, gave our name to the hostess in colonial dress, and sat down to wait on a bench against the wall. Fiddle and fife music sounded from somewhere within.

I smiled at the young man sitting next to me, and he smiled back. Unlike most tourists, he was wearing a suit, dress shirt, and necktie, and his black wingtips were polished to a high gloss. His hair was meticulously combed in the retro style that so many his age are adopting. He was one of those people who look instantly familiar, like someone you might have seen on television in a supporting role for years, but to whom you had never attached a name.

'Lousy night,' he said without a trace of true complaint. He might rather have been observing that the evening was beautifully clear and balmy.

I agreed, and Caitlin smiled empathetically. 'Warm and dry in here, though,' I added.

'Yeah. You ever eat here?'

'Oh yes,' I said. 'It's very good.'

'Try the peanut soup,' Caitlin advised.

Both the man and his wife gave little laughs of discomfort. The wife was wearing a flowered print dress and low white shoes unseasonable both in terms of weather and style. She was slim everywhere but her abdomen, a rounded mass that told eloquently of her pregnancy.

'How long now?' asked Caitlin with a warm concern that expressed her motherly (or grandmotherly) instincts. They were, I reminded myself sourly, young enough to be our children.

'Two more months,' the girl said, her voice as vaguely familiar as her husband's face. I was trying to figure out where I might have seen them before, and was about to ask where they were from, when the hostess came into the room and said that our table was ready.

'Enjoy your meal,' I told them as we followed the woman, who led us to the second floor and seated us at one of the two windows in the room that faced the street. Rain still pattered against the glass, and Caitlin and I could just make out the occasional passersby hurrying through the downpour, dimly seen in the tavern's pale, evocative front porch lights, and the residual beams of candlelight that fell onto the street from the windows where we diners sat.

We had ordered our meals, and when I looked up from the Sally Lunn bread I was buttering, I saw that the young couple from downstairs had been seated at the other window table, so that the man and I were facing each other. I smiled and nodded, and he raised his hand in a shy wave.

Throughout the meal, I found myself looking out the windows, focussing not on the kaleidoscopic surface of the glass, where raindrops struck, exploded, and made uneven rivulets as they ran toward the bottom sill, but past and through and around them, out onto the dark street, made darker by the extinguishing of the front lights. No one moved on the street below. The tourists who on previous visits had wandered the ancient streets until quite late, soaking in the ambience that darkness sealed upon the town, had been discouraged by the rain and cold. No one would walk the lanes of Williamsburg tonight out of pleasure.

Still I looked, as did Caitlin. Our attention meandered from the plates before us to the darkness on the other side of the panes, and was claimed at times by the coming and going of our server and the fiddler who drifted through the rooms, playing, I assumed, colonial airs.

Though I hadn't noticed the young couple being served, my attention fixed as it was on the windows, my plate, and the silence that lay between Caitlin and me, their courses kept pace with ours, despite our earlier seating. I occasionally glanced over, and a smile passed between the young man and me signaling a shared appreciation of the food. When I continued to watch, I observed his solicitousness toward his wife, whose back was to me. He spoke quietly to her, frequently took her hand, and on occasion fed her from his own fork when he thought himself unobserved.

As Caitlin and I sat together over our coffee, her expression was sadder than I had ever seen it. Her hand was resting on the tablecloth inches from mine, and I moved until our fingers were just touching. She smiled, just a small flower in the grim winter landscape of her face, and took my fingers in her own, then shook her head and said quietly, 'What's wrong with us?'

What indeed? I still loved Caitlin, and had no doubt that she loved me. I had no answer, and only turned and looked out the window once more.

At first I thought that what I saw was a trick of the light, a car's beams whispering across the dark street, or a soft reflection in the glass from inside the room. I then realized that I was seeing a person walking across Duke of Gloucester Street, a person who was gleaming in the rain and the night as though lit from within. I pressed my face against the glass, cupping my eyes with my hands like blinders to close out the light from within the room.

The tension of my movement alarmed Caitlin, and she leaned toward me, but when I whispered '*Look*,' she too turned her gaze to the pane. From her hissed intake of breath I was sure that she too saw it.

The Raleigh Tavern, open only during the day as an historical site, was across the street, and the figure was moving past it, toward a wooden gate to the right of the building. It was a man, as far as I could tell, wearing a three-cornered hat, a shirt, a vest, and knee breeches. I could make out no colors other than various shades of gray. The figure moved slowly, but with a sense of purpose. It was as though he were walking briskly, but in slow-motion, as though time had slowed for him. We could not see his face, but he carried himself as though he felt no rain. His head was high, his arms swung loosely at his sides.

The monochromatic glow from him illuminated the descending curtain of rain, the wet surface of the street, and, as he drew near to it, the gate, which he did not pause to open, but instead passed through. In another few heartbeats he was out of sight.

Caitlin and I slowly drew back from the window, and over her shoulder, behind her pale, shocked face, I saw the young man with the same expression of surprise and disbelief that Caitlin (and certainly I) wore. He was staring at his wife, and they both turned and looked out the window for another moment. Then the young man saw me, and his wife turned, as did Caitlin, both with trepidation, the two women wondering what their husbands were looking at now.

Understanding shot through us. He knew that we had seen it, and I knew the same was true of them. When I looked back at Caitlin, her pale, startled look had been replaced with a pink sheen of excitement. Her posture was erect, and her hands hovered over the table as though she would spring up at any second. Her head jerked toward the window. 'Let's go,' she said.

I yanked out my money clip, glanced at the bill, and tossed down enough twenties on the tray to cover it and a generous tip. Then, with a conspiratorial grin at the young man, I raced down the stairs, Caitlin behind me. We retrieved our coats, threw them on, and went outside, opening the umbrella as we scurried down the porch steps. Caitlin's arm was wrapped around mine, and I saw the puffs of her excited breath in the cold, damp air.

We paused at the edge of the street, thinking about our next step. The silence between us now was electric and communicative, not sad and awkward as it had been upstairs. We had both seen something unexpected and wanted to see more. Across the street was The Raleigh Tavern, and between it and the building on its right was the small wooden gate through which the ghost, for as such I had naturally come to think of it, had passed.

I looked at Caitlin and gave a small nod, and she nodded back. We had just stepped into the street when a voice behind us called 'Hey . . .', just loud enough for us to hear over the attack of rain on our umbrella. We both turned and saw the young man and his wife a few steps behind us, huddled under their own umbrella.

Caitlin and I knew what they wanted, to come with us in search of whatever we had seen. I felt disappointed, yet also relieved that we would not be alone, and voiced my sole concern. 'Will you be all right?' I asked, looking at the young woman, whose pregnancy was all too obvious beneath her raincoat.

'Oh yes,' she said, clutching her husband's arm as tightly as Caitlin did mine.

I gave a shrug of acquiescence, turned, and headed for the gate. It was locked but low, and we were able to climb over, giving extra help to the future mother, who got stuck halfway across. 'Oh Tommy . . .' she said, more in frustration than pain, as her husband and I bodily lifted her over the obstacle.

I recalled that this gate led back to a bake shop that we had visited earlier that day, and also assumed that we were now trespassing on private property, off limits after hours. *We were after a ghost*, I was certain, would not prove an effective motive were we to be apprehended.

The bake shop was on our left as we walked along the path. It was dark, as were the other buildings around us. Ahead of us lay an open space, with a broader area to our right, between Duke of Gloucester and Nicholson Streets. We stood, uncertain of how to proceed. It was so dark that I could see the young man and woman beside us as only blacker figures against the black night.

Then, to my right, I saw a glimmer of light moving slowly in the direction of the old public gaol across Nicholson Street. 'Come on,' I whispered, and went toward it. With a thrill I saw that it was the male figure we had seen earlier, and I glanced back at the young couple to share my delight. They were scarcely a yard behind us, and I saw a tense alertness in the way they moved.

I had no sooner turned back to look at the figure, which by now had reached Nicholson Street, than it seemed to flicker and fade, and then wink out entirely. I gave a moan of disappointment and stopped, then turned to Caitlin, who was gripping my arm so hard that I winced. Her attention, however, was not focused on the disappearance ahead, but on the one behind us.

I followed her gaze and saw too that the couple who had been only a matter of feet away from us were now gone. Though we stood in an open area twenty yards from the nearest buildings, all of which were locked and dark, the pair was nowhere in sight.

I stood there slack-jawed. It was obvious that they simply could not have run away without our being aware of it, yet they had vanished as quickly and completely as the glowing figure we had seen and followed.

Before this, I would have said that the most dreadful, disconcerting, and alarming feeling in life would be to suddenly be thrust face to face with the inexplicable, a phenomenon that had no logical first cause. Now I know that is not true.

On the contrary, as Caitlin and I stood there in that sopping, muddy lot, the cold rain still pounding down on us as though it would never stop, I don't believe we had ever felt more thrilled and vital and alive. We held onto each other like children on a roller coaster, and perhaps for the same reason, that if we were to let go, we would be yanked away, over the edge of the little conveyance in which we passed through life, and down—or *out*—into some great abyss.

I put my face close enough to hers so that, even in the dark, I could imagine that I saw her expression. She gave a laugh that held a shudder, the kind of laugh you give when, to use another amusement park allusion, you've come out of the house of horrors frightened but unscathed. I laughed too, not because the situation was funny, but because *she* had laughed, and because we were alive.

I felt her lips on mine, and though they were cold, she kept them there long enough for them to grow warm. We held each other, the umbrella listing to the side and finally falling, so that the raindrops drenched our hair and faces, and gently bonded our cheeks together.

Then we began to shiver, and that made us laugh more. We didn't understand what had happened, but it didn't matter just then. 'We'd better get out of here,' I said, 'before we get arrested.'

We found a path that led back to Duke of Gloucester Street, and followed it, our umbrella back up, arms around each other's waists. I was still frightened, yet revived, and I knew Caitlin felt the same, for she told me later. I didn't want to see another ghost—or ghosts, as I now suspected. Three were enough.

Still, the coda was necessary, the confirmation required, as it is in all these types of stories. We returned to The King's Arms. Its interior lights were still on, and the front door was unlocked. I created the pretext that the couple who sat next to us were acquaintances, and that the woman thought she had left her glasses case at the table and we had said we would check for her, as we had to pass the tavern anyway.

We were not disappointed by the response. The hostess fetched our waiter, who looked slightly puzzled, but led us upstairs. The tables at which we and the other couple had been sitting had been cleaned and cleared, and the waiter crouched down and looked at the darkness of the floor under our table.

'No no,' I said, 'not us—the couple at *this* table,' and I crouched, pretending to look under it.

The waiter seemed hesitant to speak. 'Sir,' he said at last, 'what couple would that have been?'

'The young couple,' I said, and I could feel my heart beating in my chest, 'who were sitting right here. The woman was pregnant. They ate at the same time we did.'

He raised his eyebrows and shook his head. 'Sir, I'm sorry, but there's been no one at this table since around eight o'clock.'

'Really?' I said, and looked at Caitlin. Her eyes were wide, and she was smiling so that I could see her teeth. 'Well,' I said, and again, 'Well.'

We sat in our car for a long time, holding each other's hand on the arm rest. The rain still fell heavily on the roof of the car. I felt Caitlin's hand leave mine, and then felt her fingers passing through my wet hair. I kissed her, long and deeply, and we drove back to our room, frequently glancing out the window, but seeing nothing out of place. Still, it had once more become a remarkable world.

In our room, Caitlin luxuriated in her bath, using the full contents of the complimentary bottle of bubble bath. I took off my wet things, slipped on a bathrobe, and waited to succeed her. Sitting at the round table that seems to be a fixture in every motel room, I idly continued to flip through the photo albums that I had brought in from the trunk the previous day. The album I chose was an older one, filled with black and white photos I did not remember ever having seen. When I turned over the second page, I stopped.

Few of my generation really know what our parents looked like when they were young. Our visual knowledge is usually limited to a sepia wedding picture and an early portrait or two that hung on the walls of our childhood homes for so long that they became iconic and unique, always presented, never noticed. So I suppose it's not unheard of that I hadn't recognized them, those old images made young flesh, moving, speaking, smiling.

Oh Tommy, she had said. She had always called him just Tom for as long as I could remember, or Thomas when she pretended to be peeved.

There they were, held to the page by photo mounts in each corner, looking shyly at the camera, standing holding hands in front of the Governor's Palace, wearing what Caitlin and I had seen them wear tonight at The King's Arms Tavern. My mother's belly was full with what would prove to be her only child.

Wmburg 1947 read the hand-inked caption beneath the small photo, and I looked at it for a long time, until I felt Caitlin's hand on my shoulder, her fingers pressing tighter as she saw too.

I can't explain it, but to note that good parents never stop loving their children or wanting to help them, far beyond the point at which they're capable of doing so. Or maybe what we experienced says that there is no such point.

I won't pretend that the feelings over what we saw that night will be permanent in Caitlin and me, but they certainly provide an emotional base on which to rebuild. What we expect will always come, so every day we look for a trace of the *un*expected, and if we don't find it, we create it, for ourselves and for each other.

Sundowners

IF YOU KNOW ANYTHING ABOUT the history of fantasy and science fiction, you know the name of Lewis Becholdt. His first story appeared in a 1929 issue of *Amazing Stories*, when he was eighteen, and he had several dozen tales published during the heyday of the pulps. He is best remembered, however, for his creation of SFPC (Science Fiction Publishing Company) in 1944.

Financing himself on a shoestring, Lewis became one of the first people to publish exclusively in the genre of science fiction and fantasy, setting the gold standard for the specialty presses that followed him. He was the first to publish, in hardcover, most of the science fiction giants of the first half of the twentieth century; he was the first to offer signed, limited editions; and he was one of the few old-timers who were able to retire in sound financial condition.

Lewis's career in fantasy had always been a deeply loved sideline. He came from a conservative farming family, and realized young that the penny-a-word rates paid by the pulps were no way to build a nest egg. He took a job as a salesman for a major textbook publishing house with which he worked until his retirement as sales manager, but also made his avocation for science fiction a supplemental vocation as well. His writing earned him some extra money, and the publishing brought a small return on his investment.

By the mid-1950s, however, the major houses were listing science fiction titles. Lewis folded SFPC, to the secret delight of his wife Emma, and, as she had hoped, spent more time with her and their two children. He retired in 1974, and returned to writing, producing a Celtic fantasy trilogy, the first volume of which appeared in 1978.

That year brought tragedy along with triumph, when Emma died of an unsuspected heart condition. Lewis's children were grown with families of their own, and he tried to bury his grief in his writing. He wrote more novels and short stories, as well as a history of early science fiction fandom and the small publishing houses that proliferated in the wake of SFPC's success.

Still, in the midst of this activity, he continued to mourn Emma's absence. The hurt lessened, but would never fully leave. His religious faith, a strong force throughout his life, supported him, as did his certain knowledge that he would one day be with his wife again, and they would live together in joy throughout eternity.

Until that time came, he would continue to write and to attend science fiction conventions, traveling to see old friends and playing host when they visited him, graciously giving interviews and accepting life achievement awards, and answering the letters of new and old friends of the genre.

It was not until he turned ninety that he decided he should no longer live alone. He still did his own shopping, cooking, and cleaning of his large apartment, and drove his immaculate 1975 Plymouth to church, the store, and the several restaurants he frequented, and he relished that independence. Still, he was growing more forgetful, and his mobility had decreased.

Though his son Franklin had invited him to come live with them, Franklin and his wife both worked during the day, so Lewis looked into the possibility of the Brethren Retirement Village just a few miles from where he lived. As a lay pastor, he was well known within the surrounding congregations and at the home, where, as he learned, there was an opening. Lewis tried not to think of the opening for himself as a closing for his predecessor.

The 'village' was quite nice, Lewis thought as he and Franklin were given the tour by Mrs Meyer, the ebullient residence manager. It was divided into three sections. First was the cottage wing, a row of one-storey townhouses, larger living units intended for couples. This was connected to the large central hub that contained the chapel, cafeteria, social rooms, offices, and the constant care rooms on the second and third floors. These were large rooms that each housed two residents, with a toilet and shower. At least one nurse was always on duty on each floor.

The area in which Lewis would live was the resident wing on the other side of the hub. On each of its two floors, the wing held eighteen mini-apartments, with a living-room adjoining a kitchenette, a bedroom, and a bath. The available, first-floor apartment had only one window in the living-room, but that suited Lewis since he would have more wall space for bookcases.

He had already sold the vast majority of his volumes, but still retained several boxes of his favorites. The day he moved in, he was just wedging the last of them into his final bookcase when the doorbell rang, more loudly than Lewis though necessary, for his hearing was good. Lewis adjusted his necktie and gave the green stone of his tie-tac a quick polish with his shirt cuff before he answered.

Standing in the carpeted hallway was a thin, elderly man a head taller than Lewis. The man stuck out a long-fingered hand and said, 'Hi, neighbor!' The voice didn't fit the man's gaunt frame. It was hearty and jovial, slightly phlegmy, and the hand, when Lewis took it, was warm and dry, exerting just the right amount of pressure.

'Don't tell me,' Lewis said smiling. 'You're a *salesman*.'

'Whoops,' the man said. 'You got me dead to rights—in sales for forty-four years.'

'Forty-three for me. I can always tell. Like knows like!' They both laughed, and Lewis invited the man in.

His name was Joe Fenneman. 'Like Groucho's sidekick,' he said. 'If I don't say it, whoever I'm meeting will—if they're over fifty.'

Lewis learned that Joe Fenneman was eighty-four, had no children, and had been a widower for three years. 'I'm sorry,' Lewis said. 'My Emma's been gone over twenty now, and I still miss her. She was a very dear person.' He looked out the window at several sparrows sitting on a dead branch of an otherwise thriving oak tree. Putting a smile back on his face, Lewis turned to Joe. 'Would you like a Coca-Cola or some iced tea?'

'Wouldn't have any beer, would you?'

'Sorry, haven't had a drink in, oh my, let's see'—he pretended to recollect—'over ninety years now.'

'I like that, Lou. You're a kidder!'

'Please, make it Lewis. Not even my mother called me Lou—though she called me plenty of other things.'

The banter continued through several servings of iced tea. Just before Joe left, Lewis gratefully accepted his invitation to join him and his friends at dinner in the cafeteria. 'Usual assortment of codgers,' Joe said. 'Pretty nice fellas, and nobody drools, what more could you want?'

They *were* pretty nice, Lewis thought, when Joe let them get a word in. He was definitely the alpha male in the pack of six, seated around one of the round tables in the large room. Lewis enjoyed the dinner. The meat loaf and macaroni and cheese were nearly as good as homemade, and reminded him of the fare at the Pennsylvania Dutch restaurant where he ate every week.

The only negative was the unfriendliness of some of the other residents. There were several, men and women alike, who waved at Lewis's messmates, or who stopped by and said hello and introduced themselves to Lewis. But there were others who sat and threw hostile looks at Lewis's table, after which they would say something to those around them, though Lewis was unable to hear the conversations.

What surprised Lewis most was Dorothy Horst's reaction. Before Dorothy entered the village, she had attended Lewis's church, and had always been sociable and friendly toward him. But when he caught her eye as she entered, raised his hand, and said, 'Good evening, Dorothy,' she looked surprised, and then glared at him and looked away.

'Sure some old cranks in here,' said Joe, who had noticed the slight.

'Well, I don't know what *that* was about,' Lewis said, feeling chagrined. 'We always got along fine.'

Ed Saunders shook his head. 'This place changes some people. Seen folks come in here who were fine, and a month later they think the closet's the toilet. They're a lot worse up in constant care, and that's where that old lady's from.'

It was true. The constant care patients who were able to come to the cafeteria rather than eat in their rooms were a sorry lot. Nearly all of them were either in wheelchairs or leaned heavily on aluminum walkers. They ate slowly and methodically, as though every bite were a newly attempted effort. It saddened Lewis. There were people there, fifteen years younger than he, who ate like crippled babies, every movement causing pain whose source some of them no longer comprehended.

The worst were those whose movement was mechanical, who concentrated solely on their food because their debilitated minds could not allow two areas of focus at once. As Lewis watched them, pretending to listen to some story with which Joe was regaling the table, he thanked God that He had seen fit to bless Lewis with comparatively good health. The thought made him feel guilty, and he prayed instead that the ill should recover their faculties or that God would help them to bear their infirmities. Perhaps Lewis could do something to help.

After dinner, Joe and his cronies headed to the social room to watch the news, play cards, and talk some more. Lewis declined the invitation, claiming weariness and the need to finish organizing his books. But instead of returning to his room, he went to the constant care wing, and asked one of the nurses to direct him to Dorothy Horst's room.

Dorothy was dozing in a high-backed chair with wood and metal arms, and her roommate was sleeping in her bed near the window. *Entertainment Tonight* was blaring from a small color TV on a wheeled stand, and when Lewis turned it down Dorothy opened her eyes and looked at him.

Finally recognition came and Dorothy smiled. 'Lewis Becholdt,' she said. 'I didn't know you were here. Is Emma here too?'

Lewis forced a smile. 'Emma's gone, Dorothy. For some years now.'

'Oh. Oh yes.' Then she seemed to think of something, and the sour look she had worn in the cafeteria returned. 'You don't play with those boys and girls.'

'What boys and girls, Dorothy?'

'The boys I saw you with. And there are girls too.'

'Why, Dorothy? Why shouldn't I play with them?'

Dorothy closed her eyes and shook her head. A pale tongue came out to lick the dried remnants of dinner from the wrinkles at the corners of her mouth, and her fist rubbed at what she could not lick away. The flesh of her hands looked as thin as tissue to Lewis, the blue veins as distinct as on an anatomist's chart.

Her hand fell back in her lap and she opened her eyes just wide enough to peer at him. 'Sundowners,' she whispered, and nodded twice. Then her head fell slowly onto her chest.

'What?' Lewis asked gently. 'What do you mean?'

Dorothy didn't answer. She was asleep, the thin blanket over her shoulders rising and falling with her breath.

Lewis found out what she meant that night. He went back to his apartment and tried unsuccessfully to read himself to sleep. He had furnished the bedroom with the bed he had slept in for many years, and the heat in the room made no noise other than a gentle rush of air. Still, Lewis did not feel at all drowsy. He blamed his restlessness on the excitement of the first day in his new residence, and turned out the light and closed his eyes.

Sleep would not come. Lewis sighed and sat up in bed, looking into the darkness enlivened only by the brief flashes in his left eye, the permanent result of his retinal surgery ten years earlier. He had just put on his glasses and was reaching for the light when he heard the sound of a door opening and then closing again. It was not in his own apartment, for his bedroom door was open, and no light had disturbed him.

He turned on the bedside lamp and saw that his alarm clock dial read ten minutes past two. Lewis got up, slipped his flannel bathrobe over his pajamas, and walked quietly to his front door. He looked through the spyhole and saw, distorted by the fisheye lens, Joe Fenneman standing in the hall, fully clothed and wide awake.

Joe gave all the appearance of a man who was looking, or rather, Lewis decided, listening for something. The long oval of his head rose above his hunched shoulders, stretching his wrinkled neck, and his lean jaw stabbed forward. He was not looking down, but out, and often up. All his senses seemed alert, and Lewis thought that at one point Joe even sniffed the air. Then he walked on slowly, down the hall and out of sight.

Lewis turned on a lamp in his living-room and sat on the couch. Perhaps, he thought, Joe Fenneman was not quite as normal as he had first appeared. He decided to wait and see when Joe returned, and retrieved his book from the bedroom, lay back on the couch, and resumed his reading.

Before he knew it, he had awakened from a dream in which he was with Emma. They were in the living-room of their home, seated at either end of the couch, and they were talking to each other. In the dream, he knew that Emma was still dead, but had been able to come back and talk to him, and he was telling her how grateful he was that he could visit her in this way. Then he heard a noise and asked Emma to excuse him so he could see what it was. He stood up and walked into the dining-room, and heard the noise again. It was a dry cough, and it woke him so that he realized he had fallen asleep.

Lewis blinked to clear his vision, then stood up, his legs stiff, and went to the spyhole just in time to see Joe Fenneman returning to his apartment. He walked with his head down and his eyes nearly closed, passing from Lewis's sight. Lewis heard a door open and close, and there was silence again.

The clock on the top of the bookcase read 5:37. Joe had been gone almost all night, but where on earth had he been? Lewis made himself a cup of tea and sat at the small dinette, thinking about it, and was still sitting there at 7:30 when there was a gentle rap on his door.

He was pleased to see the round, friendly face of Mrs Meyer, the residence manager, through the spyhole, and he tugged the sash of his bathrobe, covering his pajamas, opened the door, and invited her in. She explained that she liked to drop in on new residents first thing in the morning to make sure they had a pleasant night. *And to try and cheer up the depressed ones*, Lewis thought, though he didn't say it.

He told her that he had spent a quiet and comfortable night, and she was glad to hear it. When she asked him if there were anything she could do to make his stay more pleasant, or if he had any questions, he thought a moment.

'You know,' he said as though it had just entered his mind, 'I did hear a phrase in a conversation last evening that was new to me, and after ninety years there aren't many of those, I'll tell you.' Mrs Meyer laughed along with his chuckle, and he went on. 'Sundowners.'

Mrs Meyer's reaction was one of recognition mixed with mild annoyance. 'Oh yes,' she said, 'They're one of the minor crosses that the staff here has to bear, or *can* be. They're patients who grow more alert—and upset—at night. It's an occasional condition of Alzheimer's or dementia. A lot of these folks sleep during the day because they feel more secure in the daylight, hearing the hustle and bustle of the staff and the other patients. But when night comes, and things get dark and quiet, the lack of stimuli makes them restless, and they can be awake all night. The ones who are still ambulatory can cause a lot of trouble, and even those who aren't can be a real disturbance to the other patients.'

'Are there any of these . . . sundowners who aren't in constant care?' Lewis asked.

'A few cases in the cottage wing, usually mild enough that the spouse can handle it. But here in the single units, no.'

'Then why would someone refer to any folks here as sundowners?'

Mrs Meyer shrugged. 'They probably heard one of the staff use the name and don't really understand it. Maybe they use it to describe night-owls.'

'Now *that* name I know,' Lewis said with a smile.

'Well, we have a lot of those. There are some folks here in the resident wing who only sleep three or four hours a day.'

Lewis nodded. 'I don't seem to need as much as when I was younger, but I still get six or seven hours. But what do these night-owls *do* all night?'

'Oh, mostly what you'd expect—read, watch TV. Sometimes they sit in the lounge. I'm not often out and about that late, but there have been times when I pass the lounge and see a good number of people in there.' She smiled. 'So I suppose they're "sundowners" too in their way. Well,' she said, glancing at Lewis's clock, 'I guess I'd better let you get ready for breakfast. They stop serving at 8:45.'

Left alone, Lewis showered, holding firmly to the safety bars as he stepped in and out. He shaved and afterward patted his face with Skin Bracer, which he had used since Gillette stopped making Sunup. All the while he thought about Joe Fenneman and his fellow sundowners, whoever they might be. The phrase, though medically incorrect, appealed to him more than night-owls. Night-owls were benign creatures who frequented twenty-four-hour diners and truck stops, who drank coffee in those clean, well-lighted places.

But *sundowners* were something else entirely. A life spent in the pages of the fantastic had, despite his religious beliefs (or perhaps, he often thought, *because* of them), predictably steered him toward the more imaginative end of the theoretical spectrum. Sundowners were a perfect appellation for vampires, and his mind raced back to the archetypal sundowner, Count Dracula, of whose exploits Lewis had clandestinely read during the Spanish Influenza plague of 1919. Years later, when he saw Murnau's *Nosferatu*, the link between the film's Count Orlok and the plague had made him shudder at his own childhood link between the vampire and the contagion which had taken his older sister at that time.

These ancient sundowners, however, certainly did not have blood on their minds. Simply for fun, Lewis quickly cobbled together a plot in which Joe Fenneman and his coven, in order to function on two hours sleep out of every twenty-four, leached psychic energy from their much younger nurses, thus hastening the eventual burnout that so many medical staffers experienced. He toyed with the idea of developing it into a story, but immediately dismissed the concept as too hackneyed. Besides, even if he could freshen it up, where would he place it? What during the thirties was a flow of markets had slowed, not to a trickle, but the kind of drip so infrequent as to not even require a call to the plumber.

Fenneman & Co. had finished breakfast when Lewis reached the cafeteria, but Joe had another cup of coffee while Lewis ate his habitual breakfast of cereal with milk, garnished with banana slices. To Lewis's surprise, Joe looked well rested. There were bags under his eyes, but that was nothing unusual at their age.

Joe asked Lewis if he had slept all right, and Lewis said he had, but had been awakened several times by what he thought were doors closing. 'Oh yeah,' said Joe, 'there are some folks who don't sleep too well, figure a little walk'll tire them out. Me, I use earplugs, sleep like a baby.'

'Really?' Lewis said with just a touch of dubiousness to see how Joe would react.

The man frowned for a moment, then a slow smile knifed across his face. 'You heard me go out last night,' he said.

'I believe I might have,' Lewis replied, 'but at my age, well, you're just not sure of anything.'

'You're pretty foxy, Lewis,' said Joe. 'You a foxy grandpa?'

'Five times over. And a *great*-grandpa six times and counting.'

'Then,' Joe said quietly, 'you know the value of family.' He stood up.

'See you later on today, Lewis. We'll talk some more.' He walked out of the room.

Lewis sipped the last half-inch of his coffee with cream and tried to make sense out of Joe's remark about family. If he had been a mafioso, Lewis might have read it as a threat to *his* family, but that certainly wasn't Joe's style. His name was Fenneman, not Fanucci. Oh well, Lewis thought, Joe had promised to talk more. Maybe later today he would reveal to Lewis the deep dark secret of his insomnia, and how he played solitaire in the lounge all night while watching old movies on AMC.

The day was more full than Lewis had expected. He had one orientation meeting in the morning and another in the afternoon, along with visits from the facility's chaplain and the doctor. Franklin and his wife Linda came over at 4:00 to visit, and Lewis assured everyone who asked that he was doing just fine, thank you, and the place was very nice, and he was sure he would be quite happy there.

At 5:00, only a few minutes after Franklin and Linda had gone, Joe Fenneman knocked on the door and invited Lewis to join him for dinner. Joe and the other men seemed interested in how Lewis had fared in his first full day, and gave him helpful tips on meal schedules, which staff members were pleasant, and which were less so.

Once again Dorothy Horst came into the cafeteria and glowered at the men. None of them mentioned it, though Lewis thought they couldn't help but notice. When they were finished with their meal, Joe invited Lewis back to his apartment, saying only, 'There's something I'd like to show you.'

Joe's rooms were laid out the same as Lewis's. His furniture was inexpensive but well cared for, and Lewis was heartened to see a small bookcase filled with hardcover and paperback novels, mostly westerns and mysteries. 'Sit down here,' Joe said, and Lewis sat at the small dinette table.

Joe entered his bedroom and came back out with a photo album. He sat next to Lewis and placed the album on the table. It was dark green, with gilt around the edges. 'Lewis,' Joe said, 'did you love your wife?'

That question, asked in a different tone at another time, might have made Lewis angry and defensive in its implications, but Joe had asked it kindly and sincerely, as though he already knew the answer was yes. 'Very much,' said Lewis. 'She was the . . . sweetest and most gentle person I've ever known. And I think she loved me as much as I loved her.'

Joe nodded. 'I felt the same about my Mary. Still do.' He opened the album then. It was filled with photographs, the earliest from the thirties, and the latest taken just a week, Joe told him, before Mary died.

'She had a heart attack,' Joe said, 'and *I* was supposed to be the one with the bum ticker. She woke up in the night, said she didn't feel well, stood up, and fell right back into the bed. Dead, just like that. I didn't get a chance to say goodbye or to tell her how much I loved her. Oh, she knew all right, but

I couldn't remember the last time I'd actually *told* her. And now I couldn't. It was just too late.'

'It's not too late,' Lewis said, looking at the last photo Joe had taken of his wife. She was kneeling in sunlight next to a rosebush, a worn throw pillow beneath her knees. She was wearing khaki overalls and a man's blue shirt, and her gray-brown hair was tied in the back. She was smiling at the camera, and her eyes were a pale blue. In her right hand were a small pair of garden shears and in her left she held three white roses. Her features were sharp, but in their harsh lines were still traces of the young beauty Lewis had seen in the earlier photos.

'It's not too late,' Lewis repeated, 'to tell her. She'll hear you.'

'You mean in *heaven*?'

'Yes, in heaven. And in dreams. God sends Emma back to me in dreams.'

'Heaven and dreams are poor substitutes for reality,' Joe replied.

'Not if you believe that heaven *is* reality.'

Joe leaned toward Lewis, a vulturine grimace creasing his thin face. 'You want to see reality, Lewis? You go to bed now and set your alarm clock for three. Then you come down to the lounge. Very quietly. Don't come in. You just look through the glass, and I'll show you reality.'

Joe didn't sound friendly anymore. He sounded angry and mean, and Lewis felt scared. 'I'm sorry,' Joe said, sitting back. 'I get a little worked up. Look, Lewis, just do what I asked, okay? I promise you, you won't be sorry. In fact, you may be very glad. What do you say?'

Lewis stood up. 'I say maybe. If my alarm works,' he added with an attempt at levity.

As he left Joe's apartment, he felt as if a knife blade might slip between his ribs. He had not suspected this side of Joe, though the man's nocturnal wanderings the previous night should have been a tip-off.

But even though Joe had frightened Lewis, he interested him as well. Lewis knew that he had no choice but to go to the lounge at three a.m. to learn precisely what delusion was possessing Joe Fenneman.

In his apartment, Lewis watched *Jeopardy*, then set his alarm for 2:45 and lay in bed with a book. In a surprisingly short time, he felt tired enough to turn out the light and try to sleep.

The alarm woke him, and he turned it off and got up. At the front door he looked through the spyhole, but saw nothing. The hall was as empty as it was quiet. Lewis put on slippers, opened the door, and closed it softly behind him, then walked gingerly down the hall toward the lounge.

It was a large room, forty by twenty-five feet, and was filled with tables and chairs for card playing and socializing, several couches and easy chairs, a TV and VCR, and an upright piano. Against one wall were juice, soda, and snack machines. Large, waist-high panes of glass allowed passersby to look in, but those were on the other side of the door at which Lewis now stopped.

A four-inch wide, vertical strip of wire-reinforced glass was set into the door, and it was through this that Lewis peered.

At first, Lewis thought Joe was sitting alone at one of the tables, his back to Lewis, lit only by the light from the hall and the glow of the vending machines' front panels. But when Lewis looked more closely, he could make out another figure at the table, sitting directly across from Joe.

Lewis couldn't quite grasp the image, and quickly looked off to the right, then back, to try and clear the vitreous floaters from his central vision. It helped. He could see her more plainly now. It was a woman with brown hair and sharp features, a woman in her forties who looked so much like Mary Fenneman in those old photos that Lewis instantly thought that it was Joe's daughter, until he remembered that Joe was childless.

Then his imagination went to work again, and he fancied that he was seeing Joe's wife, looking as she did when she was in her prime. As the thought took him, her figure grew more indistinct, not wavering but thinning, contracting in upon itself until, in a few more seconds, it was gone, and Joe sat alone in the lounge, his slim figure stiffening.

Lewis gave a half-gasp, half-moan of amazement and shock, and when he did, Joe Fenneman spun around in his chair, his eyes wild with fury. But when he saw Lewis's face through the strip of glass, his own face took on a look of victory. Joe knew that Lewis had seen what he wanted him to, and he slowly relaxed, his shoulders slumping forward.

Lewis backed away, then turned and walked as quickly as he could down the hall. He heard the sound of the lounge door opening and Joe's footsteps, faster than his own, coming toward him. 'Lewis!' Joe's voice hissed, and Lewis felt the man's hand on his shoulder a moment after he grasped and turned his own doorknob.

'*Yes!*' Joe whispered. 'It was her—it was Mary.'

Lewis did not turn around. He stood there trembling, still clutching the doorknob, wincing as Joe's fingers dug into the meat of his shoulder. 'It can't be,' he said, and heard himself as though in a dream.

'It was. It is. And it will be again. Every night, Lewis. Every night I see her and talk to her. And not in some dream, and not with her in heaven, but here on earth.' The force of the fingers on Lewis's shoulder had diminished, and now Joe only patted him.

'Let me tell you how, Lewis. Let me tell you. So you can see Emma again. Go on. Open the door. Let's go in.'

Lewis felt his hand turn the knob, felt himself walking into his living-room, Joe behind him. Then they were seated side by side on the couch. 'All right,' Lewis said. 'Tell me then.'

But before Joe would tell Lewis anything, he made Lewis tell him about Emma. He wanted to know what Lewis remembered most clearly about her, about the things she did and said that were most dear to him, about the moments when he knew that he could not go through life without her, about how much he missed her, and what he would do to see her again.

'Anything,' Lewis finished softly, tears in his eyes. 'I'd give anything to just . . . be with her again.'

'You don't have to give anything,' Joe said. 'In fact, all you have to do is take something. Just take it for the asking.' Lewis wiped away his tears and looked at Joe, puzzled. 'We're not the first, Lewis—me and Ed and Pete and Jimmy. There are some women here too. Irene and Rachel—they missed their husbands as much as we missed our wives.'

'What are they?' Lewis asked. 'Are they ghosts?'

'I guess they are, Lewis. I don't know what else to call them. But how can you be scared of the ghost of the person you loved and spent your life with?'

'How did you find out about . . . whatever it is?'

'Same as you. Somebody saw I was hurting and told me. Old Tim Heisey. He died two years ago. And somebody did the same for him. I have no idea how far back. A long way, I guess. It *feels* like something that goes back a long way, doesn't it?'

The thought made Lewis shiver. He thought of witchcraft and sorcery, of deep secrets learned in fire-lit hovels during centuries of darkness and fear, of all the tropes of fantasy and horror slouching in stark contrast to the other tales of bright and informed science fictional futures. He had spent his life reading and writing both, and now was he to learn at the end that the darkness was the reality? Nevertheless, his curiosity, and a deeper longing, proved unquenchable.

'How do you do it?'

Joe smiled again. 'At night, in deepest night; it won't work any other time. You just *want* her to be there badly enough, and she is. Almost until dawn, or until something happens. Like tonight. I knew you were coming, and that was more important to me than keeping her there, so when I knew you saw her. . . .' He lifted his hands and let them fall on his lap.

'Why don't you meet her in your room? Why the lounge?'

A webwork of lines crossed Joe's face as he frowned. 'It's not good. It's not good to have her where you spend most of your time. Old Tim told me that, and I think he was right. This way, you see, makes it more special, like a *visit*.' He gave a thick chuckle. 'Some nights there are a few of us down there. Things get . . . pretty sociable.' Joe paused and gave Lewis a sidelong stare. 'You haven't asked what I thought you'd want to know most.'

'I think I'm afraid to.'

'You don't have to be. Like I said, you just *take* a little something. Now you know that Dorothy Horst, right?' Lewis nodded. 'Well, you just go visit her in her room sometime, and you get talking, and you take her hand, and you think about your Emma and how you want to see her again, how so very very *bad* you want to see her, and then you squeeze that woman's hand, and keep squeezing. You squeeze it hard, until it hurts her. You don't have to break anything, but just till you know it hurts, and that's enough.'

'Enough for what?' Lewis asked. His mouth tasted of cotton and metal.

'Enough so you can do it. Bring back Emma.'

'By hurting someone else.'

'You're not *killing* anyone, Lewis. It's just a little pain, and then it's over.'

'And who did you cause pain to, Joe?'

'She's not even here anymore.'

'Is she dead?'

'*No*. They . . . she went somewhere else.'

'What was her name?'

'Esther Zerphy, all right? That was her name.'

'Esther Zerphy who's up at Safehaven?' Safehaven was a state mental hospital. Though Lewis had never met Esther, he had heard his pastor speak of his problems counseling the family when the woman had been committed two years earlier.

'Yes,' said Joe Fenneman. 'That Esther Zerphy.'

'Did you have anything to do with that, Joe?'

Joe didn't answer. He just looked at Lewis. Finally he said, 'Maybe. Or maybe not. That woman was right on the edge. If it hadn't been me, it would've been something else. The next week, or the next month. Same with your Dorothy Horst. The cracks are showing there, Lewis my friend. It won't be long before she's no good to you, or to anybody, if she even is now.'

Joe stood up and crossed the few steps to the door. 'I've told you how, Lewis. Now it's in your hands. Literally. A little squeeze, Lewis, and you've got Emma back. That simple. I saw that you were hurting, and I wanted to help you. I know what it's like to have back the woman you love, Lewis, to have her back sitting across a table from you, to look into her eyes, and be able to tell her that you still love her. I just wanted to share that, that's all. I'm just'—he held up his right hand in front of his face, its back to Lewis—'just holding out my hand. Like a friend. And now, Lewis, now you got to hold out yours.'

Joe looked at his own right hand as though he hadn't noticed it before, then dropped it to the doorknob, opened the door, walked through, and closed it behind him, leaving Lewis as alone as he had ever been.

His mind, however, was crowded with thoughts. What Joe Fenneman had told him was terrible, the option he had given him reprehensible. It would be like making a deal with the devil, and Lewis had, throughout his long life, shunned such things.

On the other hand, he had never before been offered what he wanted most in the world, to be with Emma once again. Would it be such a terrible thing to deprive someone like Dorothy Horst of a little more of the lucidity that was already rapidly diminishing? Joe was probably right about that. A few more weeks, another month or so, and Alzheimer's or dementia would lay full claim to Dorothy's wandering wits. Would God frown so sternly on such a spiritual misdemeanor, made solely out of love?

Lewis sat fully awake for several more hours until, just before dawn, he decided what it was he had to do. He left his apartment, walked from the resident wing into the hub, and up the stairs to the constant care section. There was no reason for stealth, and he said hello to the woman at the nurses' station, who observed with a smile that he was up early. He replied that the early bird catches the worm, and continued down the hall. He had not expected to be detained.

The door of Dorothy Horst's room, wide enough to accommodate a gurney, was open, and uniform night lights lit the room well enough for Lewis to see the two beds, and the two women sleeping in them. He looked at Dorothy Horst's deeply lined face, at her white hair fanned out on the thick pillow that cradled her head. Her mouth was open, and Lewis heard her quick, shallow breathing.

The sheet and blanket were pulled up to Dorothy's neck, but her left hand had slipped from underneath the covers and was resting on the metal safety bars that ensured she would not roll out of bed in her sleep. The pale yellow flesh was stretched tautly over the bones, and a worn gold band hung on the knuckle of the ring finger.

Lewis closed the door, then sat in the chair and contemplated the fragile left hand of Dorothy Horst. After a moment, he took it in his right hand and let it rest there. Dorothy's fingers twitched, though her eyes remained closed, and, as she muttered a word that Lewis could not make out, her fingers closed around his own.

He sat holding her hand, wondering if the hand she held in whatever dream she dreamed was that of her husband, gone many years before. With his left hand, as gently as he could, he patted the back of her hand, hoping it would make her dream all the better, then slipped the fingers of his right hand out of hers.

He watched her sleep for a minute more, glad for her and for himself, glad that he had not done what he feared he might, glad that he had passed his self-imposed test. He had taken the hand, as Joe had said, but in love, not in selfishness, and he would not be tempted again.

He passed the day making new friends and avoiding Joe Fenneman and his companions, who looked at him with hooded and hostile eyes in the cafeteria, until he returned their glares with a determined look of his own and a brave half-smile that said he knew what they were.

That night, after he finished reading, Lewis turned out the light, but slept only fitfully, his slumbers filled with half-remembered dreams. At 4:00 he got up to use the bathroom and get a drink. As the water cleaned the night taste from his mouth, he realized that in his half-sleeping thoughts, despite all of his ethics, he had been berating himself. Although he knew he could never let himself become one of Joe Fenneman's sundowners, a small part of him still longed for that forbidden fruit of cheating death in a dark hour of the night.

Even now, those who had had the necessary lack of scruples (or the gumption, he thought in spite of himself) might be sitting with the ones they loved and lost and found again, sharing sweet memories, talking of old times, seeing the wives or husbands smile and look into their eyes as they had in days past.

Suddenly he wanted to see, to see what he had missed, what his morals and his faith had cost him, not with an eye to changing his mind, but just to live vicariously by observing, and to consider what might have been. He put on a robe and slippers, and once again walked down the hall to the lounge where he had seen Joe and his wife Mary the night before. This time, however, he did not want to be seen, did not want to disturb the single or multiple tête-à-têtes that might be taking place.

So when he neared the door with the vertical glass panel, he laboriously knelt, and lifted his head so that only his left eye looked from the bottom corner of the opening. Lewis saw them then, three couples, all sitting across from each other at separate tables.

Joe and Mary were there, as well as Pete and his wife and Ed with his, or so Lewis assumed. There was, however, no joy in any of the faces. No hands were touching, no lips were moving with words of love or tales of memory. The faces of the women were blank. Their eyes were as empty and devoid of expression as the worst cases in constant care, whose memories and minds lay buried too deeply to ever be heard or heard from again.

The expressions on the three men's faces were also similar, a combination of sorrow, pain, and the dregs of a frustration borne for so long that it had grown familiar and common and altogether suitable. Joe had promised Lewis that he could talk to Emma, but he hadn't said anything about her talking back. There was no communication in that sad and empty room, and if there was love it was only one-sided and slavish.

Lewis continued to watch, but he heard no words, and the only motions he saw were those small, nervous tics of the doomed and desperate. He slowly pulled back his head and pushed himself to his feet.

As he shuffled back to his room, he did not once wonder why Joe had wanted him to join them in the lounge long after sundown. He knew that the more people there are in hell, the less lonely the damned have to feel. Damned they were, going back night after night, drug addicts still taking their poison out of habit and need, long after the initial euphoria has faded and gone, never to return.

Back in his room, Lewis lay down in the darkness, closed his eyes, and went to sleep, hoping for good dreams.

He welcomes visitors, and is happy to talk of the old days of writing and publishing, when the impossible was still fiction, but he will not speak of the sundowners and their hell. He approaches his own sundown gracefully, on his own terms and on God's. He sees Emma in frequent and blessed dreams, and waits patiently for the day he knows will come, when he will see her and hear her and hold her, and not wake to this world again.

Story Notes and Sources

OFFICES
(*Twilight Zone*, October 1981)

This was my first professional publication. When Ted Klein, then editor of *Twilight Zone Magazine*, called me one night and told me that he was buying this story, I hung up the phone, giggled hysterically, and rolled on the kitchen floor. My wife Laurie was at a rehearsal, and my son Colin, then a toddler, was sleeping soundly. Even though I couldn't immediately share my glee, it was the biggest high that I've ever had in my writing life. Even now the original illustration for the story hangs framed in my office, as does the cover of that issue.

What made it even more delightful was that writing eventually proved to be my ticket out of the offices that I had written about. The story is autobiographical, and accurately reflects my feelings toward the corporate life after living it for several years. My present opinion of major corporations, now that they seem to have successfully purchased the U.S. government, is even lower than in 1981. They're stealing more than the souls of their workers now.

Odd, isn't it, how one's chain of thoughts can lead from so much recalled joy to so much present despair in the space of one small paragraph?

A LOVER'S ALIBI
(*Twilight Zone*, May 1982)

To tell the truth, I'd forgotten the details of this story (let's face it, it's been over twenty years), and recalled it as an EC horror comic-style story about a man who kills his wife and is then haunted by her until he commits suicide. On rereading it, I was pleasantly surprised to find that there was a bit more to it than that.

Like many of my earliest stories (many of which remain mercifully unpublished), this one's set in New York City. Though I lived there only a short time in the mid-70s, there's something about the city that gets a grip on you and won't let go. I frequently return there, at least in my fiction.

LARES & PENATES
(*Twilight Zone*, December 1983)

This is a *Twilight Zone*-style story, as close to *Serlingesque* as I've ever come. I can easily imagine it airing in some alternate universe in 1961, with Hume Cronyn and Jessica Tandy playing Abner and Dorothy. It's gentle and quiet, with a nasty little bite, like so many of Serling's own creations for the series.

Unfortunately, many of the problems that plagued the Morgans nearly twenty years ago still plague the poor and elderly, very few of whom have their own *lares* and *penates*. Perhaps in that alternate universe?

I'LL DROWN MY BOOK
(*Twilight Zone*, August 1986)

And what's more tedious than a writer writing about a writer? I haven't done it too often, but here it was necessary for the underlying conceit. I consider this one a purely psychological story. The actual reclusive writers whom I name herein were its inspiration, and I tried to imagine what would make such well-respected authors eschew the fame and adulation their work had brought them. The story is the result of that imagining.

I wrote the story after visiting Basil Wells in western Pennsylvania (the story is set in my own Lancaster County). Wells wrote for the science fiction magazines of the '40s and '50s, stopped writing in the late '50s, and was somewhat reclusive, though he greeted me warmly. I suppose I derived Wingarden's farmhouse from Wells's home. I bought a number of pulp magazines from Wells, many of which had a nail hole in the upper left corner from when he had used them to insulate his garage, a case of fiction being literally warming.

PROMETHEUS'S GHOST
(*Afterlives*, ed. by Pamela Sargent and Ian Watson; Vintage, 1986)

One of my very favorites. Wilson is based on a street person I used to see when I went to New York City much more frequently than I do now, and the manifestation is a variant on M. R. James's face of crumpled linen.

It's the only story I've ever written that a reviewer has actually called 'sublime'. I like to think it's a different take on ghosts, and after all the ghost stories that have been written, I'm perhaps overly proud of whatever small amount of originality it possesses.

MISS TUCK AND THE GINGERBREAD BOY
(*Magazine of Fantasy & Science Fiction*, May 1988)

My wife Laurie has been an elementary school teacher for many years, and this is one of her favorites. I have no recollection of where this story came from. I guess I just opened a closet door and there it was.

THE MUSIC OF THE DARK TIME
(*Twilight Zone*, June 1988)

There can be a fine line between empathy and exploitation, and in this story I wanted to take a look at the kind of people who crossed it. It was inspired by Beethoven's *Grosse Fugue* for string quartet, an immensely powerful piece of music in which I immersed myself before writing the passage in which Weissman listens to the tape.

The supernatural element now strikes me as unnecessary, but that was the way my mind worked back then, so, in addition to the story of one man who transcends his guilt and another who realizes his own culpability, it became a more formulaic 'biter bit' story as well.

Somewhere between my manuscript and the magazine, the last two sentences were reversed, reading: 'He did not want to hear the music. He did not want to hear it ever again.' The change destroyed the sound of the ending for me, since, in a story *about* music, I wanted it to end with the natural break after the word 'hear', followed by the heavily stressed syllables of 'the music', for a final 'da-DOM-DOM' effect. Now, finally, I get to see the correct version in print, and you get to read it. Please, humor me—go back and reread it aloud, as dramatically as possible. . . .

. . . See, wasn't that better?

RETURN OF THE NEON FIREBALL
(*Silver Scream*, ed. by David J. Schow; Dark Harvest, 1988)

A nostalgia trip for me, taking me back to the Comet Drive-In Theater between Elizabethtown and Lancaster. One of my most vivid memories concerning this story was a reading that Dave Schow threw for the anthology's launch at a World Fantasy Convention. Several of us, including me, read our stories aloud, but the highlight of the evening was Joe Lansdale's reading of his 'Night They Missed the Horror Show'. No bones remained unchilled. Now every time I think of my story, I think of Joe's, which is not a bad thing.

THE HOUSE OF FEAR
(Footsteps Press chapbook, 1989)

When Bill Munster, editor of *Footsteps* and Footsteps Press, asked me for a story to publish as a chapbook, I already had the perfect piece. 'A Study in Comparative Religions' was an allegorical tale that I had written a year or two earlier, but had never tried to market, since it really wasn't a piece of commercial fiction, and was, I felt, sure to be turned down by such markets.

Fortunately, Bill liked the story, but was afraid that the title might label it an essay rather than a work of fiction, so it became 'The House of Fear', with the original title as a subtitle. It's an allegory about superstitious behavior, of which I count myself a victim. Long before this story was written, I had fallen into both the finishing-a-book-and-immediately-starting-a-new-one ritual, and the cat-petting ritual described here, maintaining it through eighteen years of Mehitabel, our Siamese, and twelve years (and counting) of Gus, for three continuous decades of kitty-stroking.

The 'House of Fear' is an amalgamation of the houses of my two sets of grandparents. My maternal grandparents, the Hersheys, lived in a double house on one side of which was their grocery store, and there were a number of empty rooms on the second floor, including one that could be reached only by descending from the attic or by passing through a long dark closet to a door at the end. There was also a stairway that led nowhere, and two ways to reach the coal bin, the darkest part of the cellar, where the stock boys told me Edgar Allan Poe stories when I was little. Hardly any wonder that such a dream-inducing place should eventually pop up in my fiction.

The final chapbook was a lovely piece of work, with evocative full-page pen and ink illustrations by Douglas C. Klauba, and Bill even had t-shirts printed to promote the book at conventions. I'd like to tell you that I continued to wear one unwashed until the chapbook sold out, but I didn't.

BLUE NOTES

(*Night Visions 7*, ed. by Stanley Wiater; Dark Harvest, 1989)

As this story proves, I love jazz (I'm listening to Stanley Turrentine as I write this). I became exposed to jazz when I researched it for *Dreamthorp*, and quickly got hooked. The Sonny Rollins imagery in this story extends further than *The Bridge*, way back to his *Way Out West* album in which he posed in a cowboy hat in the desert, his trusty tenor sax taking the place of a six-shooter, just the way Luther faces down Mickey and his boys.

When you look beyond the final metaphysical musings, what we have here is basically your EC horror comic return-from-the-dead-for-vengeance story. I like to think that artist Graham Ingels would have had a good time drawing water-bloated, lank-haired Todd.

Unfortunately I can never listen to music, jazz or otherwise, when I write fiction. It intrudes too strongly, and I find its rhythms taking the place of my own, so I write in silence, envying those who are able to use music as a soundtrack to their own work.

O COME LITTLE CHILDREN

(*Spirits of Christmas*, ed. by Kathryn Cramer and David G. Hartwell; Wynwood, 1989)

Every year since 1980 I've written Laurie a short story which I give her on Christmas Eve. They're fairly personal, and are not written for publication. Still, several have appeared in Christmas anthologies when I've received a request for such stories, and one, *Pennsylvania Dutch Night Before Christmas*, was published as a picture book. This is one of those Christmas stories, and, in the tradition of Dickens and James, a Christmas *ghost* story.

The setting is modeled after a huge farmer's market/flea market only a few miles from our home, and there, just before Christmas, we did indeed once see such a decrepit looking Santa Claus. My son Colin was a babe in arms then, so no explanation of the bargain basement Santa was necessary, but I wondered what other parents were telling their children who were old enough to idolize Santa. That thought and the maxim about seeing traces of the divine even in the most lowly led to this story.

OTHER ERRORS, OTHER TIMES

(*Magazine of Fantasy & Science Fiction*, January 1990)

This one's a bit prophetic. Although it was published after Boston first baseman Bill Buckner let a grounder roll through his legs to lose the game and ultimately the 1986 World Series to the Mets, it was actually written before that dire (for Red Sox fans) event. I had been thinking more of the famed Snodgrass muff when I wrote the story (and if you don't know your baseball history, just ignore me).

The setting is all too real. My in-laws owned a cottage on Lake Shawanaga, twenty miles north of Parry Sound in Ontario, where we used to vacation. It was sold, alas, after my father-in-law's death. The Terwiliger cabin of the story is based on an abandoned cabin on the lake that appears exactly as I've described it. Even in daylight, with the sun shining brightly, it was a sad and lonely place. I went inside once and once only. Even though I'm a confirmed skeptic and usually love old, forsaken places, I was uncomfortable there, and wouldn't have liked to have been inside that cabin at night. I think my discomfort comes through in the story.

EX-LIBRARY

(*The SeaHarp Hotel*, ed. by Charles L. Grant; Tor, 1990)

A story from a shared-world anthology, the world in this case being Charlie Grant's Greystone Bay. An ex-library edition of M. R. James that I once owned gave me the basic idea. The '*face of crumpled linen*' from '"Oh, Whistle, and I'll Come to You, My Lad"' has always been my own personal touchstone of visual horror, since it lets you form the image yourself, and create what you personally find most frightful. It's James at the height of his genius.

JABBIE WELSH
(*Weird Tales*, Fall 1990)

Jabbie stepped right out of a nightmare that I once had. I awoke and immediately wrote down her name and *modus operandi*, and the old idea of belief giving a manifestation corporeality and the ability to harm brought her to fictional life. The story appeared in a 'Special Chet Williamson Issue' of *Weird Tales*, which contained two more stories of mine and an interview. *Weird Tales* had always been my favorite pulp, with the great triumvirate of H. P. Lovecraft, Robert E. Howard, and Clark Ashton Smith all debuting their best work there back in the '20s and '30s, so I was delighted with the honor.

THE CAIRNWELL HORROR
(*Walls of Fear*, ed. by Kathryn Cramer; Morrow, 1990)

This one's from the grand old heyday of theme anthologies, the theme in this case being houses. What more intriguing house, thought I, than Glamis Castle, which has fascinated people for years with the legend of its resident monster? So this is my take on the Glamis Mystery, and an attempt to stand the Gothic on its head while still working within its confines. Editor Kathryn Cramer hit the bulls-eye when she introduced it by saying, 'this is a story about the power of inheritance.'

HIS TWO WIVES
(*Iniquities*, Autumn 1990)

This is what might have happened if Roger Corman had played Poe's 'Morella' for laughs the way he did with *The Raven*. I grew up on Poe, both in print (my parents had the '40s collection with the grim Fritz Eichenberg woodcuts that I mention in the story) and on screen (thanks, Roger!), so it was only a matter of time before I got around to deconstructing him.

It was great fun to pastiche Poe's florid style and to drop tidbits of Poe scholarship throughout the story, and even more fun, of course, to drop the bomb on the narrator at the end. And, in the last sentence, is that not one of the most dreadful semi-puns you have ever read?

Roger, screen rights are still available. . . .

FROM THE PAPERS OF HELMUT HECKER

(*Lovecraft's Legacy*, ed. by Robert E. Weinberg & Martin H. Greenberg; Tor, 1990)

We tend to forget that H. P. Lovecraft was a very *funny* guy, as may be seen in his letters and essays, and in the memoirs of his friends. Though I've been a Lovecraft fan forever (and was a member of the Esoteric Order of Dagon, a Lovecraft amateur press association, for eight years), I'd never written any Lovecraftian *fiction*, as that area seemed to be well covered by dozens of Grandpa Theobald's other acolytes. The offer to write a story for this anthology changed all that, giving me the opportunity to pastiche the styles of serious HPL, whimsical HPL, and that of the ghastly Helmut Hecker, the writer we love to hate. And, unlike many of my stories, I was able to give this one a deliriously happy ending!

THE BOOKMAN

(*Obsessions*, ed. by Gary Raisor; Dark Harvest, 1991)

Except for the supernatural element, this story is true. The events occurred in 1977, Laurie was pregnant with Colin at the time, and I was at the height of my collecting frenzy. This particular collection kept me busy for a long, long time.

'Nevin Huber' was actually Henry Nauman of Elizabethtown. Unlike Huber, he was a constant reader as well as collector, and he did indeed call his collection the Victoria Library, stamping many of his books with that name. The 'Jim Brubaker' of the story is Kinsey Baker, who with his wife Kelly owns The Book Haven in Lancaster, Pa., still a marvelous used bookstore that must be visited when you come to the area. Lucky me is the narrator.

I got some other treasures at the Nauman auction, including several dozen hand-colored magic lantern slides from silent films (for a time, Nauman managed a movie theater) which I had designed into a light-box. There was other film memorabilia that I now wish I'd bought, but I was saving my money for the pulps.

I seem to have quickly recognized the dangers of obsessive collecting, but it didn't stop me. Only in the past few years have I been weeding out things that I know I'll never want to read. So far I've heard no whimpers or low screams as I've taken them out of my house, but I keep listening. . . .

A FATHER'S DREAM

(*Final Shadows*, ed. by Charles L. Grant; Doubleday Foundation, 1991)

Charles L. Grant's *Shadows* anthologies had always been among those I enjoyed most, so I was happy to appear in the last volume of the series. The story really is based on a disquieting dream that I had, and a dreadful, coffin-like wardrobe in an old furnished apartment in which Laurie and I lived years ago. I've always found this a very uncomfortable story, not so much for what actually occurs, but for the doubts the reader has about the trustworthiness of the narrator.

By the way, among Gogol's *Cossack Tales* mentioned in the story is 'Taras Bulba', about the Cossack who kills his own son.

COVENTRY CAROL

(*Ghosts*, ed. by Peter Straub; Borderlands Press, 1995)

It wasn't until I was rereading these stories to write these comments that I realized how thematically close this tale is to 'The Cairnwell Horror'. The stories are very different, but the endings are almost identical, with their sense of peace in acceptance of what we are given to love, no matter how dreadful it may seem at first.

I think that 'Coventry Carol' is one of the most emotionally disquieting stories I've ever written, not to everyone's taste. Not even, perhaps, to my own.

A PLACE WHERE A HEAD WOULD REST

(*Dancing With the Dark*, ed. by Stephen Jones; Vista, 1997)

Time for my midnight confession. The stories in this anthology were supposed to be true, but I embellished this one, just a little. I related everything just as it had occurred, except for one detail: Mr Picard had a heart attack all right, but as far as I know he *didn't* fall into the pond out back. I added that flourish when I used to tell this story around a campfire full of impressionable kiddies, and retained it for the print version.

Frankly, I think it was a mistake to add it in the first place, at least for an adult audience, since it feels too fabricated and allows everything to click into place at the end. Life's too random for that; things don't click that easily.

Still, the rest of it's true, especially the final sentence.

THE BLOOD-RED SEA

(*The Crow: Shattered Lives and Broken Dreams*, ed. by J. O'Barr and Edward E. Kramer; Ballantine, 1998)

During the mid-90s, my interest in writing horror novels was waning, and the horror market was faltering anyway, so I wrote a pair of novels that were not easily categorized, and, as a result, not easily sold. To retain my sacred status as 'professional' writer, i.e. one who writes for money as well as for love, I wrote several licensed novels during those years. These were books about characters or concepts that already existed, and among those concepts was James O'Barr's *The Crow*.

I first wrote a novelization of the script of the second film, *The Crow: City of Angels*, in a white-hot two weeks. The script by David S. Goyer was a fine piece of work, and I had an intense fortnight embellishing and expanding on his concepts. Unfortunately, somewhere between script and screen, a great deal was lost, and the film was a disappointment. Though now out of print, the novel is available on the DVD-ROM portion of the movie's DVD.

Next I was asked to write an original *Crow* novel, and agreed for the same reason I had agreed to do the novelization: I was *simpatico* toward the concept, and its themes of lost love and redemption had figured strongly in my own original novels. Besides, the concept gave me total freedom in terms of characters and setting, something that nearly all other licensed properties did not. *Clash By Night* explored the right-wing militia underbelly of the United States while using a female lead character and telling a tragic love story, and I was pleased with the result. For better or worse, it turned out to be a Chet Williamson novel.

Then along came an invitation to do a *Crow* short story for a new anthology. Though I still liked the theme, I was starting to question how coming back from the dead to kill your oppressors could continue indefinitely to 'make the wrong things right,' so I decided to write a pacifistic *Crow* tale in which the protagonist ultimately declined to use violence against those who had wronged him. In order to have a main character with such a love of life that he would refuse to take that life from others, I wanted to make him blind from birth and allow him to regain his sight with his second life, and also make him intelligent and sensitive enough to value the sanctity of life. At that point the Greek poet Homer stepped forward and volunteered, and I accepted his offer.

The story turned out to be not only my farewell to the Crow, but my farewell to licensed work as well, at least at novel length. Though I've been offered some since, I've declined in order to pursue my own writing. This is not to say that I'll never be lured back to cast a new light on someone else's creation, but at this point, in the words of that other reluctant scrivener, I would prefer not to.

EXCERPTS FROM THE RECORDS OF THE NEW ZODIAC AND THE DIARIES OF HENRY WATSON FAIRFAX

(*999*, ed. by Al Sarrantonio; Avon, 1999)

I actually own a copy of *Records of the Zodiac: 1915–1928*, which was published in an edition of fifty copies for the members of that club (which may still exist for all I know—I don't generally run in those circles). That volume naturally inspired this story, along with my own dismay at the lack of civility in this new century, as well as my belief that corporate vultures are capable of *anything*.

As serious as my intent was, I think the story turned out quite funny, at least to those of us with a warped sense of humor. Since you've read it here, you may want to enhance the experience with the limited edition of *999*, which used different colors and varieties of type for the various headings, nicely suggesting the lushly printed real and fictional *Records of the* (Old and New) *Zodiac*, and making you feel as though you're drooling over the actual menus.

Bon appetit!

A COLLECTOR OF MAGIC

(*Imagination Fully Dilated: Volume II*, ed. by Elizabeth Engstrom; IFD, 2000)

This was written for an anthology in which invited writers were asked to select a painting from artist Alan M. Clark's *oeuvre* and write a story around it. In this way, it hearkened back to the days when pulp writers were asked to write a story based on a painting which would be on the next issue's cover.

Instead of choosing one of Alan's delightfully grisly trademark concoctions of bone and dried flesh, I picked a painting that was done for a convention program. It showed a giant top hat rising out of a forest on the edge of a river, and from the hat was spewing magical apparatus: linking rings, scarves, a wand, playing cards, and more. I thought it might be fun to treat the picture literally rather than symbolically.

Once I had devised the plot, I decided to play with form by writing it as a *New Yorker* personality piece. I've always loved *The New Yorker*, and actually had a humor short story published there in the '80s, a credit that *always* appears in my mini-bios. 'A Collector of Magic' is also unlike any of my other stories in that it's written in the present tense, a device I usually despise, but which was a necessity for the style.

I'm not a collector of magic myself, though my own 1940s copy of the National Magic Company's catalogue suggested the 'Perfection Rabbit', and, by extension, Dwayne Orgel's 'Perfection Assistant' as well.

And, by golly, I *still* managed to get in one of Alan's trademark concoctions of bone and dried flesh!

SUBTLE KNOWING

(*Strange Attraction*, ed. by Edward E. Kramer; Shadowlands, 2000)

This story was written for another art-oriented anthology, based on a sculpture by Lisa Snellings. Writers were asked to select one of the riders (or hangers-on) of a giant ferris wheel, and do a story based on the character. I selected a mysterious, cloaked figure holding up a mask in front of its blank face.

The theme of the masks that we wear to hide our true selves is one that I've always gravitated toward, and the story is an exploration of that theme, which seems to have infinite permutations.

FIGURES IN RAIN

This story, one of two new ones written for this collection, recalls our most recent trip to Colonial Williamsburg. Laurie and I had gone before, but had had with us pre-adolescent Colin, who suffered less than valiantly through the old buildings for the future promise of the rides at Busch Gardens. This time, however, we were on our own, free to eat, drink, and linger at will, just like my protagonists. Unlike them, however, we went on Easter weekend and our weather was much better, although we did suffer through a storm while having dinner at The King's Arms.

Williamsburg is a town where you really do expect to see ghosts. Alas, we didn't, so I had to create my own. Instead of terrifying, I like to think of this ghost story as illuminating, if only as much as the light of a single candle.

SUNDOWNERS

The second story written for this collection, it was inspired by and is dedicated to Lloyd Arthur Eshbach. I met Lloyd in the early '80s, when I discovered that he lived in Myerstown, about a forty-minute drive from my home. Lloyd has just celebrated his ninety-second birthday and still lives in Myerstown, but in a retirement home just across the street from the apartment in which he lived with his late wife for many years.

His first short story was published over seventy years ago, and his tales frequently appeared in the pulps during the 1930s and '40s. He's best known, however, for his creation of Fantasy Press in 1946. This small press was the first to publish many science fiction giants in hardcover, and also published, under Lloyd's editorship, what is considered to be the first book on modern science fiction, *Of Worlds Beyond*, a collection of essays by Heinlein, van Vogt, and others.

In the early '80s Lloyd started writing again, and his best known later works are the *Gates of Lucifer* tetralogy, which appeared from 1984 to 1990, and his memoir of early publishing days, *Over My Shoulder.* He's also a skilled gemstone craftsman (I proudly wear a black tiger-eye ring of his creation), and a minister in his church. He's also one of the kindest people I've ever known.

I got my first agent through Lloyd, who was willing to share his with me, and I went to many SF and fantasy conventions in his company. He's shared his time, his talents, his good humor, and his gifts with me, and I hope that this story shows some of the affection I have for him.

Understand, Lewis Becholdt is *not* Lloyd Eshbach. Although there are some similarities, 'Sundowners' is a work of fiction. What both the fictional character and the real man do share, however, is that strength of spirit that marks the heights we can reach when we look beyond ourselves.

FIGURES IN RAIN
WEIRD AND GHOSTLY TALES

The first printing of the Ash-Tree Press edition of

Figures In Rain
Weird and Ghostly Tales

was published on 29 July 2002
and is limited to Five Hundred copies
with additional copies produced for
legal deposit and contract purposes.

Ash-Tree Press

Titles Published

1994

Lady Stanhope's Manuscript and Other Supernatural Tales
(Card Covers)

1995

The Five Jars
by M. R. James

The Alabaster Hand
by A. N. L. Munby

Intruders: New Weird Tales
by A. M. Burrage

They Return at Evening
by H. R. Wakefield

Nine Ghosts
by R. H. Malden

1996

Sleep No More
by L. T. C. Rolt

Randalls Round
by Eleanor Scott

Conference With the Dead: Tales of Supernatural Terror
by Terry Lamsley

Forgotten Ghosts
(Card Covers)

The Executor and Other Ghost Stories
by David G. Rowlands

Old Man's Beard
by H. R. Wakefield

Ghosts in the House
by A. C. and R. H. Benson

The Stoneground Ghost Tales
by E. G. Swain

A Book of Ghosts
by S. Baring-Gould

The Occult Files of Francis Chard: Some Ghost Stories
by A. M. Burrage

1997

In Ghostly Company
by Amyas Northcote

Under the Crust
by Terry Lamsley

Unholy Relics
by M. P. Dare

Imagine a Man in a Box
by H. R. Wakefield

The Rose of Death and other Mysterious Delusions
by Julian Hawthorne

Midnight Never Comes
edited by
Barbara and Christopher Roden

The Haunted Chair and Other Stories
by Richard Marsh

Someone in the Room:
Strange Tales Old and New
by A. M. Burrage

Annual Macabre 1997
edited by Jack Adrian

1998

Binscombe Tales:
Sinister Saxon Stories
by John Whitbourn

Out of the Dark: Volume 1
by Robert W. Chambers

The Night Comes On
by Steve Duffy

The Clock Strikes Twelve
and Other Stories
by H. R. Wakefield

Ash-Tree Press Occult Detectives
Aylmer Vance: Ghost-Seer
by Alice and Claude Askew

Twilight
and Other Supernatural Romances
by Marjorie Bowen

The Fellow Travellers
and Other Stories
by Sheila Hodgson

Nightmare Jack and Other Tales
by John Metcalfe

The Black Reaper
by Bernard Capes

The Terror by Night
by E. F. Benson

Lady Ferry
and Other Uncanny People
by Sarah Orne Jewett

Annual Macabre 1998
edited by Jack Adrian

Nights of the Round Table
by Margery Lawrence

1999

Six Ghost Stories
by T. G. Jackson

Ghost Gleams
by W. J. Wintle

The Night Wind Howls:
Complete Supernatural Stories
by Frederick Cowles

Binscombe Tales II:
Sinister Sutangli Stories
by John Whitbourn

Ash-Tree Press Occult Detectives
Norton Vyse—Psychic
by Rose Champion de Crespigny

Out of the Dark: Volume 2
by Robert W. Chambers

The Terraces of Night
by Margery Lawrence

Strayers from Sheol
by H. R. Wakefield

The Wind at Midnight
by Georgia Wood Pangborn

The Passenger
by E. F. Benson

The Phantom Coach:
Collected Ghost Stories
by Amelia B. Edwards

Annual Macabre 1999
edited by Jack Adrian

The Talisman
by Jonathan Aycliffe

Warning Whispers
by A. M. Burrage

2000

Phantom Perfumes and Other Shades: Memories of *Ghost Stories* Magazine
edited by Mike Ashley

The Horror on the Stair and Other Weird Tales
by Sir Arthur Quiller-Couch

Dark Matters
by Terry Lamsley

Reunion at Dawn and Other Uncollected Ghost Stories
by H. R. Wakefield

The Cold Embrace and Other Ghost Stories
by Mary Elizabeth Braddon

In the Dark
by E. Nesbit

We've Been Waiting For You
by John Burke

The Lady Wore Black and Other Weird Cat Tails
by Hugh B. Cave

The Moonstone Mass and Others
by Harriet Prescott Spofford

Summoning Knells and Other Inventions
by A. F. Kidd

Ash-Tree Press Occult Detectives
The Secrets of Dr Taverner
by Dion Fortune

Annual Macabre 2000
edited by Jack Adrian

Shadows and Silence
edited by Barbara and Christopher Roden

2001

Where Human Pathways End
by Shamus Frazer

Mystic Voices
by Roger Pater

The Golden Gong and Other Night-Pieces
by Thomas Burke

After Shocks
by Paul Finch

The Far Side of the Lake
by Steve Rasnic Tem

The Shadow on the Blind and Other Ghost Stories
by Mrs Alfred Baldwin

Mrs Amworth
by E. F. Benson

A Pleasing Terror
by M. R. James

The Floating Café
by Margery Lawrence

Annual Macabre 2001
edited by Jack Adrian

The Five Quarters
by Steve Duffy and Ian Rodwell

Couching at the Door
by D. K. Broster

2002

The Invisible Eye
by Erckmann–Chatrian

Hauntings
by Vernon Lee

Sinister Romance
by Mary Heaton Vorse

Ash-Tree Press Occult Detectives
The Amazing Dreams of Andrew Latter
by Harold Begbie

Not Exactly Ghosts:
Collected Weird Tales
by Andrew Caldecott

No. 472 Cheyne Walk
Carnacki: The Untold Stories
by A. F. Kidd and Rick Kennett

Figures in Rain
by Chet Williamson

Titles in preparation

Crimson Flowers
by Tod Robbins

Ghost Stories of Chapelizod:
Ghost Stories 1838–1861
by Joseph Sheridan Le Fanu